THE WINDING

TIME CORRECTOR SERIES BOOK 1

AVI DATTA

Edited, designed and distributed by Bublish, Inc.

ISBN: 978-1-64704-391-9 (Paperback)
ISBN: 978-1-64704-390-2 (eBook)

ACKNOWLEDGMENTS

Music plays a vital role in how I perceive the world around me. I plotted the whole story while listening to Hans Zimmer's "Time" and "Chevaliers de Sagreal" while placing the ticking sound of my Seamaster's Caliber 8800 against my ear. Compositions by Liszt—especially Consolation no. 3 and Liebestraum no. 3—helped sculpting Akane. Without Chopin's Ballade no. 4 (Op. 52), Raindrop Prelude, and Liszt's La Campanella, I could not have sketched Emika.

To create the three interconnected lives of Philip Nardin, I kept staring at the intricate dial of the Grand Seiko SBGH267 while constantly listening to Hans Zimmer's "Dream is Collapsing." The paintings described as Philip Nardin's are my own. I have often marveled at looking at the mechanical movements inside a watch, especially while winding it. The time and memory loops in this story are an homage to the intricate art of watchmaking.

I must thank my wife, Priyanka, for her patience with everything while I struggled between shifting between my world and Vincent's. I am not sure how she might react when I tell her that two more books are planned in the series. Life is an absolute dull affair without Brucie—my furry child. Yes, Hulk is modeled after him. I am indebted to my friends, who gave me invaluable suggestions on the earlier drafts of this work. And of course, my fantastic editor—Anna Vera, for her sharp insights.

Lastly, this may sound a bit odd. Emika and Akane, I would have preferred if you existed beyond the confinements of my imagination. Our only encounters were in a dream I had in the year 1994, which reappeared in 2020. Maybe one day, the past and the future will converge, and you can reveal yourselves.

CONTENTS

CHAPTER 1

TODAY (EPISODE 1)

Hope played a cruel game of hide-and-seek with me.
She did not want to be found, so I stopped looking.

(August 15, 2024)

I AM RETURNING HOME FROM THE talk show, *What's Tonight with Maurice Johnson*—where I'd been the guest.. Hulk is napping in the front passenger seat. My watch is displaying the perfect time—local on one side and GMT on the flip side. This will all end in a minute, as soon I enter my house. Since the evening of August 13, all my mechanical watches have been acting erratically while on my property. I know what it means.

My car automatically plays Chopin's Ballade no. 4, an opus I removed from my playlist six months back. That's not supposed to happen. Up ahead, I see my brightly lit Pacific-Northwest house peeping through the evergreens.

"Porsche, open garage door." I turn into the driveway. Hulk lifts his head, barks, and wags his tail. He's usually calm when we reach home. I touch his forehead. "What's wrong, bug?" He whimpers, desperately trying to free himself from the harness.

"OK, bug, let's inspect."

I wrap my scarf around my neck and get out of the car with Hulk, holding tightly to his leash. As I walk toward the front door, Hulk pulls with all the strength he can muster from his sixteen-pound body, and I let him loose. He runs toward someone sitting on the bench by the door. And there she is—my Emika—after six months. She is wearing a tan suit with an untucked, white chiffon shirt underneath. When Hulk reaches her, she picks him up, letting him lick her face. After a moment, she sets him back down on the grass and walks toward me. She touches my shoulder. "You look so different."

"Still your Vince, Emi." I tilt my head. My eyes widen with joy. "But you are here."

She shrugs. "Well, whatever. I was just in town for an interview."

"With?"

"Nardin Robotics—about leading their memory transfer division."

I take a deep breath. Will she come back to me? Placing my hands on her shoulders, I ask, "Are you taking it?"

"Six months, and that's what you ask?" She removes my arms, smirking.

"I left a voicemail two days back. Did you check it?"

"Nope." Her phone rings. "Hello, this is Emika." She turns to me, covering the speaker, "It's Nardin Robotics. Can I quickly get in and talk?" She knows the door will recognize her thumb.

I wait as she goes inside, sensing that she will decline the job.

Less than a minute later, she comes back out. "It's cold inside. Not that I care. I just came here to return that." She points at Akane's violin case, resting by the front door. Her eyes well up, and she pauses before adding, "Your pocket square is in there."

A white Camry pulls up on the driveway. "That's my Uber." Her tears reach her chin as she turns back to me. "I saw you on TV today. You said your love is unrequited. But you're wrong."

She starts walking toward the cab, but I outrun her and grab her hands. I can feel each throb in my heartbeat. "Can't you stay for one day? At least let me drop you?"

"It will be hard for both of us," she says, giving me a brittle smile. "Like last time." She picks up Hulk, kisses him. "Take care of Daddy for me." After gently placing Hulk on the grass, she looks at me one last time through her teary eyes. "See you later, Vince." She gets in her Uber and leaves me.

"Goodbye, Emi," I murmur, watching the disappearing rear lights of the Camry.

I collect the violin and Hulk, and I enter my home. Walking toward my bar, I notice that my wristwatch stopped ticking at 8:00 p.m. I fetch a whiskey and then look out the window. It's morning already? I take out my cellphone to check the real time. My heart almost stops, and my jaw drops. The phone screen reads November 15. It was August 15 when I pulled in my driveway just moments ago. I see a robin pecking at my glass wall, and it flies away as soon as I hear my doorbell three times in succession. I open my door and see a petite woman in a cobalt blue jumpsuit staring at me. She has a smile that I have never forgotten. Her brown eyes, her beautiful mole above her lip and to the left—they are etched in my mind. She comes to me and wraps her arms around me. "Found you, silly. *Watashi no ai. Watashi no amai*, Vincent!"

I take her arms from my shoulders and kiss her palm. "What took you so long, Akane? Thirty-three years?"

She wipes my tears, shuts her eyes, and kisses my cheek. "I was caught in the time turbulence, silly. Been trying to free me since December."

"Free from what?"

Her smile shuts her eyes into think lines of eyelashes, and she tilts her head. "Emika. We were the same… till August 14."

I take her hand in mine. "Let's go in. Tell me everything." Notes of Debussy's Claire de Lune ring in my ears, and I look at my hand to find it empty. Where is Akane? I turn back, but there is no one, and it's evening again. Dropping to my knees, I begin to breathe hard. I recheck my cell phone, and I am back on August 15.

The notes of Claire de Lune get louder, and I can feel Hulk licking my face. Yes, I'm home. Yes, I'm awake. Did I once again dream about my future? Have I already attended the talk show? My cellphone tells me I haven't. It's August 15, 6:30 a.m., and I am due at the studio at 3:00 p.m.

Since childhood, my dreams have given me fragments of my future before it happens. I wish they didn't. I wish I didn't wake up. It's far better to die while dreaming than wake up every day to find my dreams are dead.

Wait. Akane said that she and Emika *were* the same until August 14. So what I did on August 13 worked? I had to free Emika. I had to end her suffering—at the cost of her forgetting me altogether.

But what about Akane trying to free herself since December last year? That was the time when Emika's behavior changed. And how come Akane was back? And as an adult, no less? Was that a dream within a dream? Fuck it. I have a busy day ahead.

It's 3:00 p.m., and I am at the studio, sitting on an Eames Lounge Chair overlooking a large glass wall. My briefcase is resting next to me, with my scarf just beside it. The girl at the reception desk assured me that someone would escort me in.

I look around. The TV is broadcasting a documentary on Swiss watch movements, reminding me of my childhood. I was raised in a boarding school in the Montagnola village of southern Switzerland. When I was eight years old, one inescapable incident scarred me for life on November 23, 1991. I was never the same again.

(Boarding school, November 23, 1991)

I was missing Akane too much to even taste my lunch in the school cafeteria. We did everything together. If she learned a new violin piece, I would be the first one to listen. If I drew something new, I would rush to show it to her. We studied together. We were partners in the culinary club. In her presence, I never felt like an unwanted orphan. Why wasn't she back? She'd promised. *Just two days, Vince, I will be back before the first snow.* And yet, it'd been nine days. I kept staring at my food as my tears soaked my eyeglasses.

I looked out the windows at the majestic view of snowcapped mountains, watching the snow flurry—the first one of the season. We had always played together on the first day of snow. I kept looking around, hoping she would spring from somewhere and say, "Found you." Her maroon and mustard striped scarf was still wrapped around my neck. I touched it. *When will you be back?*

I felt a tap on my shoulder and looked up to see Fred, my roommate. "Hey, Vince, let's go and play in the snow."

"I can't. Where is she?"

My classmates Sasha and Krista joined us. Krista gently rubbed my hair and wiped my tears. Sasha tilted her head at me and smiled. "She'll be back, buddy. Come see the flurries."

"She promised me that she would be back before the flurries." I took off my glasses. "I won't talk to her when she comes back."

Sasha lifted one eyebrow, smiling sarcastically. "Right. You should tell her that."

The three of them and the rest of the students went out to see and touch the first snow. I was struggling to eat, my shoulders were shaking, and my eyes were soaking wet. A heavy hand landed on my shoulder. I looked up and, through my tear-stained eyes, could make out my culinary teacher, Chef Marcel.

He touched my face. "Hey, what's wrong?"

"Why isn't Akane here, sir?" I asked, sniffling.

"Why don't you ask Mr. Kruger? I will get someone to collect your plates."

I rushed to the restroom to wash my face before seeing Mr. Kruger. Then I checked my uniform—no visible wrinkles on my maroon blazer, clean school emblem on my left pocket, spotless white shirt, and one inch of cuff visible under the blazer sleeve. My gray trousers were ironed, and my black shoes were polished. I was allowed one personal effect—Akane's scarf.

I climbed the stairs to Mr. Kruger's office. On the right of the stairwell stood a majestic, tinted-glass wall, depicting the tree of life that spanned across ten floors. When I reached his office, I could hear that he was listening to Chopin's Ballade no. 4 on vinyl. I knocked hard on the door, under the nameplate—David Kruger–Headmaster.

"Come in," Mr. Kruger answered in his baritone voice that resonated through the door. As I opened the creaking door, I saw him put on his thick black eyeglasses and then pause the vinyl. He pointed at the sofa by the fireplace. "Shut the door and take a seat, Vincent."

He came around his desk and sat on the chair perpendicular to the sofa, then touched my shoulder with a trembling hand. "This is not going to be easy. And you need to be strong—stronger than ever." He took four deep breaths. "Akane is not coming back."

I could suddenly feel every beat in my heart. My eyes widened, yet the sudden tears dampened my vision. Running my fingers across my eyes, I asked, "Why, sir? She promised me. She is my best friend." *Have I lost her?*

He coughed as if to hide the tremble in his voice. "Vince… she can't come back. She and her parents were taken by time turbulence on November 15."

"What's a time turbulence?" My voice quavered.

He placed his hand on my wrist as he explained. "It's a tear in time that swallows people. Akane and her parents went to see the World Clock's repair and launch in Berlin at Alexanderplatz. Small turbulence occurred, and a few people were taken, including them. I am so sorry, Vince."

"Taken where?"

"We don't know."

That's it. I won't see Akane again. *Why? Why can't I have one person who loves me? The one person who calls me family.* I shut my eyes, and I could see her smiling face, her bright eyes. Every moment we'd spent together flashed behind my eyelids—the first time I saw her, the moment she wrapped that scarf around me, up until she came to my dorm room to say goodbye before leaving for Berlin. Would that be my last memory of her? I'd only known her for two years. I could not accept that. It had to be a lie.

I got down on my knees and clasped my hands together as tears flooded my eyes. My lips trembled. "Sir, please take me to the time turbulence. I will beg it to give her back. Sir, I will clean your office, arrange your records, and polish your shoes to repay you. Please take me to Berlin." I nudged his cuffs. "I have no one. Tell me where I can find her."

For the first time, I saw tears in Mr. Kruger's eyes. He held my face with both his hands and wiped my tears with his thumbs. "Why would you ever think of repaying me like that?" he croaked. "I know what she was to you, and I would trade my own life to get her back. I wish I could find her for you. But the time turbulence appears randomly. You can't bargain with it."

How could that be acceptable? Why must I lose everything? Why was the world so cruel to me? My breaths came rapidly. I clenched my fists and felt a sharp tingling in my palm. Spreading them open, I saw lightning-like sparks jumping from my fingertips. My jaw dropped as I looked up at Mr. Kruger. "What is this?"

Mr. Kruger clenched his jaws and bolted up from his chair. "Don't move." He rushed into his private restroom and fetched two towels. Coming back and kneeling in front of me, he wrapped them around my palms, extinguishing the sparks. "Thank God, it's not electric," he muttered. Then he met my gaze. "Did that hurt, Vince?"

"No, sir. But what were they?"

He shook his head. "I am not entirely certain, but I feared this day would come." He shook my shoulder. "Vince, listen to me carefully. When you see these sparks, put your palms under your thighs or wash them. Then divert your mind. Solve the puzzles I sent you or draw something. Get your mind off it. OK?"

I nodded.

"Vincent, no one must find this out." He grabbed both my arms and shook me. "Do you understand me?"

"Yes, sir."

After a moment, he rose to his feet and went to his desk. "You know some people come back from the time turbulence."

My tear-stained eyes widened. "She'll come back, sir?"

He took out his pocket square and dabbed his eyes. Turning back toward me and forcing a smile that didn't match his broken voice, he said, "She can't stay away from her sweet Vince forever, can she?"

I wiped my tears, my lips wobbling. "No."

He got behind his desk and brought a cardboard brown box marked 'Akane Egami.' "Till then, why don't you keep some things that'll remind you of her? If she comes back, you can give them back."

I picked two items from the box. One was a photograph of Akane and me sharing a bowl of ice cream. Her scarf was wrapped around both of us. It was encased in a platinum photo frame. The other item was her violin. "Can I keep these two?"

"Can I see the picture?" he asked, pointing at the frame.

I handed it to him. Blinking back tears and pressing his lips together as he looked at it, he said, "I took that picture, remember? Two days before your eighth birthday. Perfect Kodak moment." He handed the frame back to me. "Take care of them and always keep them with you. That scarf, too."

As I stood up to leave, he came close to me and formed a fist. "From this point onward, I want my Vincent strong. It's going to be difficult, but can you do that?"

I ran Akane's scarf over my eyes. "Yes, sir."

"Then go to your dorm room and wash your face. I will let your teachers know that you won't attend today's remaining classes."

"Thank you, sir."

I shut the door behind me as I left and placed the violin and picture frame on the bench just outside his office. A knot in my stomach tightened. Trying to steady my breathing, I sat down, heart pounding against my sternum. I'd become an orphan again. I took some deep breaths, stood up, and climbed onto the bench. I brought the photo frame and violin case close to my chest and shut my eyes to picture her face—large brown eyes, black hair, lips red like an apple, and smile like the sunshine. I pressed my face into her scarf. *How could you leave me, Akane?*

I hugged her violin tighter. *Please come back to me. I miss you. I am begging you. When will I ever see you again?*

A robin pecked on the window, seeking my attention. The clock struck noon—Westminster chime followed by twelve dings. Mr. Kruger resumed his Chopin's Ballade no. 4. A ray of sunlight pierced through the clouds and entered the hallway, forming a shimmering image of a young lady. She had short black hair and was holding an umbrella. She looked at me, smiled. Then in the next second, her image vanished, and the robin flew away. Who was that sparkling lady?

I climbed down from the bench. Tightening Akane's scarf around my neck, I placed the violin in my left hand and the photo frame in the crook of my right arm. I descended the stairwell and walked across the campus to my dorm room. I kept my head down to hide my tears. I should have stopped her from going to Berlin. I'd dreamed she wouldn't come back. This was my fault.

(Back to the studio, August 15, 2024)

With time, that memory almost faded away. Before Emika's arrival last year, all my struggles had been limited to moving on from my partner's death in a plane crash and my resulting inability to invent something pathbreaking. She'd been everything to me, and to cope, my only goal had been to make my center the best AI facility in the world. And then came a barrage of political shit and conspiracy from the last December. I had to protect Emika by not sharing anything about it. She misread, and I found out the extent of her suffering. My mission became clear on August 13—I had to end her torment. I became the time corrector in the process, and I found out who I was beyond a worthless orphan.

"Sir, Dr. Abajian… We are ready. Could you please follow me?" asks a young man while gently nudging my shoulder. "I'm Jim, and I'll be escorting you to the dressing room, then to the studio, back to the dressing room, and your exit." He has curly hair and is wearing tortoise-framed eyeglasses—he looks overqualified for this job. I get up, straighten my trousers, pick up my briefcase, and follow him. We start walking, but he stops and points at the lounge chair. "You forgot your scarf, sir."

I run back to pick it up and then hold it to my chest, closing my eyes. I lift my glasses to sniff the scarf and hold it against my face. Walking back to Jim, I touch his shoulder. "I can never thank you enough."

I can barely keep my eyes open with the makeup lights glaring at my face. Sophie, the show's stylist, is struggling to make my face presentable, using all kinds of pigments. She sees a little sweat on my forehead and quickly rubs it. The chair is squeaky, with no lumbar support, and I shift uncomfortably. I've placed my briefcase and scarf on the chair next to me. The wall opposite the mirror has eight posters of Maurice Johnson, the host.

"Nervous, Dr. Abajian?" Sophie asks around the makeup brush in her mouth.

"A little."

"I didn't think you would be." She takes the brush off her mouth. "I saw how you rebuked the senators in the hearing. That was totally awesome." Her eyes glow.

I shut my eyes and recall every incident that led me to the Senate floor in April this year. "They had it coming."

"Dr. Abajian? Did you mean it when you said that politicians can be replaced with algorithms?" she asks, squinting at me.

I smile. "Yes. And it doesn't have to be a complicated one either."

She fans the brush across my face. "It will be just a sec." As she leans closer, the top note of her perfume is revealed—jasmine. Then she leans away again to look at her art, smiling. "You have nice wavy hair."

"Thank you, Sophie."

She puts her brush back, contemplates for a second. "Can I ask you a favor?"

"Sure."

After reaching into her bag, she hands me a paperback of *The Time Fixer: Three Lives of Philip Nardin*. I scribble, "Dear Sophie, The future has already happened. But you can change it, Vince—August 15, 2024."

Grabbing the book with both hands, she jumps up and down. "Thanks so much. Can I take a selfie with you?"

"Absolutely, but you should know, I am not on social media."

She tilts her head. "I know that." Then she gets uncomfortably close to me, pouts her lips, and snaps a selfie. "Jim will come and get you soon. It was totally awesome to meet you."

I blink. "Likewise, Sophie."

She leaves, waving at me as she goes out the door.

Alone again, my mind starts racing, and my chest begins to pound. What questions will Maurice ask? About my book? About my performance in the Senate that put three senators in jail? Those are easy ones. What if he asks about my personal life?

I snap my fingers. Sparks transform into a miniature core—a white luminant sphere levitating an inch over my palm. As I examine the sphere I think about what it means. I am the key to the time turbulence, a secret I discovered only a few days back. Inside the time turbulence, I can change the past and the future. Closing my palm, I dissolve the core. Mr. Kruger never revealed what I could do with the sparks, and only recently had I understood why—I had to find out myself.

I straighten my necktie and adjust my pocket square. The necktie button has gotten looser. I've lost fifteen pounds, five of which were since August 13, when I did the unthinkable. Yes, given the task's magnitude, I'd had my doubts—my incompetence with the sparks to create turbulence. And, even if I could muster the power, should I? Emika would forget me. But, as my resolve strengthened, I could create turbulence through these sparks. There was no stopping me. Emika is now free, and I am OK with her not remembering me. Maybe that's why she never returned my voicemail that I left on August 13. But, that dream this morning… Is she coming back?

I lift my cuff to look at my watch. It's 4:25 p.m. My JLC Reverso is now ticking beautifully at 21,600 vibrations per hour, 6 ticks per second. But, it stops when I enter my property, just like all my mechanical watches. It means only one thing—my action on the thirteenth removed my property from this reality.

Which dial goes better with my blue shirt and charcoal plaid suit? The white dial with local time or the black dial with GMT—Emika's time? Let's toss a coin. I throw a penny into the air, and there's a knock on the door. As soon as the door opens, I can hear the crowd chanting "Maurice, Maurice" against the poorly orchestrated sound of the trumpet, drums, and bass guitar. Jim comes forward. "We are ready for you." The coin lands on my left palm. Showtime.

CHAPTER 2

CONSOLATION NO. 3

Happiness is the longing for repetition.
—Milan Kundera

(About thirteen months before today)

"COME ON, HULK, LET'S FIND Mommy." Date: January 15, 2023. Location: the local airport. Elise should take Flight 0606 from Bangalore to Seattle through Tokyo, with a connecting flight here. There she is in her olive-green parka. Her blonde, wavy hair can't be contained by her hood. I pick up Hulk and touch her shoulder, and Elise turns to me. Her face is all burnt. Her eye sockets transform into an aircraft's engines and move past me. Her body turns to ash and is on the floor. The floor disappears, and I start to descend, with Hulk in my lap. We are free falling. I hear someone playing Für Elise in the background.

That's my alarm clock. It's 6:30 a.m. Sitting up, I massage my temples. Everyone seems to leave me but my migraines. Hulk is sitting in my lap, panting. He wags his tail, licks my palm, and jumps off the bed. With his torso down and butt raised, he whimpers—time for him to go to the terrace lawn.

While he's out, I prepare his food. I sit on the floor next to him, watching him eat with tiny bites and finishing off by licking the bowl spotless. Time for my breakfast—a doppio. Twenty grams of beans converted to forty milliliters of heavenly syrup extracted in precisely thirty seconds through my Lelit Bianca Dual boiler. A little stir, three sips, and it's gone. Hulk drops his favorite toy, "Lambchop," by my feet. I throw it across the room, and he barks, then fetches, wagging his tail. We continue this game until he gets tired when I get ready to leave for work.

It's a bit cold in late July. Maybe a mixed fabric of linen, silk, and wool in burgundy, over a charcoal mock neck long sleeve shirt, pair of Donegal trousers, and oxblood cap-toe oxfords. Wristwatch time: Back Omega Seamaster-professional—a gift from Elise when I'd made tenure. I lock the door and leave with Hulk.

We are now in the elevator, accompanied by a teenage girl engrossed in her cellphone. When she notices Hulk, she starts to approach him but finds shelter behind my legs. I smile. "He is a bit shy." Although really, it's her perfume—too jarring for both Hulk and me. The elevator predictably informs us, "You've reached Parking Level 1."

I walk toward the parking sign "Abajian" and notice that My BMW I7-M is sandwiched between a Hummer and an F-150. "BMW, pick me up." The vehicle reverses out of the space, and I get in, lifting Hulk with me and harnessing him in the passenger's seat. I scroll through my texts to fetch the last one I received from Elise almost eight months back, on January 15. "Missing you and Hulk. I love you."

I hold my trembling left hand with my right hand. "BMW, navigate to Little Paws and play Bach Cello Suites by Yo-Yo Ma." The sound of a cello, especially Bach, soothes Hulk. He lifts his head as soon as he hears, "You have reached Little Paws."

He won't walk, so I carry him to the reception area, where one of the attendants takes him from me. "Hi baby, how are you?" she croons. Then, to me, "Just for the day, right?"

"Yep, I'll pick him around five."

It's 9:25 a.m. I am sitting on a chair outside Dr. Rebecca Kauffman's home office. She is my psychiatrist, who recently moved her practice to her home to take care of her husband, Bernard—a Field's Medal-winning mathematician. I see Bernard in the room across the hallway from Dr. Kauffman's office, working on an equation while scratching his head. He is constantly shouting at the whiteboard, "Fuck, what's wrong with you? You were right here. Come back this instant." What's on the board looks like a variant of the Black-Scholes Equation.

By the time I was fourteen, I could recognize and derive all significant equations and identify major art movements. I could also acknowledge almost all opuses and symphonies from the first two or three notes. Every equation has a specific color. Every number type has a particular sound—prime numbers stand out as clarinet notes in a symphony. Will I end up like Bernard? At least he has Dr. Kauffman. If I lose my memory, who will find the Vince in me? I have no anchor, no family. I'll be alone, surrounded by trinkets that I won't recognize. Hulk will be long gone.

Dr. Kauffman peeks outside the door. "I'm ready, Vince."

I follow her in and sit on the couch, and she takes her place on a chair opposite. Between us is a coffee table with a bottle of Fiji water. Dr. Kauffman's scrutinizing eyes are piercing through her red-framed glasses. She removes a few strands of white hair from her eyes and continues to smile, hoping I will break this silence. This is not a contest, but I have nothing to say. Life has been at a standstill ever since Elise died. Dr. Kauffman opens her yellow notebook, uncaps her fountain pen, checks the time on her Rolex two-tone Lady-Datejust, and sighs at a wasted five minutes. Suddenly, Max, her goldendoodle, jumps next to me and exposes his belly. I scratch him.

Dr. Kauffman takes off her glasses. "How was your week?"

"Lonely, productive, and uneventful. Just the way it's supposed to be." I continue scratching Max.

She scribbles in her notebook while putting the fountain pen cap is in her mouth. "It's interesting how you chose those three words. Why does it have to be this way?"

"It's lonely because Elise is gone." I lean forward and rest my forehead on my palms. "Since childhood, whenever I was upset, I buried myself in work. Now, it's a productive diversion that gives me a purpose—to make the Center of Inventive Studies the best research facility in AI. And it's uneventful, as I haven't had the urge to invent anything—that's the part I need to change."

She tilts her head, squints her eyes. "That's the only part? What about friends?"

"I like to deal with my problems alone. But, I am in touch with three of my school buddies, Fred, Krista, and Sasha." I shut my eyes and inhale deeply. "Because of them, my high school graduation was more memorable than my undergraduate, master's, and doctorate."

"How so?" she asks, lifting her eyebrows.

I feel my pulse speed up, and I take some deep breaths to calm myself. "I always felt like an unwanted stray, except when I was with them. There was another one, too, but only for a couple of years." I pause and gulp. Taking the water bottle from the coffee table, I swallow down half of it. It's been thirty-two years now, but I can't bring her up. I can't stir up those memories and relive a fantasy that she will come back. Fantasies are not for those born to nothing. Dr. Kauffman observes all this and writes her notes.

Massaging my temples, I continue, "During my high school graduation, Fred, Krista, and Sasha might have asked their parents to cheer when my name was called." I look straight into Dr. Kauffman's eyes while bringing my thumb and index finger close together. "For a tiny smidgen of a second, I felt like I mattered—that I had a family. It was a beautiful lie." I stretch my neck, sip more water. "At Cambridge and MIT, I was hit with deafening silence when my name was announced—the thunderous cheer of orphanhood and poverty."

Dr. Kauffman pushes a box of tissues toward me. "If you need."

I wave my hand and smile. "I won't." I don't cry in front of humans. "And here, my colleagues are my friends—Anna, Chris, and Ravi. They are extremely talented scholars."

She scribbles something in her notebook and then looks at me. "Tell me something about Ravi, Chris, and Anna."

I lean back into the couch. "Anna and I were close. She was my first hire. She is incredibly perceptive of my feelings, and she also has no filter.

She calls me an idiot, but in the most endearing way. Chris and Ravi initially saw me as a boss rather than a friend. I was determined to change that as we hung out together. You know, playing pool and tennis in the country club, movie night—all five of us." Pausing, I take some deep breaths and finish the remaining water. "By five, I also mean Elise." I look down and rest my forehead in my hands again, trying to conceal the quaver in my voice. "And then it happened. Elise died, left Hulk and me. And I distanced myself from all the social activities."

"It's been almost eight months since Elise's departure." Dr. Kauffman squints at me. "What comes to your mind when you think of her?"

I rest my chin on my palm. "She was gone too soon, leaving Hulk and me to pieces. Her relentless pursuit of developing a cure for malaria, filariasis, and cholera ended with a plane crash. Maybe she was too good for this fucked up world." I pause and shut my eyes. "But in the end, it was fucking unfair to me and, more importantly, Hulk."

"Have you ever talked about this with your friends?" Dr. Kauffman asks, leaning forward.

I blankly stare at her notebook. "Will they allow me in? They gave me space to recuperate. But I guess I took too long… I am taking too long. I may have fractured the bond."

"Stop imagining the worst is out there to get you. Don't be so risk-averse. Ask them out to dinner. Show them that behind the pile of inventions and publications rests a breathing, vulnerable human. Trust me, they will be glad to see you back. Maybe then you will slowly learn to share your problems with your friends. Can you do that for me?" She then looks at her watch. I know what it means.

I stand up. "Absolutely."

"Take care, Vince. And give Hulk a big hug from me."

Bernard comes in, holding pruning shears. "I need to prune those roses. But they're gone."

Dr. Kauffman sighs. "We replaced them two years back, honey. Remember, they never came back after a harsh winter. So we have hydrangeas now."

Bernard slaps his head. "I remember." Then he leaves the room again.

Dr. Kauffman dabs her eyes with the pashmina throw resting on her chair. "Sometimes, he can't even recognize his daughters. He spent his entire life chasing complex problems, and now he forgets the simplest of things. But in his way, he's beautiful, and I'm so grateful to have him."

I take a few steps toward her. "Are you alright?"

"Oh, I'm fine, Vince. You go and conquer the world."

"BMW, take me to work."

"Certainly. Do you want me to order a Reuben and get it delivered to your office before we arrive?"

"Sure."

The time to destination is fifteen minutes, which I cover in under ten by breaking the speed limit and tight cornering. What's the point of a powerful car if I can't drive it the way it was meant to be driven? I park my car in my reserved spot: "Professor Vincent Abajian, Director, Center of Inventive Studies." I walk toward the College of Business, which houses my center.

A group of five grad students greets me, each with variants of "Good morning, Professor."

"Morning."

I walk past about twenty professors—same protocol. They know who I am, and I pretend to know them. I even feign interest in their derivative and subpar research.

I created this center from scratch from a single grant from Philip Nardin about eight years back. Then I hired Anna. Chris and Ravi followed a year after. After that, we studied the potential of robots replacing humans as managers. Our current work's primary focus is to transfer consciousness from an organic body to an artificial one while keeping all the knowledge and nuances intact. We are now testing if we can replicate a dog's personality from organic to artificial bodies. Nardin Robotics, a division of Nardin Applied Sciences, is funding the whole project. So far, we have received about $950 million from the generosity of Mr. Nardin. He's had only one condition: no mention of his name anywhere in any buildings. This center is my raison d'etre, my *ikigai*. I can make it the best facility in AI if I can free us from the clasp of the university's bureaucracy.

As I enter my suite, Linda hands me my sandwich. She peeps behind me. "Where's Hulk?"

"Little Paws. Thanks, Linda."

I unlock the door to my office, cross the sitting area by the fireplace to my desk, and switch on my four-screen computer.

Linda follows me. "The dean called, and so did the senator."

"Tell the dean I'll be there in half an hour. Ignore the senator." I take off my jacket and hang it on the back of my chair.

"OK, Dr. A. Is it OK if I leave a little earlier today? I have a stats class at four."

"Sure. But you will be here for the next three hours?"

"Yep, Dr. A."

As I'm pulling a second double shot of espresso through my other Lelit Bianca, I hear footsteps nearing my office.

"Is he in?" I hear Anna ask Linda.

"Come in, all of you," I shout.

Anna steps forward, hugs me. "We just dropped in to see you." She's cut her hair short and colored it red. She sits on the chair by the fireplace while Chris and Ravi take a seat on the adjacent sofa.

Stretching his arms like he's completed a victory lap, Chris announces, "Our new hire is joining us on August 3." He has a blue folder in his right hand.

Ravi smiles. "You'll love her. She's brilliant."

I tilt my head. "Guys, I need help. What new hire?"

"For our work in memory transfer. And we needed help in setting up experiments and analytics. So we needed a postdoc." Anna shakes her head. "Remember, genius?"

I snap my fingers. "That's right. I had to fight tooth and nail with the president, and the dean, to get it approved. They hated that we offered $150,000 to a postdoc. One day, guys, I will meet with Philip to get us out of this bureaucratic mess. I need full control of the funds."

Taking over, Chris says, "She's a recent Ph.D. from Caltech."

"Caltech!" I smirk. "So, what's the name of this brilliant mind that couldn't get into MIT?"

Anna smirks back at me. "Emika Amari. I think she can balance your skewed opinion about Cambridge and MIT."

I lift my eyebrows. "Challenge accepted. Hey, we haven't eaten out in a while. How about dinner, just the four of us? Or you can invite Emika too if you want. Friday or Saturday. My treat. You guys decide where. OK?" That name Emika... I have heard it before, sometime way back, but I can't place it.

Anna's eyes brighten up. "Sure. Let's do it, Vince. It's been so long."

Chris gets up to hand me the blue folder. "This is Emika's file."

"We should get going now." Ravi stretches his arms, and everyone stands up with him.

I turn to Anna. "Can you stick around?"

"You guys go ahead. Mommy and Daddy need to talk." Anna comes closer and sits across from the desk. "What's up?"

"What's with the new hairdo?" I point at her head.

"I ended things." She runs her hands through her shorter hair. "What a waste of two years. Needed this new look."

I click my tongue. "Did I meet this one?"

Anna shakes her head at me again and touches her forehead. "Yes, and you snarked that she has the emotional depth of a doorknob."

"And?"

"Yeah, yeah, you were right." She rolls her eyes.

I lean forward. "You wanna talk about it?"

"Nah." She hesitates, though. "But, I miss hanging out with you."

I breathe in. "Me too. Maybe the dinner will get us back to old equilibrium."

As she stands up, I notice her eyes gather tiny drops of tears. "I'd like that. I know, it's difficult without Elise."

I hand her a tissue. "Thanks for all your support."

"We are all with you, Vince." She wipes her eyes and then reaches across the desk to touch my hand. "You don't always have to be the strong one. It's OK to ask for help. We all love you."

I place my other hand on top of hers. "I'll remember that."

"Idiot." She pulls away and opens the door to leave but then turns back. "Quit being a stranger." She exits before I can reply.

I never realized how much I missed them until this moment. Sighing, I collect my jacket and leave my office. As I pass reception, Linda's head is buried in paperwork. "I am heading out to the dean's office."

"Don't stress him out, Dr. A."

Six years back, I chaired the committee that hired our dean, Dr. Vikram Murthy. He'd done his Ph.D. in economics at Princeton decades back. The man never forgets to mention that he studied Nash Equilibrium under John Nash and that the members of his dissertation committee were all Nobel laureates. As soon as I open the door to his suite, the shrilling noise of drillbit on drywall pierces through my eardrums. Shutting my ears, I ask one of his secretaries, "What's going on?"

"Mrs. Murthy found some feng shui guy to redecorate his office. They're taking down shelves, and he's upset. You can go in, Dr. Abajian."

Vikram exits the room before I can step into it, though. "Let's go to my conference room." We enter his twenty-four-chair conference room overlooking the rolling hills, the evergreens, and the mountains.

"Vince, I need a favor."

I sit. "Go on."

He drinks half a bottle of water before continuing. "OK, you know Philip Nardin, right?"

"Who doesn't?"

"So, President Alyson and I convinced him to let us write a piece about him and his business for the *Business Review* magazine. But he has one condition. He wants you to do the interview."

I lean toward Vikram. "Why me?" This could be the perfect opportunity for me to voice my concern about my center to Philip directly.

"He's fascinated by you and your work. He read some of your papers. You want to expand this center. So, meeting him might help you, Vince." Vikram takes a breath. "Please, man. My credentials are better served by not arguing with bureaucrats like Alyson… I studied under Nash, and all my committee members were Nobel Prize winners. So, please do this for me, Vince."

"Why are you getting worked up?" I say, lifting my shoulders. "I never said I wouldn't—just wanted to know why. So, when's the interview?"

"Tomorrow. Sorry, Vince."

"I can be there. Just ask one of your assistants to ping Linda or me the location."

Vikram grabs my hand. "I will. Also, Vince, thank you."

"You're welcome. But what's this sudden need?"

"Well, you may know that he is the only person who's come back from two time turbulences. Also… our readership is decreasing. So we are not getting that much ad revenue. This might boost things up."

"I will get it done." I leave Vikram's conference room and head back to my office suite.

I lean back in my chair as I flip through the pages of Emika's folder. Her name is written in both English and hiragana on her CV. She was born in November 1991—the year and month Akane disappeared and the last recorded event of time turbulence. Bachelor's in mathematics from Kyoto University in 2010, master's in mathematics with a specialization in combinatorics and number theory from Oxford in 2012, and a Ph.D. in artificial intelligence from Caltech in 2023. That's brilliant. So, what is she doing at a lower-tier school, like this one? Well, I am here, too. I take off my glasses and rub my eyes. But I had my reason.

(Ph.D. defense at MIT, May 2010)

"Congratulations, Dr. Abajian!" Dr. Bovet hugged me. "You're now officially one of us."

Joining him were the members of my committee: Dr. Ashis Sengupta (Nobel Prize-winning physicist), Dr. Amy Choi (Fields Medal-winning mathematician), and Dr. Ezra Freeman (Nobel Prize-winning economist). Dr. Bovet continued. "You can sit down now. You're the best doctoral student I ever had. But it disappoints me to see you're going to join a broken program. You could've joined any school—Carnegie, Stanford, Caltech, even the one across the road, that community college for the entitled brats. Why, Vincent?"

I sat with Dr. Choi on my right and Dr. Freeman next to her. Dr. Bovet is on my left, and Dr. Sengupta is next to him. "As a child, I was left outside the gate of an orphanage. Someone took a chance on me and paid for my schooling."

Dr. Choi raised her eyebrows. "I had no idea, Vincent. I am so sorry."

Dr. Sengupta's jaw dropped, and Dr. Freeman took off his glasses. But Dr. Bovet knew.

I paused to gather my thoughts and conceal the imminent tremble in my voice. "At the age of eight, time turbulence took my friend. She was my world. My friends and my headmaster helped me through that. Then Cambridge gave me a chance. And then, through you, MIT did. Every broken thing deserves at least one chance, and I have gotten several. I'll try to fix that program. Though, I will leave if it's beyond fixing."

Dr. Choi touched my right hand. "So, Dr. Abajian, can you share a bit about your friend?"

(Back to the present)

What brings you here, Emika? I put my glasses back on and flip through Emika's CV. From 2012 to 2014, she was a private maths tutor in Japan. Why? I turn a page: two papers under review at *Nature Machine Intelligence.* Any hobbies? Yes, last page. She plays the violin and enjoys tea-making. Proficient in Japanese, English, Finnish, and German. Fascinating. But that name—Emika—where have I heard it? I must meet her.

It's 3:30 p.m. I go over to Linda's desk to speak with her before she heads out for the afternoon. "I need a favor."

She looks up. "Yes, Dr. A?"

"Can you add a meeting between Emika and me on August 3 at 10:00 a.m. to my schedule?"

"What's the subject of the meeting?"

"Hmm… How about 'exploration?'"

She rolls her eyes. "Aha."

"What?" I ask, leaning forward.

"She might be confused, but who's not when it comes to you?" she shrugs.

I snap my fingers. "Hey, you want some coffee before you leave for class? I have carryout coffee mugs."

"No, Dr. A, your coffee will keep me awake for seven days."

I lift my shoulders. "Your loss."

"I know." She collects her bag from under her desk, "How can I live with myself?"

"You should get Mr. Nardin's address from the dean's office. I need to drive there."

"I already got it, and I emailed you the address. You can share it with your car before you drive there."

I shake my head. "What'll I do without you?" She'd be leaving me soon to spend more time taking care of her kids at home, and I was dreading the change.

She smiles. "Well, don't make a robot to replace me."

"I won't. And good luck with your class."

It's 4:00 p.m. I still have one hour left before I need to pick up Hulk. Let's look up Philip. I turn on my computer. "Ludwig, pull up everything you've got on Philip Nardin. And order it by relevance." Anna programmed Sir Patrick Stewart's voice into Ludwig. The agent often uses phrases, such as "Ahh," like Professor Xavier or Picard. Right now, all the patents surrounding Ludwig belong to us and the startup we funded. Anna made some modifications to Ludwig's mannerisms, which she sarcastically mentioned I'd love.

"I have collated all the information you need. Is it OK if I call you Vincent?"

"Absolutely." I lean back in my chair, ready to listen. "I don't need all the information now. But tell me about his firms and inventions."

"He pioneered the commercial use of intreton—an element absent from the periodic table. He mainly uses a synthetic version called intreton-c, which has breakthrough applications in healthcare. He invented synthesized ceramic-oxide-electrolytes from intreton-c to power electric cars, cellphone batteries, energy infrastructure, and 3,000 operational satellites. Every car company uses his battery technology. He is the founder, president, and CEO of Nardin Industries."

"Any hobbies?"

"He is a painter and a race car enthusiast. What else do you want to know?"

"Tell me about his properties."

"He has mansions in the US and Iceland. He owns numerous jets and helicopters as well as two submarines. Also, he holds a private island in the northeast of Iceland. No satellite can observe any of his properties. There is a rumor that he is building a spaceship."

Besides the invention, Philip sounds like my boarding school classmates' typical parent—spoilt brats offspringing more of their kind. So how many does he have? "Family?"

"No mention of any on the Internet. And as you know, Vincent, if it's not on the Internet, it's nonexistent."

Anna programmed Sir Patrick's sense of humor as well, apparently. "Ok, Ludwig, print out a summary. I will read at home."

I haven't researched anything on time turbulence since my Cambridge days. Pragmatism took over the fantasy of meeting my Akane, so I stopped caring. But Philip is tied to this phenomenon, and I want to be ready before meeting the most powerful person on the planet. "Pull up everything you've found on time turbulence. And order them by relevance. Also, print the summary."

"Do you have any specific questions?"

"What caused it?"

"No one knows, Vincent. But, some Historians and Classics Professors believe that turbulence caused World Wars. Ahem! The actors behind it were Hades."

Shaking my head, I comment, "Morons."

"Ah! That's an apt sentiment, Vincent. The last recorded turbulence occurred in 1991."

That's the one that took my Akane. "Other than it being a tear in the continuous flow of time, do we know what it looks like?"

"Philip Nardin commissioned a study. Physicists from MIT and Caltech created a simulation. It's like a wormhole—"

"Stop it there, Ludwig. Can you project the 3D image onto my left bottom monitor?"

A hologram appears. The light blue, almost white, looks a lot like the sparks I experienced when I learned about Akane's disappearance. I put on my wireless sensory gloves and pull the hologram from the screen. It looks like an Einstein-Rosen Bridge—two funnels connected by a single tunnel. "Ludwig, so to suck people in, there needs to be a powerful centripetal force. Does that force tear time?"

"You got that right, Vincent."

"So there must be a centrifugal force to balance it out on the other end?"

"Yes. But the speed is slower on the other end."

I release the hologram and press my temples with my fingertips. Why would it be slower? That would cause an imbalance, which is why only a few people make it out of the turbulence. Something must account for this loss. "Ludwig, what happens to the place after turbulence?"

"Rich deposits of intreton are found."

So Philip's wealth is a direct result of this basic physics equation. On one side, you have high speed and a lot of people getting sucked in. On the other, you have maybe one person, a slow pace, and copious amounts of intreton.

"Ludwig, can you tell me about the characteristics of people who survived turbulence?"

"Once a turbulence-affected soul enters a different body, the host experiences severe headaches and challenges in their lives such as split personalities. They become deeply confused individuals, often conflicted between the host's independent thoughts and the turbulence survivor."

"When do these hosts experience these symptoms?"

"Ahh! That can happen anytime in their lives. Usually with some strange inciting incident."

"Like what?"

"Someone who had no talent in spelling suddenly becomes a spelling bee champion. It gets more complicated."

I tilt my head. "Like what?"

"The vast majority of those who come back from turbulence are born into a reality different from the one they departed. So the symptoms they experience cannot be traced to anyone in the reality they are born into."

Fuck. So even if Akane came back, she would be in a different reality. I guess I will never meet her. But things do occur at the fringes.

"Any social, economic, or political impact, Ludwig?"

"Hah! The world is fucked up with or without the turbulence, Vincent. Other than Philip Nardin, there isn't any record of noteworthy people getting sucked into turbulence. Unless we meet someone who has been experienced multiple realities, we wouldn't really know anything."

"I will read the rest at home. Ludwig, can you install yourself on my cell phone? I don't think my BMW iDrive will be able to navigate me tomorrow."

"Ahh, sure. Can I bypass all the security protocols on your cellphone?"

"Absolutely."

Ludwig continues. "Thank you, Vincent. Also, I won't tell BMW that you're cheating on her with me."

I smile. "Thanks, I was worried."

It's 4:45 p.m.—time to pick up Hulk.

I am home, with Hulk sitting next to me. My all-home surround sound is playing select pieces from Chopin, Liszt, Saint-Saëns, and Satie. Today's research on time turbulence has stirred memories that I thought were behind me. I take out a wooden box from the top shelf in my walk-in closet. It has a lacquered imprint of cherry blossoms and houses a priceless object—Akane's scarf. I haven't allowed myself to look at this for the longest time—I had to move on. Since leaving the boarding school, I've never spoken of this scarf to anyone. I told Elise it was a parting gift from my headmaster that I cherish. After taking out the scarf, I sit on the floor, placing the box next to me. Hulk comes to sit beside me. I cover my face with the scarf and breathe in.

(Summer of 1989)

It was just another gloomy Monday. It was the middle of Grade 2 math class, and I was already bored—I'd finished the whole syllabus during summer break. I was looking out the window, watching the sun's game of hide-and-seek with the clouds. Suddenly, a robin flew to the sill and pecked on the window glass. It was looking straight into my eyes like it was trying to tell me something.

Sasha, who sat behind me and next to Krista, poked me with a pencil.

"Ouch?" I turned to look at her.

"Stand up. Headmaster is here."

I came to my senses and was the last person to stand up. Mr. Kruger motioned behind him and spoke in a low, soothing voice. "Don't be shy, Miss Egami, please come in."

From the corner of my eye, I saw the robin fly away. And at that very moment, the sun pierced through the clouds, reaching the door of my classroom and shining its light on the prettiest face I'd seen in my six years of existence. She was shimmering brighter than the light shone on her. Slowly, she walked in, wearing a backpack and carrying a violin case in her left hand. Her right hand was attached to a maroon and mustard scarf. Mr. Kruger placed his hands on her tiny shoulders. "This is your newest member. Her name is Akane Egami. Yes, the same Egami name that our auditorium and music room bear. She is the third generation to come to this school. What do we say?"

"Welcome, Akane," we all chorused.

She bowed. "*Ariga*... Sorry... Thank you."

Mr. Kruger then turned to her. "Let me find you a benchmate." Looking straight at me, he said, "Scoot over and let Akane sit next to you. Help her catch up with the syllabus."

"Yes, sir."

I made space for her as she came close. She had large brown eyes with thick lashes, and her lips were red like an apple. As she smiled, her eyes became a double layer of thick lashes. She extended her hand. "I am Akane."

"I am Vincent."

She tilted her head. "*Vu-insento*?"

"Please sit." I swiped my hand across her seat to clear it. "I will teach you how to say my name."

She lifted her shoulders and sat. "OK."

Krista poked me with her ruler. I turned to her. "What?"

Moving closer so that only she, Sasha, Akane, and I could hear, she whispered, "Vincent has a girlfriend."

I squinted at her. "What's a girlfriend?"

All three girls started giggling. Akane chuckled with her hand covering her mouth.

"SILENCE." Our math teacher banged on her desk.

I shared my textbook and notebook with Akane as our class resumed. But she kept looking at me and then touched my hair. She smiled and whispered, "Wavy hair." I ran my fingers over her scarf, and she said, "This is my favorite scarf. I wear it all the time."

I touched a small, dark brown spot above her upper lip, to the left. "What's this?"

She smiled and lifted her shoulders. "It's a beauty mark, silly."

(Back to present)

From that day, I was her silly Vince, and we were inseparable. She would insert her jade chopsticks into my hair and laugh, looking into my eyes as she said, "*Ooki na midori to aoi no me.*" Later on, she revealed what those words meant—big green and blue eyes. I kept feeling blissful around her, despite her constant usage of Japanese expressions. And then, one day, she called me her family.

(Spring of 1991, No dress code day)

It was the first day of spring, International Culture Day, which meant no uniforms. After school, parents accompanied their children for dinner and a gala. Besides my uniform, I only had one shirt, one pair of trousers, and one sweater—all gifts from Mr. Kruger. If I was cold, I had my school blazer. Most students made fun of me because I wore the same clothes for such occasions. As an orphan, these days, or Christmas or Thanksgiving, meant nothing to me. I locked myself in my room, scribbling in my sketchbook, with my radio playing Liszt's Consolation no. 3.

I peeked through my glass windows, witnessing the return of leaves and birds. A solitary robin was pecking on my window. It flew away as I heard a triple knock on my door. I knew it was her. I was hiding from her, but the radio blew my cover, so I opened the door. And there she was, standing in front of me wearing a navy-blue satin kimono, with her red-and-white polka dot obi tied like a bow in the back.

She smiled and pulled my cheek. "Found you." She came in and sat on my bed. Looking up at me as she touched her hair, she asked, "How do I look?"

I gently placed my fingers on the top of her head. "Like one of your porcelain dolls."

She got up and stepped out of the room, then dragged in a four-by-two-foot purple parcel. Nudging my hand, she said, "It's for you. Put it on. Time for dinner."

I opened the box to find a navy tux with a black velvet peak lapel, a white shirt, and black patent shoes. Tears rolled from my eyes as I touched the fabric. "When did you get this?"

"Last month, silly." She touched my cheek and wiped my tears. "There is a place called Saville Row, where *pa-pha* gets his suits. I saw this in a window and asked him to buy it for you. Now get dressed."

After I changed, she brought Fred, Sasha, and Krista to help cut the labels and wrap the cummerbund. Fred, too, was wearing a tux. Krista and Sasha were in ball gowns. We were kids dressed as adults.

Akane clenched and pulled my sleeve. "Never hide from me. Sit next to me during dinner."

I grabbed her obi and turned to her. "But everyone sits with their family."

She tilted her head, smiled—her eyes transforming into just a line of lashes. "*Kimi wa kazoku desu*, Vince."

"Huh?"

She ruffled my hair. "Silly."

(Back to present)

I don't know what I did to earn such love, such that she would call me family. Nor what I did to be robbed of that love a few months later. She'd bought me my first suit—I will never part with it. I put the scarf down, place my arms right at the center of my forty sports jackets and thirty suits, and squish them to two sides. And there it is—the purple parcel. I take the tux out, remove the dust from the shoes, and steam and iron the shirt and the tux. Tears form at the corners of my eyes as I touch the cuffs of the jacket. "I will never forget how you nudged my cuffs that evening," I whisper. I hang the tux and come back to the scarf. As I wrap it around myself, I smell it. The scent takes me to the moment when she wrapped it around my neck—the fall of 1991. It's been with me since that evening.

(Late fall 1991)

It was raining, and I rushed to the music hall to see Akane right after my classes. She wanted me to listen to a new piece she was practicing—Méditation by Massenet. But my classmates, Jean Laurent, Luther Brehme, and Rudolf Von Stein, stopped me. Luther pulled me by my lapel. "Where're you heading, Vincent?"

"Get out of my way, Luther." I pushed back.

"Else, what?" Rudy lifted his brows, pulling my necktie. "Will you tell your parents? Oh! I forgot you don't have any, bastard. And what kind of name is Abajian?"

Luther smirked. "The type the help has. How did you even get into this school?" He pulled me by my collar and punched my face. And before I could react, he hit me again. I covered my face, struggling to stop my lips from bleeding.

Why were they doing this? All because I was an orphan? Because my skin was different? Or because I was poor? Rudy pulled my hair. Luther removed my hands from my face and struck the third punch, and kicked on my belly.

I fell. I shut my eyes as Luther shoved my head into the ground, and water, mud, and grass gushed into my mouth. Then Rudy sat on top of me, landing another blow, just missing my left eye. Jean, the quiet one, started to breathe heavily and pulled Luther by his sleeve. "I think we should stop now." I opened my eyes.

With his eyes bulging out, Luther turned to Jean and yelled. "Why?"

"I think I saw Mr. Kruger," Jean shrieked, may be out of sympathy for me. Then, without even investigating, the three guys ran off.

Using my hands to support my body, I got up. There was no one around—Jean had lied. My face was sore, and my body ached. My blazer and trousers were all wet from blood, rain, and mud. All I could hear was a constant beeping sound. I limped to the music hall's restroom to clean my face. Slowly, the beeping sound was replaced by Akane's playing. As I left the bathroom and walked down the hallway, the music became louder. She was practicing without a piano accompanist, like always. I sat on the chair closest to her.

Her eyes were shut, with a tiny smidgen of tears at the corner, as she pressed her trembling lips together and continued to play. She, her violin, and Massenet's Méditation became one. I shut my eyes as her violin wiped away my pain. She transported me to a world that I could only see through her eyes and sense from her words—a world where the cherry blossoms resembled snow flurries in pink. The images became vibrant and sparkled with every note of Méditation. I felt tears running down my cheeks, not from the pain but from the pure joy she brought through her music and the world she shared.

I opened my eyes again to see her smile, sensing my presence. After the final note, she opened her dazzling eyes. "How was it?" she asks, tilting her head.

I bowed. "Thank you for playing that." She picked up her violin, and her scarf touched the floor as she picked up the case with her left hand. As she came closer, her smile disappeared. She narrowed her eyes. "Who did this to you?" Her voice echoed across the hall.

"Rudy and Luther."

She ran to the bathroom, gathered some tissues, and wiped my blood. Once my face was clean, she used her scarf to wipe her own tears. Touching my shaking hands and my burning forehead, she asked, "Are you cold?"

"A little."

She took off her scarf and wrapped it around my neck. In that moment of kindness, something changed in me. She and her scarf were inseparable. Yet, she showed no hesitation in parting with it for me. Tears rolled from my eyes as I asked, "Why were you crying when you played Méditation?"

She made a ball out of the tissues and dabbed my tears. "Silly." Coming closer, she kissed my forehead and touched my hair. "Let's go to the doctor."

"I'll be fine."

"Shut up." She pulled me by my blazer sleeve, and we headed out.

I hold the scarf. "When do you want this back?"

"When I come back from Berlin."

"Can you not go there?"

She stopped, put her index finger on my lip. "Shut up. You're bleeding."

The doctors in the infirmary had put me on some sedatives because I woke up maybe a day later. As I opened my eyes, I saw Akane holding my right hand with both of hers and resting her head on them. Fred, Krista, and Sasha were standing to my left and Mr. Kruger by my feet. As my vision cleared, Fred pointed at me. "He's up."

Akane removed her face from my palm and changed the wet cloth on my forehead. Her eyes were red and stained with tears. I was about to open my mouth, but she put her finger on my lips. "Shh, you are still hurt."

Mr. Kruger came forward and touched my head. Then he pointed at Akane. "This one saved your life—you had fractured ribs. She was up all night, next to you."

I struggled to look at Akane through my swollen eyes. She hid her tears with a smile. "Silly."

Every day for the next few weeks, she got my notes from class and ensured I had my meds and food. When I woke up, I saw her face, and it was the last thing I saw before I went to bed.

(Back to present)

I do not know or care if the bullies were racists. All I knew was that when I was hurt, Akane rescued me—through her music and her love. Growing up, I'd never felt the warmth of a home. But then she'd been my home. Her large glittering eyes and bewitching smile were the closest to a feeling of family that I'd had. On that day, I didn't know how to repay her warmth and love. And then, just a few days later, she was gone forever.

When I finally realized how my feelings had bloomed, seven years had passed since she left. She was gone before I could fully know her. A gaping void remained in my heart that longed to know her beyond her warmth and her sweet, kind face. I spent my life moving from one place to another, carrying her violin, scarf, and that photo frame. They became fragments of a soul that I could not stop loving. And, with time, they became a part of mine.

Now, I lift the scarf to my nose and breathe in. Her aura from the scarf is long gone, same as the hope of seeing her again. All I can feel is the moisture from my tears. "I never forgot you. How could I? I just stopped looking after a while."

Hulk places his paw on my knee. I lift my head from the scarf and lean down to kiss Hulk's button nose. "Thanks, bug."

As I moved from one place to another, I hoped for a miracle. I kept looking for Akane in restaurants, in airports, in hotel lounges, in conferences. I so often wished she would spring and surprise me with those sweetest words, "Found you." Since school, Cambridge and MIT, I could never forge meaningful relations in my life. I measured everyone by Akane's warmth, her vibrance, and I could never love anyone for who they were. But by the time Elise came, all my hopes of seeing Akane had vanished. I'd carefully crystalized all our memories. All I cared about was if our paths ever crossed by any chance, I didn't want to be the person who saddens her.

The music shifts from Gnossienne to Liszt's Consolation no. 3. I kept waiting for the day when this music would play, and Akane would knock on my door, just like she did in my dorm room. And we will restart life where we left off, maybe even exploring the possibility of a life together.

My phone vibrates with a message from Emika, startling me. "Thank you, Dr. Abajian!

I look forward to exploring with you."

CHAPTER 3

YAMAZAKI-55

The measure of a man is what he does with power.
—Plato

(About thirteen months before today)

ANOTHER DAY FOR HULK TO be at Little Paws. I hate to leave him.

I take out my Rolex OP-41 from the winder. Opening the drawer under the winder, I take out a Breguet pocket watch from my childhood. No watchmaker in town has been able to revive it. It's now a relic. I can't remember how I got it, but I've always been fascinated with the white porcelain dial and cursive inscription *Depuis 1775*. Did Mr. Kruger gift it to me? I put the relic back and shut the drawer. So, the list of things I can't recall is the name Emika and this pocket watch.

It's been fifteen minutes since I reached my destination. Yet I'm standing in front of 50-foot-tall hedges, spreading as wide as the eyes can see. What a colossal waste of time. Ludwig senses my anxiousness. "Ahh, perhaps I could narrate you a sonnet, Vincent."

I clench my fist, grind my teeth. "Anna!" I can almost picture her grinning.

As I leave my car, I can hear birds and crickets. The temperature is at least two degrees lower than in town. I touch one of the hedges, and it moves a horn-speaker appearing. "Please identify yourself," so speaks a woman's voice with a Nordic accent.

"I'm Vincent Abajian..." The hedge begins to retract, revealing a massive gate constructed with bronze and steel. Underneath the entrance is a contraption of wheels connected by a piston-like one would find in a steam engine. The piston, in turn, powers a mainspring, just like a mechanical watch. There's a 5-foot diameter balance wheel and hairspring, but with no indication of showing the time. Is it linked with the clocks in his house? The escapement is comprised of rubies the size of small bricks. I see no winder. But there are three flaps on top of the gate, moving with the direction of the wind. It's an ingenious apparatus—an entrance with a steam engine's wheels controlled by movement in a mechanical watch, powered by the wind. The wheels roll, and the gate opens.

The voice informs, "Please get inside your vehicle and continue to drive until you see a house."

My heart is racing. I drive for three minutes on a paved road that resembles a Formula 1 racetrack. It's flanked by a beautifully manicured lawn with evergreen coniferous on both sides.

Am I getting close to the mansion? There it is. I can now see a protruding portico. The estate looks like a rotunda, with a large dome on top of it.

The paved pathway transforms into a cobblestone driveway, alternating Italian cypress trees and Renaissance-era sculptures on each side leading up to the front door. I recognize the works of Rodin, Bernini, and Michelangelo. Just how wealthy is this guy? He did surpass Bezos and Musk four years back. I turn left and park right in front of the entrance, next to a Bugatti Chiron, a Pagani Huayra, a Ferrari LaFerrari, a Ferrari Enzo, Koenigsegg Jesko, and a Rolls-Royce Phantom. Fuck, he doesn't even care to put them in a garage. I get out, collect my briefcase, and walk toward the main door. The Ferrari Enzo bears a license plate spelling, "TIME-FIXR." I am positive that I've seen this license plate before. But when and where? What's happening to my memory?

The main door is about 10 feet tall and 4 feet wide. A stained-glass border, exquisitely tinted with blue, red, and purple, outlines the two sides. Skirting the top of the door is a 4-foot-wide semicircular cut of tinted glass. The designer used a single crystal to construct each leaf of the tree. The door itself has nine rectangular, raised wooden panels. Right in the center is a carved lion's head with a knocker. I knock.

A penguin suit-clad, well-built, and chiseled-jawed gentleman answers the door. I lift my head sixty degrees to see his face, judging him to be in his early sixties. He stretches his hand, and my palm gets engulfed by his enormous grip. "I am Edward Tealeaf." South London accent. "Mr. Nardin awaits you in his studio." He points me in the general direction.

The flooring is made with red mahogany wood. I see ten rooms, five on my left and five on the right. Each has a French door in crimson red. On the left, each of the five doors is flanked by a samurai armor and a 5-foot-tall Kintsugi. The doors on the right are lined by a terracotta warrior and a 5-foot-tall vase from the Ming Dynasty. On top of each artifact is a light bulb encrusted with Tiffany's crystal shade attached to the wall. On top of each door is a painting. On the right side, I recognize Vermeer's "Allegory of Painting," Goya's "The Third of May," Friedrich's "The Wanderer Above the Sea of Fog," Monet's "Sunrise," and Van Gogh's "Café Terrace at Night." On the left are paintings by Mr. Nardin. I saw then in Ludwigs' summary report from last night. The first is a cubist style called "Gnoseinne 1, 2, and 3." The second is titled "Starry Night Over Manhattan." The third is a surrealist work called "Moonlight Sonata." The fourth is an impressionist style depicting a man riding a bicycle titled "Homebound." The last one is a portrait of a woman called Amara. She has wavy brown hair and piercing blue-green eyes, painted in spontaneous realism.

"He's in the second room on the left," Mr. Tealeaf reminds me. I pass the first room, which looks like a study. The door to the second room is ajar. I enter. The room freshener exudes a smell of an oud, birchwood, and oak in the room.

The room is an enormous hall with five doors, each flanked by a giant clock. The other side of the wall has several 10-foot-tall glass windows, sealed. The windows end 3 feet above the floor, allowing a window seat with blue cushions. I can tell that the room is soundproof, just the ticking of the second arm of all the clocks. They all tick as if there is only one clock.

I see a relatively short individual—about 5 foot 6 or 7—in the center of the room. His face has a full beard, all white, that comes to a point about an inch below his chin. His hair, also all white, is neatly parted on the left. Wearing a white linen shirt, cream linen trousers, and Birkenstock slippers, he's dressed casually. He's holding a palette in his left hand and a brush in his right, contemplating a canvas depicting a woman emerging from the fire. Mr. Nardin used Pollock's splatter painting method to represent the fire. The woman's skin is blue, her eyes a mixture of green and blue, and her hair is orange and yellow like the fire but flows like waves. Upon closer inspection, I see that the woman's face resembles the one outside, called Amara.

Mr. Nardin turns his head slightly and stares at me with his glinting eyes, hazel eyes that can pierce through one's soul. They deceive the smile on his face. "Ah! You found me at last, Dr. Abajian." He winks. "I hope the directions worked." I can't place his accent, and his deep voice vibrates through the floor and the furniture. Why did he wink?

"Thanks for having me. You live on an enchanting property."

He shrugs and points at his painting. "What do you think"?

"It's marvelous." I tilt my head. "What do you call it?"

He puts his palette and brushes on a table next to his easel. "'Risen from Fire and Ashes.' Do you mind if I call you Vincent?"

"Absolutely not."

He lifts his eyebrows. "I'm famished. Do you like *tamagoyaki*?"

"Yes."

While wiping the paint from his fingers with a cloth, he asks, "Espresso, brewed coffee, tea?"

"Espresso, double shot, please."

He walks to the door. "Edward, can you ask Gai to make two servings of *tamagoyaki* with dashi, one double shot espresso with Kona peaberry beans, and a cup of Darjeeling first flush, please." He turns to me. "Please sit, Vincent."

I sit. "So painting is your hobby?"

"Yes, I was an artist in one of my previous lives and a mechanic-cum-amateur racer in another. Some of the skills from my past life have transferred to this life as hobbies. The remnant of the former two comes and goes, like flashes in your memory. Sometimes they come in a dream."

"I have seen your cars outside. Where do you race them?"

"I have a replica of the Le Mans on my property. My Iceland property has an imitation of the Nürburgring track."

"So, you transport the cars with you there in case you want to race?"

He chuckles. "No, I have the same cars there."

Of course. He can buy every car Ferrari produces. I scratch my head. "Why don't you simply go to the Nürburgring?"

"It's too crowded."

"I see."

Edward brings some food in. Philip lifts one small portion of his *tamagoyaki*. "So, what do you want to know, Vincent?"

"My university wants to do a feature on you, so that'll be mainly about your business." I pause briefly. "But I would personally like to know more about you."

He looks at one of his clocks. "That might take longer than a meeting."

"I understand. Did you make that clock?"

His eyes glint. "I made all the clocks in this house and fixed all the important ones on this planet."

"What's so special about your clocks?"

"They can be synchronized to a millisecond using mechanical movements."

"How?"

He waggles his eyebrows. "Through intreton."

I lean forward. "What exactly is it? It's not on the periodic table. Not even listed in rare earth minerals."

He stretches his arm, cracks his fingers. "You will learn a bit about intreton today. And if you are more interested in my previous lives, that has to be another time."

I nod. "Absolutely. I can make a few trips."

"You can bring your dog if you want to," he says, pointing at the white hairs on my trousers.

"Are you sure?"

"I am wary of humans, especially politicians. Dogs are fine."

I finish my last bite of *tamagoyaki*. "OK, I'll bring him next time."

Philip crosses his legs and takes off his slippers. "So, where do we begin?" The glint in his eyes is visible through his glasses.

"Well, how about we start with your discovery of intreton?" I take out my notebook and uncap my Montblanc fountain pen.

He leans back. "I will get to it. My uncle, Louis, raised me in France. He repaired watches and occasionally made them. His shop was close to the Sarthe River, near the Le Mans track. I was his only family. The name of his shop was Louis-atelier.

"He sent me to an école d'horlogerie in Switzerland to learn watchmaking. I finished the program in two and a half years. Then, I got an offer from Jaeger-Lecoultre in 1968." He pauses. "Would you like anything else to drink? Whiskey?"

I hesitate. "It's early, though."

He smiles. "I did not make that rule. Edward, can you get us one of the Yamazaki-55 and two tumblers, please?" Then he looks back at me and rubs his palms together. "Oh, you'll love this, Vincent."

Edward arrives, pushing a whiskey trolley. He opens the bottle, dispenses two ice cubes in each of the tumblers, and pours the dark amber whiskey. Philip gestures to stop. I note the exact amount. When Edward reaches it with my glass, I say, "That's it, Mr. Tealeaf. Thank you." Edward hands us our glasses and walks from the room, leaving the trolley.

I taste the smooth, woody profile. "You wouldn't save this for someone close to you?"

He tilts his head, his eyes piercing through his glasses. "Well, maybe we will become close. So, where was I?"

I glance at my notebook. "Your employment with Jaeger-Lecoultre in 1965."

"I had to decline." He clicks his tongue. "My uncle was sick, and he needed help with his shop."

I straighten my glasses. "What happened afterward?"

"Every day was the same. People would bring me watches to fix. And then something strange happened. It was 1970 when Porsche won the first Le Mans. I received two watch repair orders. One Omega Speedmaster caliber 321, and the other was a Rolex Daytona 6262. The watches suddenly brought a glimpse of a life that I never lived."

"Two watches were placeholders of your previous lives?" I ask, lifting my pen.

"I will reveal this paradox later."

"Sure."

"Now, let's get to intreton. It was accidental." He takes a sip of his whiskey. "My search for my literal former lives took me to places where I could remember I was. I noticed that in places where the turbulence occurred, some dark-blue crystals formed. They looked like asphalt with a blue sheen. I collected a handful and took them to my shop. I extracted two crystals from the dirt and placed them apart. They were trying to distribute the dirt equally. Then I put one needle on each of the crystals. The needles stood straight. When I moved one needle in one direction, the other one moved in the opposite direction. So, I thought, can this help keep better track of time, overcoming the obstacles with mechanical watches?"

I lean forward. "So, what'd you do?"

He presses his glasses back up his nose. "There had been some unclaimed watches from customers. It hurt the shop but provided me the fodder for experiments. So, I replaced some components with the newfound crystal, discovering that if I replaced the escapement and balance wheel with this crystal, keeping the mainspring, the watch would never stop winding. And you don't need a battery, either. I could increase the frequency from 21,600 to 36,000 vibrations per hour. I'm sorry if this is too technical."

"Not for me," I smirk. "That's the frequency of a Grand Seiko Caliber 9S."

He claps. "You know your watches."

"My headmaster taught me to fix watches. So did you make any intreton-powered wristwatches?"

He pauses, taking cuts a dry smile. "I just made one."

"For?"

"Me." He smiles. "But I never got to wear it. It has many complications—time, perpetual calendar, and a reset date of your choosing."

I look into his eyes. "Why haven't you worn it?"

His eyes grow gloomy, and he looks down. "Long story. Another day?"

"Sure. Let's continue?"

"After I managed to assemble one watch, I did the same with another. So, when I reset the time on one watch, the other watch's time could be automatically reset. It's almost like the crown attached itself to multiple watches."

"How far apart did the watches need to be to counter the influence?"

"For a crystal the size of two square millimeters, two watches can sync up to one hundred feet. I traveled across Europe and collected more of the crystals. Then I spoke with a professor of materials science at the University of Paris, who said that the crystal is an element unknown to humanity." He pauses, stands up, stretches his arms. He looks remarkably fit for his age.

Sitting back down, he continues, "A few days later, I noticed an ad to fix the Elizabeth Clock—Big Ben. Several clock makers applied for the job. My design had the least modification to the current movement, and I promised it would run for eternity. I got the job. I replaced the parts with exact replicas and changed the balance wheel with a large crystal."

He takes another sip. "My next big job was the fixing Prague Astronomical Clock."

I am getting curious. Will he mention the Berlin project—the one that took Akane? "Among all the clocks you fixed, which is the closest to your heart, and do you regret fixing any?"

"There're two. The closest to my heart is the Conciergerie Clock in Paris, and the one I regret is the World Clock in Alexanderplatz, Berlin."

"Why are they significant?"

"After fixing Big Ben, my reputation reached across the Atlantic and the Pacific. I got a few international jobs, mainly synchronizing multiple time zones in stock exchange offices, including New York, Sydney, and Tokyo. Then in 1984, I got the contract for the Conciergerie Clock. After fixing the clock, I met Amara. Only for a moment, though." A blank look comes over his face. "I have one regret in this life. And that's being unable to share it with Amara."

"Who's Amara?"

He points to his work 'Risen from Fire and Ashes' swallowing hard. "Her. She was my girlfriend in my first and second life. In my second life, however, her name was Iman. In my current life, I only met her for a few days. But that won't interest your readers unless you're writing a book."

So, that clears my suspicion that they are the same person. "Do you want your story in a book?"

"Depends if someone writes it. Will you?"

"I've never felt inspired to write a book."

"So, if the story is inspiring, will you give it a go?"

"I may." I push back my glasses. "So, what about the Alexanderplatz?"

"Yes. I'll come to that. Following my New York, Tokyo, Sydney, and the Conciergerie Clock job, I received a letter from Ronald Reagan inviting me to move my business to the US. I would share my research findings with National Labs, and in return, I'd get full access to all the intreton. I guess the US wanted to know the true potential of this element."

"You accepted it?"

"No, I had my lawyers draft a counteroffer." He stands up, paces 10 feet, then comes back. "I wanted him to sign an order that no politician or weapon manufacturers would ever have access to this technology." He hammers his left palm with his right hand. "And if this executive order was ever revoked or challenged, I'd destroy all the stockpiles of intreton."

"I believe he agreed since you did move to the US?"

He nods. "After I moved to the US, the tensions around the Berlin Wall amplified, and the wall eventually came down. Around September 1991, Helmut Kohl contacted me to fix the World Clock in Alexanderplatz, synchronizing multiple time zones. I accepted the offer. I decided to unveil the clock on November 15, 1991, with a reset time of June 13, 1990, commemorating the fall of the wall."

I form a fist under my notebook. I was robbed of my life on November 15, 1991. Trying to resume my regular breathing, I ask, "So, what was the significance of this job?"

"Managing multiple timezones meant more intreton. Also, the clock is only 16 feet tall, making it much closer to humans than the other clocks I fixed. So, I asked the police to create a 100-foot perimeter around the clock so that no one came close to it. But when I unveiled it, people broke the perimeter. Turbulence occurred due to the abundance of intreton, and about a dozen people were lost. It's my only professional regret. I wish there had been more police, a better perimeter. I wish people could control their emotions."

Then he leans forward and touches my hand. "I'm sorry, Vince."

How could he possibly know that I lost someone in that turbulence? Or was it a generic apology for the loss of a dozen people? Should I ask?

Perhaps not. "How come the turbulence did not suck you in? You must've been closest to the clock."

He chuckles. "I wore an intreton-powered vest, which is a repellent to the turbulence. I still have it, but it is now powered by intreton-c. It has enough intreton-c to power a city for a hundred years."

I look back at my notes. "What's the significance of this reset time?"

"It's a token reset time of your choosing—something that's noteworthy to you. For example, it may remind you of something important that happened on a particular day."

"So, what's in the interest of the US government when you've got access to all the resources?"

"They get my knowledge. Intreton, in its pure form, is electromagnetically unstable. So I created a synthetic version of intreton-c, developing it to meet mass-market needs. It has virtually all the benefits and almost none of the hazards. Our scientists have also created a ceramic oxide electrolyte using intreton-c for powering electric cars, cellphones, satellites, and such."

"So, what are you doing with the large stockpiles of natural intreton?"

He looks at the time in his A. Lange & Sohne Lange 1-time zone, then leans forward. "Do you have time, Vincent?"

"Of course."

"A handful of senators and defense contractors have been pressuring the White House to revoke my privileges. Since this isn't an issue that's important to voters, none of the presidents have cared. Technically, I cannot own intreton. But I own all the technology to excavate it, transport it, and store it. And we have been very crafty in filing new patents with updates every five years so that the technology stays with us. That has protected me from any attempts to steal this intreton. But the attempts have increased considerably in the last five years."

I narrow my eyes. "But what would they do with the natural one if the artificial one is as good?"

"Weaponize! You need the pure one to be able to do that. And I won't allow it." He shakes his head. "Because it is unstable, intreton can only be transported in my proprietary canisters. But of late, one defense contractor from Lombard Tech convinced some senators that their canisters are just as good."

"Is it any good? They make drones for the military, right?"

He chuckles. "It's garbage, just like their drones."

"Then how did they convince the politicians?"

"Through lobbyists, who run the country and own the politicians. The senators pressured the DOD to accept a contract with Lombard Tech to transport intreton. Soon after that, I received an order that I must grant Lombard access to pure intreton. I moved it before they could find it. But, last December, about 10 kilos of intreton went missing from one of my storage facilities in Bangalore, India. A month later, a flight from Bangalore to Seattle via Tokyo went missing—Flight 0606."

Everything goes silent. I can hear each of my heartbeats and even the movements inside Philip's clocks. Did this government conspiracy kill Elise? I try to swallow, but my throat is dry. Philip is at the center of both my losses. How much more do I have to pretend? I take a sip of the whiskey. I try to regain my voice, free it from all the wobbling. "Do you know what happened? The government said it was a terrorist attack."

He leans forward and forms a fist. "That was a cover-up. I'm sure whoever stole the intreton used the Lombard boxes to transport it. Because their shielding is rubbish, the electromagnetic interference was enough to destroy the plane. So the question is, how did those boxes get past security?"

So, Philip is key to my finding out what happened to Elise. I turn a page in my notebook. "So what do you want to do with all the natural intreton now, as it can lead to global war?"

He points at my notebook. "I can tell you if you promise that it won't be in print."

"Absolutely." I snap my notebook shut.

He pushes the nose bridge of his glasses. "I wanna destroy them."

"Isn't that dangerous?"

"Of course. Have you heard of the Nardin Space Program?"

"Your $150 billion space project."

He starts whispering. "I can't destroy all the intreton without a catastrophic impact on the planet. I have collected most of it now, and I plan to take it outside the solar system. That's the whole point of the Nardin Space Program."

I follow his lead and start whispering as well. "Who will pilot such a spaceship?"

"If need be, I will." He narrows one eye to a slit.

"What? How will you return?" I cannot hide my surprise.

"I'm currently working on an autopilot system. But even if I fail and I'm unable to return, it will still be worth it."

I see no regrets on his face. I have never seen such a selfless act from a human, let alone someone whose personal wealth might be enough to buy a small continent. However, I'm still curious about the space program. "Why did you choose to create your space program in such a remote area?"

He leans back, relaxing a bit. "Two main reasons. But this is to be off the record as well. Have you ever wondered why all the time turbulences occur in mainland Europe?"

"No."

"I, too, had no idea. But then, I found a rich deposit of intreton in the North Atlantic, Norwegian Sea, and the North Sea. At the center, close to the Faroe Islands, is a core. It's a luminant-white mass constantly vibrating and communicating with the intreton, a pure source of energy. I own all the islands around it and forbid any commercial activities, so the world is oblivious of its existence. Else they will rush into weaponizing it—especially this country. The core forms a time mesh, where past and future are variants of the present. But, at times, there are disruptions when the core reacts with the surrounding intreton, which creates time turbulence."

"What type of disruptions?"

He stares at me and lifts one eyebrow. "You will find out soon enough."

I tilt my head. "How?"

But he just keeps staring at me silently, smiling.

I can tell he won't reveal anything more there. "What else can you tell me about the turbulence?"

"Because of its location, the turbulences are centered in Europe alone. And I found that in Europe, the turbulence was nonexistent at higher altitudes. Maybe that's why enrollments in boarding schools in the Alps increased. So, I wanted my station close to the core and carefully removed all the intreton tangled around it. I believe the core can create alternative timelines for turbulence survivors. Time turbulence creates a wormhole into the core, you see. Some people are absorbed into the core, and some come back anew, newborn, or like me. When someone emerges anew from turbulence, they are usually a part of a different reality."

These scenarios all sound like science fiction. But the entire notion of time turbulence would be science fiction to me if Akane hadn't been taken. "What's the second reason?"

"I wanted to avoid politicians and news media. They all believe that I'm driving cars, enjoying deep-sea diving, all that. But I sneak onto my island and work on my space program."

"I have some other questions, Philip."

"Sure."

"Why do you fund academic research when it sounds like you have other important places to put your money?"

"The world will become a better place only through education and research. Beautiful minds like yours can freely work if they don't have to worry about funding. And I'm proud of what you and your team have accomplished for the center."

I could achieve more if it weren't for the bureaucracy in the uni. "Thank you, Mr. Nardin. I have one more question… and a request?"

"Please go on."

"I see you wearing an A. Lange & Sohne time zone. Is that your favorite watch?"

"Yes, this and the JLC Reverso. The wristwatch that I made for myself has some design cues from the Lange."

"I planned on buying a Reverso after becoming a full professor."

"You're a full professor now, so what happened?"

"I'd made plans to buy it with Elise."

"Elise?"

"She was my late partner."

He squints. "Was?"

"She was on Flight 0606."

"I'm so sorry, Vince. I tried everything in my power to stop it."

"I believe you. It's just that I had no idea a tragedy connects us."

He stares at me with his penetrating eyes. "Well, other things may connect us as well."

"Like what?" I don't break his gaze.

He waves his hand between us dismissively and changes the subject. "What's your request?"

"I have a Breguet pocket watch that I've kept as a memento. Can you have a look at that?"

"Of course. I'll require a bit of time, but absolutely. Do you have any more questions, Vincent?"

I put my notebook back in my briefcase. "I have numerous questions, Mr. Nardin, but none for the interview piece. So, can I come by again for intellectual thirst?"

"Of course, just drop in. Let's exchange numbers. I'll let you know when I'm here. Edward has a more updated schedule. But before you come, let me know so that I can make the property visible."

"Visible?"

He grins. "You'll get it when you leave the property."

"Thank you, Mr. Nardin."

He leans forward and grips my hand. "Call me, Philip. I insist."

"Alright, Philip."

I take my leave after shaking his hand.

Mr. Tealeaf shows me the way out. "It was great meeting you, Dr. Abajian."

I look up. "Please call me Vincent." He must be almost a foot taller than me.

"Certainly, Vincent. Enjoy your day."

As I drive off, I look in the rearview mirror. Suddenly, the mansion and sculptures are engulfed by the earth, leaving only the trees behind. The main gate opens as I reach it, and, as soon as I cross, it hides again behind the 20-foot-tall hedges.

That was perhaps the best meeting I'd had in my life, and I couldn't wait to meet him again. It almost seemed as if I knew him.

It's just me and Hulk in the office. I pick him up and nuzzle my nose against his. He licks my nose and then the tears on my cheeks. I stare deep into his amber eyes. "Can you imagine, bug? Of all the things that could have happened, a political conspiracy took your mom." He tilts his head, trying to make sense of my words. "Elise was such a gentle soul. I have you with me because of her."

(August 2019)

Elise sat next to me and ran her finger across my face. Then she loosened my tie and wrapped her arms around me. "How was your day?"

I gazed at her kind blue eyes. "Nothing spectacular, except for my visit to the Humane Society."

She kissed my forehead. "You keep going there almost every day. What's there?"

I touched her hand. "There's this two-year-old discarded puppy with no name. He's a Shih Tzu and bichon mix, champagne, and white, with the sweetest face. I just spent some time with him. He doesn't want to walk, just wants to climb on my lap, that's all."

Elise got up to fix me a glass of port. "What's so special about him?"

I unbuttoned my collar. "We are the same, two unwanted orphans." I took out my cellphone and showed Elise a picture of the puppy.

"He's adorable. He looks like you." She stood in front of me and narrowed her eyebrows. "Also, you are not unwanted. You have so many people who love you—me, Anna, Ravi, Chris. Your friends from school. Stop saying that."

"You're right." I kissed her hand.

Two days later, I stopped by the Human Society with some toys and a $100 check for the puppy's vaccinations.

At the front desk, I asked, "Can I see the little Zuchon boy?"

"I'm sorry, sir, but he's adopted."

"No, don't apologize. I'm glad the pup found a home. Please keep the toys and the check."

I was genuinely thrilled that someone had chosen the pup. But I still wanted to see him, at least once. I would miss how he licked my face.

I headed home, and as I turned the knob to my apartment door, the screaming of the word "Surprise" reverberated through the space. I covered my ears and saw Anna, Chris, and Ravi. I'd forgotten that it was my thirty-seventh birthday. Where was Elise? The three moved to make way for her. She was holding the pup, the one that had been adopted.

My face crinkled with joy. After Akane's departure, my birthdays never meant anything until that moment. All I can see is the sweet puppy and the kindness and love in Elise's eyes. "When did you adopt him?"

Elise smiled, came forward, and kissed my lips. "Yesterday. Anna kept him for the day. I couldn't separate you two on your birthday." She grinned. "By the way, they've no record of his fellow's birthday. So he will share yours."

Anna rolled her eyes. "Whatever. I kept calling him 'Dog' all day. Name him now, or I swear that I will call him Vincent Junior."

Chris turned to me. "He's little and looks docile. So, you should name him something contrary."

I snapped my fingers. "How about Hulk?"

"Hulk it is," approved Elise.

Ravi raised his glass. "Happy birthday to Vincent and to Hulk."

Everyone joined in the chorus. Elise released Hulk, who smelled the carpet and walked toward me. He stood up on his hind legs while touching my knees with his front ones. I picked him up and held him close, kissed his button nose. "Hi, Hulk! I am your Dadda."

(Back to the present)

Maybe Philip knows more about this conspiracy. I scratch Hulk's chin. "What do you think, bug?"

I create two MS Word files. One I title "Philip Nardin: An Interview by Vincent Abajian," and the other I save as "The Time Fixer: Three Lives of Philip Nardin." The first one is for the *Business Review,* but the second one may reach a greater audience. I liked the license plate on his Ferrari Enzo. As I think back, I know I have seen that license plate somewhere before. Just like I have heard the name Emika before. So now I can't recall three things: Emika, the pocket watch, and the license plate.

A while back, our center offered accelerator funding to a group of engineering students who developed a program that can translate thoughts into words. It's a combination of a headpiece and a program called Prose. "Engage Prose for one hour on file, 'The Time Fixer: Three Lives of Philip Nardin.'"

CHAPTER 4

BALLADE NO. 4, OP. 52

It is a part of the probability that
many improbable things will happen.
—Aristotle

(About a year before today)

JUST AS I STEP INTO my suite, Linda jumps up from her desk, and her eyes lighten. "Oh, Hulk is here." She comes forward and ruffles his luxurious coat. After he gets a good petting, I enter my office with Hulk. I hang up my drenched trench coat, and Hulk shakes off the water from his furry coat and jumps onto his buffalo plaid bed by the fireplace.

I turn on my piano playlist, with the first song being Chopin's Raindrop Prelude. It sounds immersive through my Bang & Olufsen Beolab 20. The raindrops splashing on my window create an amalgam with the gorgeous melody. It's 9:54 a.m. I start to edit "Philip Nardin: An Interview by

Vincent Abajian." I have always used the length of songs as a measure of elapsed time. This one is six minutes long.

As the clock turns to 10:00 a.m., a robin appears outside my window and pecks on the glass, seeking attention. *Where were you hiding for thirty-two years?* The song on my system changes to Chopin's Ballade no. 4. A ray of sunlight pierces through the cloud and reaches my office door as I hear three knocks in succession. I haven't heard that specific knock since 1991.

"Please come in."

The robin flies away. A young woman enters, folding her transparent umbrella. She is shimmering in the sunlight. It's the same image I saw outside Headmaster Kruger's office on November 23, 1991. The same song was in the background. Every strand of hair on my arms and neck rises as I see the spitting image of Akane in front of me. Has she come back? Did she find me? And there she is, smiling. That smile—I never thought I'd see it again. This is Akane, with shorter hair and a beauty mark shifted from the left of her top lip to the right.

She's wearing an olive suit with folded sleeves. A tan shopper bag with the logo Gurkha hangs from her left shoulder, with a laptop and a few papers peeping out of it. Around her neck is a rose gold necklace with a Tiffany-blue pendant resembling a puppy. On her left wrist, she has a smartwatch—rose-gold with a brown rubber strap. On her right is a bracelet, this one rose gold with a Tiffany-blue heart-shaped pendant. I can feel every beat of silence between the notes of Chopin's masterpiece. Her burnt sienna irises can illuminate a dark room—I have seen it before. Her hair is straight, black, cut to an inverted short bob, with a few locks of hair covering a portion of her right eye.

She walks over to me, tucks a lock of hair behind her ear, and extends her arm. "Professor Abajian, my name is Emika Amari. You wanted to meet me?" Her accent is a mix of Japanese, British, and Northern European. We shake hands. Am I touching Akane after thirty-two years?

"Please call me Vincent or Vince. Take a seat."

"Thank you, Vince." She sits. The reflected sunlight from my floor-to-ceiling windows touches her face, and her sienna-colored irises turn golden in the sunlight. Her thin black eyebrows look almost maroon, and her black hair resembles the color of sugar maple leaves that turn red in fall. The pointed tip of her nose casts a long shadow, crossing her lips to her chin.

The sight in front of me is far more elegant than Seong-jin Cho's divine interpretation of Chopin's Ballade no. 4.

Hulk alerts us of his presence with a yawn as Emika turns to him, cups her cheeks with her hands, and tilts her head, her eyes widening. The pitch of her voice goes up with the words, "*Kawaii.*" She turns to me and points at Hulk. "Can I? Please."

"Sure."

She walks toward Hulk. "What's your name?" She notices the collar and stretches her arms, puffs her cheeks. "Oh, you're Hulk, big and strong?" Hulk hates strangers, but he proceeds to sniff her. Emika scratches his chest and, after a moment, comes back to the chair. She closes her eyes. "Hmm, Chopin's Ballade no. 4, my father's favorite."

I tilt my head. "Is he into music?" Damn, I should have asked what her favorite is.

She shrugs. "He was a pianist then became a conductor with the Tokyo Philharmonic Orchestra."

I need to be professional. "So, Emika, what brought you to us?"

"Well, my dream job would be at the Alan Turing Institute. But your vision and ambition made me apply here. I heard you speak several times. And I thought 'I wish I could work with him.'" Hulk leaves his bed to sniff Emika's feet. His cold, wet nose must've tickled her because she laughs while looking down.

"Thanks for choosing us. In the next two years, we will make this center the premium research facility in AI."

She lifts her brows. "Anna keeps telling me how ambitious you are."

"Why did you choose mathematics? Unfortunately, it's not popular these days." I place my hand on the desk, trying to appear unaffected by her praise.

Her smile reaches her eyes. "You'll laugh at my reasons."

"Try me." I rest my chin on my palm and blink.

"My father always emphasized that music is the true language that doesn't hide behind words humans create. His idea was that music is the language of God. My mother, being a linguist, was far more pragmatic."

"Your mother is a professor?"

"Yes. The University of Kyoto, and she did her doctoral studies at Oxford."

"Is that why you chose Oxford?"

She leans forward and narrows her brows. "Yes. But we were talking about my choosing mathematics."

"Sorry, please go on."

"Oh, that's fine." She smiles through her eyes. "So, I thought that if I studied mathematics, I could bridge the gap between words and music through numbers." She picks up Hulk and pets him gently. "I had a Japanese spitz as a kid. His name was Haru, and he meant everything to me. My parents were always busy, so it was just Haru and me. He was my brother, my son, and then he left me."

"I am so sorry, Emika." I wish I could reach across the desk touch her hand. "Haru, as in Spring?"

Her eyes brighten. "You speak Japanese?"

I cough to conceal the tremble in my voice. "A little. I had a friend who taught me a few words, and then I learned a bit more to impress her if she ever came back."

"Where did she go?" she asks, slanting her head.

"Long story. Some other time?" Maybe she has come back. If she is Akane, does she know that?

She blinks. "OK." Then she does me the favor of changing topics. "Vince, I have some questions about transferring consciousness."

I lean forward. "Fire."

"I would like to experiment with transferring consciousness with successive iterations. And for that, we'll require more synthetic bodies unless one can create a restore point, which I can make easily."

"Go on."

"Say John wants to transfer his consciousness at the age of eighty. But his brains have already degenerated. But if he had created a transfer when he was forty, we transferred a fully working brain. Now, if someone wants to have a restore point, we could do it. Or someone can create multiple entities with the same consciousness, say at ages of forty and fifty and so on. I believe the transfer is the wrong term and strategy. We should copy the consciousness from the human to the machine. What do you say, Vincent?" She lifts one shoulder and grins, exuding the confidence of a brilliant mind.

"OK, let's do it, Emika. We'll have the resources soon. I am expecting a large shipment from Nardin Applied Sciences."

She leans forward. "Also, can you call me Emi?"

"Sure, Emi, it is. What are the others calling you?"

She slants he head, smiles. "Emika." Her expression hinting that I am different from others—unless I am reading too much into this. My playlist suddenly changes to Chopin's Concerto no.1 in E-minor.

She shuts her eyes and smiles. "That's one of my favorites. When I close my eyes, I can picture cherry blossoms."

I can't help leaning toward her. "Did you ever watch this opus live?"

"Yes, I did. My father was a solo pianist and then became a conductor and composer."

Why didn't this occur to me earlier? Amari and Tokyo Philharmonic Orchestra. Where are my faculties? "Don't tell me Hiroshi Amari is your father? He is my favorite pianist and conductor."

She nods and smiles. "Yes, he is."

"I have all his recordings. You must be proud to be raised by him."

"He is just my pa-pha, who was not too pleased with my career choices."

That word, *pa-pha*—I had heard it before. Form the one who was engulfed in time-turbulence.

"Anyway, what's done is done." She waves her hand, dismissing her father. "Is Chopin your favorite?"

"Chopin and Liszt are at the top. But I also love Sarasate, Massenet, Saint-Saëns, Kreisler, and many others."

She grins, and her eyes become a double line of lashes. "Wow! Most people would simply say, Beethoven and Mozart."

I look into her eyes. "I am not most people." I am lost in her eyes, and I need a diversion. I lean back, breaking eye contact. "Do you play any instruments?"

She pauses, taking a deep breath. "As a child, I took piano lessons under papha. But then I gravitated towards the violin. But I struggled. I realized that I couldn't be professional."

"What type of struggle?"

"I'll tell you the whole story some other time." She smiles to bury something deeper.

"OK, that's a date." I'm not sure if I should've used the word "date."

She snaps her fingers. "Sure. My violin saga and your Japanese friend." She points at a picture of Elise holding a four-month-old Hulk. "By the way, who's she?"

"She's Elise, my late partner."

She bows her head. "I'm so sorry, Vince. I had no idea." She holds Hulk tightly and kisses his forehead. Hulk, of course, continues his inertia of siesta.

"It's fine—just a fact of my life. Been almost eight months."

Linda knocks and comes in. "Sorry to interrupt. Emika, can I bring in your luggage from the reception?"

Emika stands up. "Let me do that." She brings in two pieces of luggage, red and blue, and a black Samsonite carry-on, while Linda returns to her desk.

I squint my eyes and point at the luggage. "Why are you lugging these around?"

"I stayed in a hotel last night because my townhome wasn't quite ready. It will be in an hour or so, though. After that, the building manager will deliver the keys to Linda."

I stretch my arms. "And where is this townhome?"

"It's on NE Street," she says, tucking her hair behind her ears again.

"Give the details to Linda, and as long as you are here, the center will pay for your lodging. Also, give her a copy of your hotel bill, breakfast, air ticket, all expenses. We will take care of it."

She smiles. "Thank you, Vince."

"You're welcome. Also, do you have a car?"

She shakes her head. "Sorry."

"OK, I'll drop you off. Do you mind spending another torturous hour or so with me?"

"Nope." She then points at my left hand. "That's a beautiful watch."

"Oh! Thanks. It's an Omega Seamaster."

"Can I see it?"

I stretch my arm out, and she places her ear on the dial. I am not sure if it's appropriate behavior to do that with your boss's boss. But if she is who I think she is, I wouldn't care if she bites off my arm.

"My mum gifted a Grand Seiko to my father."

"What's your mom's name?"

"Siri Jokinen. She is originally from Finland but moved to England for her education. She's also fluent in Japanese." My espresso machine catches her eye. "You make your own espresso here?"

"Yes. Want a shot?"

"Let me think." She shuts her eyes. Then, after about three seconds, the bright eyes open. "Sure, why not?"

I shout, "Linda, do you want an espresso?"

"No, Dr. A, I need my sleep," she shouts back.

Emika covers her lips, and her shoulders shake.

I reject three beans that are too large and weigh precisely twenty grams of beans inside the Faustino grinder.

Emika narrows her eyes. "Are you this anal about everything?"

"I am particular about a few things, yes."

"I see."

I pull two double shots and give one to her. "I hope you like the content befitting the art on the cup."

She stares at the cup, which reveals Van Gogh's "Wheat Field with Crows." Then she swirls the cup, sniffs the coffee. And she drinks it in precisely three sips. "I'm sure old Vincent will be proud of the new one," she says, curling her thumb and index finger into an OK sign. "Perfect espresso." She dabs her upper lip, feeling the crema there. "Can I have a tissue?"

Without thinking, I hand her my white and navy pocket square.

She extends her hand but hesitates before taking it. "That'll get damaged."

I look into her eyes—the ones I knew for only two years and have longed to see for more than three decades. "I don't mind."

"OK, I'll clean and give it back. It will be an excuse to come to your office." She looks around the room, taking everything in. "Your office is just a reflection of what you like outside academia: watches, cars, art. I read about you in *Poets & Quants*. The music bit wasn't there."

"You don't need an excuse. Just drop in anytime."

She looks at the pocket square. "This matches your navy suit and your white shirt. You're very well dressed. Anna was right." Then she sniffs the air and turns to me. "Your office smells like a coffee shop. How much do you consume?"

"About four to six double espressos a day. Keeps me awake."

She lifts her eyebrows, shakes her head. "That's not good for you. One double shot fine. Two is pushing it, but four to six is damaging, Vince. You could try tea instead."

"I could."

Linda comes back in. "Your townhome is ready, Emika. I will get your keys here in about five minutes."

"I'll drop you off after the keys come." I want to cherish every microsecond.

"Thanks, Vince."

"Hey, you two, can you guys join Anna, Chris and Ravi, and me for dinner? Unfortunately, I'm not sure of the venue."

Linda sighs. "I'm sorry, Dr. A. I hardly get any time with my kids."

"It's fine, Linda. You don't have to apologize." She leaves, and I turn to Emika now. "You have kids?"

She tucks that hair behind her ears, shrugs her shoulders. "No. And Anna already invited me. Sichuan Palace, right?. By the way, they're already betting on how overdressed you'll be. They wanted me to bet after I met you."

"The odds are stacked against you. They have more data points than you do."

"I'm sure the odds will even with time as I see more of you. By the way, what type of beard is that?" She uses her index finger and thumb to draw the beard pattern on her face, imitating mine.

"It's a mix of Balbo and Anchor."

Linda shouts, "Keys are here."

I turn to Emi. "Let's get you settled in."

She gathers her things, collects her umbrella. I take her blue luggage and the black carry-on, and she carries the red one.

On reaching the parking lot, I take my cellphone out. "BMW, pick me up." The car arrives in thirty seconds.

She laughs at the license plate, "HULKSDAD." Turning to me, she offers, "I can hold Hulk unless he prefers the harness in the rear."

I turn to her. "Hold him. He wants to be held by those he loves."

She smiles, blushing.

Hulk jumps on her and starts licking her throat. She kisses his nose. "Yes, Hulky, I love you too."

We reach her townhome in almost no time. I should have taken the longer route—I am an idiot.

"You wanna come in, Vince?"

"Sure." And I disembark.

She opens the dark green door. The living space has a sofa and a loveseat set perpendicular to it. Opposite to the couch is a 40-inch TV. The kitchen seems well-equipped. There's also a powder room, and dining space. And the stairs going up must lead to a couple of bedrooms.

"You think this will do?" I ask.

"Sure. This place is much bigger than my apartment in Pasadena."

"Let me get your luggage."

"Please don't spoil me."

I bring her luggage inside. "It was great meeting you, Emi. I'll see you at dinner tomorrow or the day after."

She comes close and hugs me. "Thank you so much, Vince. You're so different than what I imagined."

Why is she hugging me? Is she truly Akane who missed me all this while? Or is she over-friendly with everyone? And why don't I feel uncomfortable? I can smell her perfume: amber, vanilla, vetiver, and sandalwood. Her hair, I know that texture. "Settle down, and if you need something, let me know."

"Vince, I have one question."

"Sure." I don't mind prolonging this introduction.

She clasps her hands in front of her. "Please don't think I'm stalking, but when I search your name on Google, no social media profile comes up. Any reason you shy away from such platforms?"

I sigh. "After Elise passed, I left those platforms."

"I'm sorry, Vince."

"It's fine. See you soon."

"One last thing, Vince—can we share our phone numbers?"

I hand her my cell, and we exchange numbers. I assign Chopin's Ballade no. 4 as her ringtone. Fitting, I suppose.

She hugs Hulk. "I'll see you soon, baby boy."

I collect Hulk and enter my car. Then I turn back to see if Emika is looking at us through her window. She is.

"Hey Ludwig, back to work, and can you play the playlist, 'Akane's favorites?'"

"Ah! Just four opuses. But good ones."

That's right. She'd mastered them by the time she was nine. And played them for me. I wish I'd had a device to record her violin back then. Itzhak Perlman isn't bad either.

I am back in my office, and I lean my head on my desk. Philip Nardin has had multiple lives, and he even remembers past ones. Is it possible that there is a fragment of Akane in Emika? And in this reality, no less? Does the Akane in her remember me? Like Philip, does Emika have those flashes of her past? Am I in any of those? If Emika gets Akane's violin, will she remember anything? Does the violin need servicing?

Why am I electing emotions over reason? I have work to do. Over half a dozen papers need revising, patents to submit. I want to take this center to the top, but I haven't invented anything in a year. That's shameful! My team depends on my leadership. I need to get down to work.

But how did Philip know Iman was Amara? I can feel my pulse quicken. How to find out if Emika is Akane? I pick up my cellphone. "Ludwig, who is the best violin restorer in town?"

"That'd be Hans Effennberg & Sons in uptown. They close at 5:00 p.m."

I turn to Hulk. "Let's go for an adventure?" He wags his tail and jumps on me. Unlocking a drawer, I take out Akane's violin and the photo frame. I bring the photo to my chest, and I shut my eyes for a few moments. When I open them again, tiny droplets of tears fall on the glass frame. I move my fingers over Akane's face. "So you found me, right?" I gather up the violin case. "Are you really back? After all these years."

(2018)

Elise decided to move into my apartment. As her eyes fell on Akane's violin and our picture, she wrapped her arms around me. "Hey, remember what I said about moving on?"

"I do." I took a deep breath. "But I cannot throw those away."

She pulled my head toward her shoulder and whispered. "I will never ask you to do that. Can you just move them? So that we can create our own memories, detached from your past?"

I pulled back to look into her blue eyes. "Sure." I did not want to argue with someone who wanted to spend her life with me—or try to anyway. I took the violin and the photo frame and locked them securely in my office at the university.

When I came back, Elise asked, "So where'd you put them?"

I looked at her. "Far from us."

She came close, hugging me again. "It's for your own good, Vincie, and you should realize that."

"I guess." I shrugged begrudgingly.

(Back to the present)

I lock my office door. "Enjoy your evening, Linda."

She peers over her computer monitor. "Wait. Is that a violin case? Yours?"

"Not mine. But stayed with me for the longest."

"Whose is it?"

"Childhood friend."

"Where is he?"

I shake my head. "She. And it's a paradox."

Linda rolls her eyes. "You and your puzzles."

The store is squeezed between a watch repair shop that couldn't fix my pocket watch and a used vinyl store. Between the three stores, I am the only customer. The McDonald's and the Pizza Hut at the two ends of the strip mall are packed.

As I open the glass door, an attached bell rings. I see about twenty violins, a dozen violas, two cellos, and one double bass lined up for restoration. An elderly gentleman wearing a rumpled shirt comes to the front. He has gray curly hair, almost touching his shoulders, and a thick beard with no mustache. His cheeks are recessed, and he reeks of tobacco. Glasses, round like Gandhi's and thicker than Sherlock's magnifying glass, rest on his hooked nose. His watch is an old Seiko automatic.

With a weak voice, he says. "I'm Hans. Jr., Are you lost?"

I squint at him. "Why would I be lost?"

"People usually knock on my door when they're lost." His swollen eyes and dry smile depict a sadness that the world pays no attention to in his art.

"I am in the right place."

He pulls a high stool forward. "Sure, what do you have?"

I put the case on his table, and he opens it. The violin breathes life into his soul, his eyes brighten, and his mouth opens wide. "*Wunderbar*, this is a Lorenzo Carcassi from the mid-eighteenth century." He turns to me with his eyes all moist. "This is a million-dollar violin, sir."

"Hans, I want to unite this with its rightful owner. I want to make sure it sounds like it's supposed to." Never had I had so much confidence in the quivering hands of a human.

He presses his lips together. "I am surprised you haven't sold it."

I shut my eyes and see Akane playing this violin. Opening them again, I smile. "It has memories that no dollar amount can surpass."

"I'll do my best to restore those memories. I don't know how much it will cost, but I need a small deposit. And I'll call you when I have a full estimate."

"That's fine. Do you accept credit cards?"

"I do, sir. I should have more information to give you in about seven days."

He charges $1,500 on my card and takes the case and its contents into his workshop. My hands almost resist letting go of what has become a part of my soul.

☀

With homemade miso ramen in one hand, the TV remote in another, I settle on the couch with Hulk to watch *What's Tonight with Maurice Johnson.*

"We have a wonderful show for you tonight. We have Senator Dick Graham with us. He's running on the GOP ticket for the US presidency. Ladies and gentlemen, Senator Dick Graham."

Let's see what Dick has to say. He's been bugging Linda for the last few months to set up a meeting with me.

The fake smile from his dentures is unmistakable. He parts his hair in the middle and uses a yellow-blond dye to conceal the gray. A phony tan makes his teeth glow. Clad in his ill-cut blue suit and long red tie, Dick waves at the crowd. There are more boos than cheers from the left-leaning crowd that Maurice caters to.

After a few moments, Maurice fires, "So why do you wanna run for president?"

The camera zooms in on the senator as he spews utter garbage in his Oklahoma accent. "I believe in public service, and I have worked so hard to bring people together. But, we need changes in the country, we need tax cuts, we need to make it America's time."

"Mr. Graham, you have deep ties with some of the most notorious lobbyist groups in the US. You pushed for a genetically modified wheat that changed the soil. You pushed for authorization of an Alleren's allergy drug, Clear-day, that killed tens of thousands of people. How do you answer for that to the American people?"

"Well, science is tricky. If we'd known then what we do now, we would not have approved the drug."

"Tricky? Your daughter, a reputed epidemiologist, published a report on the drug's ill effects a year before you approved it. Didn't you discredit her findings in public?"

Dick shakes his head while keeping his fake smile. "Liberal fake news like yours misconstrued my words."

"I'm not the news, Mr. Graham. How is your fundraising going?"

"I'm grateful for all the millions of hard-working Americans supporting me as the people's candidate." The crowd boos him.

Maurice fires again. "What do you have to say about using your daughter's funeral as a platform to raise funds and meet lobbyists?"

"Again, those are rumors concocted by your left-biased media."

It seems that the serpent is out of his depth today. Let's do something better—load my dishwasher. I see pending notifications on my cell—a text from Emika, an email from Ravi regarding a revision request, and another from Anna about a grant application. Which should I read first? Logic dictates Anna, Ravi, and then Emika.

I open Emika's text. It reads, "I decided to attend orientation. Wish me luck. Please."

"Good luck. You may die from boredom or bad food."

Emika: If either is terrible, I'll come to bug you in your office.
Me: I can be boring, too.
Emika: Not from what I saw.
Emika: Vince, there are four Sichuan Palaces in town. Which one are we going to?
Me: It's the one I'll take you to.
Emika: Thank you, Vince.
Me: *Doitashimashite.*
Emika: *Oyasuminasai.*

(My orientation at the uni, Fall 2010)

I stretched my arms, yawned, and shook my head to stay awake. I took out my laptop and began to revise a paper. A woman sat next to me, placing her bag on the empty chair on the other side of her. She was wearing an orange floral top, tan blazer, and navy khakis. She poked me and bent her head. "Bored?"

I looked at her—blue eyes, blonde wavy hair tied in a knot at the back of her head. Pretty. I smiled ruefully. "Can you blame me?"

"Nope," she said, extending her hand. "I'm an assistant professor in epidemiology."

I shook her hand. "I'm Vincent Abajian, assistant professor of something far less intriguing."

She smiled and released my hand. "Wanna cut this for some lunch? And tell me about your less intriguing subject?"

That was forward. I lifted my eyebrows. "Sure. Do you have a name?"

She smiled. "Elise Graham."

CHAPTER 5

UNMEI

I lost my way all the way to you.
—Atticus

(About a year before today)

"HI, PHILLIP."

"Hi, Vincent. Did I wake you?"

"No, I was up."

"Your editor contacted me. I approved the article."

"Thanks, Philip. Where are you?"

"In Iceland. Checking on my spaceship and racing. Have you ever raced, Vincent?"

"I haven't."

"Then let's change that. If you want to drive fast, just drop a text to Edward, and you can come to the property and race. You can even try one of my cars. Then, once you have enough practice, you and I can race."

"That sounds amazing."

After Akane's disappearance, I delved deeply into my studies. First, I went to Cambridge for my undergraduate and master's in computer science and mathematics on a full scholarship. Then I did my doctoral studies in innovation, analytics, and artificial intelligence at MIT. I came to this town as an assistant professor, and I met Elise. She was estranged from her parents and did not want to be associated with her corrupt father.

Her body had never been recovered. Dick Graham put together a memorial that he transformed into a fundraising opportunity. The official story was that the fund would go to the families of the Flight 0606 victims. But the families received nothing.

Later on, I bought a small plot in a local cemetery and had a headstone made. We'd loved each other in our own flawed way. In a perfect world, I don't think we would have found each other.

I need to move—something Anna's told me several times. Each piece of furniture here has a memory of Elise attached to it. Should I simply discard them? And move to what?

My phone beeps with a text from Emika.

Emika: Dinner at 6:00 p.m. today.
Me: Yep, Anna told me.
Emika: How is little Hulk?
Me: He's fine, resting on my leg. We are watching TV.
Emika: Anything specific?
Me: Pink Floyd's *Pulse*.
Emika: My parents met at a Pink Floyd concert.
Me: I must thank Mr. Gilmour for bringing you to me.
Emika: Do that. I'll be ready by 5:30 p.m.
Me: See you then.

I pick out a light-blue chambray sports jacket, a white poplin shirt, brown suede shoes, and my Rolex Oyster Perpetual 41 for dinner tonight. It's August, and twenty-two years have passed since the last time I ever begged for anything.

(August 2001)

On my graduation day, I went to the music room with some blue and purple bellflowers—her favorite. I placed the flowers on the exact spot where she'd stood to tie the scarf around my neck. My voice trembled, and my eyes got moist. "You can hear me, right? Ten years have rolled by since I heard you say, 'Found you.' Ten years of ignoring flurries, fresh spring leaves, the bellflowers, and the autumn leaves. How could you leave me? How could you be so selfish? How many more years will you keep me waiting? I still don't believe you're gone. It feels like a lie—a very long lie." I took out my pocket square and dabbed my eyes. "All I want is to see you—maybe just for a minute. Is that too much to ask?"

As I began to turn away, I saw the setting sunshine on the flowers. The colored hue created an image of a little girl, about eight years old. She wore a knee-length navy dress with white polka dots and puffed sleeves. Her shoes were pink with a white bow, and she was holding a violin. She looked at me with tear-soaked eyes. "Who are you?"

As I walked toward her, her image disappeared.

(Back to the present)

I have programmed the dog feeder robot for Hulk in case I'm late coming home. As I step into the empty elevator, I can't help wishing it were just Emika and me in the restaurant. Maybe through Emika, I can understand a little bit more about Akane.

It's 5:29 p.m., and I'm standing outside Emika's townhome. The days are getting shorter. The streetlights are on, and the setting sun is painting the sky with purple, orange, yellow, and red. She emerges just as I am about to knock on her door.

Wearing a pair of suede boots, a white T-shirt, and a tan utility jacket over her jeans, she looks stunning. Around her neck is a Burberry scarf. "Hi, Vince." She stretches her arms out and hugs me. I open the passenger door, and she climbs in. Is it possible that Akane is sitting next to me? Emika turns to me. "How was your day"?

"Papers, patents, and grants. Yours?"

She crosses her arms. "Got some groceries delivered, changed my address, and thought about you."

"Me?"

She shrugs. "Yep. After meeting you, I felt like I've always known you."

My heart skips a beat, and I grab the wheels hard, doing my best to interrupt my chain of thoughts. "You know, Emi, I once saw your father conducting. It was in the Cambridge auditorium, as a celebration of its 800th year. I traveled from Boston to see it."

"Oh, I remember that. My mom and I went with him. I was looking at colleges. Chose Oxford over Cambridge. Sorry!"

"We all make mistakes." I wink. "You only made two—Oxford and Caltech."

"Hey, those mistakes made me sit here next to you." She turns her entire body toward me and crosses her legs. "I think we didn't meet earlier because we were destined to meet now."

"You believe in destiny?"

She touches my shoulder. "Of course."

"You've reached your destination," my car informs.

Emika and I walk toward the main door of the restaurant. Upon entering, the maître d' asks, "Abajian—party of five?"

Emika's eyes sparkle, and she claps. "Yes, yes."

We reach our table to find Chris sitting between Anna and Ravi. Emika sits next to Anna, and I sit next to her. I keep my jacket on. Emika takes hers off and hangs it from the back of her chair.

Ravi turns to Emika. "So, are you all settled in?"

She nods. "Yes, Ravi, thank you for asking."

Emika with Rs and Ls. Luckily my name has neither.

Anna touches Emika's wrist. "Let me know if you need any help finding groceries and stuff. I can—"

Chris interjects, "Yes, if Anna can't find it, she'll grow it for you, especially potatoes." We shake our heads, trying to conceal our laughter.

I turn to Emika to let her in on the joke. "Anna loves growing things, and she's from Idaho. You know, the Potato State."

"I had no idea Idaho was called the Potato State."

Chris continues, "That's why we all dine together, Emika. To learn and broaden our—"

Ravi interrupts, touching Chris's belly, "Horizons and bellies."

Emika covers her mouth and shakes her shoulders as the server makes her appearance.

"Hi, I am Sharon. What can I get you to drink?"

Everyone looks to me to order.

"Do you have Dom Perignon Vintage, anything before 2000?"

Sharon slants her head. "We do have Dom Perignon, but let me double-check we have some of that vintage left?" She goes back.

Anna turns to Emika. "See, what I mean? He won't say 'champagne' or even dress like normal people do."

Emika twinkling eyes glance at me, and she gives me an endearing smile. I can tell that Anna notices.

Chris turns to Emika. "I once saw him discarding coffee beans whose sizes and shapes didn't match the description in the packet."

I give him a look. "Hey, they were supposed to be Tanzanian peaberry beans, not miniature bananas."

Sharon comes back. "We have 1998 and 1999."

"Two bottles of 1998, please," I say, raising my fingers.

She brings the bottles, and I open the first one and pour everyone's glass. Raising mine, I say, "Emika, welcome to the team of misfits."

"To Emika," four of us chorus.

Emika takes a sip before asking, "Misfits?"

Ravi takes a sip and turns to Emika. "Vincent likes to fix things. He created this center from scratch. When I interviewed, I was certain that I wouldn't get this job because I had no authorization to work in the country. Vincent sponsored my work visa. Without him, Dr. Bose would be on a flight to India."

Anna takes over. "My adviser at Yale made sure I was unemployable."

Emika turns to Anna, tucking her hair behind her ears as she does so. "How?"

"He published my work in his name." Anna drinks a few sips before continuing. "I filed a complaint, but that made things worse. He wrote derogatory comments to each place I applied. I had no offers after I graduated. With almost no hope, I applied to this center and came for an interview." Anna places her hand on top of mine while looking at Emika. Her voice trembled slightly. "This guy gave me five equations to solve. He looked at my approach and told me, 'Dr. Calimaris, let's out-publish and out-invent your adviser.'" Anna moves her hand to point it at my hair. "Also, those waves are delicious. Couldn't keep my eyes off them during the interview."

Ravi shakes his head. "Anna."

Anna shrugs. "What? They are. Ask any woman." She turns to Emika. "Don't you find them, delish?"

Emika's face turns pink.

I turn to Anna. "Two sips of champagne, and look where you are."

Chris speaks up. "My advisers told me that I would never get published because my research did not fit within the silos of the Wharton School. I wrote to Vincent, and he could see the connection. He fought with Vikram to create a course AI for managers. And now, I am a co-author on all of Vincent's publications." Chris turns to me and touches his chest. "Thank you, Dr. Abajian."

I bow my head. "You deserve it, Dr. Washington."

"So, we were pieces that did not fit together," Ravi concludes. "But somehow, Vincent assembled us to create a perfect movement, like in a watch. Without him, we are just misfits."

"I see," Emika says, her eyes fixed on me.

Sharon appears. "Have you decided on your food?"

Anna is the first to order. "Chef's special chow mein with beef and an entrée of dry chili chicken."

"Chef's special chow mein with shrimp and an entrée of dry chili chicken and cumin lamb. Everything super-hot," Ravi follows.

Chris turns to Sharon. "Chef's special chow mein with barbequed pork, an entrée of sole fish fillets."

When Sharon turns to me, Anna tells Emika, "Pay attention to how he orders." While Emika widens her eyes, Anna rolls hers.

I take off my glasses and look at Sharon. "Everything should be cooked unbearably hot, please. I'd like the chef's special chow mein, with beef and shrimp. I prefer noodles made with buckwheat. If not, it's fine. Each noodle should have a coating of red chili powder. I also want dry chili chicken, where the garlic cloves should be halved, not whole. Lastly, I want cumin lamb, with whole and ground cumin."

It's Emika's turn. Her mouth is wide open, and she rests her face on her palms. She blinks. "Wow, you are specific, Vince. Poor chef!" She turns to Sharon. "I want the chow mein, just like his." She points at me. "But with only shrimp and a side of spicy Sichuan green beans."

Sharon takes meticulous notes and narrates the orders back before heading back to the kitchen.

I turn to Ravi. "Hey, how is your mom?" A month back, she suffered a minor cerebral stroke.

"She's fine now." He shrugs.

"If you need to take some time off to visit, please feel free, irrespective of how you feel about her."

Anna turns to Ravi. "Yeah, I was surprised you never went to see her."

He takes a few sips before responding. "We weren't close. She was downright abusive. At the slightest provocation, she would hit me. It started when I was three and continued until I went to the Indian Institute of Technology. After that, I was glad to leave home."

"What about your father?" Emika asks, leaning toward Ravi.

"Oh, yeah. Father was all philosophical. He asked me to divert my mind into happy things when I was beaten." Ravi shakes his head. "He was an enabler. I never even informed them when I finished my Ph.D. from Carnegie."

"That's terrible, Ravi. I thought mine was bad," Chris says.

Anna touches Chris's shoulder. "What about you?"

"Well, my parents weren't thrilled that I chose a field different from theirs when I went to Berkeley and UPenn." He sighs.

I lift my eyebrows. "They are all lawyers, right?"

"Yes, and they do a great job representing those who can't fight against police brutality or are affected by systemic racism. They believe that my work will bring unemployment, and African Americans and other minorities will be the most affected. Barring official emancipation, they have disowned me. They didn't even show up for any of my graduations."

I press my lips together. "I see." Maybe not having parents isn't that bad?

"Well, if it makes you feel any better, mine didn't show up either," Anna offers.

I place my hand on hers. "I know."

Emika turns to Anna. "Why? If I may ask."

"My family ostracized me when I came out."

Emika covers her mouth in disbelief.

Anna takes some deep breaths as I squeeze her shoulder. She turns to me, forces a smile. "Boy, I am hungry."

Fortunately, our food arrives.

Emika turns to me. "Do you wanna try some beans?"

"Sure."

She picks some and transfers a few to my plate. Then asks, "Anyone else?"

Anna notices how she first offered some to me and then to the rest of them. She won't mention this in my office. I turn to Emika. "Wanna try my chicken and lamb?"

"The only non-vegetarian things I eat are fish and eggs."

Anna takes her first bite of the peppery Sichuan chicken, shuts her eyes, and goes into a food coma. "I could just die now. Vince, you are a godsend." She turns to Emika, "Do you know he has a heart of gold?"

I rest my chopsticks on my plate. "Anna. No."

Emika turns and lifts her eyebrows. "Let her speak, Vincent-*san*."

Anna presses on Emika's arm and continues. "Three Christmases back, Linda suddenly thanked us for a Christmas check for $5,000. Ravi, Chris, and I had no idea. Soon after, we learned from Elise that Vincent paid Linda's student loan and that every Christmas, Vince was giving her a bonus out of his own pocket."

Emika turns to me. "Why?"

"I did not want to take all the credit, Emika. So I put their names on the card," I say, deciding I should call her Emika in public.

Emika shakes her head, then clarifies. "I meant your reasons for your generosity."

I take a sip of the champagne before answering. "She is a single mother, raising little ones while battling enormous student loans. I am not belittling her ability to raise her children. And every case has its own unique challenges. I wanted to minimize her children having my fate."

The gleam in Emika's eyes made way to curiosity. She squints. "Your fate?"

Anna, Chris, and Ravi lean backward as I clarify. "Maybe if someone like me helped my parents or parent, I wouldn't be dropped at an orphanage."

Emika dabs the corner of her eyes, then stands up, leaving her napkin on the table. "Excuse me."

I turn to the rest, looking for some clarification. "Why would that upset her? What did I say wrong?"

"Makes no sense." Chris leans forward, lowering his voice. "It's not like she's known you very long."

Ravi shrugs. "Absurd."

Anna shakes her head. "Guys, have you seen how she looks at Vince?"

The men all look at her. "What?"

Anna looks at me. "Idiot." Then she turns to Ravi and Chris. "More on this in the office. I seriously hope she is OK."

Chris smirks at Anna. "At least she's not wearing tons of makeup."

"Jerk," Anna says, staring daggers back at him.

I wave my hands. "That's enough.

Emika comes back, and once she's sitting again, Anna rubs her shoulder. "Hey, you OK?"

"Yes, I'm fine. Thanks for asking." But there is a tremble in her voice.

Sharon shows up. "Any desserts, anyone?"

Ravi, Chris, and Anna pass, but Emika turns to me and points at the dessert section. "Can I get a mango mochi and a green tea mochi, please?"

"Sure, Emika. Let's get five mango mochis and five green tea mochis for the table."

Anna puffs out her checks. "We are full, Vince."

"The fuck you are. There's always room for mochi."

Emika smiles widely. "You read my mind, Vince."

"Of course he did," Anna quips, rolling her eyes.

When Sharon brings the desserts a few minutes later, Emika picks hers up immediately, using her chopsticks. She shuts her eyes, opens her mouth, and touches it with her pink lips after spending about ten seconds sucking the mochi, like a child sucks a lollypop. Then she bites into it. She opens her eyes again, looks straight at me. "Vince, eat yours."

Sharon brings the check. I raise my arm. "That's for me."

Ravi straightens his leather jacket. "So, how much will you be tipping her?"

"How about fifty percent?"

"Isn't that high?" Emika notes, lifting her eyebrows.

Anna shakes her head. "Here we go."

I click my tongue and place the napkin from my lap on the table. "Despite being an orphan, I had a privileged upbringing. Someone paid for my expensive boarding school. Look at Sharon. She is in her twenties and has felt pen marks on her arms. So maybe she is raising a child or maybe babysitting in addition to toiling through a couple of low-paying, thankless jobs. She may have amassed enormous student debt. Despite its numerous other benefits, our research may eventually take this job from her." I pause to see Emika's inquisitive eyes against the other's nonchalant. "We from the educated class have pushed the doctrine that humans will be freed to tackle larger problems when machines do menial jobs. Look around you. Are all humans equipped to solve larger problems? So, yes, I pay a little extra."

"Anna was right." Emika's eyes brighten. "You are beautifully complex."

Anna sighs. "And an occasional idiot."

I sign the bill with a seventy percent tip.

I check on Anna, Chris, and Ravi, "You guys OK to drive?"

They all nod.

"What's stopping you from getting an autonomous vehicle?"

Chris smiles at me. "We will do that as a celebration of your next invention." He winks. "No pressure, boss."

Within a few minutes, Emika and I are back in my car.

Emika touches my wrist. "Vince, are you free this weekend?"

"Sure, what have you got in mind?" Is she asking me out?

"Remember when we met that first day in your office, and you said we could meet and talk about things?"

"Yep."

"So, can you come to my place tomorrow or Sunday? Also, please bring Hulk. I know what he eats—I asked Linda—so, he can have his food as well."

"That was very thoughtful of you. Tomorrow, then?" I don't think I can wait until Sunday.

We reach her townhome.

I touch her hand before she gets out of the car. "Let me walk you to the door."

She tucks her hair behind her ears and looks at me. "It's just 20 feet."

"So?" I have waited for more than three decades. I have earned every inch of those 20 feet.

"OK." Her smile is so wide it completely shuts her eyes.

We walk toward her green door, and she unlocks it. She looks into my eyes and bites her lips. Then, making a decision, she comes forward and hugs me. "Thank you, Vince. Thanks for dinner, and thanks for being you."

Does she recognize me? Should I ask her? Is it too early? In the end, I say nothing.

She pulls back, "See you tomorrow."

Walking into her townhome, she closes her door behind her. I can see her silhouette behind the blinds, waiting for me to drive away. My feelings are muddled. If she is Akane, does she realize who I am? After all, Akane knew me only for a couple of years—and we were both children. That may not be long enough for a lasting memory to travel across the turbulence. And even if Emika does realize who I am, she could simply dismiss it as the past. And as a past, that's not even her own.

It is tomorrow—Saturday—and Hulk and I are now standing in front of Emika's townhome. He's wagging his tail. I've brought a small vase with some flowers in it. Let's see if she likes them.

The sound of a piano recital comes through the door. I knock. She pauses the music and opens the door, glowing as always, clad in sweatpants, a navy t-shirt, a thick multicolored cardigan, and Birkenstock slippers. As she looks at the flowers, her eyes glimmer. "How did you know I love bellflowers?"

"I took a chance."

"It was a good one."

She collects the flowers in one hand and takes Hulk's leash in the other. "Come in."

Under the kitchen counter, I see a set of dog bowls. She must have bought them just for Hulk.

"Emi, you can continue Rachmaninov's no. 3. I won't mind."

"You could tell that from outside?" She lifts her eyebrows. "Do you want some tea?"

I sit on the sofa. "Sure. Whatever you'll have."

She opens a kitchen cabinet door, and inside I see at least eight jars of tea marked in hiragana. She takes out a jar and measures one teaspoon for each cup. After placing a filter on each cup, she pours water through the tea from a goose-neck kettle. "Three minutes," she says, looking at me.

Her hair covers her right eye, and she tucks it behind her ears as she leans over to check the color and smelling her concoction. After she is satisfied, she discards the tea leaves in the compost bin. I have not witnessed such extraordinary beauty in the art of making a simple cup of tea before. She seems content with the final product—the smile at the corner of her lips is the one of a concert pianist when they hit the last, defining note. "Ready."

I am about to get up, but she says, "Keep sitting. You're my guest."

She hands me the cup in her right hand and gives me a coaster. With me on the sofa and her on an armchair, we are sitting perpendicular to each other. Hulk jumps onto her lap. She smiles and then kisses his forehead before picking her cup up with both hands and taking the first sip. Her eyes shut, and her hair covers her right eye again. "What do you taste, Vince?"

I breathe the tea's aroma in and take a sip. "Matcha, water, and rice."

She touches my shoulder, "Bravo, Professor."

"What tea is it?"

"Genmaicha." Then she asks, "Vince, how could you guess that blue bellflowers are my favorite?"

I look in her eyes and touch her hand, "You remind me of a friend who loved bellflowers."

"Loved?" She squints. "As in, she's in the past?"

I take a deep breath. "I lost her to a time turbulence."

She tilts her head, "Yes, the last known turbulence occurred in Berlin."

"That's the one that took her. Her name was Akane Egami. Her initials would be just the opposite of yours."

She puts her finger on her chin and looks up. "There is a very influential Egami family in Japan. They own the largest media conglomerate in Asia."

"Yes, Akane was from that family. She only flew on private jets. You could say she was the 'princess' of our school who made friends with this poor orphan."

"So you were close?" She touches my hand.

I shut my eyes as every single moment between Akane and my flashes behind my eyelids. I open them again and look at Emika. "We were inseparable."

"Can you tell me more about your childhood? Unless it will upset you."

I lean in the backrest and crack my fingers. "Akane was an accomplished violinist. Her music made me forget all my misery and struggle. I used to dread summer breaks. All my classmates went home, and I'd stay back, wandering the corridors and the library. Sleep in my dorm and eat with the staff and headmaster. I looked forward to the school reopening, just to see her again. When she'd come back, she would enchant me with stories from places she'd been. She promised that when we grew up, we would travel together. And then, after November 1991, she never came back. Her violin is with me. I learned to live with the void... until recently, when I met someone who's lived through three lives, across two turbulences."

"Wait, you know Philip Nardin?"

"Yes, actually."

She begins scratching Hulk's belly. "Do you know I was born after the Alexanderplatz incident? November 23, 1991. Against the doctor's order, my mum accompanied my dad to Berlin for his debut composition—Waltz in D-minor. A month later, she went into labor. I was born right at noon Central European Time. *Pa-pha* believed my birth ended the turbulence."

That was the exact time I came out of Mr. Kruger's office and saw that robin. Was the robin telling me that Akane was reborn? And the image that appeared, just for a second, was Emika folding her umbrella. She is Akane.

She nudges my shoulder. "More tea?"

"I'm fine, thank you."

"Did Elise know about Akane?"

"Yes, she did. But she wanted me to move on and maybe forget her."

Emika tilts her head. "Why?"

"As someone who was estranged from her family, she believed forgetting could be the key to moving on."

"Why was she estranged from them?"

"Have you heard of Dick Graham, Emi?"

"The GOP senator?"

"That's Elise's father. The apple could not have fallen any farther from the tree."

She touches my arm. "Do you mind telling me what happened to her?"

I shake my head. "Plane crash on January 15, Flight 0606," I say and leave it at that. I'm not going to reveal to her the conspiracy that Philip told me.

Emika lifts Hulk and nuzzles her nose into her fur. I haven't seen such acts of endearment toward a dog someone has only seen twice. Hulk licks her forehead. Emika pulls back to scratch his belly and looks at me. "Vince, do you have a picture of Akane?"

"Yes, in my office. Come by any time you want."

She squints. "I don't recall seeing any such pictures."

"I kept it in a drawer." I smile. "Didn't take it out until after I dropped you here, after our meeting."

She tilts her head. "Just like that?"

I nod. "As of now, I would go by the theory of coincidence. Let me gather some data."

"I understand." She removes her hand from my arm. "And the violin? Is it in your office?"

"I just took it to a repair shop for tuning," I say, sighing.

"That's a coincidence too?"

I touch her hand. "For the time being." Our eyes lock—there are so many emotions in her eyes, joy, sorrow, anticipation, hope, despair. She tries to conceal them all with her smile. I wonder… if she is Akane, is there an Emika free from Akane?

"Anna, Ravi, and Chris know about Akane?"

"They do. But they don't bring her up. They've not seen her picture or her violin."

She looks at her smartwatch. "Are we hungry, Vince?" she asks, changing the subject.

"Yes. What do you want to eat?"

"I am craving deep-dish pizza. Do you know any place?" Her eyes gleam with anticipation.

"That will be Godfather's." I hand her my credit card. "Feel free to order your favorite toppings for both of us and add a thirty percent tip."

She takes out her cellphone and calls in the order, choosing onions, mushrooms, artichoke, garlic, and spinach as our toppings.

I just notice that she didn't turn on the AC, and I can hear cicadas, the chirping of birds, and the sound of leaves against the wind. I feel warm and content. Is this the life I want? Though I know nothing about this beautiful woman, everything indicates that she is my childhood friend. But I really want to know her beyond that.

"Emi, now it's your turn."

"For?"

"The story of your violin?"

She rests her forehead on her thumbs. Then she looks at me and smiles. "I never thought I'd share this with anyone. So, can you keep everything to yourself?"

I touch her hand. "Of course."

Closing her eyes, she begins. "OK, it started in August 2001, when I was almost ten. I was taking piano lessons under *pa-pha*, and his friend Suzuki-*san* was with the violin." She presses her temples with her thumbs. "About three minutes into Chopin's Raindrop, I stopped and turned to Suzuki-*san*. 'Oji-*san*, can I play your violin?' He first looked at my *pa-pha* and then handed me the violin. So, I picked it up, and I tucked the chinrest under my chin." She mimes the motion, holding an imaginary violin. "Suzuki san handed me the bow, and I started to play. I played a tune that I had never heard before, but somehow it came to me. Then, after about three minutes, I could hear cries and voices, and my head started to hurt. And I stopped. *Pa-pha* and Suzuki-*san* looked at me with eyes wide, and jaws dropped. Their surprise faces scared me, and I ran from the room to find my mom."

"Why were they so surprised?"

She pauses and looks at me. Her lips smile against her moist eyes. "That was the first time I ever played the violin. No one taught me, Vince." Hulk licks her hand, and she pets his forehead.

"Do you remember the tune, Emi?" A part of me hopes that it's one of those Akane played. But I also want Emika to be free from Akane's predicament.

"Yes, at dinner that night, my father told me. He said it was the first three minutes of Massenet's Méditation. Then he asked me, 'Why did you stop?' I replied, 'I heard voices, *pa-pha.*' I don't think he believed me. But he looked at my mom and said, 'Our Emika is blessed. I am taking her off the piano. She will be a violinist.' The next day, he bought me a violin and signed me up for music lessons. I could play any piece with ease by the time I was twelve. All but four pieces."

"Which four pieces?" But if she is Akane, I already know the name of the pieces.

Suddenly there's a knock on the door. I'd forgotten about the pizza. She opens the door, and I collect the pizza. "Where should I put it?"

She points at the kitchen counter. As I open the lid, she stares at it like a child opening a Christmas present, a feeling that I never experienced. The pizza's been cut into eight slices. She takes one out for herself and hands me two.

"Do you wanna go to the deck and eat? It's nice and sunny."

"Sure."

She opens the sliding door off the kitchen, and a spectacular view greets us—an array of rolling hills and snowcapped mountains beyond. A warm breeze caresses us, and Emika's hair dances in the wind. I take her pizza while she tucks her locks behind her ears. She stares at the horizon as her eyes grow brighter, her pupils smaller. Her hair transforms from black and burgundy to the color of maple syrup. We sit on the lounge chairs, and she takes her plate back from me. "Eat, Vince. Else, I'll finish all of it." I take a small bite. She turns to me. "You wanted to know what pieces I couldn't play?"

"Yes."

She shuts her eyes. "Besides Massenet's Méditation, the other ones are Paganini's no. 24, Sarasate's Zigeunerweisen, and Saint-Saën's Introduction & Rondo Capriccioso."

The breeze stops, and I can feel every beat in my heart. Those are the exact four pieces Akane had mastered by the time she was nine. The four pieces on my playlist are titled 'Akane.' If Akane could play these pieces, why couldn't Emika, if she is her? "What specifically went wrong with these pieces?"

"Well, about halfway through each piece, I would get a severe headache. And occasionally, I could hear voices. I tried many violins, but the problem persisted. But if I chose to play something else, then I was fine."

I take a bite, chewing thoughtfully. "What do you think was happening?"

"I don't know, Vince. I loved those pieces, yet I could never play them. So I withdrew from music altogether. The decision did not go well with *pa-pha*. In Kyoto and Oxford, I studied mathematics until I met Benjamin, a concert pianist." She takes a bite.

"Benjamin? How did you meet?"

"I met him in a music bar in Oxford. He was playing Mozart's 21. He saw me, bought me a drink, and we started dating. A couple of months later, we moved in together. He was practicing to become a concert pianist."

"Once," she continues, "My parents were in Oxford, and I introduced Benji to them. He was delighted to meet his idol—Hiroshi Amari. And *pa-pha* revealed that I was a violinist. Benji insisted that we play together at the next party. But it was a private party with close friends, family, and some of Benji's influential musician mentors.

"The day arrived—Benji on piano, me on violin. The music was Ravel's Sonata for Violin and Piano no. 2. But then Benji wanted me to play Zigeunerweisen. Despite my resistance, he insisted that every violinist should do it. So, I started, and after ten minutes of perfection, the voices and the headaches became too strong for me to keep playing. I sat on the floor holding my head, and instead of attending to me, Benji accused me. His words were, 'How could you insult me like that in front of my teachers and friends. We are done, Emika.' I tried telling him about my condition, but he did not believe me. Even *pa-pha* never believed me. I never had a serious relationship after that. The whole idea of commitment frightens me to the core. I gave up on violin, too. It's who I am now." Her voice trembles as her eyes well up.

I can't bear to see tears in those eyes. I hand her my pocket square.

She dabs her eyes and continues. "I finished my master's at Oxford and then took a break, returning to Kyoto to teach mathematics to school kids as a tutor, living there from 2012 to 2014. On weekends, I met my parents in their *machiya*. Pa-pha was visibly ashamed of me. Every day, I could see the disapproval in his eyes. I couldn't continue like that. Then, in Tokyo, I saw a presentation on how AI can be used to change businesses. You were the presenter, Vince. You looked so confident. I admired you immediately. Even at such a young age, you were at the top of your field. Your command of the subject got me interested in the mathematics of AI and machine learning. I applied to several schools, and Caltech was the first one to accept me. And that brought me to the US." She pauses. "Remember, you asked me why I took this job?"

"Yes."

"The job mentioned that Vince Abajian ran the center. And, today, you're sitting next to me." She places her hand on mine. "You saved me from a joyless life."

I place my other hand on top of hers. "I can't take all the credit. You are exceptionally brilliant and have worked very hard."

"I wouldn't have worked this hard if I hadn't seen you. So, maybe I'm here because I saw you at the conference."

I don't know what to say to that and blurt out. "So, Emi, tell me your dreams?"

"I wanna be happy, Vince." She points at the mountains. "And I would like to have a house with large glass windows that give a closer view of hills, those mountains, the snowcapped peaks. I want a backyard full of cherry trees that will bloom pink in spring. Ideally, I would like to play my violin. But if I can't, that's OK, too."

Turning back to me, she forms a wicked smile at the corner of her lip. "And, by the way, I now have two of your pocket squares. Do you hand them to women regularly?"

I look at her. "I don't mind losing them to you."

Emika takes a deep breath. "I'm glad I met you, Vince."

"Me, too." My calm tone underplays my feelings. The truth is my heart is racing.

"You know my birthday, now. When's yours?"

"August 30, 1983."

"Oh, it's just around the corner! I'll remember that."

I wonder if her headaches and voices would disappear if she played Akane's violin. "Emi, do you talk to your parents?"

"Not really. I couldn't forgive them." She shrugs.

"It's not my place—but find a way to forgive them. If you don't, then twenty years later, you may regret it."

She narrows her eyes. "Would you forgive yours if you found them?"

I lift my shoulders. "I already have. I don't know under what extenuating circumstance they gave me up, but I assume it was difficult."

She stares at the mountains again. "Then you are much kinder than I am."

"It's free—kindness, patience, and tolerance. Just my two cents."

She smiles. "I'll think about it, professor. Did you ever try to find your parents?"

I glance at her slender, delicate fingers, still resting on mine. "Nope.

"Why?"

I click my tongue. "Who I am should be determined by my work, not my genes."

We grab some more slices, and Emika offers me some iced tea that she brewed. I take a sip. "Where is this tea from?"

"It's Darjeeling, first flush. Spring tea."

I take another sip. "Beautiful subtle flavor. If I were to compare it with music, this is Satie's Gnossienne of teas."

She nods her head. "Elegant metaphor."

I am not sure what's going on in her mind. "So, Emi. You barely know me, yet you revealed a lot. Why?"

She touches my watch with her index finger. "I don't know why, but when I saw you for the first time in your office, I felt I had known you forever." She leans back. "Vince, did you ever visit the World Clock in Berlin?"

"I went there in 2001, right after finishing my schooling and before attending Cambridge. I bought her favorite flowers and placed them under the clock."

Time passes, and the sun hides behind the mountains, giving us a beautiful starlit sky. The view could put the soul of Van Gogh within the depths of the most apathetic humans. Emika calls, "Hulk, baby, come and sit with us." He jumps on her lap.

The sky is clear tonight, and I point upward. "That's Scorpius."

She turns to me. "When did you learn the constellations?"

"I spent all the summer in school, playing chess with my headmaster, doing math, and spending tons of time in the library. The only condition was I could not mess with the ordering of the books. So, one day, I learned about the stars."

"When you stare at the stars, what comes to your mind?" she asks, looking up.

"I think our understanding of time is flawed. It's not linear at all. Maybe the past and the future are happening simultaneously, or perhaps the future affects the past. After all, we are probably looking at stars that don't even exist. And in the vastness of all, how insignificant I am."

"Why do you think you're insignificant?"

"Because I am. Everything that I am involved with will continue its path, whether I exist or not."

Deeply absorbed in stargazing, she comments, "Well, I wouldn't be sitting and talking with you while holding this fluffball in my lap and staring at the sky as if you were insignificant. I wouldn't have this job if you were insignificant. I wouldn't tell stories of my past to anyone insignificant. So, Vince, you are more than what you give yourself credit for."

"What do you feel when you look at stars, Emi?"

"Sorrow, hope, and joy. Sorrow because I couldn't play the violin as I wanted to. Hope that one day I might and that a day may come when I'll stare at the stars from my own home. And joy because I'm thankful for all the paths I traversed that led me to this moment—enjoying a cup of tea with someone I've just met but feel I have known forever." She keeps looking at the stars, then blinks and bites her lip.

I am sure she is Akane. But I would really like to know the Emika that is free from Akane.

CHAPTER 6

ONIGIRIS

Hope, in reality, is the worst of all evils
because it prolongs the torments of man.
—Friedrich Nietzsche

(A year before today)

DR. KAUFFMAN ADJUSTS HER GLASSES. "How come you've never mentioned Akane before?"

I give her a half-smile, not knowing where to begin. "Her departure broke me. I kept hoping that she would turn up one day, and we would start from where we left off. But with time, pragmatism took over fantasy, and I slowly gave up the hope of ever meeting her. Even mentioning her name would derail me from the realistic path that became my sustenance."

"So, this new colleague, Emika, how does she remind you of Akane?" Dr. Kauffman asks, turning a page of her notebook.

I start scratching Max's belly. "She doesn't just remind me of Akane. I think she is Akane. So I guess this is the correct place to inquire if lunacy has plagued my mind."

Dr. Kauffman takes off her glasses and stares at me. "I don't know what crazy is. But tell me why you think she's Akane?"

"It's not just the looks. It's the way she talks, laughs, asserts herself. Akane always ordered me around. I believe if I weren't Emika's boss, she might do the same." I close my eyes. "There were four pieces of music that Akane played for me. Those're the exact four pieces that Emika struggled to play. When Emika played those pieces, she heard a voice asking her to find something. I think if I were to unite her with Akane's violin, she would be able to play these pieces."

She puts her glasses back on. "You realize that my expertise isn't in the metaphysical or paranormal?"

"Neither is mine. But recently, I met someone who's lived through three lives across the two time turbulences. You may have heard of him."

"Philip Nardin? You met him?" Her voice pitches higher with each question.

"Yes."

Dr. Kauffman scribbles something, then squints her eyes at me. "Vincent, tell me what you feel when you see Emika?"

I scratch my beard and involuntarily smile. "I see her as an opus where logic and emotions don't fight but give in to each other. She reminds me of brush strokes in Starry Night or the notes on Chopin's Ballade no. 4."

"That's a high pedestal." She smiles. "Do you see a future for you two?"

I lean back. "I will be happy if Emika can play those four pieces on the violin, and I can live the remaining years of my life, knowing that she'll not disappear again."

"Why don't you try separating Akane and Emika and see how you feel about Emika?"

"I want to do that, but all I see is Akane in her."

"Why don't you ask her out?"

"Maybe I will."

She looks at her watch. "Anything else, Vince?"

I lift my finger. "I did my homework."

"Homework?" she asks, tilting her head slightly.

"Yes, you asked me to find out about my colleagues. So, I took them to dinner. I also took Emika. I found out several things about them. Do you want to know?"

She adjusts the frame of her glasses. "How did you feel when they opened up, Vince?"

"I felt that they trusted me with their past. I am indebted to them for all the support they've shown me in the last eight months. Especially taking my teaching responsibilities after Elise died. Maybe I can share a thing or two with them."

"That was the point, Vince," she says, smiling. "You are not alone—open up to your friends. And I see how you separate Emika from the rest."

"What do you mean?"

"You said, 'So, I took them out to dinner. I also took Emika.' Is she not your colleague or friend?"

"Well, she only recently joined the group, so maybe because of that?"

She gives me a hard stare. "Is that it? Maybe you'll feel differently in a few days or months."

I lean forward. "Are you insinuating that I have romantic feelings toward her because of Akane?"

"No." She shakes her head and closes her notebook. "I think you want to know her beyond the confinements of Akane. And you will never know unless you try."

"I'll keep that in mind. How is Bernard doing?"

"Well, there's no going back to where he was. We are just managing our expectations. Is there anything else you want to talk about?"

"Nope." I stand up.

She smiles. "You conquer the world."

A week has passed since my interview with Philip Nardin hit the press. It's 8:00 a.m. Hulk and I are in the office. Linda usually comes at 9:00 a.m. I have my four-screen computer open. Today, I'll be working on two research papers—one with a conditional acceptance and a revision request. Hulk growls. Does he hear footsteps? He doesn't bark at Anna, Chris, Ravi, or Linda, and if he senses Emika, he wags his tail. Someone new is approaching us. The sound of the footsteps is getting louder. It's someone with a heavy gait, possibly a male. The footsteps come to an end with a loud knock on my door, making Hulk stand up and howl.

"Come in," I shout.

A twinge of nausea hits me at the sight of Dick Graham. As he walks in, he points at Hulk. "How do you keep this mutt quiet?"

"Well, he isn't a fan of walking, talking trash."

"I read the interview you did with Philip Nardin."

"Congratulations," I say, stretching my arms wide. "You can read now."

He sits on the chair opposite my desk. "Did Philip Nardin mention me? Did he say anything about Flight 0606?"

I prop my legs up on the desk. "You are too insignificant for him to have mentioned, and what we said about Flight 0606 is none of your business."

"He's an enemy of the state, you know? And we'll bring him down." He bangs on my desk. "It's better if you tell me what he told you about the flight."

I snap my finger, and Hulk growls. "First, behave yourself. This is my office, not your brothel in Capitol Hill. Second, go on, bring him down, Dick. I'd love to see you try."

"You'll regret this."

"Go fuck yourself, Dick."

He points his finger at me, "I will bring you down too, you worthless orphan." He slams my office door as he leaves.

What a worthless fuck. Wasting his time, taxpayers' money, and what is infinitely more important, my time. Finally, I can be with my papers.

Another interruption. This time it's Chris peeping through my door. "Busy, Vince?"

I wave my hand. "Not at all, come on in." I bet that I will lose my work rhythm. That's why I like to stay home and work.

Chris enters, and the other two follow.

Ravi sits in the chair Dick recently vacated. "Thanks for dinner. We should do this more often."

I lean back. "You're welcome. What else, guys?"

"Vince," Anna pulls up another chair and takes a breath of exasperation, "we are tired of Cameron."

I need to get back to my work and am losing patience. "Who the fuck is that?"

Chris leans forward. "She's one of the associate deans who sign documents when shipments come, in the absence of you or Vikram. She wields her power by delaying, and we keep waiting endlessly."

"Why would she do that?"

Anna rolls her eyes. "Jealous of the success of our center and our salaries being higher than hers."

I take several long breaths to calm down. "I see." Then I pick up my phone. "Linda, can you bring the signature transfer digital letter to me? We need to remove Cameron and add Anna, Chris, and Ravi to proxy for me." Linda brings her tablet with editable and biometric-enabled files. I cross out Cameron while Anna, Chris, and Ravi insert their signature and thumbprint. Then, I authorize the whole action with my thumb.

I turn to my three musketeers. "You should get an email, and Cameron will be notified now."

Chris smiles. "Thanks, man."

I smirk. "It's not over. Stay with me." In the next instant, my phone rings, and Linda informs, "Cameron is on the other line. You wanna speak?"

Anna's eyes gleam with the imminent broadway show as Ravi leans forward, and Chris starts to nod.

"Sure, connect us." I put my finger on my lips and tell the three musketeers, "Shh."

"Vincent, is that you?"

"Guilty."

"What's next? Coming up with a robot to replace me?"

"I don't need a robot. A *maneki-neko*, with a rubber stamp attached to the waving arm, should suffice."

"What's that?"

"I am sure your online Ph.D. program taught you to Google. Use that invaluable skill." I hang up.

The musketeers whose hands were pressed against their mouths begin laughing. As the sound echoes through the thin walls, Linda rushes in, "What's funny?"

Anna turns to her. "It's just fantastic when Vincent is on your side."

Ravi's expression suddenly turns somber. He gets up and crosses my chair, picking up the photograph of Akane and me. He takes the frame and shows it to Anna and Chris. Chris raises his eyebrows while Anna covers her mouth with her hand in astonishment. Their eyes reveal it all.

Chris squints at me. "This is Akane, right?"

I look into the eyes of Anna, Chris, and Ravi. "Yes. Emika is the spitting image. Not just a spitting image, a reflective one. Akane had her beauty mark on the left, Emika on her right. They're both violinists." I feel a load sliding from my shoulders.

Anna bats her eyes. "Well, Vince. We didn't pay close attention to the coordinates of her beauty mark. But we did notice how she looks at you."

Ravi tilts his head at her. "What do you mean *we*?"

Anna shrugs. "OK, so only I noticed." Then she turns to Chris and Ravi and exhales in exasperation. "You two are pathetic. Is this how I raised you?"

"Noticed what?" I place my elbow on my desk and rest my head on my palm.

Anna leans forward. "So, I offered to pick her up for Sichuan Palace the other night. And she was like, 'No, Vince will pick me up... Vince this, Vince that.' And in the restaurant, her eyes were fixed on you." She turns to Chris and Ravi, "Right, guys?"

Ravi shrugs. "I didn't notice anything."

"I plead the fifth," Chris says, shaking his head.

"Vince, do you think, Emika is Akane?" Ravi asks, almost in a whisper.

I rest my forehead on my palms and shut my eyes. "The collected evidence is too strong to dispose of the hypothesis." I lift my head and open my eyes. "She has not seen this picture. So, please, can you guys not mention anything?"

Chris claps his hands together. "You got it. Since we selected her, it's like we three brought Akane to you."

"She *likes* you, Vince," Anna adds.

I lift my eyebrows. "Really? How do you know?"

Anna looks sideways. "I just do."

"So, where is she? I didn't see her today?"

"Ooh, someone is missing, Emika." Anna stands up.

Ravi gives me an answer instead. "They've some new faculty staff retreat for the new hires."

I sigh. "Fuck, that's boring."

After nodding their agreement, the three musketeers leave my office.

Yes. I've loved the time I've spent with Emika. She revives a memory of a warmth that I only felt for a couple of years. Maybe I can spend another day with her. With this train of thought at the back of my mind, I finish reworking my papers. Revising papers is second nature to me. It's almost involuntary, like breathing. It also makes me escape my life. Did I forget something? Yes—lunch. I do feel a little hungry, but I really have no time to waste. I can suppress the appetite with a doppio and a biscotti.

"Linda, how about a biscotti?" I shout.

"Sure, Dr. A, just one."

I take out two Nonni's biscotti, place them on a paper plate, and walk toward Linda's station. She looks up at me, "I could've come and got those, Dr. A."

"It's OK. I could use some moving around. You know what goes great with biscotti?"

"I know, but I need my sleep. I don't get much given my kids, classes, and this job."

"You're getting tuition waivers, I hope."

"Yes."

"I know textbooks are expensive, and so is software. Let me know if you need help."

She touches my hand. "You're very kind. I don't know how I can ever repay you."

"You don't owe me anything, Linda."

Philip is wearing his watchmaker loupe and closely inspecting my severely oxidized Breguet watch, with a tight smile on his face. Has he seen this watch before? Today we are sitting in the study portion of this large room. Behind Philip are bookshelves over thirty feet tall and about forty feet wide, with two ladders to reach the top. I notice books on travel, watchmaking, art, anthropology, architecture, quantum mechanics, in fiction, Dickens, Murakami, Mishima, Shakespeare, Shelley, Irving Stone, and Tolkien.

The desk is made of agarwood, and Philip confirmed that it was built in the eighteenth century. His chair is swivel, and the backrest is made of tufted leather. The one I'm sitting on is similar, except it doesn't swivel. There's a Tiffany lamp on each side of his desk. Hulk is napping by my feet. Philip is wearing a gray linen suit with penny loafers. His pointy beard is neatly combed, and his hair is parted on the left.

"Philip, can I take a glance through your books?"

He waves his hand. "Of course!"

I reach for the Tolkien collection. All the books are leather-bound. And, after turning a page or two, I see it was printed in 1954. I can't contain my joy. "Is this the first edition?"

Still deep in the watch, he says, "They all are." He takes off his loupe and puts his prescription glasses back. "I can easily fix this. But I have two questions."

My own eyes are buried deep in Tolkien's works. I'm trying to feel the texture of the paper.

"Sure."

"I'll be busy for the next few months. So, can you wait? I promise to hand it to you at the most fitting moment."

I reshelve the book to come back to my chair. "I can wait. What fitting moment?"

Philip smiles. "You will know."

"What's the other question?"

"You want it in its original form or powered by intreton-c?"

"What's the advantage of having intreton-c?" I ask, tilting my head.

He leans back, stretches his arms. "You won't ever need to wind it. And, if you possess any intreton-powered clocks, you can use this to adjust all of those."

"I don't have any intreton-powered clocks, but I do prefer the second option." It's surreal that the wealthiest and perhaps the most powerful individual on this planet will fix my watch.

"I have a few intreton-powered clocks. I can give them to you." He puts the watch on a tray.

I lean forward. "Do you know how much it will cost me to get the watch fixed?"

He chuckles. "It will cost me a bit of my time and your patience. But, first, what do you want to eat?"

I shake my head. "I had cereal, thanks."

"Let me know if you change your mind. Gai can cook anything."

"This Gai, where was he trained?"

"Gai is not a human. He's a robot, coded with the finest recipes from three Michelin star chefs—one from France, one from Japan, and one from Morocco. Copying consciousness is still a distant future." He then leans toward me and winks. "Maybe you will invent the technology for a two-way transfer of consciousness between humans and the machine."

If only I could remove my inventor's block. I stay with the topic. "These chefs are all alive, right?"

Philip shakes his head and laughs. "Of course they are—they volunteered to share their recipes with me. Would it be a stretch to say that the best chef in the world isn't a human? I don't think so. But that only opens a more fundamental question. What makes us humans? The ability to talk and look like humans? Or the capacity to love, feel, and be imperfect?"

"I just have a new colleague in the center. She was also talking about consciousness copying rather than transfer. And she also spoke about creating a restore point where the donor's mind was most active, free from Alzheimer's."

He smiles, intrigued. "She sounds bright. What's her name?"

"Emika Amari. I met her on August 3. She reminds me of a childhood friend, someone I lost in the small turbulence in Alexanderplatz."

He grows quiet. I should not have mentioned this. He shakes his head and turns to me, "Vince, I hope one day you can forgive me."

"None of them are your fault, though."

"This childhood friend of yours, what was her name?"

"Akane."

He goes silent and stares at Hulk. And after a moment, he asks, "Does he need any food?"

"No, I fed him in the morning, but thanks." I lean forward and whisper. "Is Mr. Tealeaf a robot, too?"

He laughs and shakes his head. "Well, he can be. Sometimes he shows no emotions. He's a war vet who lost both legs in 2006. I made him robotic legs, powered by intreton-c. We could cut the intreton-c using a laser tech to a diameter of three nanometers. Each strand was capable of carrying an electric pulse to create an optimal connection with his neurons. We haven't commercialized this technology as yet. Edward was so indebted that he chose to stay here and serve me. I tried to look for work for him. But his expertise is too specific to get any job."

I cross my legs. "What expertise?"

"He was a long-distance sniper for NATO and the British Army. He can shoot a moving object a half-mile away, and when he's also in motion. His choice of weapon was Accuracy International AS-500."

I would've never pegged the soft-spoken Mr. Tealeaf as a sniper. "How did he lose his legs?"

Philip narrows his eyes to slits. "It was 2006, and he was waiting for his target, Abu Musab-al-Zarqawi, to show up in a building about three hundred meters from his. But there was US intel that the building he was waiting in had another target. The intel from the UK and Mossad was contradictory. The secretary of defense chose to ignore the opposing view and order the bombing using a drone strike. Edward lost his legs."

"Why would the defense secretary act like this?"

Philips exhales in deep despair. "After this bombing, Lombard got the majority of the defense contracts for drones. I believe this was their way of showcasing their capability to the DOD. Their lobbyists must've paid the defense secretary. They'd already done one strike, and a second one sealed the deal."

I raise my eyebrows and ask, "Who was the defense secretary?"

"Dick Graham," Philip answers through a clenched jaw.

Is Philip privy to more secrets on Dick that I don't know? Is this why Dick was so interested in Philip when he came to my office? I don't want to reveal that Dick's estranged daughter was my partner. Or maybe he already knows.

"Philip, do you think Dick Graham will win the primary for GOP?"

He looks off to the side and smiles. "I'm certain his end will come before that."

"End of a political career?"

Philip clicks his tongue. "What end means, in the most simplistic way."

I scratch my sideburns. "What about the first drone strike? Any casualties from that one?"

He tilts his head, "Oh, yes. But we will discuss that later, OK?"

"Sure."

I take out my fountain pen and notebook from my briefcase and turn to an empty page. "What do you remember about your first life?"

Philip breathes deeply. "My name was Victor Constantin. And I was an artist."

"How did you figure out your profession and name?"

"By the time I discuss all my three lives, you'll know."

"OK."

He leans back, settling into the story. "I was born around 1950. My mother was a curator, and my father, a mechanic. I didn't recall their names, but they always fought. Once, they were fighting about her getting a job as a curator in a museum in Paris. We lived north of Paris, and my father didn't want to leave his drinking buddies." He wets his lips with his Assam tea and continues. "When my mother threatened to take me away, he agreed to move. Over the next few months, things seemed normal. Mother was happy in her job, and my father worked as a mechanic in a local shop. Occasionally, he assisted in tuning cars used by the French Le Mans team for some additional income." He pauses there.

"Well, that must have been nice to have extra money for the family."

"Except, he blew most of it on alcohol and prostitutes. Their fights resumed, and I took solace in doing my sketches. My mother encouraged me to pursue the arts, and when I was fifteen, she got me enrolled in École des Beaux-Arts." He pauses and sips his tea.

I push back my glasses. "So, did you finish art school?"

"I did. And I got a job as an art teacher in a local school. The salary was modest, but it was deeply satisfying to escape the pompous art teachers who stifled creativity more than embraced it." He seems lost in thought as he stares at his desk. "Soon after, my mother died when a car hit her. She was crossing the road, and a car ran a red light. Although she's not my mother in this life, I still feel the pain. I don't fully recall the details of her accident or the funeral after her death. After that, my father became an obnoxious drunk. He would come home, hit me, and steal my money. After a few months, I left and got my own place. And then something changed." His eyes flicker.

"For the better?" I ask.

He smiles slightly. "Only for a little while, but it was worth a lifetime, Vince. One morning, in 1969, I saw a pamphlet for an art competition. Picasso, Dalí, and Man Ray would be the judges. The first prize was five hundred francs, and the work would be showcased in the Yvon Lambert gallery. So I bought a two-by-four-foot canvas, colors and began painting. I painted using an expressionist style and splatter technique. Can you guess what I painted, Vince?" He lifts his brows.

I take a guess. "Was it something to do with Amara?"

"Splendid." His voice echoes through the 50-foot-long room. He points to the painting he was making when we first met. "Not just any portrait of Amara, but that one, and I called it 'Risen from Fire and Ashes.'

I scratch my head in confusion. "But in that life, you were yet to meet Amara, right? So does this artwork from 1969 exist?"

Philip leans forward. "In this reality—where you're Vincent, and I'm Philip—there's no record of that painting. The only one that exists is in this house. And to answer your question, I, Victor Constantin, was yet to meet Amara. I painted her from my imagination. Then we met. In this life, I painted her from my memory of a different life—Victor's life."

"So, how did Victor meet Amara?"

He drinks some more tea before answering. "I won the competition. I went to Yvon Lambert to see my painting, make some connections, and meet the judges. None of the judges came. As I walked toward my painting, I saw a beautiful lady standing there and keenly observing it. She had gorgeous wavy hair, tan skin, and Turkish blue eyes. She turned toward me and asked in North African-accented French, 'Can I help you?' Then I introduced myself as the painter. She laughed, 'I'm possibly the model of your painting. But we have not met. My name is Amara Idrisi. I'm a sculptor.'"

I scratch my head. "How come you could imagine her, paint her, and then she appears, staring at the painting?"

Philip smiles. "Improbable things happen in life, Vince."

"What happened after that?" I ask, turning a page in my notebook.

"It was the year Apollo 11 landed on the moon. The gallery sold the painting to an automobile engineer, Olivier Journe. Amara and I began dating. I was slowly getting a bit of a reputation as an upcoming painter. To celebrate my new feat and the moon landing, I got myself an Omega Speedmaster caliber-321. Amara introduced me to her parents, who were immigrants from Morocco. I became a part of their warm and loving family. Then it was 1970. Both she and I went to the Le Mans race. That's the year when Porsche ended the dominance of Ford GT-40." He pours some more tea into his cup and asks, "Espresso?"

I wave my hand. Coffee is far less intriguing than the story. "What happened?"

He continues. "I noticed the name Olivier Journe in the Porsche roster, and I thought that he might have been the one to buy the painting. I shared that with Amara, and we waited for the race to finish. Afterward, Amara and I could only get to a hundred meters from the winning team. From that distance, we couldn't tell who Olivier Journe was. At that time, my Speedmaster stopped ticking. No amount of winding brought it back. Amara and I asked around, and we found a watch repair shop called Louis-Atelier." Philip pauses, letting me catch up.

I stop writing and lift my head. "That's your uncle's shop?"

He nods. "Yes, Vince. My uncle in this life."

This is exciting. "So, did you meet Louis? By you, I mean Victor."

"Yes. Louis said that his nephew Philip would look at the watch, which would cost about two hundred francs. He recommended that I should contact the dealer, but I wanted it fixed sooner. So, I wrote a check of two hundred francs and handed it and the watch to Louis Nardin. Then I went back to the hotel to meet Amara. We planned on dining together. In the hotel register, I saw the signature of Olivier Journe. As I turned around, I saw the Porsche team signing autographs. I ran toward them and asked if they knew where Mr. Journe was. One of them pointed me toward the elevator. I chased after him. I dodged three people, I apologized, I tripped, but I couldn't reach him. The next thing I remember was people getting sucked into nothing like dirt in a vacuum cleaner. Yes, turbulence took me." He takes off his glasses and cleans them.

While Philip had been talking, I'd used my phone to do some quick research on Olivier Journe. I turn to Philip, "There's no record of Olivier Journe on the Porsche team, so who was he?"

Philip gives me a dry smile. "You see, just like there's no record of Victor Constantin, there would be none for Olivier Journe, either. We live in the universe of Philip Nardin and Vincent Abajian."

I take off my glasses. "Who was Olivier Journe, then?"

"I'm Olivier Journe," Philip says, his eyes glinting. "That was my second life. If I'd known what I do now, then I wouldn't have tried to meet Olivier. Victor, Olivier, and Philip could only co-exist if their paths never crossed. I don't know if my coming close to Olivier caused turbulence or if the turbulence chose its destination to stop Victor's encounter with Olivier. But the stopping of the watch was a warning that I should not meet Victor."

We sit in utter silence, which makes the pendulum sound louder with every passing second. I can sense that everything Victor cared about was centered around his life with Amara. Finally, I break the silence. "Do you remember having any last thoughts upon entering the turbulence, Philip?"

He exhales slowly. "I wished I could see Amara one more time."

I lean forward. "And you did, right? I remember you saying that you two were together in your next life."

"Yes. Her name was Iman Alami."

"How did you recognize her in your next life?" I ask.

He stares blankly at the tinted glass. "One was the spitting image of the other. And it went beyond just looks."

My mind is racing. "Philip, is it possible that one emerges from the turbulence and may not recall much of the former life but experiences it in the form of headaches, hearing voices, et cetera?"

"Of course. Iman hardly remembered anything, but she had memories of a life unlived and frequently had severe headaches. According to her, the symptoms subsided after we met. But again, every case will be different. It's a curse to remember your former life. People have split personalities."

I squint. "Can someone be born into the same reality from where they were taken? Amara and Iman were born into different realities."

"It's not impossible." Philip lifts his eyebrows. "You're trying to decide if Emika is Akane, right?"

"Yes." How could he read my mind? I look at my watch. "I have one question before I leave."

"Go on."

"Philip, why do you hide your property?"

He looks at his now empty cup. "To conceal it from those who will come to seize everything."

"Who will come to seize it? And how do you know they will?"

He leans forward. "The future has already happened. I just experience it before most." He changes the course of the conversation. "So, will you still be interested in my second and current life?"

"Of course."

"Just text me, and I'll be here. I wish I could tell you everything now, but I guess you have a lot to digest, and I have to meet my lawyers."

I close my notebook and cap my pen, placing them in my briefcase. "Lawyers? I hope everything is fine."

He chuckles and stretches his arms. "I'm a substantial source of their revenue. They're making sure that I'm still their client."

As I start flipping through my notes on today's interview with Philip, Hulk lifts his head and whimpers, warning me of inbound traffic. A set of three knocks follows. "Come in, Emi."

She peeps in. "How did you know it was me?"

I lift my head from the notes. "Lucky guess. I had no idea you wore glasses."

"They're just for my computer usage. I look terrible in those." She takes them off.

"It will take a lot more than a pair of glasses to make you look terrible."

Her cheeks turn pink. She comes forward and points at my notebook. "You have amazing penmanship."

"*Arigato*, Amari-*san*."

She places two bags on my desk and then sits across from me, opening the first bag and taking out two plastic zipper bags, each housing one of my pocket squares.

I have not seen such meticulous care for something as simple as a pocket square. I look at her gorgeous burnt-sienna eyes. "You didn't have to do this. They are just pocket squares."

She leans forward. "But they are yours, and you never hesitated a second before handing them to me."

"Emi, any other person would've done the same."

"I don't think so." Then she takes out four tea samples marked in English and Hiragana: Darjeeling first flush, Genmaicha, Oolong green, and Assam second flush. "Do you have a sieve?"

I shake my head and smile. "For ramen and rice."

She smiles. "I'll bring one next time." Then she goes for the second paper bag, taking out a lunch box. "I made *onigiri* for you. One with salmon, one with tuna, and one with eggs."

They're stylishly wrapped in an envelope of rice, which is tied with seaweed. "Thank you, Emi. You seriously didn't have to go to this much trouble."

She tilts her head, "I thought of you while making them. There aren't many people I care about—" Before she finishes her sentence, something behind me catches her eye. She walks past me and picks up the picture of Akane and me, covering her lips with her other hand. Turning to me, she points at the little boy in the image. "This is you?"

"Yes."

Then she points to the girl in the picture. "And this is Akane?"

"Yes."

Emika takes the picture and sits on the chair by the fireplace. Shutting my office door, I sit perpendicular to her. I touch her hand, I ask, "What're you thinking?"

She looks at me. "I looked exactly like that as a kid."

"I know. The pieces you struggled with are the ones Akane used to play for me when we were kids."

She pulls my jacket sleeve—I know that nudge. "So you think I may be Akane?"

I place my other hand on top of hers. "I don't know what to think. Yes, it would be lovely if you were her, but I don't want you to hear voices when you play the violin, either."

She runs her fingers over the photograph. Not over Akane's face, but little Vince's. She stands up, places the frame where it belongs, then turns to me. "Let me know how you like those *onigiris*."

Why this transformation? Have I done something wrong? I stand up as well and touch her shoulder. "Are you OK?"

"I'm fine." She gently removes my arm. "I just need to process this."

"Do you need a ride home?" I ask.

She shuts her eyes briefly. "I'll Uber. Don't worry. And take care. Please eat in time and sleep." Then she leaves.

I don't understand what ticked her off. What did I do wrong? All that I said was that she could be Akane. I haven't been spending time with her only because I thought she was Akane. Or have I? What does she need to process? She's told me so much already. Why can't she tell me this? Fuck that. I have no time to dabble with this. I have work.

After about thirty minutes of working, Linda knocks. "You've some envelopes, Dr. A."

"Like what?"

She shrugs. "Who knows what you're into? Porn, maybe?"

I smile back. "Yes, I have been waiting for my stash."

She hands me the envelopes. Two of the three are garbage. The third is the real deal—a full concerto recital for Beethoven's Fifth and Seventh for his 253rd birth year. Nice.

"That's the porn?" Linda asks, pointing at the envelope.

"Oh yeah!"

She rolls her eyes. "What kind?"

I waggle my eyebrows. "Eighteenth-century porn where Beethoven will make everyone strip."

"So, classy porn?" she fires back as she leaves my office.

As a member of the Symphony Center of the city, I get two box tickets each month.

I check the dates on the tickets. August 30—my birthday. Should I ask Emika to join me? Will she come? I pick my cellphone. "Ludwig, can you create a nested event? Event: Date night with Emika, on August 30. Subevent 1: Concert at 6:00 p.m at Opera House, and Subevent 2: Dinner at Chez-Giraud at 8:30 p.m."

I'm home. The delicate balance of rice and fish makes *onigiris* melt into my mouth. She must have put a lot of love into prepping these snacks, which is my dinner. Should I call Emika? I should since she left so suddenly. And I miss talking to her. Let's first text her and see if she's available to speak?

Me: The *onigiri* was great.

Emika (a few minutes later): You're welcome, Vince.

Me: Hey, are you OK? You left so abruptly.

Emika: I'm fine. Vince, can we chat later? I'm on a date. Please?

Sparks at my fingertips. Hello old friend, where were you? You never appeared in Cambridge, MIT, not even when Elise was gone. I quickly sit on my palms to suppress them. Why should I feel uneasy that Emika is on a date? What's to say that if Akane had lived that we wouldn't have drifted apart? Maybe the fragment that is Emika, who is not Akane, is on a date? The fragment I want to know, but I may not. Is there ever a conflict in her mind between what she wants and what Akane wants from her?

(August 2001)

We were done with the high school ceremony, and I paid my respects to Akane in her music room. I was still baffled by the image of the girl in polka dots that had appeared before me. I was heading to bid goodbye to the man who practically raised me. I knocked on Mr. Kruger's door.

"Come in," he answered.

He looked at me through his black-framed glasses. "Ah! Vincent. All ready for your new journey? You will love Cambridge."

I sat across from his desk. Desperately trying to hide the tremble in my voice, I said, "I just wanted to see you before I left. Thank you for all your support, sir."

He left his desk, came toward me, and hugged me. "I am so proud of you. The other brats, children of politicians, celebrities, business tycoons, the royalty will never amount to anything on their own. You are different."

I handed him a book, *Watchmaking* by George Daniels. "I got this for you since you love watches."

His eyes brightened. "That's so thoughtful of you. Thank you." He looked at my scarf, touched it. "I saw you enter the music room with bellflowers. It's been ten years, Vincent. I know it's not my place, but don't you think you should move on? You can't tie your happiness with an improbable hope."

I looked at the scarf, then looked at the violin. "Move on? What's that? Is that something my parents did after discarding me? Would Akane move on if I were sucked into turbulence? It's the hope that she will be back that keeps me going, sir."

He placed his hand on my shoulder. "Is that why you did not mention Akane in your valedictorian speech? You still can't fathom that she's gone?"

I bent my head, dabbed my eyes. "Yes."

"I'm sorry, Vince." He went back to his seat. "Are you heading straight to Cambridge?"

"I'll make one stop, and then Cambridge."

He took off his glasses to peer at me. "Where?"

"Alexanderplatz. I need to see the place that took everything from me. I will be leaving tonight."

"I see. You have to let go of her memories, Vincent. Else you won't surge ahead. She is not coming back."

We had gone over this many times, and prolonging it seemed like a waste of everyone's time. So I changed the topic. "Sir, do you know why I get these sparks in my fingers? I've found nothing on that topic."

He put his glasses back on. "All I know is that you need to control it. They only appear when you are emotionally agitated. You remember the drill, right?"

"I do, sir." I paused. "This place was my home, sir. And I'm leaving. Do you have any advice for me?"

He gave me a stern look. "Keep toiling till you are the top of your field. Then when you are, you will realize that the work has just begun. And there is the only way to get there—between logic and emotion, always choose the former. Work hard, expect a lot from yourself, and nothing, I repeat, nothing from others. Logic over emotions, hard work, and let go of the past."

(Back to the present)

Mr. Kruger's continued insistence on forgetting Akane fractured our relationship. But, his works on logic over emotions became the bedrock of my life. Emika, with her text, saves me from an imminent cesspool of mawkishness. Her being on a date helps me nip this feeling in the bud before it blossoms into something unmanageable.

I have so much work to keep my mind occupied. My research, this book I'm writing, the center, forthcoming publications, patents, meeting with Philip. I haven't invented anything in a year. I must change that. Maybe I'll attend the concert solo. Frivolous thoughts are terrible company for those who come from nothing.

Hulk jumps on my lap and tilts his head. I scratch his belly. "It was a long day in the office, bug, you know what happened?"

He tilts his head and whimpers.

CHAPTER 7

SPRING DRIVE

Time is a storm in which we are all lost.
—William Carlos Williams

(About a year before today)

TODAYS' PLAYLIST—PINK FLOYD. MY SLEEVES are rolled, and I hold a CPU severed from one of the Nardin robots and compare that with the hologram of an average human brain. We cannot achieve a two-way transfer of consciousness between humans and machines with his configuration. We need to replace silicon or germanium with something different. With what? I have to invent this. I cannot afford any distractions. Why can't I simply skip to the day where I have already invented this? I take a bite of my Reuben and take a sip of long black.

(Third semester at MIT, Fall 2007)

I knocked on the door.

"Come in," answered Dr. Ulysses Bovet, my doctoral adviser. Books, journals, and coffee-stained loose papers poured out from his shelves and spilled over the floor, desk, table, chairs, and even under his coffee machine. He was the editor of *Nature Machine Intelligence.* His shirt was crumpled, and his hair and beard had been uncombed since World War II ended or his third divorce, whichever happened earlier. He looked at me through his glasses. "Have a seat, Vincent."

In the background, I could hear Rachmaninov's Second on his Bose radio. He moved two dozen books and freed a chair for me. Smiling and nodding at me, he said, "I read your paper on two-way memory transfer and its impact on the global economy. Compelling. If only someone could invent the damn thing."

A deep feeling of accomplishment ran through my veins. My eyes widened. "So, Dr. Bovet, is the paper publishable?"

He shook his head but kept smiling. "No, it's utter garbage in its current stage. It's speculative, and it reads like an Asimov novel rather than an academic paper." He stretched his arm across his desk and fished out the paper from the piles. "I have a few suggestions. Follow them to the dot if you want me to coauthor this." He handed me the paper with his corrections in red ink. I couldn't even see my writing anymore.

I turned to him. "Thank you, professor. I will work on it till it becomes perfect."

Dr. Bovet narrowed his eyes. "Mr. Abajian, I picked you from a pool of seven hundred applicants. So don't make me regret my decision."

"You won't, professor."

He tilted his head and yawned. "Publishing this won't make me proud." Then he leaned toward me, eyebrows lowered. "This is MIT, so every idiot has a Ph.D., so that won't make me proud either. But, when you invent the two-way memory transfer, I will be proud. I will be long gone, though."

I got up from the chair. "I will give my best shot, professor."

He smirked. "What are you willing to lose to invent that?"

I shut my eyes, and I smiled. "I have already lost everything, professor," I replied as I reached the door of his office.

"Stop."

I turned back. "Yes, Professor Bovet?"

He pulled his eyeglasses down. "When was the last time you ate?"

I looked up to think.

He interrupted my thinking. "Well, it's definitely not today or yesterday." Getting up, he collected his crumpled herringbone brown Harris tweed-jacket and touched my shoulder. "You will learn two things—why a long black taste better than an Americano and a delicacy called the Reuben."

(Back to my office)

I take a second bite of my Reuben and sip my long black, then go back to reviewing the hologram. *I am trying to make you proud, Dr. Bovet.* What else is there to lose?

Three consecutive knocks interrupt my thoughts. Fuck!

"Come in, Emika." She walks in, tucking her hair behind her ears. She is wearing a gray linen suit and a pink blouse under her jacket.

She points at the CPU and looks at the hologram. Her eyes widen, and her jaws drop. "What are you working on?"

She doesn't need to know. I shrug. "Some random stuff." I swat away the hologram, and I cut a dry smile. I don't want to lose my inventive inertia. So I rush. "What can I do for you?"

She hands me a small box. "Open it."

I open the box to find a Japanese bamboo tea strainer. My heartbeat increases, but I remember that she is with someone else. I look up. Logic over emotion, Vince. My words are battling between how I feel and how I think I should feel. "Thank you, Emika. You didn't have to."

Her smiles reach her eyes. "I wanted to. You pour boiling water in a cup through the strainer filled with tea. And don't keep tea leaves submerged for more than three minutes for green tea and five for black tea. Also, just use one teaspoon of tea for every eight ounces of water."

"*Arigato*, Emika-*san*. I'll remember this like a manual."

She comes close and snaps her fingers. "Remember, more tea and less coffee. It's good for you."

I wonder why she cares. She smells different, like musky old-spice. I know what it means. She pulls a chair across to my desk and sits. "Vince, you were so quiet over the weekend. No texts. Are you OK?"

I lean back. "I was waiting for you to text me."

"Why?"

I pull our entire conversation history up and show her the last text. 'I'll text you later.'

She looks at the log, laughs. "Sorry."

"What's funny?"

She points to my cellphone. "About that, I meant to text, but Jason and I went out on a weekend trip. So, I didn't get the time. Sorry."

I smirk. "Well, in that case, I did my best not to disturb you and Jason on your rendezvous."

"Did I mention Jason?"

"Nope," I say hurriedly.

"Do you have time? Can I talk about him?" she asks.

Fun fact—I don't give a fuck. Is it not already bad that she likes someone else? So now I have to learn about this loser guy while interrupting my inventive rhythm. I sigh. "Sure, go on." Why couldn't I say no?

She smiles and raises her eyebrows in delight. "His name is Jason Taylor, and he works in the diversity office. He has a master's degree in college student personnel."

Another specimen with fake academic degrees designed for two-digit IQs. Whatever the fuck happened that higher degrees were designed for the intellectually gifted ones? How the fuck can Emika even pick him? I lift one eyebrow. "How scintillating? I wonder how rigorous that program must be."

She waves this away. "I don't really know. But we met at orientation, and he took me to lunch on Friday."

I lean back and sneer. "Friday as in the Sichuan Palace night?"

She snaps her finger again and smiles through her eyes. "Yes."

Wonderful. So she lied about thinking about me when I picked her up on Friday. And what was all that about getting so emotional about my being an orphan?

She tucks her hair behind her ears. "We went on another date on Sunday."

I press my lips tight and smile to hide my discomfort. "That's the day after I was in your townhome, right?"

She lifts her right shoulder and smiles. "Yes. That was when we felt something special. And, we were on another date when you texted."

I have walked out of meetings that were far less exhausting emotionally and intellectually. How long do I have to maintain this charade of curiosity? I can't be rude. How can I switch the topic, or better yet, ask her to leave? I crack my knuckles and yawn.

She points at my left wrist. "What watch is that?"

Why is she interested? "It's a Grand Seiko-Godzilla limited edition, powered by a spring drive."

She tilts her head. "What's a spring drive?"

Can't she Google? Better, ask her semi-illiterate boyfriend. "A spring drive is where the quartz oscillator and electromagnetic brake replace the escapement and balance wheel. It's hand-wound. It vibrates at 36,000 vibrations per hour." So, why the fuck did I give in?

She leans forward, touches my hand. "Are you OK? There's something different about you."

"I'm fine, Emika. Why?"

She taps on my desk. "You are calling me Emika. Your music is different. You are so matter-of-fact. You don't seem like the Vince, I know."

I shrug to conceal my discomfort. "Sorry, Emi. I once told you that I'm a Pink Floyd fan. And, facts are facts."

She stands. "I guess. But you are hiding something." She goes to pet Hulk. He sniffs her, turns the other way, and continues to sleep. Emika turns to me, helpless. "Even he's different. Is he OK?"

"He is just exhausted." *He hates Jason's stench on you. He has better taste.*

On her way out, she points to my jacket. "New?"

I shake my head. "Only to your eyes."

Her eyes shimmer. "Enjoy the strainer." She closes the door and leaves.

Now let's back to my futile attempt at inventing a two-way transfer of consciousness.

Philip takes a sip, shuts his eyes. "You're right. Long black tastes much better than an Americano."

"I discovered that during my Ph.D. years."

"Can you guess what coffee you're drinking?" Philip asks, pointing his finger at my cup.

I inhale the coffee's scent. "Jamaican Blue Mountain?"

Philip claps. "Splendid." He is wearing a plaid navy suit, a maroon tie with a blue paisley design, and his white shirt has a French cuff. Rubbing his palms together, he says, "So, Vince, let's get to it. My mother was a history teacher in my second life, and my father was still a mechanic."

I take out my pen. "Still in France?"

"Nope. Modena, Italy. But still in 1950."

I scribble in my notebook as Philip takes a sip from his coffee mug and then continues. "One morning, I woke up dreaming that I was an artist in the future, around 1970. I talked about this to my father, and he rebuffed it and asked me to help in his workshop. He specifically said, 'We don't have time for dreams. We are born to work. Dreams are for those who make us work."

Philip pauses and takes a sip. "Around that time, Enzo Ferrari decided to expand his racing team, and my father got a job as a contractor mechanic in the Scuderia Ferrari factory. He fixed and tuned cars for long endurance races like the 24 Hours of Le Mans and 24 Hours of Daytona. My mother had no interest in her husband's life or mine." Philip pauses, takes his glasses off, cleans them, and puts them back on. "I often accompanied my father to his work. And one day, I saw two engineers arguing about reducing the cars' weight. I just casually mentioned replacing steel with aluminum. That caught the attention of their drivers. As time went by, I was helping with making the vehicles lighter and testing the cars. I got better and better at driving. So, whenever the main drivers weren't available to test, I would. I know I was allowed to do this because my life was expendable, but I enjoyed it nonetheless. I would drive, listen to the engine, fix it, and drive some more." He pauses. "More coffee, Vincent?"

I wave my arm. "No, I'm fine, thanks."

He smiles and looks at Hulk. "Does he fetch?"

"The bichon in him wants to, but the Shih Tzu in him forbids."

Philip laughs, then continues with the story, leaning back. "Enzo's patience was running thin after his two consecutive losses in 1966 and 1967 to Shelby American, Inc. He ended up firing the entire team of mechanics and engineers, including my father. After losing his job, father hung himself, and my mother left with her boyfriend."

I look into Philips's eyes. His eyes are blank, devoid of the grief that he felt about Victor's mother. Is a sons' love for his mother a reciprocation of the mother's love? And does that carry across realities? Well, what would I know? *Come back, Vincent.* I lift my eyebrows. "I so sorry, Philip." By the way, who am I sorry for? Philip? Olivier?

Philip swats his hand. "Oh, forget it. Who are you sorry for, Vincent? Me as Philip or Oliver?"

How the fuck did he read my mind? Anyway, let's get back. I look at my notes. "But you—I mean Olivier—worked for Porsche, right? So when will that happen?"

He takes several deep breaths. "So, I took up my father's shop and began fixing cars as a sole mechanic. And one day, a Porsche showed up in my shop. The owner saw some of my photographs on the wall with Ferrari drivers. He asked me, 'Hey kid, how do you know them?' I explained how I fixed their cars and had been on the Scuderia Ferrari as a mechanic and test driver. He was impressed with my work and asked me if I wanted to move to Stuttgart, Germany. I said yes in a heartbeat."

I tilt my head. "Did you move right away?"

"Yes. I was in Zuffenhausen at the end of 1967. They paid me well, and we won the 1968 Daytona-24 race. I bought myself a Rolex Daytona 6262 panda dial. We did lose the 1968 and 1969 Le Mans race, but Porsche did not fire me. For a change, I was doing well. Then, during a visit to Paris, I stumbled upon an art gallery."

I turn the page and smile. "Yvon Lambert gallery, I suppose."

Philip nods. "Yes. So, I saw this painting, titled 'Risen from Fire and Ashes,' and bought it. I don't know why, though. I thought I knew the artist and the woman in the painting. I wanted to meet Victor Constantin, but he was unavailable. Then in 1970, right after we won the Le Mans, my Rolex Daytona stopped ticking. No amount of winding brought it back to life. Can you guess what happened next, Vince?" He looks at me after pulling his glasses down.

I lean forward. "It stopped ticking because Victor came close to you. And then you went to Louis-Atelier, and he said that his nephew Philip would look, and it may cost around two hundred francs to fix? Am I correct?"

"Yes to everything—except the charge was 350 francs because the 6262 was an automatic movement."

"So, did you go to the hotel where Victor disappeared?" I ask, turning a page in my notebook.

"That turbulence didn't occur in my second life. I left Paris and went to Stuttgart to start prepping for upcoming races. And one day, while I was driving on a regular road, I had a head-on collision with a Saab. The accident burnt my face beyond recognition. The other car driver died, and the passenger, a lady called Iman Alami, had a spinal injury, disabling her from the waist down. Later, I found out that the driver was Victor Constantin. Now, I realized that I had an accident with myself. Weirdly, I killed myself and came out alive."

He cuts a dry smile and continues. "After many months, I mustered the courage to meet Iman. As soon as I saw her, I couldn't help but notice her resemblance to the painting I'd bought. She was calm and quiet and said that it was not my fault and I shouldn't blame myself. Then I asked her what she would do after she was released from the hospital. She said that she had no idea. I offered for her to stay at my place as penance."

"Did she agree?" I ask.

"She first asked my name, and when I revealed I was Olivier Journe, she burst into tears, stating that Victor had always wanted to meet me—that I'd been his first patron. She said my purchase of that painting springboarded Victor's artistic career. And she thanked me for that. And yes, she then agreed to move, after a year. Our relationship was fulfilling. We would sip tea or coffee and watch the rain splash against the window. We never made any marital promise. We lived a quiet and peaceful life. Until a stupid idea hit me." Here he pauses, shuts his eyes, and takes his glasses off, pressing the bridge of his nose with his fingers. He is quiet for a few long moments. All I hear is Hulk snoring and the sound of the pendulum in the hall.

After a couple of minutes, he breaks his silence. "Sorry, Vincent."

"It's alright. Please take your time."

He puts his glasses back. "I'm fine now, thanks. So, news reached me that this watchmaker, Philip Nardin, had created a perpetual movement using crystals found in turbulence sites. So, I convinced Iman that we should see him fix the Prague Astronomical Clock. And so we went. Everything would've been fine if I hadn't had the urge to meet Mr. Nardin in person. As we neared him, we got sucked into turbulence. But, remember Vince, because I emerged as the final me, turbulence in this reality didn't happen. So, there's no record of it. The only time turbulence that happened near my work, in this reality, was the one in Alexanderplatz."

I glance through my notes. "But, you did meet Amara in this life."

"Yes, I did. Only briefly, though. I will tell that story on a later day." He exhales and changes the topic. "How's work, and the center? Does the school need any funds?"

This is my opportunity. "Work is fine, and so is the center for the most part. The challenge is the red tape and bureaucracy."

"Go on," he says, adjusting his glasses and leaning forward.

I take a few deep breaths. "The provost and the VP of foundations have found a way to circumvent me and fund things that have nothing to do with my center."

He crinkles his eyebrows. "Such as?"

"Paying for the president's and provost's vacations. Worthless events like 'get to know the parents.' Even finding meaningless academic programs with nothing to do with my center." I hake my head in dismay. "Money from the center was diverted to create a so-called 'doctoral program' in education management. Even hiring has become a nightmare." I pause for a breath. "And with the annual spending rate at only 2.25 percent, I can only do ten percent of what I want to achieve. I have contacts in Silicon Valley, Seattle, and Boston, and they want to support us. But the university dictates that all monies should be handled by the provost and the president's office. Trust me, Philip, if these angel investors ever met the provost or Alyson, they would run away. Their stupidity is a repellent to any species."

Philip is silent, and his eyes are closed. What is he thinking? He wrinkles his forehead and slowly opens his eyes. Then he smiles. "Let me talk to my lawyers and revise the draft of the endowment. You'll have full autonomy with decisions related to the center. If you move, the endowment will move with you."

I squint. "Will the university allow redrafting?"

He smirks. "They can't fight me. The best legal minds represent my interests."

"That sounds wonderful, but why're you doing this?" I ask as I close my notebook.

"I read your papers, your patents, and you struck me as someone who can make academia a better and more efficient place. You cracked a sweet spot where universities, and industry, can all benefit from each other. I'd rather have you control the endowment than some half-brained bureaucrat. It's also a little thank you for giving me an audience, Vince. People only come to me for money. You did not."

I get up. "Thank you, Philip."

He snaps his fingers. "Hey, next time you come, I'll show you the Omega 321, the Rolex Daytona 6262, and the wristwatch I made."

"I do have one question about the 1970 Porsche win, Philip."

"Go on."

"What modification did you make to the car?"

"I replaced a lot of steel with aluminum, reduced the tail's length, removed the engine intake cover, and replaced the windscreen with 1.2-millimeter fiberglass. We built a 638-brake horse-power car that weighed only 800 kilos. That was no easy feat in 1970."

I tie Hulk's leash to his collar. "I think the world benefits a lot more from Philip Nardin than it would've from Victor Constantin or Olivier Journe."

Philip stares into my eyes, smiles. "I can see that."

What kind of material should replace silicon to carry a seamless neuron charge? Or will the next generation of Nardin robotics modify silicon in any way? This is the key to the two-way transfer of consciousness, but it's perplexing my mind, and I press my temples while the ambient song changes to "Shine on You Crazy Diamond." My eyes fall on the concert passes. Will it be OK to ask her out? If she agrees, that could be the most beautiful birthday present. Why is this problem inhabiting my mind when the consciousness transfer is a far more elegant question? My mind takes a break as I hear three consecutive knocks. Oh, fuck! I must pretend to be happy for her. She was perceptive last time. "Come in, Emi."

She peers around the door. "Busy?"

"Not at all. What do you want?"

"Nothing, Vince. I thought that I'd check in on how you are."

She is wearing a black short-sleeved top, maroon trousers with blue polka dots, and a Burberry scarf. Her hair is now chestnut brown. She points at her head. "Do you like my new hair color?"

I tilt my head. "Yes, but I still prefer the old one."

She pouts. "Sorry, Vince. Jason thought I would look good in chestnut brown."

"Well, ultimately, it's your choice. If I were him, I wouldn't change a thing about you." I should not have said that.

She turns to Hulk. He sniffs her and walks behind my chair. She has come from a date with Jason. "Do you know why he's ignoring me?" she asks in dismay as she sits across from my desk.

I shrug. "Well, he can be quirky."

She points at the symphony passes. "What are those?"

"Two concert passes to Beethoven's Fifth and Seventh. Box seats."

"Wow! When is it?"

I shrug. "It's August 30, a Wednesday."

She surely has forgotten my birthday. And she doesn't seem too keen on attending it with me, either. She tilts her head, "How did you get those? Every seat for all concerts seemed sold out."

I sit up straighter. "I'm a member of the symphony. I donate to their benefit charities."

"Of course you are," she says, rolling her eyes.

She wants to go. And, if she changes the color of her hair to please him, maybe she would love to attend the concert with him. "Emi, why don't you and Jason attend it? Go and have fun." And a moron, I remain. My plan for a perfect date, a concert followed by dinner, comes crashing down.

She lifts her eyebrows. "Are you sure?"

Logic over emotions, Vince. I manage to smile. Under the desk, I form a fist. "Absolutely."

I can sense the sparks in my fingertips. Emika must not see them. I place my hands under my thighs, hoping the sparks extinguish.

"Jason and I owe you big time." Then she leans forward. "Something is bothering you, and you are not telling me."

Yes, it's you. My sense of logic disappears around you, and my sparks appear at the prospect of you being with someone else. "I'm fine. Enjoy the concert."

She places the tickets inside her Gurkha bag and leaves.

Dr. Kauffman pushes her glasses higher on her nose. "Let's not stray from what's in your mind. When she told you she was on a date, how did you feel?"

I look at Max, who seems to be smiling. "Like I lost someone with whom I'd shared some of my deepest feelings, vulnerabilities."

"So, you thought she won't be available to you anymore. Or, even if she was, you can't be transparent with her?" She scribbles on her notebook with her fountain pen.

I can sense my blood rising to my head. I form a fist, and I clench my jaws. "How can she be available when she couldn't even drop me a line of text? She said she would. Isn't a promise a contract? So, I must be OK with this. And why? How much shit must I accept? Dropped in an orphanage? Beaten to a pulp in school? Akane promising she would be back in a couple of days? Elise said she would be back on January 15? And now this? Don't words mean anything these days? Why're people so shallow?"

She takes off her glasses and leans toward me. "Vince, close your eyes, take a deep breath, and listen. None of this is your fault or Emika's. You are too bright to compare your challenges with a text. Don't let this be the straw, Vincent."

I bang on her coffee table. "No, Dr. Kauffman. People must take responsibility. This entire doctrine of 'good job,' 'there are no dumb questions,' 'there are no wrong answers,' will only set us up for mediocrity and failure."

Dr. Kauffman smiles and turns a page. "So why didn't you ask her to join you at the concert? You wanted to take her out, even after she texted that she was on a date?"

"My desire disintegrated once she went on and on about this, Jason. And after a few minutes, I stopped paying any attention. I'd planned to take her to dinner after the concert, but I feared she would keep rambling about this illiterate idiot while we ate." I massage my temples. "I don't want that image of Emika. I want to remember her as she was the first day she walked into my office, the first group dinner with her Anna, Chris, and Ravi, and when I went to her townhome and spent a whole day there."

Dr. Kauffman shakes her head. "But two people can enjoy a concert or dinner even if it's not romantic—unless such involvement was in your mind. You put Emika on a pedestal in our last meeting, where falling is only a natural course. Perhaps, Vincent, deep down, you wanted this to fail. Tell me, do you hold yourself responsible for Akane's disappearance?"

"Yes, it was all my fault. I dreamt she would not come back. I should have stopped her. I should have thrown a tantrum. Maybe then she wouldn't have gone. I often think that if I hadn't been close to her, it would've hurt a lot less. I don't want another loss. So, I'm distancing myself. And I am failing. Maybe that's why I gave away the tickets. This should be easy, Dr. Kauffman."

She puts her glasses back and looks at her notebook. "How are you failing? And what's supposed to be easy?"

"I am failing to dissociate from the scenario, where I keep thinking of a possibility of a life with Emika." I shake my head. "I have solved far more complex problems. This one should be easy."

"Your mind is instrumental in solving complex problems. This one is a bit different and does not follow the structure of logic," she says, leaning forward again. "I'll tell you what—if the opportunity presents itself, ask her to accompany you. I think she might like it."

"So I'll wait for a new set of passes from the Symphony Center?" I lean back on the couch.

She chuckles. "You are a prominent figure. You get invited to the university president's dinner, Chamber of Commerce gala—places where Jason cannot be a substitute. Why don't you ask her? If she says yes, that's fine. If she turns you down, you know you tried. Also, when you think of Jason, what comes to your mind, Vince?"

"You'll laugh."

She narrows her eyes. "Try me."

I sigh. "I think he's a turbulence, akin to the one that took Akane."

She continues to look at me. "Vince, turbulence took a little girl, Akane, without her consent. Jason and Emika are in a consensual relationship."

I squint. "Consensual. How is this supposed to help me?"

She smiles and leans back. "She has the choice of leaving Jason. Also, Vincent, can I say something?"

"Sure."

"Look, Emika is not my patient." She squints and looks at me. "But from what you've told me, it seems her mind is split—a sort of discord between her actions and intentions. I know what you see in her. But, please, be careful."

"Thank you, Dr. Kauffman."

Yes, maybe there is an Emika that is free from Akane. I guess the Akane-free one just might prefer Jason.

The conference room is ready. I have called a meeting about the possibility of reducing the red tape that the university administrators love. I see Anna, Chris, and Ravi sitting with notebooks and a plate of bagels sliced in half as I walk in. Anna's hair is back to blonde. "I like it," I say, pointing at her hair.

She bats her eyes. "It's all for you, hon."

Chris leaves his seat to offer cream cheese. "Chris, Mama needs cream cheese," Anna says. Chris hands her a pack, takes one for himself, and tosses one to Ravi.

I fold my sleeves up and sit.

"Grand Seiko?" Ravi points at my watch.

"Yeah. Elise hated it, so it hardly got any wrist time."

Anna frowns. "She was right. It's hideous." She turns to Chris and Ravi. "Are you with me on this?"

Chris crosses his arms. "I love the watch."

Anna shakes her head, rolls her eyes. "Fucking suckers, all of you."

Vikram walks in, wearing an ill-fitted three-piece suit. I turn to him. "Board meeting? Donor meeting?"

He sighs. "Both, Vince. I wish you could come to one of these."

I stretch and yawn. "No thanks. I have no interest in discussing singularity with anyone who can't solve a simple linear equation."

Vikram sits. "What do you want, Vince?"

"Given we have close to one billion in endowment and grants, I would like you to talk to the provost and the president about having a higher spending rate per year. Further, I would like to explore fundraising for this center without Alyson and her lieutenants' intervention. My connections in Silicon Valley want to meet the scientists and professors, not bureaucratic fuckheads." I want to see if Vikram can push this agenda before Philip's lawyers make their moves.

Vikram shakes his head. "Alyson and Matt won't allow that."

"Who the fuck is Matt?"

"The provost, Vince," Anna says, rolling her eyes.

I lean toward Vikram. "So, will Alyson and Matt object if Philip were to recommend these?"

Vikram stands up, loosening his necktie. "Is Philip asking this? Did he say anything?"

"Relax, Vikram." I wave my arm at his chair. "Please sit. I voiced my dissatisfaction with how the admin is creating roadblocks to my vision. So, yes, he is asking."

"How could you do this?" Vikram takes out his handkerchief and rubs the sweat off his forehead.

I pass a bottle of water to him. "Why not? When you came here, you had a bold vision. But now, you have become a bureaucrat. What will you do if Philip pulls the endowment? Will the foundation be happy managing $500? Think about it."

Vikram catches his breath. "I'll do my best to convince them."

"We appreciate that."

Vikram finishes the bottle and nods. He leaves the room, panting.

Anna lifts her eyebrows. "Wow, Vince, you almost gave him a heart attack!"

Chris leans toward me. "What if he did have one? What would you do, Vince?"

I point fingers at them. "I will blame it on you three."

"Seriously, Vince, can something be done about these roadblocks?" Ravi asks.

"Give me a couple of months."

Anna leaves her seat. "Coffee, guys?"

"Black for me," Ravi says.

Chris leans back and stretches his arms. "Cream and sugar for me."

She hands coffee to both and turns to Chris. "Get your cream and sugar, sunshine."

I smirk at Anna. "You forgot me, Mama."

"Oh, I'm sorry, hon. I wonder why." She bats her eyes. "This coffee isn't hoity-toity enough, that's why. It's not a single origin. All beans aren't the same size."

I can't help smiling. "That's not a bad impression."

Ravi takes a sip of his and turns to me. "So, what's the plan for tomorrow?"

"Nothing special. Just another day. I had a couple of passes for the symphony tomorrow, but—"

Anna grabs my arm. "So you're taking Emika to the symphony, right?"

"Anna," Chris interjects, "Vince said he *had* the passes. He also used the word *but,* which implies—"

Anna pulls my neatly folded sleeve. "You donated your tickets before asking her out. You did that, right? You idiot."

I tap on the desk. "Hey, can I talk?"

"Whatever," she says, rolling her eyes.

I shake my head, exhaling. "OK, I wanted to take her. But it turns out she is seeing some guy called Jason from the office of diversity. She is into him. I gave the passes to her, and she'll take Jason with her. I just want her to be happy on my birthday."

Everyone is silent. Anna stands up, clicking her tongue she turns to me. "You are the world's most brilliant idiot. And I love you for it."

CHAPTER 8

KODAK MOMENT

We're just two lost souls swimming in a fishbowl year after year.
—Pink Floyd

(August 28, 1991)

EVERY WEDNESDAY, AKANE AND I would ice cream together. She would come from her violin practice, and I would come from my art class. But unlike other times, she did not reveal what she was practicing. "It's a secret. You will know it," she kept saying.

I stood in the queue with a large bowl as per her instructions. "We'll have the ice cream together, like we do every week, and get the biggest bowl. One bowl for both of us."

Chef Marcel's assistant looked over my shoulder. "Where is the rest of you?"

I shook my head. "Violin practice."

Fred, Krista, and Sasha were already in the queue.

Fred turned back to look at me. "Why do you guys share one bowl?"

Krista slapped Fred on his head.

"Ouch." Fred touched his head.

Then Krista lifted her brows and touched her platinum blonde hair, and rolled her eyes. "Stupid. Because Akane loves Vince." She emphasized the "O" in the word "loves."

Sasha pulled my cheek. "And this one has no clue."

Their words seemed meaningless as I began to miss her. I looked outside the window and saw the robin. Turning to the door of the cafeteria, I wondered where she was.

I started jumping to spot her beyond the tall students. And then I saw the top of her violin case. The entire cafeteria grew brighter as she hopscotched toward us. Her smile, her bouncing hair made me make the world around me beautiful. At that moment, time stood still. She high-fived Krista, Sasha, and Fred. Then she ruffled my hair and kissed my cheek. "Found you. *Watashi no*, Vince." She handed me a bunch of purple flowers. "Hold them."

She took the bowl, inspected it, and smiled. "You did well, Vincent."

I pointed at the flowers. "What're these for?"

Her eyes widened. "These are blue and purple bellflowers—my favorite. I will keep them in my dorm room. Keep holding them."

It was our turn for the ice cream. Chef Marcel kneeled to reach our height. "And what's my favorite couple want?" Akane tapped her finger to her lips, looking up. She then smiled through her eyes, compressing them to double lines of lashes. "I know what we want. Three scoops of Tahitian vanilla, one scoop of dark chocolate, and four maraschino cherries, please."

After we collected our dessert, she pulled me by my blazer sleeve and looked for a table. She nudged my sleeve. "There, found it." We sat, and Akane tied her hair into a bun. She inserted two jade chopsticks to hold the bun. Taking the bellflowers from me, she put them in a half-filled glass. Then she used her spoon to cut my cherry in half and scooped up a quarter spoon of chocolate and three-quarters of vanilla. Bringing the spoon in front of me and smiling with her incandescent eye, she said. "Open your mouth." She gently placed the spoon between my tongue and upper lip. "Eat up, Vince." Suddenly she squinted and tilted her head. "Why are you sitting far away?" She took off her scarf and wrapped it around us. "Try and move now."

Suddenly everything went quiet as Mr. Kruger walked in. His presence intimidates everyone. Except for Akane, who waved at him. "Hello, Mr. Kruger, sir." He came forward. "There are my favorite students. Having fun?"

"We are, sir. Can you take a picture of Vincent and me, please?" she implored with batting eyes.

"Of course. Do you have a camera?"

She reached for her backpack, pulling my neck along with her, and handed him her camera. "Here, sir."

Mr. Kruger peeped from behind the camera. "Smile."

Akane looked at the camera while posing to eat ice cream and pressing her cheeks against mine. And I was staring at the ice cream with profound attention. We were both sharing one scarf. Mr. Kruger handed her the camera. "I have captured the perfect Kodak moment."

Midway through our dessert consumption, I pointed at her bun. "Hey, how do you tie that with two chopsticks?" She took the chopsticks out, and silky hair fell onto her shoulders. Then she inserted them into my wavy hair. "Like this, silly."

I squinted my eyes. "You're silly."

She smiled and pulled me by my cheeks. "*Watashi no amai*, Vincent."

CHAPTER 9

YAKITORI

The two most powerful warriors are patience and time.
—Leo Tolstoy

(A year to eleven months before today)

"HELLO, MR. HANS EFFENBERG."

"Am I speaking with Mr. Vincent Abajian?"

"Yes, you are."

"I have tuned the violin, and I have kept all the parts original."

I thought he'd call me with an estimate first. But I guess it's OK. "Can I come and pick her up today?"

"Yes. But don't you want to know how much it cost?"

"It's immaterial. I'll be there before you close, sir."

"See you soon."

I hang up. Well, that's the best news for my birthday. I was missing a part of my soul.

I've never tested my car's acceleration of 0–60 mph in under three seconds. Now is the time. Philip modeled his track after the Circuit de la Sarthe, except for the Michelin Chicane and the Forza Chicane. It's a befitting homage to his earlier life.

I arrive at the Mulsanne corner, a sharp left. My entire body shifts right. The seat belt pulls me back, hurting my collarbone. Now I can drive straight. Sixty, eighty, a hundred, hundred thirty. Han Zimmer's futuristic sound effects in my electric car are fabulous. One hundred fifty. The surrounding trees are now a single line. One hundred eighty. My BMW I-7M and I are one. Sharp left at the Tertre rouge. Slow drive across the curves, and I am back at the Mulsanne straight in less than a few seconds. I am not sure if Beethoven's Fifth and Seventh would come close to this. But that's not why I wanted to go here, right? I should not be thinking about that. A hundred and fifty. My body is fixed to the backrest. My feet feel light; I feel weightless. I reach two hundred miles per hour, the maximum in my car at 8,000 RPMs. Then I leave the track and park beside Philip's Enzo.

It's windy today. I'm holding my hair away from my eyes. Edward is patiently waiting with Hulk. Hulk's luxurious coat and Edward's penguin coat are also dancing in the wind, but Edward's cropped hair is unfazed by it. I walk toward them. "Mr. Tealeaf, I hope that was not too inconvenient."

"Certainly not, Vincent. Please call me Edward. You could've taken one of Mr. Nardin's cars. They're quicker, you know."

"Maybe next time. Thanks for taking care of Hulk."

He looks at Hulk, smiles. "He is a fabulous fellow."

It is difficult to imagine a trained sniper becoming a caretaker of an estate in gratitude to his savior. I stretch my neck. "Where is Philip?"

"He was in London and is now in Hong Kong. He'll be back tomorrow."

"So, what's he doing there?"

"He wants to buy Formula E-Holdings. And if that goes successfully, he'll buy some of the Formula 1 team, transform them from gasoline to a ceramic oxide electrolyte. Then he plans to invite Red Bull and Mercedes to a race and beat them, hoping that they too ditch gasoline in favor of ceramic-based. He's on a war against gasoline. And he is not making any friends among oil and gas lobbyists and politicians."

A second gust of wind whips up, reminding me that summer is ending. I zip my jacket and hold my hair again. "Edward, does he take care of all these business initiatives, personally?"

"His lawyers accompany him. You will meet them soon." So, Edward is privy to a lot more than I'd thought. I guess they're more like friends. We shake hands. "See you in a few days, Edward."

Why will I meet the lawyers? For the endowment revision? Hulk and I climb in my car, and we head to Effenberg and Sons.

Hulk and I sneak into my office with the serviced violin. The lights and the fireplace switch on automatically after sensing my presence. Linda put the cards and bouquets on the coffee table by the fireplace. I take inventory—a bouquet from the Foundation, one from the Chamber of Commerce, one card from Vikram, one from Linda, and one large one from the three musketeers. They wrote: "Happy fortieth birthday to the one for whom buying a gift is impossible. Happy fifth to Hulk." It's signed by Ravi, Anna, and Chris. And there's a postscript: "We messed up the alphabetical order, on purpose." They'd omitted Emika from the card. The evening sky lights up against the thunder, and within seconds the defining sounds echo through all the floor-to-ceiling windows in my offices. Hulk jumps on me and buries his face between hi shand and my waist.

I sift through the other cards. Lack of cursive penmanship indicates Vikram's card is written by one of his secretaries. Linda acknowledged me as the best boss. The cards from MIT and Cambridge Alumni association are templatized. I open the envelopes to see if there is a donation form. They never miss a chance. Classy. I put everything back on the coffee table and sat on the chair by the fireplace. Hulk jumps on my lap, and Akane's violin is on the sofa next to me. I touch the violin case.

My phone glows.

> Sasha: Happy Birthday, little one.
> Me: Thanks, Sasha. Not little anymore.

Krista: You will always be my little brother.
Fred: Our.
Me: I am so sorry for not keeping in touch, guys. I am sorry for not attending school reunions.
Sasha: It's OK, bud. We know it brings memories.
Me: I am sorry, Fred, for not attending your MBA graduation. Krista, Sasha, I am sorry for missing your wedding.
Fred: You missed my wedding, too.
Krista: Fred, be specific. Your weddings have become an annual event.
Fred: Not funny. I lost my Murcielago in my last divorce.
Sasha: At least she got something out of you.

After his mining degree from Manchester and MBA from INSEAD, Frederique Deschamps now oversees a leading iron and steel company—his grandfather's company. Krista Gallo and Sasha Cheng are married to each other, against the wishes of their families. They now own Thyme & Cumin, a Michelin one-star restaurant in Copenhagen. I can feel the tears in my eyes as I think of how much they helped survive the tragedy of November 1991. They sacrificed their own family gatherings and parties to be with me all because I had no one. I don't know if they perceived me as needy, but I wanted my absence to be a reward to get back to their lives. They did not need a child, not when they were children themselves. But did I take a path of no return?

Me: It's been so long since I saw the three of you. Have I fractured our bond? If I want to meet you, will you take me back?
Sasha: You haven't broken anything. No one can break our bonds. Not even you.
Fred: I will break your arms before you break our bonds.
Me: Thanks, guys. I can't ever repay you.
Krista: Shut the fuck up.

(August 30, 1991)

It was an exhausting Friday, with classes, drawing, soccer, and cooking, so I went straight to bed after dinner. I changed into my PJs and got under the covers. As I shut my eyes, my last thought was about the lowest point of the day—not seeing Akane even for a minute. Krista had told me she was still busy practicing the new piece. Why the secrecy from me? I always listened to her practice. Suddenly the door creaked open, and Fred turned back to the corridor. "Found him." He switched on the lights, removed the blanket, and scooped me out.

I looked at him with half-open eyes. "What?" Behind Fred were Krista and Sasha—all three clad in their uniforms. I rubbed my groggy eyes and yawned. "What do you want?"

Sasha pulled my slippers from under the bed. Then she shook my shoulders. "Get up, sleepyhead. Chef Marcel wants to see you. He is furious."

My pulse increased, and my eyes widened. "What did I do? OK, let me change."

Krista opened my wardrobe and handed me my blazer. "Just wear this. We don't have time. He wants you right now." She helped me fit the blazer over my PJs, and we headed toward the culinary classroom. Sasha stretched her arms and pushed me from behind, ensuring I didn't fall asleep while walking.

Fred opened the door. "Enter, buddy."

I walked to the room, which was sparingly lit. After a few steps, Chef Marcel stopped me. I inclined my head almost ninety degrees. My hands were shaking in fear. I could feel my heartbeat as my voice quavered. "What have I done, sir?"

His eyebrows were down, but slowly a smile appeared at the corner of his lips. He began to laugh as his voice resonated through each corner of the kitchen. Sasha pointed at my face and covered her mouth. Her shoulders shook. "You look like you saw a ghost."

Chef Marcel moved and revealed a chocolate ganache cake with eight candles.

He ruffled my hair with his enormous hands. "Vince, make a wish and blow these out."

I looked around. "Where is Akane? I won't unless…."

My words were interrupted by the sweet melody of "Happy Birthday" on a violin. I turned back around. And there she was, her eyes shut, a smile on her lips. She was seamlessly adding notes from other pieces and modifying the original song. So, that was the secret piece? For me? Then she stopped and opened her eyes. She hopscotched toward me, pulled my cheeks. "Happy birthday, silly."

Chef Marcel placed his heavy hand on my shoulder. "She has been practicing that violin piece the whole week. She planned this whole thing. You're lucky, Vince."

Fred interrupted. "Yes, yes, but we want cake."

Chef handed me a knife. "Make a wish."

I shut my eyes, joined my hands, and made my wish. *Please let me be close to Akane all my life.* Then I blew the candles. I gave my first piece to Akane.

She broke it into two and whispered, "We will share this."

Headmaster Kruger walked in. "I want a piece, too."

(Back to the present)

I have etched those notes she played into my heart to this day. She wasn't even nine, and she mixed parts of Méditation and Zigeunerweisen to make "Happy Birthday" sound like a piece written by Massenet or Sarasate. And she'd done it for me, a worthless orphan. That day had been perfect—she'd made me a part of her life, music, and love. At that moment, I was not an orphan, all because of her.

I take out my handkerchief and cover my face. "Why did you have to leave? It hurts, Akane."

Hulk nudges my hand with his nose, and I bring him close. He licks my tear-soaked face. "I'm fine, bug. Look around me. I have you. I have everything a worthless orphan could want." Hulk is the only one in my recent history to witness my tears. It's raining. Hulk climbs up and nests his face under my neck. The soothing sound of the rain is calming his pulse.

"Happy birthday, Hulky," I whisper into his warm ears that smell like butterscotch.

(August 2001)

I shut Mr. Kruger's office door after handing him the book. Fred, Krista, and Sasha were sitting on the bench by the door. I asked, "You guys in trouble?"

Sasha stood up, hugged me. "We are here for you, bud. Akane would be so proud of you."

I shut my eyes to hide my tears. But they knew better. Fred took out my pocket square and dabbed my eyes. "It's OK, bud."

Krista pulled me forward to show me the contents in her backpack. "I have Riesling and Cabernet Sauvignon. Let's go to the dorm room one last time."

That was my last visit to the room where I'd spent most of my life. Sasha and I sat on what used to be my bed. Krista and Fred sat on the one that had been Fred's.

Sasha took out four coffee mugs from her bag. "I came prepared." Fred opened the bottles, and I poured the cups. After two rounds, Krista came over to my side of the bed and kissed Sasha.

Fred's eyes widened, and he looked at me. "You had any idea?"

I shook my head. "Not the slightest."

"So, what do we do after this, guys?" Sasha asked, straightening her jacket.

Fred raised his glass. "I will expand our iron and steel company globally. And maybe buy a yacht and a Lambie."

"I'm going to Cordon Bleu to be a chef. All I want is to open a restaurant with Sasha and spend the rest of my life with her." Krista said, raising her own glass.

To that, Sasha added, "I'm going to Cordon Bleu as well. I'm doing that against my parents' will. They want me to run their real estate business, but I want to cook and open a restaurant. And with Krista by my side, I can."

They all turned to me. I had a dry smile, but my eyes were wet. "I am going to Cambridge. My home, from one dorm to another. After that, who knows, maybe MIT or Caltech. A school campus is all I know, and I will stick to it. But my dream is something metaphysical. My life will be worth it if I can just meet Akane one more time."

They all kept quiet. Fred interrupted the silence. "Bud? That's beyond your control, right?"

"I know. But what else could I want? I don't know what it feels like to have a home, car, or parents. But I know how I felt when she was around me for two years. Every minute since that day, I have missed her. I don't know what I will accomplish in my life, but I am willing to trade everything for just one minute with her. Is that too much for an orphan to ask?" I took out my pocket square and dabbed my eyes.

They all came close and wrapped me in their arms.

I looked at them. "Aren't your families waiting for you?"

Sasha ruffled my hair. "You are family, and you are coming with us. Who knows when we'll meet again?"

(Back to the present)

That was the last time humans witnessed my tears. Twenty-two years have passed since then, and thirty-two years have passed since Akane disappeared. She did come back, right through my office door. And we did talk for more than a minute. She did not recognize me, but that's OK. I have gotten more than what I had bargained for. I will give her the violin. But I don't think I will ever get the chance to wrap the scarf around her if she is cold. "Scarf," "cold," and "Emika,"—I've heard those words before. But where? Should I tell Fred, Krista, and Sasha about Emika? Maybe later. So, now there are four things I can't remember: where have I heard the name Emika before, Philip's license plate, the pocket watch, and the juxtaposition of "scarf," "cold," "and "Emika."

"Ludwig, can you play Liszt's Consolation no. 3 six times in a row?"

"It's too somber for a birthday."

"I am missing someone, and it reminds me of her."

I walk into my suit and fold my dripping umbrella. Linda is showing something to Emika on her computer, and both are giggling. I stop before unlocking my office door. "What's funny?"

Linda stands up. "I am showing Emika old pictures of you, Anna, Ravi, and Chris."

Emika comes closer to Hulk, and he hides behind me. She tilts her head. "Still ignoring me."

"Don't you think, Emika looks beautiful?" Linda asks, turning to me.

I look at Emika, attired in a woolen burgundy knit dress with short sleeves folded and stitched. The dress goes down to her knees and is complemented by suede boots and her Burberry scarf. I turn to Linda. "Not my place to comment."

Emika lifts her brows, looking surprised. She tucks her hair behind her ears and asks me, "Can I come in?"

"Sure."

She follows Hulk and me. Why is she here? To thank me for the concert passes? A text would have sufficed.

"Nice trench." She points as I hang up my coat.

"Thanks." I hang my sports jacket as well and take out my cell phone. Then I roll my sleeves and sit.

She points at the cards and bouquet. "Occasion?"

I sit on my chair, switch on my computer. "Why don't you read them?"

She inspects the contents, comes back, and sits across from my desk. "Thanks for the passes."

"You're welcome. I hope you guys had fun."

She ignores my comment and leans toward me. "Vince, can I see your cell phone?" I hand it to her, and she asks. "Now, can you please unlock it?"

"You can do it. It's the first five of the Lucas series."

She unlocks it while I get back to my computer. After a few seconds of staring at my cell, she covers her lips with her hand. She hands me the phone, pointing to the calendar entry on August 30, and asks, "Why?"

I squint at it. "Why, what?"

"Why didn't you tell me it was your birthday, and why did you not ask me to go with you?"

"I told you about my birthday at your townhome." I shake my head. "And I didn't ask you because you are seeing someone."

She looks at the phone some more, then says, "You also reserved a table at Chez-Giraud for us? Don't they have a waiting list of several months?"

"Antonio Giraud is a friend, and I have equity in that restaurant." Then something strikes me. "I am so sorry. I should have transferred the reservation to your name instead of canceling. If you and Jason want to go there, just let me know, and I can get you a table."

She props her elbow on my desk and rests her chin in her palm. "I don't wanna go there with Jason." And then she keeps quiet. After a brief pause, she gives in. "Won't you ask why?"

This shit again? I should not delve into this—I have to work. "Alright, why?" Fuck, why did I ask?

She leans back and crosses her arms. "He has no etiquette. He kept texting his buddies throughout the recital. He knows I don't eat red meat yet still took me to a cheap steak place. He ordered a large steak, beer and kept talking about NASCAR and his pickup truck. Other than French fries, I had nothing to eat. After dinner, he wanted to take me to a sports bar to meet his buddies, but I excused myself and Ubered home. He also lied that he listened to classical music—he doesn't know Beethoven from Boy George. He is not worth my time. So, I ended it."

Ended at the first sign of discord? Just a few days back, she went on and on about this guy. So that's the Akane-free Emika? Or is it a split personality like I read about? The date didn't go well, so should I be delighted or concentrate on things with tangible outcomes like always? I lean a little forward. "Emi, the new normal is that people will check their cellphones, and people lie during dates."

She quickly reacts with, "I am certain you wouldn't."

"How'd you know?" I cut a dry smile.

She looks away and points at Hulk. "Why's he ignoring me?" She looks back at me with child-like innocence in her eyes. "What've I done?"

"It's confusing for him. You sound like his favorite person, but you smell different. You ditched your perfume that had an essence of amber, sandalwood, vanilla, and vetiver to a pedestrian musky Old Spice."

"Yeah, that's Jason's cologne that he left in my apartment." She squints at me. "How do you know that my regular perfume had those notes?"

"From your first hug."

Her eyes sparkle. "Vince, about Chez-Giraud—I want to go there with you." She starts drawing circles on my desk with her index finger and tilts her head. "Not with our colleagues. Just you." She stops making the circles and stares into my eyes. "Can it happen?"

That was quick. She just broke up with Jason. But, I can't deny that I want to know her. If I tell the truth, then I risk going down a chasm of an emotional wreck. If I don't, then I'll forever wonder what if. If I damage myself emotionally, can I recover? And which Emika is asking? The one predominated by Akane, or the one which is just Emika? *For once, Vince, fuck logic.* I stare at her shimmering eyes, and I blink. "Yes, it can happen."

She extends her hand and presses my palm. "Thank you, Vince." She leaves my desk and picks up the birthday card from the three musketeers. "Why didn't they ask me to sign your card?" Then she looks at me. "I am an outsider, right?"

I leave my desk, take the card from and place it back on the coffee table. I take both of her hands and look into her eyes. "Of course not. They may have tried to reach you when you were with Jason. But trust me, you are not an outsider."

She nods begrudgingly. "Maybe."

There are about thirty pieces of military-grade luggage outside Philips's study. "You're leaving again?" I ask as I sit down.

Philip is glancing through a manual. "Yes, Vince. I'm going to the North Sea. But I must go to Basel first."

I reach for my notebook. "What's there?"

"An old friend. He is dying of pancreatic cancer." He sighs.

Basel is Mr. Kruger's hometown. It's been so long since I spoke to him. I squint. "Intreton-c can't help?"

"Too late for that, he says, shaking his head. "So, what made you come and drive the other day?"

"It was my birthday, and I wanted to do this for myself."

He takes off his glasses, lifts his brows. "Racing alone on your birthday? What about friends or Emika?"

Wow, he remembers her? And even he separates her from the others. "Emika was on a date."

The smile disappears from his face. "I see."

"Can I have a drink, Philip?"

He picks up the phone by his desk. "Macallan 30 with two glasses and a bowl of water for Master Hulk."

Edward comes in with a bowl of water and a whiskey cased in a golden box. The white bowl has the signature blue markings from the Ming Dynasty. Most people wouldn't eat from such an expensive artifact. But Philip doesn't mind using it for a thirsty dog. I sip the whiskey. It has notes of orange and nutmeg. Opening my notebook, I say, "So, Edward was telling me about your Formula E ambitions."

Philip stares into his whiskey. "He thinks I should be less ambitious and relax. He deeply cares about his adopted daughter and me."

With the pen cap in my mouth, I tilt my head. "Adopted daughter?"

"Remember Lombard's first drone strike authorized by Dick Graham?" He clenches his jaws.

"Yes."

"Well, the intel was to bomb a rural house that was hiding Zarqawi. But there were only five innocent lives. Two adults and three children. The children were two girls and one boy. Only one girl survived. I think she was outside the impact zone. Edward rescued and then adopted her." Philip gulps his scotch and pours another. "Just like other intel, Dick Graham concocted. Once again, his intel was unconfirmed by Mossad and MI6."

"No one charged Dick Graham?"

"He was good for business. His corruption led to weapon sales and military presence in the Middle East. Weapon sales mean fat commissions for politicians. If the US tried politicians for a crime against humanity or corruption, then we would have a vacant Capitol Hill and White House." He leans back. "Anyway, let's leave the politicians and talk about this life. That's why you are here, right?"

I nod. "So what do you remember as being the most striking or revelatory of your third life, besides the discovery of intreton?"

"That I had two lives that I know of. So, while working in my uncle's watch shop, I came across Speedmaster and the Daytona. I still have the watches." He opens a drawer in his desk and takes them out. "Here, have a look."

I pick up the watches. The lumens are patinaed, the hands rusted a bit, but both are keeping accurate time. Turning to Philip, I say, "The Daytona must be worth millions."

"It could be, but there is no record of its existence in this world. Same with the Omega. The serial numbers don't exist."

I crumple my brows, crinkle my forehead, and keep looking at the watches. Philip detects my perplexity, but he waits for me to voice it. "So, Philip, I am touching two artifacts that don't exist?"

"Puzzling, isn't it? Also, they wouldn't be running without the intreton powering them."

"What do you mean?" I squint at the watches.

He smiles. "Intreton is a reality-proof element. Mechanical watches, quartz watches, spring drives all behave unreliably in a reality where they were not built. The world of Vincent and Philip is an alternate reality for these watches." He pushes his eyes glasses upward and keeps smiling. "If one day you find that all your watches are behaving unpredictably, then you have entered an alternate reality."

"What about the time displayed in cellphones and smart devices?"

Philip tilts his head. "Well, all cellphones and smart devices are powered by inreton-c, making them reality-proof." He then looks at me. "If you ever enter an alternate reality, you will see the mismatch between your mechanical watch and your cellphone time."

"I don't see that happening," I say, chuckling.

Philip stares at me with his penetrating eyes. "You never know."

I turn to a new page in my notebook. "So, how did you figure out your past?"

"I could see some flashes of lives that I couldn't relate to. I often woke up with weird dreams of characters that I had never met. I had unexplained headaches, and I have woken with tears in my eyes." Philip takes a long sip. "The flashes I had from those watches gave me a glimpse of people that were in my dreams. I asked Louis about the watches. He said that he had no recollection of them."

"What about the checks written against the service?"

He lifts his eyebrows and nods. "Yes, I took the checks to the banks. The account numbers did not exist. It was easier for Olivier to decipher his past. He saw the painting and later met Iman. It took longer for me.

But a lot of things happened between finding the watches and knowing about my past."

"Like what?" I ask.

"My uncle's death. I kept the shop running. Then I came across intreton. You know that part. I sold Loius-Artelier. I recalled my past right after I repaired the Conciergerie Clock in Paris. I cut my hand while fixing it and had to go to the hospital, Hôtel-Dieu. The attending doctor recognized me and offered me a tour of the facilities. And there I saw a woman, lying almost lifeless. I couldn't recall who she was. I went closer to her. She opened her eyes and called me Victor. I asked her name. She said it was Amara. But she had a different last name." Philip pauses and pours some more scotch, then continues. "We met regularly. I began to construct a wristwatch with the hope of wearing it when we started a life together. Later on, I came to know she was suffering from AIDS."

Philip takes a few deep breaths. "You see, Vincent, her career as a sculptor never really took off. In this world, she was an orphan, and Victor died before their relationship began. So, she became a prostitute. Before her last breath, she confessed that she had had a child with one of her visitors. She asked me to take care of the child. A week later, Amara died."

Philip's eyes go blank as he stares at the desk. He revives himself with a sip of scotch. "I did four things after that. I took care of the child, completed the watch, expanded my business, and retraced my previous lives."

I turn to a new page. "How did you retrace everything?"

"I began to have flashes of my life with Iman. From there, I constructed the possibilities of two previous lives. I could make the connection with the Speedmaster and Daytona. There's no scientific method to elucidate these. My headaches already reduced when I came across the two watches. As I reconstructed my other two lives, they disappeared altogether. Maybe the headaches and the dreams are a way to connect to my past lives. Possession of an artifact or coming close to someone dear from that life may decrease the dreams and aches." He sips some more whiskey. "I think any turbulence survivor is connected to the core or the time-mesh. Some have strong connections, like me dealing with three matured lives, all occurring parallel. Others could have weak ties, like maybe your friend Emika, whose past life as Akane was relatively short."

"Philip, why didn't you start a family?" I ask, leaning toward him.

He smiles and takes a box from a drawer. "I never got to wear this—the wristwatch I built. It shows the time, perpetual calendar, and a reset date of your choosing. I made it to wear on a special occasion. But Amara passed before that. So, it has remained unworn."

He hands me the watch. It looks like an A. Lange & Sohne Langematik perpetual calendar, with two date options. "That's the reset date?"

"Yes. You can put any date of your liking. It will take your memories back to that date. Not physically but figuratively. Also, it is perpetually wound and is powered by intreton-c."

I return the watch to him and get back to my notebook. "So, what about Amara's child?"

"The moment I saw him. I could feel he was Amara's child. Same eyes and hair. I had no idea what to do with the child." He fills his glass again. "But then the strangest thing happened. A hazy image of a man appeared before me. I could tell he was from the future. He instructed me on what to do with the child. So, I did exactly that. He even told me to create a synthetic intreton. We met again, and he told me how to fix Edward's leg."

I adjust my glasses. "How do you know he was from the future?"

"He was wearing this," he says, pointing at his special wristwatch, "which I was still constructing."

I lean back, exhaling. "Maybe it was you from a different world from the future. Who else would wear your watch? And who else would tell you to fix Edward's legs?"

"That'd be the simplest explanation." He nods.

I lift my eyebrows. "Occam's Razor."

Philip sighs. "When you deal with the physical and the metaphysical, you can't help but see the limitations of Occam's Razor."

"Did you ever meet the child after that?"

He looks straight into my eyes. "Very sparingly. We had a memorable meeting in 1992."

"I see."

Philip stands up, stretches his back. "Why don't you give Akane's violin to Emika and see what happens?"

My jaw drops. "How do you know I have Akane's violin?"

"You must have told me."

I glance through all my notes and still cannot find any references to Akane's violin.

"Also, Vince, I'll be gone for a few months. But we'll meet again, I promise."

"When are you leaving?" I ask, capping my pen.

"End of this week. There are certain things I have for you. When they're ready, Edward will call you. Can you please come then?"

"Of course."

Philip takes off his glasses and presses the bridge of his nose. "Let me also confess something. It should stay out of the book."

I lean forward. "I promise."

He takes a few deep breaths. "I don't go to the North Sea just because of my space program. I have an underwater station near the core, keeping track of all the tentacles spread from the core. Every historical anomaly is a tear in the tentacle. Sometimes I decide whether to correct it or let things be."

"Such as?"

He looks straight at me with his piercing eyes and smiles. "Both world wars resulted from tears. But changing that meant half the world would remain colonized by Europeans."

"Did you make any changes at all?"

"Very minimal. Through the core, I found that Ferrari would be the sole champion in the endurance race if things kept happening the way they happened. I couldn't let Enzo have all the credit."

My eyes widen. "What did you do?"

"I convinced Ford and Shelby to put Bruce Mclaren and Ken Miles as their drivers."

"You don't like Enzo, right?"

"I couldn't let his ego engulf the arena."

"So, why didn't you alter time to be with Amara?" I ask, raising my eyebrows.

He smiles and shakes his head. "Even the one with the least invasive process will take her child out of the equation. I could not hurt the only living fragment of her. The child did nothing wrong. Being born is not a sin."

"So, you are the Time Fixer?"

His eyes glint. "Ah, so you noticed the license plate?"

I have seen it before. But I still can't remember when or where.

I am flipping through my notes in my office. I don't see anything about Akane's violin. But I don't recall saying anything to Philip either. How does he know?

The weather is beautiful and warm outside—it's the last few days before the imminent fall and dreadful winter. I go through my contact list and find a number that I haven't called in a long time. Should I? What will I say? I press call, and after three rings, I hear. "*Das ist David Krüger. Bitte hinterlassen Sie eine Nachricht.*" The baritone is evident even through the tiny phone speaker. I press disconnect. I wish he could see that Akane came back and that my not moving on did not make a single dent in my success. But why did I call him? Is it because Philip said he would be in Basel?

I get back to my work. The sound of Chopin's piano and Hulk's snoring give a sense of contentment. Yet something's missing. It's almost 8:00 p.m. I can see most of the lecture rooms from my office windows. Only one room is lit—my AI lab. It is where we invent most things. It's also where Anna, Chris, Emika, and Ravi spend most of their time. Where I want to spend most of my time. So, who is working this late?

I go past the offices of Anna, then Ravi, Chris, and Emika. All locked. After walking fifty more feet with Hulk, I reach the door with the sign "AI Lab, Authorized Persons Only." Everyone except Anna and me needs an access card to enter. The name of the lab assistant that Anna and I built is Athena. As I enter, Athena welcomes me, "Welcome back, Dr. Abajian, it has been a while."

The lab has a large lecture hall designed as a horseshoe. There are five levels of stairs, and each group has twenty seats with attached computers. I see Emika sleeping on the floor between the second and third flights of stairs. Her head is in the third, and the rest of her body is in the second. She's folded her utility jacket into a pillow and is wearing a pair of blue jeans and a white polo top. Three dormant robotic dogs marked X, Y1, and Y2 are surrounding her. Her Gurkha bag is on the central lecture console. I see an empty lunchbox next to her Gurkha bag, though some rice grains are stained with soy sauce chili oil. The four monitors in the central control are on, and I see Python, Lisp, Prolog, and Java programs on four monitors.

Before I can wake her up, Hulk knocks down the three robotic dogs and rescues sleeping Emika from an imminent threat. After that, he starts licking her face. I guess Jason's stench is gone.

With her eyes barely open, she touches Hulk's face. "Hi Hulk, where's your daddy?" She rubs her eyes and yawns, stretching as she sits up. I climb up the stairs and sit next to her. I collect her utility jacket, straighten it. "Sorry, Vince, I fell asleep." Her eyes are sleepy, her hair frizzy, but her beauty unfazed.

I touch her head. "Did anyone ask you to work this late?"

"No, I just wanted to finish up. Do you want to have a look?" She's finally awake enough to notice the demise of her robotic dogs by the paws of Hulk. "What happened?" she asks, tilting her head.

"Well, Hulk rescued you from those devils."

She covers her mouth and laughs. Then she gets to business. "I transferred consciousness from X to Y1 after teaching four commands. Then I taught one more to X and transferred to Y2. The commands in the previous transfer were sit, shake, down, and roll. Y1 can do all of those. Then I taught X to crawl and transferred all five to Y2. So, now Y2 is the latest version of X, and Y1 is the previous version. We talked about this when we first met. We can create multiple restore points for the same organism. Say X has dementia right after copying their consciousness to Y1, but before reaching the stage of Y2, there will still be a working version of their consciousness, thus a restore point. One can go to the previous version given copying of consciousness from machine to humans if possible?" She demonstrates her experiment for me.

"Splendid. So now we need to invent a two-way transfer of consciousness between machines and humans?"

"That will require a true genius, Vince. Someone like you."

If only I could solve the limitations of silicon and germanium. I remove some strands of hair from her face. "Are you hungry?"

She nods. "Famished. But I need to initiate a shutdown protocol for the lab."

"I can do that. Why don't you decide what you want to eat?"

"Dr. Abajian, you need a keycard," she says, tapping on my shoulder.

I help her fasten her jacket and then turn to the ceiling. "I am the keycard. Athena, initiate shutdown."

"Very well, Professor Abajian. Good to sense you."

Emika's eyes widen. "Wow!"

"So, what do you wanna eat?"

She looks up as her eyes expand, then snaps her fingers. "*Omurice*! I know the perfect place—House of Bamboo."

"Do they have outside seating?"

"Yes, I know, for Hulk. That's why I said it's perfect. I love him, too." She grabs my cuff and pulls me. "Let's go, Vince."

House of Bamboo is a tiny hole-in-the-wall Tokyo-style midnight café, with paper lanterns both outside and inside. We are sitting outside. Emika's bright eyes sparkle under the swinging paper lanterns. She is struggling to keep her hair in place against the wind. I take out my pocket square and form a triangle, then get up to tie it around her hair like a ribbon. She looks into my eyes and touches my hand but struggles to find any words.

A Japanese couple, Toshiki Natori and Futaba Natori, run the restaurant. Futaba comes and speaks Japanese with Emika. She smiles. "*Sumimasen*! Menu, *onegaishimasu*."

I stand up and bow. "*Konbanwa. Hajimemashite. Watashi wa Vincent desu*."

Futaba covers her mouth with her hand to hide her smile as she hands me the menu and leaves.

Emika turns to me with her mouth wide open. "How fluent are you?"

I hold her hand. "I just know a few sentences."

After a few minutes, Futaba comes back. "What can I get for you?"

I quickly glance at the menu. "Reba yakitori, mune yakitori, and tebamoto yakitori, and a bottle of your house saké. *Kudasai*."

Emika looks at her and smiles. "*Omurice, onegaishimasu*!"

Smiling, Futaba collects the menus and leaves.

Emika notices an autumn ladybug on my sleeve and gently flicks it. "How was your day?"

"I went to Philip's house, talked about his life. Then, I came back to the office and wrote about it. I'm transforming our interview into a book. The rest of the time, I worked on our papers."

"What drives you?" she asks, lifting her eyebrows.

"I remember someone telling me that if I am at the top of my field, I will find what I am looking for."

She looks deeply into my eyes. "Have you found it?"

"Maybe," I say, staring at her brown eyes, her apple-red lips. "How was your day?"

She shrugs. "I spent the whole day in the lab."

Futaba-*san* brings our food and saké. Emika's eyes gleam at the sight of the *omurice*. I pour the saké into our glasses and raise mine. "To a long-winded road that got me to sit here with you."

She lifts her glass. "To possibilities." We take our first sip. Then she joins her hands together and shuts her eyes. "*Itadakimasu*." When she opens her eyes, she catches me staring at her. "What?" she asks, touching my hand.

"You didn't say that in Sichuan Palace."

She smiles and squeezes her eyes to curved lines of lashes. "I would have if it had just been you and me." Then she tilts her head. "What are you looking at?"

"Your smile. There is no pretension, and your eyes do all the talking—they glow even in the dark."

She forms a fist and gently punches me. "Stop it." Then she focuses on her food, cutting through her fluffy omelet. After mixing the egg with the rice, she brings the fork to my mouth. "Eat up, professor. You look hungry."

She is the second person to have placed food in my mouth. Akane was the first.

"I'm sorry for not ordering anything vegetarian, Emi."

"It's fine, Vince." Then, with her eyes shut, she takes a bite.

Halfway into our meal, I turn to Emika. "I need to ask you something."

She leans forward. "Sure."

I lean towards her and look into her eyes. "Why didn't you tell me earlier that you wanted to go to Chez-Giraud with me alone?"

She takes a sip of her saké. "It's a long explanation."

"We'll make it a long evening."

Sitting up straighter, she begins. "You are a world-renowned authority in your field. When I came here, Vince, you were all over the university, from brochures to posters and on everyone's mouth. They even have a name for you—the VA syndrome. It's about dealing with someone arrogant. The rumor is that the president and the provost are somewhat scared of you.

But then, I met you, and you couldn't be any more different than what I'd heard. You were sweet and sensitive. I was conflicted between how I perceived you and how the rest of the uni did. Plus, I report to those who report to you. And... after seeing Akane's picture, I also feared that you might only see your childhood friend in me." She pauses and takes a sip of saké. "During this conflict, Jason asked me out. He's a nice guy, but we had nothing in common. And I couldn't get past your act of giving away your concert passes. You were on my mind the entire evening during the concert. Actually, you've been on my mind since the day I met you. I spoke about you to Anna, and she said that if I want to know you better, I should make the first move. Does this answer your question?"

"Sufficiently." But were those her thoughts or Akane's? Will I ever know?

Toshiki comes to greet us. "Would you like some dessert? We have house-made Tahitian vanilla and dark chocolate ice cream."

I must thank him for the food, so I stand up and bow. "*Natori-san, anata no tabe mono wa oishidesu.* I'll let the lady decide what dessert she wants."

Emika taps her chin with her finger while looking up. "Natori-*san*, we will share one bowl. Can we have three scoops of vanilla and one scoop of dark chocolate and... She shuts her eyes tight. "I'm forgetting something—what is it?"

"Maraschino cherries?" I offer. Mr. Natori bows and leaves.

Emika lifts her eyebrows. "Seriously, how did you guess the cherries?"

"Lucky guess."

"No way," she says, shaking her head.

Mrs. Natori brings the ice cream. Emika cuts one cherry in half and takes a quarter spoon of chocolate and three-quarters of vanilla. "Open your mouth, professor. And tell me, what do you think?"

All I can muster is, "It's delicious."

I am about to drop off Emika at her townhome. She turns to me, "Do you mind coming in to chat for a bit?"

I can chat with you all day for my entire life. "Sure." We walk into her townhome, into her living room, and sit kitty-corner to each other—me on a chair, her on the sofa with Hulk. Just like last time.

She turns to me. "All my childhood and adolescence, I often woke up dreaming about a life that I never lived. I had unexplained headaches. And I longed to get to that life, but I had no roadmaps. I could only see the mountains. There were days, Vince, when I woke up with tears." She exhales. "I have never shared this with anyone."

I have heard this before, just a few hours back, from Philip. I touch her fingers. "Do you still have those symptoms?"

She looks deeply into my eyes. "No, it's almost gone."

I tighten my grip. "Since?"

"A few days after I came here."

My breath catches. "Ahh! The mystical powers of this town."

"It's not the town." She looks at how I am holding her hand. "I have a theory, which I'll share later."

"Sure, whenever you want." I won't dull the conversation by bringing up my own headaches.

She leans toward me. "Vince, Anna says that you are the most naturally gifted inventor. So when you invent something, I want to be there."

"Anna exaggerates. If you are in a position to come, of course."

"I don't see why not? Sometimes you are so silly." She runs her fingers over my wrist and touches my watch crown. "Vince, can you not drive so fast? I'm worried you may hurt yourself. Please, will you be careful?"

"I'll try." I open my jacket. "Can I use your bathroom?"

"Sure."

I return to find that Emika has dozed off, hugging Hulk on the couch. Her head is on the second cushion, and she is curled up. I take my jacket, place it over her, and sit on the adjacent chair.

That must have woken her because she points to the empty cushion on the sofa. "Can you sit here, please?"

I get up and switch places. She places her head on my lap, and I run my fingers through her hair. "What about chatting all night?"

She smiles. "This is better. I enjoyed this evening. Can we do this again?"

"Yes."

"And again?" she asks.

I keep running my fingers through her hair. "Yes."

It's raining. The transient nature of things around me has always gotten in my way of enjoying the moment. I somehow know that joy shies from me. My life has always been an equilibrium of torment, punctuated by few moments of bliss, standing out as anomalies. At this moment, when Emika is resting on my lap while tightly hugging Hulk, the thought of anomaly is struggling to enter my mind. Somehow, I've blocked it. Could this be the moment where my life turns? I can hear the soft snores of Hulk, the crackling sound of the fireplace, and the tiny yet quick drops of rain outside. At this moment, I don't care if she is Akane. I just want her to be Emika—my Emi.

She grabs my palm, kisses my fingers, whispers almost inaudibly, "Found you."

CHAPTER 10

TODAY (EPISODE 2)

The distinction between the past, present,
and future is only a stubbornly persistent illusion.
—Albert Einstein

(August 15, 2024)

THE COIN LANDS ON MY left palm, revealing heads—so white dial with local time. Jim hands over some folded papers to a girl whose name is not legible under the assistant producer tag. The folded paper has handwritten notes with a header, "The Time Fixer: Three Lives of Philip Nardin." I follow her to the main curtain. She turns to me and smiles. "You will do fine, Dr. Abajian. Keep smiling—the audience loves it."

"I will keep that in mind."

She points to a spot of tape on the floor. "Please wait here and then walk beyond the curtains at my cue."

From beyond the curtain, I can't decipher Maurice's jokes but can hear the audience's laughter and the cheap sound effects made by a struggling music group. Now I hear Maurice Johnson say, "Our guest tonight is Dr. Vincent Abajian. He's the author of the book *The Time Fixer: Three Lives of Philip Nardin*. You all know him from his actions at the Senate hearing."

I cross the curtains and immediately shut my eyes against the blinding studio lights. The jarring sound of the trumpet, drums, and screeching noise of the audience hurt my ears. Somehow, I manage to walk up to Maurice and shake his hand. I can not avoid the lights to see his face that stands eight inches higher than mine. We sit. He is wearing a black suit, gray tie, and a pair of Christian Louboutin whole cut shoes. His wristwatch—a Patek Phillippe Nautilus 5712. I sit on a blue sofa next to his curved desk, bearing the slogan, *What's Tonight with Maurice Johnson*.

He leans forward. "So, Dr. Abajian, how's your day so far?"

I sit back, pull my cuffs. "Dramatically uneventful." The crowd cheers without any clue why I said that.

Maurice picks up a hard copy of my book, turns to the jacket cover. "Wow, you look different from the picture on the jacket."

I smile. "Yes, I lost a few pounds and grew out my beard."

"So, tell us about your book."

"It's about the three lives of Philip Nardin across two turbulences."

"What drove you to write this?"

I can't stop thinking about my meetings with Philip and everything that transpired after. So much has occurred in thirteen months, and a part of me wishes none of it had happened, especially the last seven months. The other part longs for someone who may have forgotten me by now. "I interviewed him for our magazine and got curious about his lives."

Maurice leans toward me. "Any reason you wrote this book in an interview format?"

"It seemed to be the most pragmatic approach. The only way I learned about his life was by asking him. So, I wanted to keep it that way. Also, I am not a creative writer."

"Why call it *The Time Fixer*?"

I need to field this question cautiously. I lean back and cross my arms. "In a way, he did repair time when he fixed clocks. But, from a symbolic standpoint, he may have preserved history—whether it's through fixing clocks or through his reset times. I think when you fix clocks, you also tinker with memories to some extent, preserving the ones that matter while disregarding the ones that don't."

Maurice places the book on his desk and taps on it. "Is there a message in this book for your readers?"

I pause and look at Maurice's eyes—devoid of any curiosity. "It's about someone who felt the non-linearity of time and how time and turbulence affect reality. Whether we use it literally or metaphorically, the turbulence only shows what we hold dear to us can be taken from us in a flash. Unfortunately, we have a reductive way of measuring time by equating it with money." The crowd is silent.

"So time is not money?" Maurice rests his chin on his hand.

"Let's look at you. You have more money now than you did ten years back. Do you have more time? Of course, money can increase with time. But time, as we perceive it, only diminishes with time. It's definitely not a cosmological constant."

"So, what *is* time?" I can tell Maurice is only pretending to be interested.

I sit up straight. "We experience time through what has happened and what is about to happen. But aren't the past and the present a function of our perception? Can they co-occur? Philip once said that the future has already happened—you just need to experience it."

Maurice leans back. "How is that even possible?"

So, now I have to make an example for this moron. "Your phone rings, and the caller tells you that you've been nominated for an Emmy. The nomination occurred before you knew it. Your future occurred before you experienced it through the phone call."

"Profound," Maurice says, lifting his eyebrows.

I click my tongue. "Not really." He has no idea what it is like to be outside the space-time continuum. I experienced it just two days back.

"Your book shows Lombard and Senator Graham through the eyes of Philip Nardin. What's your opinion about them? I'm asking because your performance in the Senate has put three senators in jail."

I straighten my cuffs. "My performance did not put them in jail. Their corruption did." Thundering cheers, whistling, and applaud interrupts, and I wait until it dies down. "Also, they epitomized what's wrong with politics and democracy in this country. The USA is a country run by lobbyists. But they are your typical politician, one who begs for your vote and forgets all about you until the next election cycle. The number of votes they get is their currency to make money from lobbyists. Politicians have two talents: begging and deceiving. Public service is just a cloak they wear to hide their true intentions."

"What about corporations like Lombard?"

I can feel my blood boiling, knowing what Lombard did. "If tax dollars pay for your entire R&D, there is no incentive to innovate. And the fact that intreton leaked through their 'tight vessels' is indicative of that. They fund politicians to doctor intelligence, kill innocent lives to showcase their technology. The evidence is too strong to ignore."

"Dr. Abajian, does your opinion extend across both parties?"

"Yes. One party is more blatant, the other slightly less so. Members of both parties are cut from the same cloth." I lean back and smirk. "You see, none of the politicians genuinely want to solve healthcare, social inequality, or justice. The market of promising something is far more enticing than delivering it. Once you deliver, these one-trick ponies are out of their game. If you look at any politician, only one thing changes when they enter prominence and leave. They become richer, settle in expensive mansions, charge enormous speaking fees, and talk in clichés. You can get such clichés inside a fortune cookie after ordering a plate of $9 fried rice. At least the fried rice tastes good. While the people who elected them remain in the same station."

More booming cheers from the crowd echoed through every corner of the studio. Long applause follows. I wave my arm in gratitude.

Maurice leans forward. "Tell us about your profession."

"With a group of extraordinarily talented scientists, we study all aspects of artificial intelligence. We invented ways to copy human consciences to synthetic beings. We also created a theoretical breakthrough in achieving the reverse."

Maurice slants his head and squints. "You are a prevalent figure now. People want to know if there is a special someone in your life?"

I smile. "Hulk—my furry child. Also three of my colleagues, whom I love as my own siblings." I look at the camera. "Anna, Chris, Ravi—I love you." I turn to Maurice. "I have three friends from school who helped me recover from a personal tragedy. I can never repay that debt." I turn to the camera again. "Fred, Krista, Sasha—if you are watching, just know that I'm nothing without you." I don't want to bring up Emika on live TV.

"I mean romantically, Dr. Abajian," Maurice presses.

Why does he want to know about this part of my life? Emika is free—free from the clutches of Akane that made her look for me. That's why she never bothered to call me. And I am beginning to accept it.

Maurice taps my wrist. "Dr. Abajian, we are all waiting for your response."

I lift my eyebrows. "I'm sorry?"

"Do you have anyone who pulls your heartstrings, Dr.?"

"It's complicated. My feelings in their structure and emotion seem too misplaced to be requited."

"Aww," the crowd reacts.

Time's up. I breathe a sigh of relief. If there's any link between my dreams and reality, I need to rush back home. Maurice and I stand up and shake hands. I turn around and find Jim waiting, ready to show me back to my dressing room. Time to face the inevitable.

CHAPTER 11

AKI

A tree branch dipped into the
pond under the bridge becomes a paintbrush.
—Japanese proverb

(Eleven to ten months before today)

I **PARK MY CAR NEXT TO** four luxury sedans, a Burgundy Mercedes-Maybach V12, a Blue BMW Alpina B7, a Black Bentley Mulsanne, and another black Audi S8 Quattro. Three chauffeurs clad in black suits service all but the S8. They are all sharing chitchat, with one showing cellphone pictures to the other two. The cobblestone is slowly getting sprinkled with fall leaves in yellow and red. A little farther away, I see Edward supervising an assembly of a Gulfstream G-400. The gentlemen assembling the plane under Edward's supervision look ex-military.

"Buying some old planes, Edward?"

He clicks his tongue and ignores my observation. "We need you in residence. Please follow me."

He takes out his satellite radio. "Bird is in."

Who is he talking to? I follow Edward into the residence. All the luggage is gone. "When's Philip expected back?"

He continues to walk. "It might take him a while this time. That's all I can say."

We enter Philip's study, and I see four gentlemen. Edward announces, "Gentlemen, the man of the hour, Dr. Vincent Abajian." Edward takes a seat and turns to me. "These gentlemen are from Bernstein, Ozawa, Toscanini, and Mehta."

The first gentleman comes forward, and we shake hands. "Vincent, I'm Jerry Bernstein. Oy can call me Jerry."

Age has not tarnished the sharpness in his blue eyes, visible through his round, gold-framed glasses. The shine on his bald head rivals that on his black cap-toe oxfords. Beneath the white french cuffs under his pinstripe suit sleeves hangs a gold jubilee bracelet of a Rolex Presidential Day-Date.

"Pleased to meet you, Jerry."

The next gentleman stands up and shakes my hand. "I'm Kenji Ozawa. Pleased to meet you. You're my son's age. Can I call you Vincent? Please feel free to call me Kenji."

I bow. "Vincent is fine. Thank you, Kenji."

His black glass perfectly contrasts his white close-cropped hair. The sharpness in his eyes and the smile on his lips reveal that he can predict an opponent's moves several stages ahead—like a grandmaster. Underneath the sleeves of his glen-plaid suit and white cuffs peeps a Patek Philippe perpetual calendar.

A slim gentleman with his hair neatly brushed back comes forward. "I'm Alberto Toscanini. Pleased to meet you, Vincent." The wrinkles around his eyes are testimony to his age and all the changes he witnessed, the artifacts he helped Philip procure, and the fights he helped Philip win against politicians. Under his cuff, I can spot the integrated bracelet of AP-Royal Oak.

"Pleased to meet you too," I acknowledge.

Then a much younger gentleman comes forward. He is holding today's copy of the *Wall Street Journal* in his left hand and extends his right. "I'm Dinesh Mehta. Glad to meet you." The confidence in his eyes is the result of the company he is surrounded by. His beefy Panerai-Luminor is not peeping out from under his cuffs and seems to be yelling, 'Look at me.' I hope his taste becomes more refined and understated with age, like those of his senior partners.

"Glad to meet you too, Dinesh."

We all sit.

Kenji speaks first. "Philip Nardin left some things for you. One of us will name the items, another will bring them to you, and Edward will take notes."

"And this requires the presence of all the named partners?" I'm not sure what's happening. Is Philip dying?

Jerry coughs and clears his throat. "Ordinarily, no. But Mr. Nardin is no usual client."

Kenji shakes his head and smiles. "Item one is a framed painting titled, 'Risen from Fire and Ashes,' sized 2x4 feet." Dinesh lifts the painting and sets it beside my chair.

"A Jaeger-Lecoultre Reverso duo face rose-gold watch with full box and papers," Alberto announces. Dinesh brings the box to me, and I open and pick out the watch. A white dial on one side, black on the other.

Now it's Jerry's turn. "Three table clocks, powered by intreton-c, handmade by Philip Nardin." Dinesh makes two trips to bring the clocks. He also gets the following items, the first editions of Tolkien's work.

The last thing was two bottles of fifty-five-year-old single malt Japanese Yamazaki whiskey. Edward brings these, then he hands me a sealed envelope with a red inscription PC. "Philip asked me to ensure that you read this in front of us, though not aloud, and confirm you understand the content."

I take the letter out—magnificent penmanship.

Dear Vince,

I'm so sorry to leave.

Well, I cannot bring Elise back, but this JLC is for you. In a few months, you will realize a deeper connection with the painting. I'm leaving you three clocks that I made and have put the reset time as of August 3, 2023—I think that's an important date for you. If you adjust the time on one watch, the others will automatically change themselves to match. I've had the first editions of Tolkien's work for too long. So, they are yours now. I felt close to you while talking, so the two Yamizakis are yours as well. I hope you find an excellent company to share them with. I know I did.

Also, I have instructed my lawyers to revise the agreement of endowment with your school. You'll have total autonomy. It will take them a couple of weeks to draft it, and they'll directly get in touch with your university foundation. A Pulitzer-winning, brilliant journalist, Tabitha, from The Tribune, *will get in touch with you in a few days. She may want your help in an investigation, but your contribution will remain anonymous. You'll hear and witness a lot in the next few months. You will have access to direct lines with any of my four lawyers if there is any need, and you won't have to pay anything. The investigation may create a severe distraction in your life, and I apologize in advance. Protect the one you care about from the case, even if your actions are misunderstood. The misunderstanding will lead to revealing something about yourself and the one you care about. You must complete your mission. Once you do, you will know your identity.*

Love,
Philip
P.S. We will meet again in a fitting moment.

I turn to the four lawyers and Edward. "I don't understand the last paragraph. What mission? What identity?"

Edward takes the letter, reads it, then hands it back to me. "You will find out in due time."

I have heard the word "mission" uttered to me many years back. So why can't I recall it? The list now grows to five things that I can't remember—hearing the name Emika the first time, Philip's license plate, that Breguet watch, wrapping Akane's scarf around Emika, now this word "mission." They must all be linked. I start massaging my temples. Fucking migraines, again.

Dinesh collects his colleagues' business cards and hands them to me. "These are all our direct lines. Have them on speed dial, but I hope you never have to call us. However, if you do, we'll take care of everything. Also, we'll be in touch with your university's foundation soon. We are done here."

I follow them to the door. Dinesh drives the Audi S8, Alberto's chauffeur opens the door to his Blue BMW Alpina B7, Kenji's chauffeur opens the Bentley for him, and the Maybach belongs to Jerry. The cars pull out of the driveway one after the other. Edward waves goodbye. In a few seconds, all I can see is dust.

I turn to Edward. "What's going on?"

A spurt of wind hits our face, and Edward covers his eyes. He looks away from the wind, turning to me. "A storm is coming, Vincent. Stay close to news channels."

With my new possessions, I leave Nardin's estate. I was hoping to reacquaint myself with my pocket watch. When will that "fitting moment" arrive, as Philip said? What could be a fitting moment to receive a pocket watch that I hardly have any memories of? Also, where is Philip? And what the fuck is my mission?

Emika is dazzling in her sapphire blue dress. I remember how she looked at the mountains from the patio of her townhome. So, I reserved a table by the window in Chez-Giraud overlooking the lake, the foothills, and the snowcapped mountains through floor-to-ceiling glass walls. "It's spectacular, Vince." She squeezes my fingers.

The server comes forward. "I'm Celine. Would you like to see our wine list?"

I nod. "Sure."

Emika keeps looking at the foothills and the snowcapped mountains radiating in gold against the setting sun.

I point at Emika's necklace and her bracelet. "Are those in memory of Haru?"

She tilts her head and smiles. "Yes, they are. I thought you wouldn't notice."

"Oh, I notice," I say, locking my fingers with hers.

The background music is Frank Sinatra's "Fly Me to the Moon," which complements the sizzling sound of fresh food coming out of the kitchen, the clinking of silverware, and happy conversations all around. I feel a sudden increase in my pulse.

Celine brings the wine list, and Emika turns to me. "Vince, can you order for us?"

"How about a whole bottle of Chateau Mouton-Rothschild 2005?"

Celine leans forward. "You said the whole bottle, right?"

"That's correct, Celine."

Once Celine is out of earshot, Emika squints and asks, "What was that about?"

I shrug. "She was making sure if I could afford it."

"Because you are not white, right?" she says, lowering her eyebrows.

I kiss her fingers, and I can feel her pulse rise. "Let's look at it differently. Maybe she checks this with everyone. She is just trying to avoid an imminent commotion."

"But you have equity here."

"That's not pubic knowledge."

A gentleman brings the wine. He opens the bottle, pours an equal quantity into two glasses, and says, "Enjoy your wine."

"To life," I toast, raising my glass to a smiling Emika.

She lifts hers. "To life."

After a few sips, we see the sun slowly retiring behind the mountains, turning the white snow into gold. A portion of the gold reflects on Emika's face and turns her black hair to burgundy. The song changes to "My Way," keeping the jazz motif. Emika is quietly observing the sunset, and I am witnessing the same through her eyes. Then she turns to me. "Thank you for coming into my life. Also, Vince, thank you for asking me to talk to my parents. It was nice to hear *pa-pha* and mum."

I press her fingers. "If you need to take a few days to take care of them, just let me know."

"I will." She regards me with glittering eyes. "Vince, do you have any parental figure?"

I swirl my glass and take a sip. "Not really." I don't want to dull the evening by bringing up friction with Mr. Kruger. The background song is now "Moon River."

Celine returns. "Have you decided what you'd like to have?"

I turn to Emika. "Lead the way."

"I'll have the miso-glazed Chilean sea bass."

Celine lifts her brows and leans toward Emika. "It comes with roasted Shishito peppers, cream sauce, garlic mashed potatoes, and Sichuan green beans."

"I want all of them."

As Celine turns to me, Emika coughs. "Brace yourself."

I shake my head and smile. "I would like the 16-ounce Wagyu A-5, medium rare, please. Also, can you ask the chef to replace porcini with morel? I'd also like the scallops poached, not sautéed, and instead of asparagus, I'd like Sichuan green beans, like the lady. Also, can you serve the veggies separately?"

Celine takes meticulous notes. "Absolutely, sir. I'll get them started for you." Then she walks briskly back to the kitchen.

"Poor chef." Emika teases. "What's the reason for this modification?"

"Morel has a woody aroma that I love. The Sichuan beans will numb a portion of my tongue further to enjoy the Wagyu beef's rich buttery texture. But, if the chef can't accommodate my request, I'll oblige and still eat."

Emika tilts her head, her eyes glinting. "And why did you want the veggies separate?"

"You will see why," I say, tapping my finger on the table.

The ambient song changes to Clarence "Frogman" Henry's "I Don't Know Why I Love You."

The food runner arrives. The Chilean bass is gracefully served on a white asymmetrical plate. The steak comes on top of a wooden block, veggies in a separate bowl. Emika makes a small incision into her fish and adds a small cross-section of Shishito pepper and a dash of mashed potato onto her fork. Then she stares at her fork, contemplating her next move.

I lean toward her. "Your next step would be to open your mouth and eat it."

"Thanks, genius." She stretches her right arm toward me. "Tell me how it is."

I take the bite, close my eyes. "It's wonderful."

She smiles. "Well, lack of customization can also lead to bliss."

"Is that why you wanted me to taste it?"

"One of a few."

"What other reasons?" I ask, lifting my eyebrows.

She tilts her head and gazes into my eyes. "Silly."

I make a bite comprising poached scallops, mushrooms, beans with Sichuan peppers and bring it before Emika's lips. "Take a bite. I made sure it's devoid of meat juice."

She moves closer, shuts her eyes, and takes the bite. After chewing it, she opens her gleaming eyes. "All this goodness from your substitutes? And now I know why you wanted them separately. *Arigato.*"

I pick up my napkin and wipe pepper from the corner of her lips. "*Doitashimashite.*"

Then I feel a tap on my shoulder. I crane my neck around and see that it's Antonio Giraud. He speaks in his French accent, "I knew Vincent was in. Who else would modify my food? How long has it been?"

I stand up, and we shake hands. "Great food, Tony. I was here last November."

His eyes turn to Emika. "And who is this special lady?"

"Ah! This is Dr. Emika Amari. And Emika, this is Tony."

Emika stands to shake his hand.

"So, what kind of a doctor are you?" the chef asks with a crooked smile.

Emika rests her palm on my shoulder. "The kind that treats this one."

"It's a challenge," Antonio acknowledges, "Although he is worth keeping."

"I will keep that in mind," Emika says as she sits back down.

Antonio takes his leave, and the ambient music changes to Miles Davis's rendition of "Autumn Leaves." We are back to our forks and knives.

Emika toches my hand. "The last time you were here was with Elise, right?"

I stop chewing and shut my eyes. "Yes."

"Do you mind telling me anything about you two?"

I open my eyes and press her fingers. I want this evening to be about Emi and me. Let's make this brief. "There was more mutual admiration than the love between us, I'd say. She was one of the kindest souls I have ever met. Not just her commitment to developing a cure for diseases that are not attractive to big pharma, but also her commitment to animal rights, building homeless shelters, and so on." I shrug. "And she admired my ability to confront obstacles and be where I am."

"She not alone in this admiration, Vince," Emika says, putting her other hand on mine.

I look down at her hand, then back at her face. "All these seem unreal."

"What's on your mind?" she asks quietly.

"I am not used to feeling this happy. And if it's all too real and it is taken from me, it will be impossible for me to come back and restart my life."

She looks into my eyes. "This is real. We are here. And I am not going anywhere." My pulse rate slows against Miles Davis's "Générique" in the background.

Celine appears. "Would you like any dessert?"

Emika shakes her head. "I'm too full."

"I'm full too," I say.

Celine brings our check, and I settle it with a sixty percent tip.

As we settle into my car, Emika turns to me. "Can we have espresso, Vince?"

"BMW, find me coffee shops that are open."

Emika lifts her eyebrows. "I thought you make the best espresso."

"BMW, cancel that. We are going home."

Hulk ignores me and jumps on Emika. I open the door to the terrace lawn to let him out.

She walks around the living room. "This is so tastefully furnished."

"It's Elise's work."

"*Sokka.* Do you mind if I walk around?"

"Of course not." I switch on my evening playlist—the first song is Saint-Saëns's Dance Macabre.

Hulk follows her as she walks around the apartment, with Hulk following her while I roast forty grams of Kona Peaberry beans. She comes back, following the aroma. Reaching the kitchen, she closes her eyes and inhales deeply. "You always roast fresh beans?"

"Only on extraordinary occasions."

She lifts her index finger at me. "You have a large closet, but your suits and sports jackets are squished. The way you arrange your shirts, suits, jackets by color, pattern, plain, stripes, and plaids is meticulous, bordering on OCD." Her voice sounds melodious, like a pianist having fun while playing Liszt's La Campanella.

"Your espresso is ready, ma'am."

Taking the cup, she swirls the liquid and drinks it in three sips. "You're a maestro barista, Vince."

I lift my pocket square and wipe the crema from her lips.

She gazes at me. "*Arigato gozaimasu.* Are these cups made of onyx?"

"*Hai, so desu.*"

The song changes to Mendelssohn Concerto in E-minor, op. 64.

"You have exquisite taste in music. *Pa-pha* would be proud of you." She looks around at the pictures of Elise with Hulk on the walls. "Have you ever thought of moving, Vince?"

I sit on the sofa. "Several times. I rent this place. But most houses that have an architecture of my liking are too big for one human and a tiny dog."

She sits next to me, touches my hair. "Well, it doesn't always have to be just you and Hulk. Also, the size of a house has nothing to do with the number of occupants. Think about Bruce Wayne."

"Mr. Wayne inherited the house. I didn't inherit a nickel. But I get your point." I stand up. "Hey, you know, I was wrong about not inheriting a nickel. However, I did receive some stuff last week. Let me show you." I hand her Philip's letter.

She reads it and smiles. "You realize that Philip deeply cares about you. But, unfortunately, I don't get the last part of the letter."

I sit back down. "I don't get it either. Philip probably just cares because I'm converting our interviews into a book."

"Anna told me that you are wary of people getting close to you." She places her hand on my chest. "You fear they will leave you, and it will hurt."

I place my hand on top of hers and look deeply into her eyes. "That's my logical response, yes, but something I am failing to attain this moment."

The music changes to Chopin's Nocturne in C-sharp minor. She closes her eyes and absorbs the music, then opens them wide and snaps her fingers. "Now, I want to see all these inheritances."

She puts on the JLC Reverso, then poses with the Yamazaki-55 and Tolkien's first edition. "Look, Vince, I am a drunk Tolkien fan who wears a fancy watch," she says, smiling ear to ear. I take her picture on her phone.

Then she gets up, looks around my desk and computer, and frowns. "You've so many network drives. What's your secret? A foreign agent on US soil?"

I lift one eyebrow. "I am a double agent." Then I break a smile. "All of them are Elise's, probably filled with vaccine test data. But none of her collaborators wanted them after she was gone. I don't think I'll ever look into those."

Emika comes back to sit next to me and stares at my hands as I fold my sleeves. "Do you work out?" she asks, lifting my arm.

"Intermittently."

"You've strong fists."

The song changes to Beethoven's Symphony No. 7 *Allegretto.*

(September 18, 1996)

If Akane lived, today would be her fourteenth birthday. It's been five years since I started Shotokan lessons. The school orchestra was paying tribute to her, with Beethoven's Seventh and Ravel's Pavane for a Dead Princess. I had a front-row seat next to Mr. Kruger for the recital.

I tripped and fell as I entered the building. Looking back, I saw Luther's right food still extended. "Where're you heading, Vincent?" asked Rudy.

I clasped my hands in front of me. "Not today, guys." Luther pushed me. "Why? Will Akane come and save you?" He mocked Akane, pitching his voice higher. "Don't hurt Vincent. I'll tell the headmaster. My *pa-pha* will throw you out of school."

Before I could react to his mocking, I reeled backward in pain. That was the most brutal punch I'd received yet. I held my lips, trying to stop the bleeding. All I cared about was not staining Akane's scarf with my blood.

"Who'll tell the headmaster now, bastard? Who will throw me out now?" He kicked my stomach with his knee. I went down to my knees as he pulled me by my hair and stared at me with his bulged eyes. “Tell me, Abajian, are you a terrorist? Your name sounds like one.”

Rudy said, “It’s so great the little runt is dead.”

Luther moved his hand from my hair to Akane’s scarf and pulled it. At that very moment, a surge of strength flowed through my veins. I could feel the muscles shudder in my arms, the heat rising to my face. To hell with the training that I should not hit those who are weaker than me. I formed a fist, and I could hear each knuckle-bone crackle. I could feel every single vein bulging on my skin. Grabbing Luther’s collar with my left hand, I punched his face with every word I screamed at the top of my voice. “Never. Touch. The. Scarf.” I kept smashing his nose until it shattered. The blood from his nose and mouth splattered on my face. In the background, I heard the *Allegretto* of Beethoven’s Seventh. The entire school was attending to celebrate Akane’s life. And I was fighting for what was left of her—the scarf. A scarf that she ever so lovingly parted with because I was hurt.

There was no one close enough to hear Luther’s grunting. He kept begging for me to stop. I paused, tilted my head, and leered into his pleading eyes. “I am not done with you. Let’s see how strong my legs are.” Jean and Rudy stood there with eyes wide open and jaws dropped. Luther extended his arm in peace. “No! Vince, I’m sorry!” I stepped back and kicked his broken and battered face, then both his shin bones, his belly. He lay there, motionless. I pulled him by his hair, and I tossed him from a flight of ten stairs. Breathing heavily, almost huffing, I turned to Jean and Rudy. “One word about this, and you two are next. I don’t need Headmaster Kruger to stand up for me.” They ran away, leaving Luther in his predicament. No one spoke a single word about it again. Luther said he fell from the stairs. He was too proud to admit that the weak orphan, whose last name sounded like the help or a terrorist, did that to him.

(Back to the present)

Every single time I hear Beethoven’s Seventh, this memory comes back. Of course, Emika’s mentioning my fists didn’t help either.

“Ground control to Major Tom… Hello? Is there anybody in there?” Emika snaps her fingers. “Where were you, absentminded professor?”

I pull her toward me. “Sorry, I got lost.”

“I had to summon David Bowie and Pink Floyd to get you back. You OK?”

I hold her palm, kiss her slender fingers. I gaze into her burnt-sienna eyes. “Thank you, Emi. For finding me.”

She returns my gaze, smiles. “Your eyes, Vince.”

“What about them?”

“The colors are both green and blue. They look like the Great Barrier Reef from the sky.”

She pulls me by my necktie. Closing her eyes, she presses her lips to mine. She digs her fingers into my hair, and I touch her waist. After a long moment, she pulls away slightly and opens her eyes. “Vince, do you have any pajamas? And any makeup remover?” The song changes to Mozart’s Piano Concerto no. 21.

“Will my PJs do?”

She shrugs. “Sure.”

I showed her my PJs and sweats to choose from, and then all the makeup stuff that Elise had, which I’ve never gotten rid of. After fifteen minutes in the bathroom, she emerges, spreading her arms. “Tada.”

“The MIT gear looks good on you.”

She lifts one eyebrow mischievously. “Only a Caltech grad could do that.”

I’m always up by 6:30 a.m., minutes before my alarm clock’s rendition of Für Elise. But, today, the alarm wins the race. I’m about to get up when I feel a light arm pulling me down. Emika whispers, “I already fed Hulk and took him out. You need to sleep.” She touches my head with her palm and plops it back on the pillow. Then she nestles her face into my neck. “Go to bed, professor. Also, time for a different tune for your alarm!” She crumples my sweatshirt with her delicate fingers. “Found you.”

Emika takes a bite of the scrambled eggs that I made. "Your new alarm clock tune is Claude Debussy's Clair de Lune. It's one of my favorites. And with time, it will be yours too. OK?"

"As you wish."

She hums after another bite. "These are so silky and buttery. I could eat this forever."

I lean across the counter toward her. "Forever is a very long time. Are you up to it, Emi-*san*?"

She smiles, shutting her eyes to two layers of thick eyelashes. "*Hai*."

I take out a duplicate key to my apartment and clasp it to Emika's key-ring. "There you go. You can come any time you want."

She takes the key, smiles, and kisses me. "Thank you."

"Can you drop me at my townhome?" She keeps staring at the keys. "I need to change before going to work."

When we arrive at her townhome, she kisses Hulk and me before getting out of the car. "See you later, boys," she smiles. She is wearing my MIT attire and dragging her dress, hanging from one of my suit hangers.

As Hulk and I get close to my suite, I can hear Linda chatting and laughing. A little closer and I can distinctly hear the voices of Anna, Chris, and Ravi.

I look at them. "What's up, guys? Wanna come in?"

"We need to talk, Vince," Anna says, standing up.

Broadway time. I stare at Anna. "So, that's it. After all these years, you are divorcing me. Are you taking my boys?"

"It's not you. It's me." She touches her forehead and looks away. "You can have the boys."

We enter the office. "Want some coffee, guys?"

Anna bats her eyes. "Professor, will you roast the beans fresh? Will you serve them in onyx cups?"

Chris and Ravi are out of their depth. Chris squints. "What?"

She looks at the clueless men. "Gentlemen, I'll fill you in."

"There's nothing to fill." I can't keep a smile from the corner of my lips. "Emi and I went on a date. That's all."

"So it's Emi now?" Anna teases, turning to Chris and Ravi. "See what Daddy did? A new girl comes in, and he tosses Mommy and his two kids out." She changes her tune. "Seriously, Vince. I'm happy for you and her. We are all happy."

I sit by my desk. "Is that why you are here?"

All three sit as well, occupying the sofa and the chair. Then Chris takes a few deep breaths to calm his imminent frustration. "Our enrollments are up by fifteen percent this year. Vikram projects another twenty-five percent hike next year. The three of us can't teach so many students next fall. Even if you decide to take on teaching, we'll still be spread too thin."

"OK, I'll ask Vikram to approve two tenure-line positions. Then we'll create a committee and move forward. I'll talk to him either today or tomorrow. Does that sound OK?"

Ravi leans forward. "Can we hire Emika? She has been great in the lab."

"Vince wouldn't have an objection to that." Anna winks.

I shake my head, smile. "Teaching is different from setting experiments. I will ask her, though."

Anna gets up, then sits on the floor by Hulk. Petting him, she says, "Do you like your new mommy?" Ravi joins her in petting Hulk on the floor.

Chris looks lost, sitting on the chair. I move to sit beside him and nudge his shoulder. "What's up?"

He takes a long blink and shakes his head. "Isn't our work in robotics putting people out of jobs? Ordinary working-class people, hairdressers, waiters all might lose jobs because of what we do."

"Some of my friends back home had jobs because of offshoring: now because of automation, they're all jobless," Ravi adds, getting up to sit next to me.

Anna ignores them and continues to scratch Hulk's belly.

It is an ethical dilemma, and I need to soften the blow. "I believe this displacement is temporary. Guys, we are a product of six million years of evolution. I'm not telling you that the jobs of your friends are safe. But that doesn't mean automation will lead to the extinction of humanity. Excess profits from automation, if taxed creatively, may lead to Universal Basic Income, which should be higher than what one makes flipping burgers or waiting tables."

Anna turns to me. "I told them the same thing. But no, they needed to hear it from Daddy."

"Listen to Mommy," I say to Chris and Ravi.

They all stand up to leave, but suddenly Ravi stops. "You guys go ahead. I need to speak with Vince."

He pulls out the chair opposite my desk and rests his palm on my desk. "So, there's this professor of molecular biology, who I am seeing. Her name is Madelyn Stevens." Then he pauses and looks at me expectantly.

After about ten seconds of silence, I ask, "OK, so what's the challenge?"

"I simply can't get a table for two at Chez-Giraud. Can you help? Please."

"When do you want to take her out?"

Ravi tilts his head. "How about Friday at 6:00 p.m.?"

I take out my cellphone and text Tony. "Done."

"Thank you so much, Vince," Ravi says, clasping his hands in front of him.

"No problem, man." Then more silence. I can tell that Ravi has something more on his mind but wants me to ask him. "What else, man? Feel free."

He takes a few deep breaths before deciding to speak up. "Vince, I'm still on an H1-B visa. However, I'm planning to apply for permanent residency through the provision of EB-1, under the category of Outstanding Professor, Researcher."

I wave my arm. "Say no more. I will write a letter, and you ask your lawyer to bill us directly."

"What if the university doesn't approve?"

I leer. "I would like to see them try."

Ravi exhales in relief. "I owe you more than one, Vincent."

"You owe me nothing, Ravi. I just want you to be happy."

I can't contain my delight at the prospect of Emika joining us as a faculty member as I enter Vikram's suite.

His three secretaries are all on the phone. I never cared to learn their names. And they never stop me from entering Vikram's office. I knock on his door.

"Come in."

"We need to hire two new faculty and start an international search. But I need approval from the clowns in the admin office."

Vikram leans back in his chair. "We can't do that. The university has a hiring freeze due to low enrollments in Arts, College of Education, and Nursing."

I pull up a chair across from his desk, sit and cross my arms. "I'm not asking for faculty to teach nursing and education. I am asking for faculty to teach in my center, remember the one with close to a billion dollars?"

He points to our uni policy booklet on his desk. "Well, Vince, we have shared governance, so hiring is a university-wide decision."

I tap on his desk. "Fuck your shared governance. Where is your shared governance when the provost takes money from my center and buys first-class tickets? Our enrollment has risen, and I can't expect Anna, Chris, and Ravi to keep teaching while still publishing in *Nature* and *Science*. Did you even talk to Alyson and the other clowns about increasing our spending rate?"

Vikram's breath starts coming faster. "The provost and VP of foundations won't allow it."

I stand up, put my fists on Vikram's desk, and lean toward him. "Tell me how this VP of foundations can manage over a billion dollars. Can he even run a lemonade stand?" I can feel the veins on my forehead throbbing.

Vikram wipes sweat off his forehead and takes a few deep breaths. "I understand your frustration, but my hands are tied. I never thought being dean meant I would have to deal with such people. I took my class under—"

"I know, under Nash, yet look at your abysmal academic accomplishments." I start walking toward his fridge. "Do the right thing. Or it will be done by force." I get him a bottle of water.

He drinks up the water, loosens his tie. "What do you mean, *force*?"

"Philip and his lawyers will draft a revision of the endowment that will grant me full autonomy. I can pause it if the president can increase my spending rates and let me hire when I want to."

Vikram's jaw drops. "The university lawyers will fight it."

"I have seen both sets of lawyers." I smile and shake my head ruefully. "The university has no chance. Philip will make the endowment a mobile one, meaning it will travel with me. And trust me, Vikram, any university, even the richest one, will love an extra nine hundred and fifty million. All

I'm asking is to get two faculty members. If you agree, I will make sure you are safe. I may allow sharing a bit of the finance, provided we have the freedom to hire and research without any intervention from the admin. Else the uni will be reduced to a teaching school, scraping for dollars through tuition and enrollments."

"This is so sudden, Vince." Vikram gasps for air. "I thought you were happy here."

"I care deeply about Anna, Emika, Chris, and Ravi. So, I won't let the ectoplasms in the admin with fake degrees make their lives difficult."

I am about to enter my office when Linda informs, "Someone by the name of Tabitha Bishara called, Dr. A."

"And?"

"She left her direct number, wants you to call her back. I didn't give her your number, though."

Linda hands me a post-it with the number. I head into my office to call her. After just one ring, I hear a slightly husky voice—accent American and a Middle Eastern or North African hint. "Hello, this is Tabitha."

"Hi, Tabitha. It's Vincent."

"Vincent! I'm so glad you called."

"What can I do for you?"

"I'm investigating Flight 0606, so I was wondering if we can meet."

"Where?"

"How about your office? In thirty minutes?"

"Sure."

If Philip is right about Lombard and their complicity in the Flight 0606 tragedy, then how can I help? I have some vested interest in the investigation. What else, besides being a victim? So, who is Tabitha? "Ludwig, open what you have on Tabitha Bishara and print out a summary." After a few seconds, the report is ready. She was born in 1994 and immigrated to the US in 2006. She received her BA in Journalism from Northwestern in 2016 and an MA in International Studies from UC-Berkeley in 2018. Since then, she has been with the Tribune. Her specialty is investigative journalism, espionage, and corporate corruption. After revealing the conspiracy behind

Alleren's clear-day, she won the Pulitzer. She'd done what Elise's paper could not. Quite an accomplishment, and she's only twenty-nine.

Linda knocks and walks in with another lady. "We have Ms. Bishara."

Tabitha walks toward me, extending her right arm. "Hi, I'm Tabi."

I shake her hand. "Pleased to meet you, Tabi." I notice a burn mark on her right wrist.

She is wearing a black suit and a white chambray blouse. A Louis Vuitton handbag hangs from her shoulder. Her hair is dark brown with light brown highlights. Her wristwatch is Omega De Ville automatic 34 mm, steel and rose-gold and steel. She wears a necklace with a battered locket that looks like a small cylinder, about an inch long. Her eyes are dark brown with thick eyebrows above them. She has thin lips and a sharp, slightly hooked nose.

"You do dress much better than all the professors I had," she notes as she pulls up a chair across from my desk.

I smile impishly. "Were they better dressers before you had them?"

Linda rolls her eyes. "Dr. A has a strange sense of humor."

"I'm sensing that."

As Linda walks out, she asks. "Can I get you anything, coke, water, tea, Ms. Bishara?"

"No, I'm fine, Linda, thank you." Tabitha kneels to pet Hulk. "What's his name?"

"Hulk."

She laughs at the contrast. "He's charming. Does he always accompany you to work?"

"Yes, almost every day."

She turns to me. "No objections from the faculty or anyone?"

"I would like to see them try."

"Impressive," she says, lifting her eyebrows.

I rest my elbows on the desk. "So, what can I do for you?"

She pulls out a yellow notebook and a microtip zebra pen from her handbag. "I believe you can help my team with my investigation. But, of course, you'll remain anonymous," she says as she flips to a new page.

"All I know is that the plane was transporting illegally obtained intreton cases in boxes made by Lombard."

Tabitha smiles contemptuously. "Lombard couldn't have pulled it off without some help, Dr. Abajian."

"It's Vince, Tabi." I lean forward. "Also, what kind of help?"

"Sure, Vince it is. I meant political help."

It's already been a long day, and I am missing my Emika. So let's get this over with. "What's your theory?"

"Dick Graham's biggest campaign contributor is Lombard. I think that Lombard used Graham's connection in India to smuggle the intreton from Philip's facility in Bangalore."

So that's why Dick called Philip a traitor—because Philip may have been privy to what he was after. I squint. "Maybe he wouldn't have done so if he'd realized that Elise was on that plane."

Tabitha places her pen in the notebook. "My theory is that Dick Graham knew Elise was on that plane."

My heart stops. "What?"

"I don't think Elise was fully truthful about her involvement in her father's political life. Yes, there was a fallout at its worst—during the Alleren era—where Dick rebuffed clear-day's side effects. But, slowly, Alleren distanced themselves from Dick to curry favor with the Democratic White House. They cut their financial contribution to Dick. I believe Dick then promised Elise that he would remove all the clear-day from every store in the US if she did him one favor." Here, she pauses, hoping for a reaction.

So, Elise lied to me about her estrangement? "What favor?"

"Elise was transporting and distributing World Health Organization vaccines. The cold canisters bearing the WHO brand are used to transport those. Most airports don't scan them. Dick Graham may have asked Elise to insert the Lombard cases carrying intreton into the WHO-marked canisters. In return, he would remove every clear day from all shelves. And, she would receive compensation that she could use to further her quest for developing vaccines for ailments in underdeveloped countries."

(Summer of 2022)

I entered the home to find Elise drinking wine and tiring to take calming breaths between sips. Sitting next to her, I massaged her neck. "What's wrong?"

"Once again, they turned down our grant application to develop vaccines for cholera, malaria, and filariasis." She took another sip, then smirked. "That's what happens when top management from big pharma and insurance firms sits on these grants."

I moved my hands from her neck to her shoulder. "How much do you need to develop a working version of a vaccine?"

"We asked for five million. They are more generous for removing wrinkles or improving manhood," she said, covering her face with her hand. Hulk jumped on her lap and started to lick away her tears.

(Back to the present)

How could the one who brought Hulk into my life, who worked tirelessly to develop a vaccine for poor nations, be capable of such a heinous crime? I turn to Tabi. "Do you have any proof to support your theory?"

She starts fidgeting with her pen. "We hacked into Dick's firewalls and found correspondence between him and Elise. Although it may not be admissible in courts, the DOJ still encouraged us to go through it. Lombard may have promised hefty campaign finances in exchange for moving intreton. We need communication dates between father and daughter to double-check the creation of shell companies in the Cayman Islands and Switzerland. We need to know the bank account number, the exact number of figures to corroborate my theories. The DOJ wants to create a solid case against Dick and Lombard." She pauses and reaches for her bag, taking out an inhaler and pumping it thrice into her mouth. "Can I get some water?"

I fetch a Fiji bottle from my fridge and hand it to her. "Asthma?"

"Something like that. Thanks." She drinks half the water.

My exasperation is transforming into admiration. "What do you need from me?"

"Can you give us Elise's phone records? Also, if there is a laptop that Elise used or any external drives, can you hand them over?"

"I'll check." Should I simply hand them over?

She clasps her hands on her lap. "If there are any drives, Vince, please don't look into them. You'll be hurt, and it may derail you from your own life."

I bite my lip. "It's difficult to grasp that an estranged daughter would go to this length for her father in a conspiracy."

"We didn't find any evidence for the estrangement. We investigated all the courts in every place Elise lived. They used the estrangement story to keep themselves at a distance to do this kind of work. They may have had a fractured relationship—but nothing abnormal to merit estrangement." She hesitates, then reaches over to place her hand on my arm. "Once again, I'm sorry to bring this upon you."

So all these years, Elise had lied to me. How could I be so naïve?

Tabitha stands up. "When you have the items, let me know, and I'll come to pick them up." We shake hands again. "It was a pleasure meeting you, and I wish we had met under different circumstances."

"We can't control the circumstances. The pleasure is all mine."

As she collects her belongings, I hear three knocks on the door.

"Come in, Emi."

I make an introduction as Emi and Tabi cross paths, "Emika, this is Tabitha, an investigative reporter with *The Tribune*. Tabitha, this is Emika, a brilliant member of my team." They shake hands and give what seem to be insincere smiles.

After Tabitha leaves, Emika pulls up a chair. "She is the reporter who Philip wrote about?"

"Yep."

She locks her hair behind her ears. "What does she want?"

"Elise may have lied about a lot of things."

I tell her about the conversation I'd just had with Tabitha, leaving nothing out. Emika tightens her grip on my hand. "Will you be OK? Do you want me to come over so that we can talk some more?"

"I can pick you up."

"No, Vince, you go home and rest. I'll Uber. Probably be there at 8:00 p.m. I'll also bring food. Don't do anything stupid, like racing." She brings my hand to her lips, kissing it. "I have some work to do. See you in four hours."

"Did you just drop by to check in on me?"

"Yes, silly."

I rub her hands. "Emi, do you wanna be a professor here?"

"I hate teaching. But let me think about it—I like the idea of being a research scientist. Why?"

"We'll talk about it."

It's 4:00 p.m., and I am home with Hulk. Tabitha's voice and her apprehensions about Elise are continually ringing in my head. Should I just hand over the drives, or should I have a look myself before handing them over? Should I deny their existence? Even if Tabitha is correct by one percent, a significant portion of what Elise had said would be a lie. Was there any truth about her? Hulk comes forward and stands up on his hind legs, bracing his front legs against my knees. I pick him up and place him on my lap. "How about we investigate a bit, Hulky? I know Tabi said not to look. But let's look." He wags his tail.

I connect all the network drives to a USB hub. "Ludwig, can you give me a rundown of types of data in these attached drives?"

After about a minute, Ludwig says, "There're photographs, bank records, and copies of emails."

"Location of banks?"

"The Cayman Islands and Switzerland. Some names are redacted, but I can decipher the bank names by the length of account numbers. Do you want me to do that, Vincent?"

So, Elise did have a double life. "No need for that. Can you search documents that have something to do with Lombard, Alleren, or any of their top executives?"

After another minute, Ludwig concludes, "There are about seven hundred such files."

"Ludwig, how many of the Lombard files are related to money transfer?"

"About three hundred of them."

So, Elise knew about the drone attacks, too. She would have been in her twenties then. Had I spent so much of my life with someone who was an accomplice to terrorism? "Ludwig, among all of those, how many are related to drone strikes or to intreton?"

"About three hundred."

My heart is sprinting, my chest pounding. I stare at my hands. My palms are shaking. "Ludwig, are there any email exchanges between Elise and Dick Graham?"

"Should I do a global search or within the returns of the last few searches?"

"Global."

"There are about four hundred emails between the two. Your name appears in two of them." So, Ludwig could predict my next question. "Do you want me to read the most recent one?"

"Sure, Ludwig, go on."

"'Dad, keep Vincent away from all this. He's nothing like us. And furthest from what you are. If you ever threaten him, I have enough on you to take you down. I'm willing to go down, too. Elise.'"

"What was the date of the email, Ludwig?"

"January 2, 2023."

Two weeks before the Flight 0606 incident. Elise was still in town. Let's look at something else. "Ludwig, can you find any legal document that estranges Elise from her family?"

"There is no such document."

"Ludwig, can you print her cellphone records between July 2022 and January 2023?"

"Most certainly, but that will require over five hundred pages. Can I print them on both sides to save the planet?"

"Save her."

"Are you quite alright?"

"I'm fine. Thanks for asking. You can disengage now."

I close my eyes. I want to remember Elise as someone who had a zeal for doing good. But I'm failing miserably. Was I blinded by the fact that someone showed a shred of interest in me? I pack up all the drives and printouts for Tabitha. Then I text her.

I pick up a framed photo of Elise from the bookshelf. I clench my jaw as I look straight at the picture, feeling the throb in each vein on my face. "Liar. You asked me to move on from Akane's memories like you did with your family. But you were with them all along. I shouldn't have mourned your death. How could I have been so naïve? You are the daughter of a politician. How different could you ever be?" I hurl the frame across the room. It shatters as it hits the wall, and the shards of glass spread across the floor.

My eyes fall on a box marked "Old Stuff" next to the network drives. I open the box; the contents are primarily sketches I drew when I was younger. And there are some trophies I won in the Shotokan karate competition. It's been a while since I've been to my dojo for a spar. A good spar would probably get Elise's deceit out of my head. At the bottom of the box is my black Karate Gi. I check the time. It's 5:00 p.m. There are three hours until Emika gets here. I clean up the shards of glass, program the dog feeder, and leave.

The dojo is only a fifteen-minute drive away. I used to come here at least three times a week to keep practicing. Sensei Dojima, a seventh-degree blackbelt, runs it. He has trained the Feds and special forces and consults with the Marines. And he's only five feet four inches. He waves at me as I enter. "Vincent, how long has it been?"

I walk over to him. "Last time I was here was January 14, 2023." We bow.

"So, what brings you here?" He winks. "You've added self-defense to your Ph.D. program?"

"It would be nice to tell my students that there are many ways you can get your butt kicked in my Ph.D. program. But I was hoping for a spar with you, that's all."

Dojima crumples his eyebrows. "That's highly irregular. I haven't seen you in almost a year. I don't know if you're in shape."

I join my hands in front of me. "Please, for old time's sake, sensei."

"OK, but I will stop if I see you're hurting. I don't want an injured genius in my dojo."

"Done."

Sensei Dojima turns to his *deshi*. "Rick, you'll be the referee." Rick is over 6 feet fall, with a chiseled jaw and closely cropped hair.

I refuse any protective gear. Dojima and I take our stance. Rick announces, "Fight stops if one is down." Then he waves his arm. "Fight."

(The year 1999)

The annual school karate finals. My rival, Rudolph Von Stein. With Luther out of school, he was the last remaining bully. Rudy was six inches taller than me. He had brute force, but I had skills. I had never sparred with him, but I'd watched him fight and could predict all his moves. We bowed. I smiled, and he grunted, "What's funny, bastard?" I ignored his question and took my stance.

The referee waved his hand. "Fight."

I threw a false punch with my left hand. He fell for the bait and used all his energy to block it in his rage to fight me. What a dumbfuck! I used my right hand to deliver a punch straight to his temple. But he remained, and the referee couldn't ascertain the extent of his injury. If I pushed him, he would fall unconscious. I wanted to inflict more pain. He called my Akane "a runt." It'd echoed through my head up until this moment. I took my position and delivered a 360-degree flying reverse-turning kick to the left side of his neck. He squealed and fell. I could hear his bones hitting the wooden dojo. I bent toward his ears. "Shouldn't have called her a runt. Enjoy the infirmary, motherfucker."

The total time between the start and finish had been less than two minutes. The crowd was silent. Then Sasha started yelling, "Vincent, Vincent." Fred followed suit, then Krista, and then over 500 students were chanting my name. It echoed across the entire hall. Every student Rudy had ever bullied or who'd seen him bullying was yelling my name. The hall was booming. But I couldn't care any less. The adrenaline rush had been for nothing. Rudd was down, all for nothing. Will my Akane be back? With every passing second, the answer was a resounding no.

I bowed to the crowd, the referee, the judges. Then, my joy quickly transformed into tears as I ran into the locker room. I opened my locker and took out my scarf, covering my face with it. "You gave me this scarf after the bullies hit me. Now, one by one, they are gone. Can't you come and get it back? You said you would be back in two days. Liar!"

(Back to the present)

Someone is lightly slapping my cheeks. "Vincent, can you hear me?" I can faintly hear Dojima's voice.

"How long did I last?" I ask, opening my heavy eyes.

"About five minutes." Dojima shakes his head as he wipes my face with a wet towel. "Vince, can you drive home?"

"Yes. My car is autonomous."

Emika enters my apartment and places her bag and two boxes on the kitchen counter. "I have made two bento boxes," she announces as she hangs up her parka. Underneath, she is wearing olive leggings, a maroon sweater, and suede boots. She is here to rescue me from Elise's duplicity. Then she glances at me, and her arms drop in surprise. Her eyes harden, turning to daggers. "Who did this to you?" she asks, her voice booming through the room.

"It's my doing. I had to get some fresh air."

She sits next to me, lifts the frozen peas to see my bruise. Upon seeing it, her eyes get moist. "Your idea of fresh air is to get beaten?" She pulls the lapel of my *gi*. "And how long have you been practicing martial arts? When were you planning on divulging this to me?"

"I'm a second-degree black belt. Been practicing since I was ten." I touch her hand. "I would've told you, Emi."

"Can you hold chopsticks?" she asks, kissing my hand.

I shake my head. "Sorry."

She opens a bento box. I can smell the intoxicating aroma of ginger-soy marinated tofu, sesame hazelnut *furikake* on rice seaweed, pickled cucumber, daikon, and sweet potato. Using the chopsticks, she carefully picks up some rice and tofu. "Open your mouth." I do so, and she gently puts the food in my mouth. "Does it hurt?"

"Yes."

"Well, then make wiser choices. Choices that don't involve a brawl."

"It wasn't brawling—rather a spar with a seven-degree black belt."

She rolls her eyes. "Wow. That's so much better." Then she puts some more food in my mouth. "Chew."

We share one chopstick set and one bento box. Then, while Emika reaches for the second box, I ask, "Can I take a thirty-minute nap before the next box?"

Our eyes lock. "Sure." She puts my head on her lap and runs her fingers through my hair.

I kiss her thigh, shut my eyes. "Can you please never leave me?"

"We can work on that," she says, gently pulling my hair.

"I need to move from this place."

"OK, we'll find you a house, Vince."

I shake my head. "How about one for the both of us?"

"OK, silly. Now, nap."

"Elise lied all along."

"Get her out of your mind, or I'll leave, Vince."

"OK, ma'am."

She bends her head and kisses me. "I found you. Now don't get lost."

CHAPTER 12

LA CAMPANELLA

Life is a winking light in the darkness.
—*Hayao Miyazaki*

(Ten to eight months before today)

MY PHONE STARTS BEEPING—BREAKING NEWS. I switch to the news channels on my computer and see that one news item is trending on CNN, BBC, MSNBC, and Fox News. There is footage of a massive object emerging from the Norwegian Sea around the northeast of Iceland and the west of Finland, hurling toward space. The footage appears to be from a tourist's cellphone and is trending all over the media. Unfortunately, there are no satellite images to corroborate the findings. The ignition is bluish-green toward the ship and yellow in the periphery. The color is unlike anything I have seen from NASA or SpaceX. Is this the work of Philip?

Does intreton propel the ship? Is the spaceship powered by the same thing that it is destined to destroy?

I pause the video. "Ludwig, create a hologram from the image." The hologram is ready in the time it took me to make my doppio. I put on my wireless sensory gloves and pull the hologram out. It's sketchy at best, given the terrible resolution of the footage. I rotate the model, move it upside down. The ship should have at least three towers, the bottom of which should deploy the anchoring gadgets if a landing is an option. The towers are also joined by a cylindrical body, from which the exhaust is coming. I can't decide on the location of the propellers—the port side and the starboard should be in one of the towers.

The ingenious part was to launch the ship from under the ocean and move the satellites—a fantastic tactic to avoid suspicion. But, of course, Philip's tech powers almost all of the working satellites. If he is inside that ship, how will he return if the spaceship is supposed to exit the solar system? He has had three lives. Now, he may be gone forever. I don't know him that well, yet I feel a sense of loss. Why had he given me so many things? Why did he facilitate the documents to hand over control of this center to me? What am I to him? Let me call Edward.

"Hello, Vince. How are you?"

"I'm fine. How about you?"

"Doing good. What do you need?"

"Was that Philip?"

"Was what Philip?"

"That footage of a spaceship—is Philip inside that?"

"I can't say anything."

"Will we ever see Philip again?"

"If he wants, yes. Is that it? I have some matters to attend to."

"Yes, that's it. Take care, Edward."

What could be more critical to Edward than Philip? Unless it's about Philip or Edward's adopted daughter? I flip across some other channels until I stumble on MSNBC. "Of course, it was the aliens. And they left because of global warming." Fuck that. I flip to the other side of the alley—Fox News. "Of course, the equality of marriage and abortion will tick off the aliens. It will tick off Jesus, too." What a bunch of fucking morons. I wonder why bipartisanship is difficult when sheer stupidity unites them. My phone vibrates.

"What's up, Tabi?"

"I was in the area, so I was wondering if you have the drives? I can come and get them."

"Sure, I have them. Come on in."

"OK, see you in ten minutes."

Tabi pulls up a chair, unbuttons her beige suit jacket, and sits. "Have you looked at what's on the drives?"

I lie. "No, I didn't." I leave my chair and pick up the bag. "Everything is here. It's somewhat heavy. Let me carry it to your car."

We leave Hulk in my office and head toward the parking deck. Midway through the car parking deck, I say, "Can I ask you for a favor?"

"Sure."

"If you find something incriminating against Elise, can you go easy on her? Of course, without compromising your journalistic integrity."

"Hm, I don't understand." She squints at me. "Wouldn't something incriminating be a clear betrayal on her part?"

I stop walking. "I don't deny it. I'll know in my heart that she did. But once it's in print, it becomes impossible to see the other side—the side where she adopted Hulk or tried relentlessly to find cures for ailments in developing countries. That's all."

She pumps her inhaler. After a few seconds, we resume our walk. "You have a sensitive side, Vince." She touches my shoulder. "Please don't lose it."

I point toward the inhaler. "Are you OK?"

"It's just a condition I've had since childhood."

We halt beside a Lexus IS 350. I place the drives on the floor by her front seat. We shake hands, and I notice the burn mark on her right wrist again. As she drives away, I wonder what will happen to those drives. Will they become evidence in court?

As I open the door to my suite, I see Emika waiting for me with my Reuben in her hand. She follows me to my office and closes the door behind us. She points to Reuben and lifts her eyebrows. "What's this?"

"It's a Reuben. It has corned beef, sauerkraut, and many other delectable goodies."

She clicks her tongue and flares her nostril. "Stop eating junk. When was the last time you had a physical?"

"Three years ago."

"I got us a salad. But, I don't want to throw this Reuben away." She steps out of my office and changes her tone to be exceedingly courteous. "Linda, is there anyone who can eat a full Reuben?"

"It's a college campus—people are always hungry."

Emika adds, "Also, if someone brings a Reuben for Dr. Abajian, don't give it to him. Give it to anyone except him." She returns to the office and looks at me. "If you don't change your lunch order, I'll hack into your car and make the change myself."

There is an indescribable charm to her fury. I show a serious face to contain my pleasure. "Who taught you to hack?"

"Friends at Caltech."

Despite my gallant efforts, a slight smile starts at the corner of my lips. "Can I meet them?"

She clicks her tongue again. "No. And don't change the subject." Then she mixes two bowls of salad and hands me one bowl. "So, what's your beef with the annual physical?"

"It's boring. All I do is sit and answer mundane questions."

She lifts her eyebrows in discontent. "You're sitting and doing almost nothing now."

"Gazing at you is the furthest thing from mundane."

Her face turns pink as her annoyance gives into a slight smile. She opens her cellphone and leans closer. "Hey, you said you wanna move, right?"

"I like the way you call me 'Hey.'" I give her a smile.

She gives me an eye roll. "OK, hey, hey, hey. Happy? I remember you telling me how you like to look at the mountains. So, this is a newly listed property. You'll love it." She pulls her chair closer and holds her phone between us. The first picture is the front of the house with the address 100 Summit View Lane. Then she begins scrolling, and I can feel the beauty of the place. But through her eyes, it seems like a paradise. Her eyes sparkle like those of a child in a candy store. "Look, Vince, you can have your office here… and your home theater. Look at this view of the rolling hills and the mountains... Look at these cherry trees... it's a four-car garage." Then she pauses and turns to me, not knowing that I was looking at her the entire time. "Do you like it?" Her eyes twinkle.

I remove the cellphone from her hand so that I can hold her hands. "Do *you* like it?"

"Yes. Though I do need to see it in person. But if the photos do it any justice, it will be perfect."

"For?" I rub her fingers.

She lifts one shoulder. "Silly."

"Call the agent and say that we are on our way."

"Right now?"

"Why wait?"

Within the next ten minutes, we are in my car. It's autumn, and the trees have changed colors—some red, some orange, and some yellow. It's a beautiful season, yet short-lived, like the joy in my life. So, why am I rushing things? Is it because I waited for Akane for so long? Or because I want to know the true Emika, who seems like a mirage lost in a desert created by Akane.

I take a right on Main Street, and we begin to ascend. First, the trees change to evergreens. Then to giant evergreens, over a hundred feet tall. The roads are curvy, and Emi moves toward me or away from me with every curve. She is holding Hulk tightly and tapping her feet in joy. During every turn, every ascent, and each descent, she's whispering into his ear, "It's OK. I'm here. I love you." Every time she says that, Hulk licks her nose. And, like a kid, she giggles.

We are now in Summit View Lane. There are fifteen houses, ranging from numbers 100 to 1500. The house Emi loves is the last one in the row, at the highest elevation. We reach it after the final left turn. The entire driveway is made from cobblestone, leading to a four-car garage serviced by two doors. The whole house is carved from bluestone and glass. Adjacent and perpendicular to the garage doors is the front entrance. Next to the front door is a bench, almost invisible from the door. There are wilted flowers in the front yard. Emika pulls my sleeve. "Vince, look. Those will become blue and purple bellflowers." I look at her shimmering eyes, and I bring her close and kiss her soft lips. "Let's go in."

I park next to the agent's Lincoln Corsair. A lady in her fifties greets us at the front door. She's short in stature and is wearing a light blue suit and tan loafers. Her hair is short and straight, and pink-framed glasses rest on her nose. She comes forward and introduces herself. "Hi, I'm Carla Smith."

Emika extends her hand. "I am Dr. Emika Amari, and this is Dr. Vincent Abajian. And the little guy is Hulk."

"Perfect! The house comes furnished, except for the master bedroom. Also, there are two fully furnished walk-in closets." She hands each of us a brochure. "Why don't you two walk around? If you have any questions, I will be delighted to answer."

The living space in the house is approximately 5,500 square feet. The foyer is on the second floor. The interior design combines sloped and flat rooflines made with timber and steel details. The living room has two levels—one central portion with a large sectional sofa by the kitchen and another a few steps higher with seating for four, overlooking floor-to-ceiling glass windows. The great room is over thirty feet tall, with floor-to-ceiling windows that enable panoramic views of the surrounding mountains from all directions. The expanse of windows also makes the home feel bright and airy. Emika's eyes are gleaming with prospects. I hold her hand and bring her close to the glass wall. Pointing toward the outside view, I whisper, "Remember this view?"

She shakes her head. "Nope. What is it?"

"This is the opposing view to Chez-Giraud's that you admired a month back," I say, wrapping my arm around her shoulders.

Her eyes widen. "Wow!"

We then head toward the meticulously landscaped backyard. I turn to Emi. "I know the evergreens, but what're those fifteen rows of almost barren trees in the backyard?"

"They're sakura, silly." She puts her arms around my waist. "They'll blossom beautifully in spring. It's indescribable beauty—the pink blossoms overlooking the mountains. Imagine golden sunshine on pink blossoms, then on the green rolling hills and the lake, and then on the snowcapped mountains. When the petals from cherry trees fall, they look like pink snowflakes." Her eyes gleam with each sentence.

We head back into the house. The kitchen lights above the counters are hung from 20-feet wire encased in bronze. The kitchen cabinetry is burnt sienna like Emika's eyes. The same cabinetry also conceals the refrigerator—making it indistinguishable.

Then we walk around each of the five bedrooms, the room that would be our office, the possible home theater room. There is also a wine cellar by the prospective home theater.

I turn to Emi. "Do you see yourself in this house?"

"Yes! But it's kind of pricey."

"Let's find Carla," I say, grabbing her hand.

She tilts her head. "About?"

"We are buying this."

She grabs me by the jacket sleeve. "Why?"

"Because of what I saw when I looked at you as you looked at the house."

We locate Carla by the kitchen counter. "What do you think?" she asks.

"If we offer three installments in electronic fund transfers, what's the best deal you can give us?"

"I'll need to talk to the builders."

"Of course."

Emika and I sit by the glass wall, gazing at the starry night and the mountains as we wait. It's the dusk hour. The lake reflects the fall foliage from the foothills, and above them are the snowcapped mountains. And on my right is sitting someone who induces feelings that I never knew existed. And she's holding a pup, who's the embodiment of unconditional love. She taps my hand. "What are you thinking?"

Are we moving too quickly? Emika told me that she's not capable of long-term relations because of the Benji incident. Isn't this too quick for her? Is Akane making her rush? Or am I rushing because she rescued me from Elise's treachery? How long should I deny myself the joys of life by encasing them with rational questions? Fuck it—enough with logic over emotions. I hold Emika's hand. "I think that we were meant to find this place."

After a few minutes, Carla finds us. "We can shave off 200K and do $1.5 million for an ETF."

I brace my palms on my thighs and get up. "Let's do this." I kiss Emika's head.

"What's a good time for you to come over and sign everything?" Carla asks.

"How about tomorrow at ten? Is that OK with you, Emi?"

She nods and places her hand in mine.

Carla looks at Emika. "Can I ask you a question?"

"Absolutely."

"Pardon my curiosity, but you two are not married, right?"

Emika squeezes my fingers with her left hand. With her right hand, she firmly grips Hulk's leash. "Not yet. But we are a work in progress with beautiful potential."

Not a minute has passed since I entered my office, and my phone rings.

"Hello, Kenji."

"We delivered the portability of the endowment document to your university admin office. I will email you a copy. You've got three options. Please have a look at them and call me if you have any questions. You can pick one option now and change your mind later. We will assist you with that as well."

"Thank you, Kenji. I'll consult my colleagues to see what's the best route for them."

"Absolutely."

"Kenji, do you know the whereabouts of Philip?"

"Vincent, the less you know, the better. He has your best interests in mind."

"Thank you, Kenji. See you soon."

I print out the pdf that Kenji sent. I need to talk to Anna, Chris, and Ravi—their jobs will be the most affected by the decision. For now, I'll keep Emika out of the loop. She's going through a lot of changes in her life.

Emika tapes up the fifteenth box marked "Books." She wipes sweat from her forehead with my pocket square that has become her bandana and finds me gazing at her. "What?" she asks.

I pull her closer.

"Eww! I am all sweaty."

"So?" I run my fingers across her face.

She pulls my sweatshirt. "How about after we get to Summit View?"

"Deal."

"Anything for a good grade, professor," she says, giving me a wink. Then she looks around. "So, what will you do with the furniture and Elise's stuff?"

"Elise's stuff will go to Goodwill. The furniture to Habitat for Humanity. I have paid the building super to take care of them. Elise's family took her jewels after she died."

As Emika and Hulk wait in the U-Haul, I enter the apartment one last time. Elise, Hulk, and I did have some beautiful memories in this house.

"This is where we'll have our TV, Vince."

"Did you ever guess house training Hulk would be this hard?"

"Let's buy your watch. You've earned it, Vincent."

"Tony is looking for investors in Chez Giraud."

"Let's call Ravi, Anna, and Chris for your birthday."

And the last thing Elise said in this house: "I will miss you and Hulk."

This is where Hulk entered our lives. This is where I got my email that I was tenured, and then two years later, my promotion to full. This is where Elise heard of her paper's acceptance at *Nature Epidemiology.* This is where I heard that Elise's plane had crashed. This is where I took shelter when I wasn't allowed near her memorial.

This is where I made Emika her espresso, and we kissed for the first time. Goodbye, my friend. Thank you for sheltering us. Please love the new occupant as much as you loved us.

We move in. I place two of Philip's clocks on the main floor and one on the lower floor. The "Risen from Fire and Ashes" painting goes on the wall above the fireplace. I don't know what deeper connection I have with this painting that Philip mentioned. But Emika loves the painting, and that's what matters.

Our first dinner is vegetarian pizza from Godfathers, with toppings of artichoke, garlic, mushrooms, onions, and spinach. I take a bite. "This pizza tastes amazing, Emi."

She lifts one shoulder. "All my choices are awesome. I chose you."

How can the same person who chose Jason also choose me? I pull her barstool closer to mine. "When are we gonna set up the master bedroom?"

She closes her eyes, lost in the taste of the pizza. "When I'm ready to move into this place for good."

When will she move in? It is just a few suitcases. Does she need more time? Or does she need to keep the townhome address to avoid the suspicion that she moved in with the boss's boss? She can simply divert all mail to her office address. What's happening in her mind? Does she regret us? She must be in this town to stay. "So, would you like to work in the center as a research scientist?"

She doesn't answer immediately. "I like my current position, and after I'm done with all the deliverables, we can talk about it." I must get complete control of the endowment to allow her this flexibility.

Every time Emika and I take a bite, we give Hulk a flaked corn. He thinks he's eating pizza.

Emika shakes her head. "Most divas have fewer clothes than you do. Do you need them arranged by color, pattern, season? How did Elise manage to live with you?"

"Maybe my OCD drove her to launder money."

She looks at me, eyebrows down. "That wasn't funny."

I hug her. "Hey, when do we organize your closet?"

"I don't have enough to merit a closet," she says, shaking her head. "Besides, most of my clothes are in the townhome."

"Let's pick them up and shop for you." I tighten my grip around her.

She ruffles my hair. "Don't rush me. We will do all those when I move in. Promise." Then she runs her finger over my forehead and down my nose. "Can I make some purchases for the house?"

"The house is yours. Do you need my credit card?"

"I can afford it, Vince. The center pays me well."

"But I can add you to my credit card?"

She looks up and thinks for a moment. "Do it when I move in for good." Then she goes back to organizing my closet. "I'll do the shopping tomorrow. Probably leave work a bit early."

"Let me rent you a car. They'll drop it at work, and then you can drop it home, and they will pick it up. OK?"

She drops a pile of my shirts and hugs me. "That would be awesome, Vince. Thank you."

(August 2001 ~ A dream)

It was graduation day. Families of all the graduating students were attending. Several flew from outside continental Europe—the USA, Canada, Australia, India, Singapore, China, Taiwan, South Korea, Japan. The crowd roared as I finished my graduation speech. The cheers of Fred, Krista, Sasha, and their families and the roaring applause of my teachers all blended into white noise as I kept searching for one face, the girl that used to say, "Found you." I saw an unfamiliar face cheering for me in the crowd, mostly hidden from the sunlight by his fedora.

After my ceremony, I rushed to the music room. I had many blue and purple bellflowers, and Akane's scarf was wrapped around my neck. The man in the fedora intercepted me, his face still in shadow from his hat. All that I could make out was his pointy beard and his chin. He was impeccably dressed in an off-white linen suit and basketweave loafers. He extended his hand, "Congratulations, Vincent!"

We shook hands, and I said, "Thank you, sir. Have we met before?"

He smiled. "Sometimes 'before' happens 'after.' Good luck with Cambridge." Then he looked at the flowers I was holding. "I won't delay your journey to the music room any longer. We'll meet again." And then he turned, leaving the way he'd come.

Who was he? And how did he know about Cambridge? How could he tell that I was heading for the music room? Finally, I reached the music room and sat in the exact place Akane had tied the scarf around me. My voice quavered as tears rolled from my eyes. "You can hear me, right?"

Someone tapped my shoulder. "You remember the bellflowers?"

I turned around. It was Akane, and she hadn't aged a day. "How could I forget?" I said, giving her the flowers. "Are you still stuck in the turbulence?"

"No, silly. I'm all anew. I looked for you all over, Vince. Then one day, you became famous—top of your field. I found you, silly. *Watashi no amai*, Vincent." Her eyes welled up.

I touched her shoulder. "Anew? Where?"

"Just open your eyes, silly."

(Back to the present)

I open my eyes and see Emika sleeping next to me, with her left hand fisting my sweatshirt. Her eyes are shut, and she's breathing calmly. The light from the east is reflecting on her hair and her bare arms, making them shine. I gently whisper. "Thank you for finding me."

With her eyes still closed, she asks, "What?"

I run my fingers along her arms, and she repeats, "What?"

I run my fingers through her hair. She asks, "*Nani*?"

I touch her lips and then her chin. She repeats, "*Nani*?"

I guess I have to speak her tongue. I remove strands of hair from her face, and I touch her beautiful mole. "*Kore ga daisuki desu*."

She opens her eyes and smiles. "What else do you love?"

"What do you want for breakfast?"

Like a kid in school, she raises her hand and, with her eyes gleaming, says, "Scrambled eggs, *kudasai*." So she gets scrambled eggs, served with fried heirloom tomatoes and mushrooms, and one piece of toast with butter. I have the same, except I substitute the tomatoes for two thick-cut slices of bacon. She takes a bite and goes for a second one but stops to investigate my plate. The look in her eyes transforms from gastronomic orgasm to anguish. "You need to stop eating this shit."

"But I like bacon."

She crosses her arms, like a child, and looks the other way. "Me or bacon?"

"Is this a trick question, Dr. Amari?" I ask, playing along.

She shakes her head and takes her first sip of coffee. "Eggs and coffee go so well together."

"A thick slice of bacon makes it even better."

"No more processed meats, understood?" she says, narrowing her eyes. Then she picks up Hulk, squeezes him, and they both turn to me. "Hulky, does he love us more than bacon?"

As we leave for work, she looks back at the house. "I can't wait to see the bellflowers bloom. I'll go out, pick them, and put them in vases. On the dining table, on the coffee table, on the TV stand, bedside table, dressers, everywhere. What do you think, Vince?"

So she plans to stay in town after all. I breathe in a sigh of relief. "You should do it. And I want to see you do it."

Her smile reaches her eyes, compressing them to just curves of lashes. "OK."

Three of us get into the car. This is my first morning heading to work with Emika. Hulk is lying on Emika's lap. "I notice you tie your shoelaces differently. What is it?"

"Berluti knot."

"Hm. Who taught you to dress like this?"

We start to descend down the road. "Well, my friend's parents were well-dressed. The headmaster taught me the Berluti knot and how to polish my shoes. A friend Krista Gallo introduced me to the pocket square when I was eight. But there's also a faint recollection of me seeing a gentleman during my graduation. He was impeccably dressed in a linen suit and wore a fedora hat. I may have inadvertently picked up his style, minus the hat."

"Good decision. I wouldn't cover those wavy locks. But, hey, who's Krista? A girlfriend?"

"She's a friend who happened to be a girl, who was also into one specific girl called Sasha, another friend of mine."

Before she heads to her office, Emika looks around for any familiar faces, then she whispers, "Come closer." She pulls me by my necktie and kisses me. "See you at home." Hulk and I walk into my suite while Emika hopscotches toward the AI lab.

I find Anna sinking one ball after another on the pool table, in the reserved section of the country club bar. I hang my overcoat beside her parka. "Nice shot."

She looks at me and squints. "What's wrong?"

I tilt my head. "How could you tell?"

"I can read you like a book, idiot." She leaves her cue stick on the table and comes closer.

"Why does she insist on keeping her townhome. Why can't she move in? It's her house too." I shake my head. "I am not even sure if she wants to work here."

"Give her time. I get a feeling that she is trapped in her twenties. Plus, this could be all too rushed for her."

Did Akane's entry stunt her? When did she enter? The day Emika picked up her violin in 2001? I can hear Chris and Ravi talking outside the pool room, interrupting my thoughts.

Anna touches my arm assuringly. "Let's talk later."

Chris and Ravi come in, collect their cue sticks, and begin sharpening the tip. Chris turns to me. "Thanks for reserving this room, man. Just like old times."

I place the triangle and rack up fifteen balls. "Anna, you break."

Anna takes a hairclip from her wrist and tightly ties her hair back. Then she picks up her stick, takes a long look at the balls, and smiles. Finally, she strikes, sinking sinks three balls. "Fuck, I'm good."

As she takes her next aim, I interrupt. "I have something serious to discuss."

With her body still in the striking position, she turns to me. "Are you dying? Can I have your parking spot?"

Chris covers his face while Ravi rolls his eyes and turns to Anna. "What the fuck, Anna?"

I sharpen my cue stick. "We are talking about $950 million, guys. As of now, Philip's lawyers have sent a draft that makes his endowment mobile. And we will have full control of all decisions."

A short-statured blonde girl—probably an undergraduate student—enters with four bottles of Guinness stout on a tray. She smiles, "Stout on the house." We collect our bottles, and I leave her a fifty-dollar tip.

Chris takes a sip. "What if the university objects?"

"Then he withdraws the whole fund, which we can then use to create a startup. Now, I want your opinion on one particular decision we need to make."

Ravi's eyes are gleaming. He leaves his cue stick on the stand and comes forward. "Go on."

Anna sinks two more balls as I continue. "We have three routes. Our first option is we can remain a part of the university. This way, we can use their resources, like office space and classrooms. In return, we teach our in-demand undergraduate and graduate classes, and we share the revenue with the university. We'll have full autonomy to hire anyone we want. We will have our Ph.D. program and be academically relevant while continuing our pursuits. How do things sound so far?"

Anna leaves the table and inspects the tip of her stick. "You weren't kidding when you said you would take us out of this mess."

"I wasn't." I shake my head and continue. "The second option is we have is to become a subsidiary of Nardin Robotics. We continue our research, both fundamental and applied. I can negotiate stock options for all of us. We three sit on the board. The pros include no teaching. But it also means no more Ph.D. students, either. Are we clear so far?"

Chris walks around the table, inspecting it. "This option sounded good till I heard no more Ph.D. students. But again, the quality of doctoral students is declining."

I take a few more sips of my stout. "That brings us to the last one. We go independent. I know enough VCs and angels in Boston, Seattle, and Silicon Valley to match $950 million. Also, Philip will most likely invest. In this scenario, the sky is the limit. We can start making our products and license IPs to other firms by creating our technology standards. And because all our inventions are made from resources not provided by the university, they can't stake a claim. If they do, Philip's law firm will help us fight. And any future inventions will be just ours. This is the riskiest and potentially most lucrative financially. But just like the previous option, no students. So, your thoughts?"

"When do you need to know, Vince?" Ravi asks, putting his bottle on the edge of the table.

"The sooner, the better. I will protect your jobs, irrespective of the choice."

Chris turns to me. "Is the decision fixed?"

"If we choose option one, we can migrate to two or three later. If we choose option two, it isn't easy to drift to one, and moving to three is likely. If we choose option three, depending on the size of investment from Nardin, we could migrate to two but most likely not one."

Chris takes a long sip of his beer before asking, "What's your choice, Vince?"

When I don't reply immediately, they start looking at each other. Finally, I ask them, "Do you want me to decide?"

Ravi sighs in relief. "Yes, Vince, please."

"I would start with option one and wait till our Ph.D. students graduate. After that, we may choose option two or three. Thoughts?"

Anna goes first. "I'll go with Vince. We have a responsibility to our Ph.D. students, even if they suck."

"I agree," Ravi says.

Chris looks at me. "Me too."

"Ok, guys. I will let Philip's lawyers know."

Anna touches my shoulder. "Thanks a lot for doing this, Vince." Then she takes aim, strikes but misses. She punches the table. "Fuck, good news can be distracting."

I smile. "Now, now. It's daddy's turn." I lean over and take my aim. I have been doing this since Cambridge. I look at my friends. "Let me show you how it's done, lads." I strike and sink four balls.

Ravi's jaw drops. "Have you been practicing? It's like you never left."

Anna comes over to me and hugs me with all her strength. "This is the best part—not the endowment. That you are back."

I move her head from my chest and wipe her tears. "I never left."

She tugs my lapel. "You did, and don't do it again. We are here to help you. We love you, idiot."

I kiss the top of her apricot-shampooed head. "I won't leave again."

Ravi breaks the awkwardness. "And, how is the new house?"

"I love it."

Anna steps away, fixes her eyeliner. "Of course, you would. With such a beautiful cohabiter."

An idea hits me. "Hey, you guys in town for Thanksgiving? It's also Emi's birthday."

They all look at each other. "Yes, we are."

"So why don't you all come and join Emi and me? Bring a guest if you like."

Chris claps. "Awesome."

"Not to burst the bubble, but I'll be cooking fish. There'll be no turkey or ham because…."

Anna, now completely recovered from her vulnerable state, touches her forehead and looks up. "Yeah, yeah. The lady of the house only eats fish, eggs, and plants. We get it, Vince. Three months with this girl, and you forget your old friends. I am heading to the bar to drown myself in my sorrow."

Ravi taps Anna's shoulder. "We are in the country club bar."

The door recognizes my thumbprint and lets me in. Hulk comes running and stands up on his feet to greet me. I ask him, "Where's Mum?" As I walk farther into the house, I hear the shower running.

I sit in my favorite spot. The smell of the house is still fresh. The new carpet, the new cabinets all have the aroma of newness and witness to embryonic memories. I look outside to view the hills, mountains, and lake. The mist from the lake must make the houses almost invisible. I see the curved roads, some cars appearing and then disappearing into the fog, then appearing again. As the slops ascend, I see fewer houses, fewer lights, barely visible under the mist from the lake. And much higher are the snow-capped mountains, glowing orange, yellow, and white against the receding sunlight. Despite the beauty around me, the responsibility of $950 million weighs on me. I hope I don't mess it all up. I haven't doubted myself before.

I feel the warmth of a hug from behind. And a kiss behind my ears. I turn around, seeing Emika wearing a satin robe with a towel covering her hair. She sits on the armrest. "You look tired. Do you need to take a nap?" I put my arm around her waist. "I'm fine now."

She leans on me. "So, Vince, is it OK for official purposes? I still use the townhome address. I don't want everyone to realize you and I have the same address. I'm asking because the center pays for the townhome."

I don't want to argue with her. She should move in when she is ready. I don't know if this is a conflict between Emika and the Akane, in her but rushing her will only worsen. "If that makes you comfortable, sure. But know that this is your home."

She stands up and pulls me by my sleeve. "Let me show you what I got." After leading me into the kitchen, she shows me the Japanese chef knives, tokoname teapot, and flower vases. Next, she offers me the added pop to the sofa with new blue, yellow, and orange cushions. I'd guess she bought over a hundred pillows. She also changed the guest room bedding. Then she pulls me over to the walk-in closet. "I got this suit for you."

She unzips the Zegna cover and reveals a charcoal plaid suit. "If I ever get mad at you, just wear this. I will instantly melt."

"OK. But you needn't have."

"I wanted to." She hugs me. "I saw this, and I thought of you, silly."

I wake to Japanese words spoken by Emika. I can only decipher "*Watashi*," "*Nando*," "*Nani*," "*Suki*," "*Mum*," "*Pa-pha*," and "Vincent." I splash some water on my face, brush my hair, and then follow the direction of her voice.

She is sitting on the carpet in the great room, with her back against the sofa. The eastern sunlight through the large glass walls illuminates everything it touches, including my Emika. Holding the phone in her right hand, she flips through a sketchbook with her left. She's wearing a short-sleeved gray t-shirt and a pair of pink shorts. Hulk is lying on the sofa, resting his head on her shoulder. Both Hulk and I are gazing at her from different vantage points. This is the postcard of my bliss. She says, "*Mata-ne*," and hangs up. I lay down and rest my head on her lap. She runs her fingers through my hair. "So, when were you planning to tell me that you are an artist?" Apparently, she'd found the box labeled "Old stuff."

"I'm not. I used to scribble and paint, and then I stopped."

"These definitely don't look like scribbles." She runs her index finger over my forehead. "You were a prodigy. Why did you not make this your profession?"

I sit up. "Not an ideal choice for an orphan with no safety net. I had to make something out of myself. So I carved out a career where the probability of starving to death is low."

She nods and continues to flip the pages. "Who's this?"

"Frederique Deschamps, my roommate."

"I see." She turns to the next page. "Who're these girls?"

"On the left is Krista Gallo, and on the right is Sasha Chen. After Akane was gone, I often partnered with them in culinary class."

"It seems you guys were very close."

"Akane's departure shattered me. But they always made sure I was OK. I was like their communal younger sibling. We haven't seen each other since we graduated high school. I became so accustomed to their helping me that I never gave them a chance to depend on me. That's why I want to make sure that Anna, Chris, and Ravi can lean on me, no matter what. I try to take care of them like they are my younger siblings. It's my flawed way of repaying Fred, Krista, and Sasha."

Emika kisses my fingers as she moves to the next page. "Who's he?"

"Headmaster, Mr. Kruger."

"Wow! He was handsome."

"Still is, I believe. He was admired and feared at the same time."

She turns another page. "And who's he?"

"That's Chef Marcel. My eccentricities regarding food come from him."

"I wish I knew you when you were in school—little Vince." She kisses me. "Did you ever paint anything?"

"I did a few acrylics on canvas, experimental surrealism, and cubism. All pre-Cambridge. They could still be in my school art-room." She flips through all the pages once again, squinting. "No portrait of Akane. I'm surprised."

(September 18, 1991)

"Akane, I can't do this if you move."

"Whatever." She crossed her arms and looked to the other side.

I had my sketchbook on a desk. Next to it were twelve graphite pencils, ordered from hard to soft.

She pointed at my desk. "Why do you need so many pencils? Can't you make do with one like everyone else, maestro?"

The moment I wasn't looking, she made faces, sticking her tongue out. She began sighing and finally banged on the desk. "How long, Vince? This is boring!"

"I want this to be perfect." I knew it was futile, but I struggled to rival the opus she'd made on my birthday.

After thirty more minutes, I lifted my pencil. "All done!"

"Let me see." She stretched her arm out and batted her eyes.

I signed my name, dated it September 18, 1991. I also dated the top of the perforation. After removing the sketch from the pad, I gave it to her. "Happy birthday!"

She kissed my cheek and hugged me. "This is the best gift, Vince. It will be with me forever."

She pulled my sleeve. "Vince, *ni iku.* Chef Marcel promised me that he'd make us a cake. You, me, Chef Marcel, Sasha, Krista, Fred, and Mr. Kruger." She wrapped her scarf, pulled me by my cuff, and we ran toward the culinary classroom.

(Back to the present)

I get up, pick up a near-empty sketchbook, turn to the very first page, and show Emika the perforated part where "September 18, 1991" is written.

"That was Akane's portrait. The date was her ninth and last birthday. She left with the sketch."

Emika touches my handwriting on the perforation. "I'm sure she cherished it. So, she was a year older than you?"

"I was the youngest in my class."

She flips through the rest of the pages of that sketchbook, all filled with tally marks, scanning them like a flipbook. Then, she turns to me and lifts her eyebrows. "What are these?"

I cough to hide the tremble in my voice. "I could only fit five years of waiting in this sketchbook."

She grabs my sweatshirt. "There's more?"

I point to a stack of notebooks. "Five more years of school, and then Cambridge days." Gulping down the imminent tears, I say, "I gave up when I entered MIT."

She pulls me close and wraps her arms around my neck. "I am so sorry." When she pulls back, she uses my sweatshirt to wipe her tears, then tilts her head. "Hey, is there something weird about Akane that you adored?"

"When she was deep in her thoughts, there were certain times that she would speak in Dutch or Japanese. Like in geometry class, when she would struggle to intersect two lines. Or, in the culinary club, when she poured too much flour in her batter." I stretch my legs out. "She would do the same when she packed for summers. She'd go to and fro between Dutch and Japanese. But mostly Japanese. Then she would look at me, tilting her head, smile mysteriously, and say something in Japanese before pinching my cheek and continuing to pack—"

"Dutch?" Emika interrupts.

"Yes, her mother was Dutch."

Emika starts packing up all the sketchbooks. "I'm sorry, I interrupted. I believe you were going to add something else."

"Oh, yes. I could never decipher what she was saying, but I found the words beautiful nonetheless. But that's the beauty of language barriers. Your interpretations aren't limited by words anymore. Words become music, music becomes numbers, numbers become colors. When I first met you, Emi, you talked about two universal languages: music and numbers. The joy of hearing her words was the same as hearing the notes of Chopin's Ballade no. 4 or looking at Euler's identity. You feel joy, sorrow, love, without the confinements of a dictionary."

Emika tangles her fingers with mine. "Is there anything else whose beauty you can compare to Chopin's no. 4?"

"Hm, where's your cellphone?"

She points to the sofa. "There."

I look at her. "Call me?" She does, and in two seconds, my phone rings to Chopin's Ballade no. 4. "Does that answer your question?"

She touches the corner of her eyes, wiping the tears before they start pouring. "Yes."

"This opus started playing exactly the moment you walked into my office on August 3. When I hear it, I can see you. And it changes when you speak."

She moves away an inch. "Hey, what's wrong with the way I speak?"

I pull her back. "Didn't say anything was wrong. It's melodic, playful, polite yet assertive, happy with a tinge of sorrow. It's a rainbow of emotions, like Liszt's La Campanella. So in you, I hear two of my favorite composers."

Emika's face turns pink as she struggles to find words.

I get up. "Are you hungry?"

She shakes her head. "I'm fasting for the day."

"If you lose any weight, you will attain invisibility."

"What are you gonna eat?"

"Just cereal and oat milk."

I still struggle to find the fridge. In my quest to find the concealed refrigerator, I am opening all the other cabinets. I looked over my shoulder to find Emika laughing at my plight. Her musical laugh beautifully punctuates my predicament. I look at her, feeling helpless. I touch a cabinet, and she says, "Colder." Then another one results in "Warmer." Finally, I hit the jackpot, and she applauds. "That Ph.D. from MIT came into some use."

She grabs two green post-its, writes "Door-L" and "Door-R" and their Hiragana counterparts "*hidari doa*" and "*migi doa*," then pastes them on the doors.

I turn to her. "I would've figured it out."

She ruffles my hair. "What if you need to open the fridge, and I'm not around to navigate you?" As she heads back to the sofa, she turns back to me, smiling. "*Watashi no amai*, Vincent."

Tabi is already waiting for me when I arrive at my office suite.

She follows me in, and I hang her black knee-length parka beside my overcoat. She then inserts her gloves and a brown beanie cap inside the pockets of her coat. Rubbing her hands together, she says, "I can never get used to the cold." Then she pulls her inhaler from her bag and pumps it three times. After putting it back, she straightens her red turtleneck and black trousers.

I point to the sofa by the fireplace. "Take a seat. I will make you a latte."

She makes herself comfortable while I make her coffee. As I hand her the latte, she asks, "So, where is Hulk?"

"Chilling at home."

She takes a sip, and her eyes glow. "What coffee is it?"

"Kona peaberry."

"I could come to your office every day just for this." She takes a few more sips. I give her a tissue to wipe the foam off her lips. Then she leans forward. "Dick Graham has numbered accounts in Zurich and the Cayman Islands. We checked the dates of withdrawals and deposits against Elise's travel records. They match."

I knew that was imminent. I'd found it with Ludwig, but I'd hoped not to hear it from Tabi. Resting my head on my palms, I ask, "Were those between December 2022 and January 2023?"

Tabi touches my shoulder. "Yes, how did you know?"

I press my temples.

(December 2022)

Elise turned to me after zipping up her cabin luggage. "Do you want me to write down the mix of kibble and veggies for Hulk?"

"I know the mix. You enjoy your trip." I smiled. "You know I could've come to Zurich with you. I could have met my headmaster, Mr. Kruger, in Basel."

She came close, ruffled my hair. "Maybe next time. I'll be too busy for fun."

"That's fine. What's the one in Cayman?" I asked.

"Epidemiological society. But it will be over before you know it." She picked up Hulk. "I know you wanted to spend New Year's Eve together. But I'll make it up to you and Hulk."

I touched her shoulder, hugged her tight. "Not a problem. Knock'em dead."

(Back to present)

Elise hadn't been busy—she'd been trying to conceal what she was up to. I lift my head. "She mentioned visiting Zurich and the Caymans over those days."

Tabitha leans toward me. "She did love you—there are emails between her and Dick Graham confirming that."

I look at her. "Please continue, Tabi."

"To summarize, Lombard agreed to pay $20 million for safe transportation of intreton to Seattle. Since they had no access to the casing provided by Philip Nardin, they used their own. To avoid suspicion in scanning, Dick Graham helped bribe the Bangalore Airport authorities with Lombard's assistance. But Lombard wanted one extra layer of assurance and was willing to pay another $10 million. This is where Elise's involvement begins. She had access to WHO canisters for vaccine transportation. Either she did the casing herself or handed the canisters to Lombard representatives. The airport did not scan a single case. Lombard deposited $15 million in a numbered account in the Caymans and another $15 million in Zurich. Elise took $2.5 from each for her research." Tabitha places her hand on my arm. "Vince, I'm sure she would not have taken part if she'd known the contents. But she was quite good at handling her father's dirty money."

"And I thought she'd emancipated herself." I shake my head. "When are you publishing the piece?"

"Next week. I won't mention you or Elise. But this article will prompt an investigation from the AG's office. Sooner or later, agents from the FBI will come and speak with you. As soon as they do, just write an SOS to Philip's lawyers. They'll cut a deal with the director of the FBI. They'll share more dirt on Dick if they let you go. If they reach an agreement earlier, then the Feds won't even bother you."

My jaw drops as I look at Tabi. "Deal for what? I'm innocent."

Tabi speaks quickly to reassure me. "You are. But agencies always look for a scapegoat. They have to weigh up between you and Dick. Philip's lawyers will make sure that it is Dick. Getting him is more lucrative for an FBI agent than catching a professor, whose genius they can't ascertain." She smiles assuringly. "Relax, Vince. You've cooperated with the investigation.

I'll make sure that no harm will come to you. You did a lot for me. Can I do something to return the favor?"

I hesitate for a moment. "So I'm writing this book on Philip Nardin, called *The Time Fixer: Three Lives of Philip Nardin*. Can you help me get a publisher? I don't have time for literary agents."

"I have some connections. Send me a copy when you can. I'm sure there's a market for a book about someone who's been through three lives and whose net worth is inching close to a trillion dollars." Then she stands up. "Thanks for the coffee, Vince. And thanks for the evidence. You're a compassionate and kind soul. One day, I'd like to do a profile on you."

I spend the remainder of the day working on the book, finishing a patent application, and working on two papers. All of them were effective in forgetting Elise and her double life. I wish I could tell Emika everything. But I remember what she told me: *Get her out of our mind, or I'll leave.* I can't lose her.

The book is done. I email Tabi a copy of the manuscript.

I am home. Hulk comes running to me, and Emika follows. "How was your day?"

"Tabi came and talked about her theory." I drop my briefcase by the door.

She wrinkles her eyebrows. "Theory about what? And why does she keep popping into our lives?"

I bring Emika close, tuck her locks behind her ears. "It's about Dick Graham, intreton, the plane that crashed with Elise in it. She cannot come into our lives. I won't let anyone."

She grabs my lapel. "Do you wanna talk about it?"

Why does she want to know? I can't really discuss this without bringing up Elise. I tighten my grip around her. "Not really. I want to talk about you and your day. What did you do?"

"I was working on our papers. Vince, I need help."

"With what?"

"I keep asking Anna, Chris, and Ravi how to write the results concisely. Anna's words were, 'You live with the one who taught us. Ask the maestro.'"

I loosen my tie. "Let's go."

"Right now?"

"There is no better moment. Remember, the tables are sheet music, and writing the results is how you choose to play it—the clock is ticking, and pages are limited."

Emika wants to work from home—play with Hulk and working on our papers. While backing out, I see a Rolls Royce from the 1990s on the road. I can't get a good look at the driver through the darkened windscreen, except that he is wearing a fedora. I call Emika. "If anyone is at the door, don't open it. Please don't open it."

"OK, my protector," she replies. "You could've stayed home and shielded us."

"You think I wanna meet the university president and her intellectually challenged lieutenants?"

She laughs. "Tell me about it when you get back home."

So, I will be meeting President Alyson Bachman, Provost Matt Sandman, and VP of Foundations Bob Millar. I have already seen their nauseating profiles that reek of fake degrees, devoid of any academic rigor. Bob doesn't even have a Ph.D., yet he refers to himself as a doctor.

Linda calls, "Dr. A, your guests have arrived." I go to the door to receive them.

Three people barge in, whose collective IQ would not match that of a barnacle. Bob Millar is the first. The buttons on his shirt can barely stay in their holes, and his undershirt is visible. His belly must protrude about 2 feet, and he fastens the bottom button of his navy blazer instead of the top one. He has short hair, dyed blond to conceal the gray. He reeks of tobacco and wears a fake Rolex Presidential. Also, he's loud and spits while talking. "I'm Dr. Bob, and you can call me Bob."

I extend my arm. "I will call what you are—which is just Bob."

Bob crinkles his eyebrows as I rob him of his non-existent doctorate.

Next, Sandman. He is just another Bob, but with a tweed jacket and a better diet. He stretches his arm out. "I'm Dr. Sandman. You can call me Matt." Both Bob and Matt take a seat on the sofa, Bob taking up almost two-thirds of it.

Next in line is our president, Alyson. She has short hair, like mine, but straight. She is wearing a red suit with a skirt, and a pearl necklace is draped around her neck. "Hi Vince, we've met before. Feel free to call me Alyson." She sits on a chair perpendicular to the sofa. That's my seat, but today, I won't object. They are already wounded.

Instead, I sit on the chair opposite Alyson, who starts with, "Is there anything you want from us?"

I smile and shake my head. "Actually, no. I am getting to a point where I don't have to ask you for anything. I'm sure you have seen the documents."

Matt smirks. "We have not signed anything."

"Your signature is a mere formality. Mr. Nardin's trust can move the endowment without it. When I was hired, I was given absolute freedom to start programs. Slowly, as we attracted more and more funds, you took chunks away. You didn't let me hire endowed chairs; you delayed my doctoral programs and used endowment dollars for personal use. I did not work this hard to seek approval from the likes of you. Your constant interference makes this center beyond fix. It will all change now."

Bob's face turns red. He struggles to reach the coffee table, but his belly forbids him, so he ends up banging on his own knee. "What do you mean the 'likes of us'? And we'll fight this in a court."

I look him in the eye. "By the likes of you, I mean those with a scarcity of intellect but an abundance of entitlement. When you say you will fight us in court, do you realize you can't use endowment money for legal fees? And without that—"

Bob stands up and points his finger at me. "Don't underestimate us, you son of a—"

"Get one thing in that thick skull of yours. Never. Interrupt. Me. Again." I shut my eyes and take off my glasses. Then I take a few deep breaths to calm down before putting my glasses back on.

Alyson turns to Bob. "Sit, Bob."

I clench my jaws. "You came here to make me reconsider by promising that you will throw me a bone. It's not your bone to give." I form a fist and continue. "My team and I will take it all. And I will decide whether to keep this center here or move out."

Sandman leans forward and squints at me. "We can fire you."

I grin and shake my head. "That'll result in a lawsuit that you can't survive."

I get a text from Tabi with the link to the article. I print it. She has also already spoken to a publisher that is a subsidiary of *The Tribune*. That was quick. People are either interested in Philip, or Tabitha is exceptionally well-connected, or both. Of course, she won the Pulitzer. I read the article, and as promised, she did not mention Elise. But now it's in print—a permanent reminder of my naiveté of Elise's duplicity.

Anna and I need to make two stops.

"Welcome, Professor Abajian," greets Diego. He is always impeccably dressed and extremely polite. "We have some new releases from Grand Seiko, a new Speedy, and a Vacheron Constantin Overseas. Would you like to see any of them?"

"Diego, I would buy the Vacheron in a heartbeat. But today, I am in the mood for something different, as I am not buying anything for myself."

After a few minutes, we leave with a beautifully wrapped box, and we make another stop.

I point at the metronome. "Is that supposed to time my responses?"

Dr. Kauffman smiles. "No, it's supposed to keep you calm."

"But I am calm."

"They all claim that." She opens her fountain pen. "Why do you think Emika is hesitating to move in with you completely?"

"I don't know. You are the doctor of the mind." I begin scratching Max's ears.

She takes off her glasses. "Well, why don't you tell her how you feel and see if that prompts any change?"

"I did. Also, I'm not sure if she wants to apply to our center. She has a bright future, and by expressing my feelings, am I not asking her to give it all up and be with me?"

She puts her glasses back on. "You can't control everything. But you should not hold back what's in your heart. If you do, you will never find happiness. Also, Vince, all humans don't mature at the same rate. From what you have told me, Emika rushes into a decision and then thinks about it and often regrets it. She may be over thirty, but it is possible in her mind she is still young. She may want to move in, but she questions why she rushed in the first place."

Did I make a mistake falling for someone who is trapped in her twenties? Should I have delayed our date? Why did I have to rush into buying the house? I will never know what's in her mind unless she is free from Akane. But, would she even care for me if it weren't for the Akane in her?

Dr. Kauffman looks at her watch. "We're almost out of time. You have anything else?"

"A few days back, I had a dream of my high school graduation. In my dream, I met a gentleman wearing a fedora. I am not sure if I have met him in person or if he is imaginary." I get up and collect my overcoat.

Dr. Kauffman stands up as well. "Well, Vince, I am not an expert on dreams. But maybe your mind is exerting his significance in your life."

I sit in the living room one more time with Tabi's article. No opinions, just facts. Facts enough for the Department of Justice to move against Dick Graham. If the FBI comes knocking on my door, I need to protect Emika. The less she knows, the better. I feel the warmth of a sweet embrace and a kiss behind my ears. "How was your day?"

I pull her around onto my lap. "Boring. How was yours?" The meeting with the three morons and Elise's deceit all fly away from my mind.

She takes the printed article from my hands and reads it while sitting on my lap. Her eyes move from the paper to me. She touches my face. "See, there's nothing on Elise. You were worried for no reason."

"That's because I asked Tabi to keep Elise out. Deep down, I know I was with someone who smuggled intreton, killed more than two hundred souls, and laundered money."

Keeping her palms on my cheeks, she kisses me. "Vince, please don't be so hard on yourself." Then she looks down at my sleeves and scowls. "Whose hairs are these?"

I touch her face and smile. "Dr. Kauffman's dog."

"Who is Dr. Kauffman?" she asks, frowning.

"My psychiatrist, since Elise's departure."

She gets up from my lap and sits on the adjacent sofa. "What else are you concealing? Since when did Tabitha become Tabi? You two a thing now?" Her knees are shaking.

That reaction is not typical of a thirty-plus-year-old woman. So, is that Akane's possessiveness or Akane-free Emika? I don't want this battle to tear her down. How can I help?

"I provided Tabi with the evidence for her article, and in return, she found a publisher for my book. There is no one between you and me."

Her expression completely turns 180 degrees. She tucks her hair behind her ears, smiles. "So you have finally written something that ordinary people will understand."

I take both her hands in mine. "Yep, that's the plan. I don't think anyone other than Anna, Chris, and Ravi has read my papers."

"Oh, shut up! I read everything you wrote and looked through all your patents."

It's 6:00 a.m. on November 23, 2023. I am awake, facing Emika, and Hulk is resting his head on Emika's neck. I run my fingers through Emika's hair. She can barely open her eyes. "What?" I touch her lips, and she asks, "What?" I feel her beauty mark. She exhales, "OK, you have my attention."

I pull out a box from the bedside drawer. "Happy birthday!" Hulk crosses her to sniff the wrapping.

Emika rubs her eyes, yawns. "What is it?"

"Open it."

She cautiously unties the wrapping paper without making a single tear. Inside is a red box with the Cartier logo. Reading it, she covers her face with one hand.

I smile. "You have come this far. Why don't you open the box?"

Inside the box, she finds an 18-carat Rose Gold Cartier Tank Louis watch. She removes the watch from the pillow and remains silent. She touches the sapphire crystal and the blue sapphire crown, then bites her lips and looks at me.

I take the watch and fasten it on her left wrist, kissing the inside of her wrist after. "You need to wind it every two days."

I wind her watch, and she kisses me. "This is beautiful, Vince. Thank you. But what if it stops?"

"I can fix watches."

She tilts her head. "When did you learn that?"

"Headmaster taught me. It was a good distraction."

"Distraction from?" she asks, touching my hand.

I wink. "Using my superpowers?"

She rolls her eyes, then pulls Hulk and me to her. "Happy Thanksgiving, boys."

I am chopping onions, and Emika comes and kisses me. "I can help with the prepping."

"Not on your birthday."

She pours a Château Lafite and swirls the glass, then sits on a barstool across the aisle. "What are you making us, professor?"

I've moved from onion chopping to julienning bell peppers. "Two appetizers—one will be seafood ceviche, and the other Shishito peppers cooked with miso, garlic cloves, and sesame seeds. I will serve two main courses. First will be fried salmon topped with yellow corn, broccoli, cherry tomatoes, and green cilantro sauce. Second, sautéed mahi-mahi cooked with Panang sauce, and morel mushrooms served on a bed of jasmine rice."

"Nothing from Japan, professor?" She sips her wine and winks.

A smile forms at the corner of my lips. "I am extremely possessive about the Japanese dish. That's only for me."

She tucks her hair behind her ears and says, "I like to watch you cook."

I smile and stare at her wine-soaked lips. "What else you like?"

The three musketeers arrive as the clock strikes six. Ravi's Madelyn remains a well-kept secret. Anna goes to the refrigerator to put the dessert in. Then she pulls me to a corner. "Did you give her the gifts?"

"One, yes, the other has to wait till she moves in."

Anna narrows her eyebrows. "Give her time. But I want full credit if she likes it. If she doesn't, it's on you."

"You are the boss."

She rolls her eyes. "Yeah, right."

The four of us sit in the living room, and our chit-chat gets interrupted by the sight of a radiant Emika emerging from the bedroom in a burgundy dress. Everyone's eyes are on her.

"Drinks, anyone?" I ask as I walk into the bar and fetch everyone's choice of drinks. Anna follows Emika to tour the house.

Chris comes close. "Has she moved in?"

"Not entirely. Sometimes she stays in the townhome."

"That's strange. I am sorry, man," Ravis says, shaking his ice.

I look down at my whiskey. "If things go south, I won't be the same again."

Ravi and Chris touch my shoulder. Ravi presses hard. "We are with you."

"Thanks, guys."

Anna and Emika are back. Anna looks at me. "It's a beautiful home, Vince. Congratulations."

"It has potential," I say, looking at Emika.

Anna stretches her arms. "I'm famished."

Emika and I serve the appetizers, then the main course. After, Chris rubs his belly. "Never thought Thanksgiving without the turkey could be this good."

I look at Emika and gesture that there is something on her lip. She stands up leaves for the powder room. "Excuse me." Anna runs to the refrigerator. Chris and Ravi get ready with the lighter.

Emika comes back to see a candle-lit, vanilla-chocolate ice cream cake with several maraschino cherries. She covers her face and takes a deep breath. "Who got the cake?"

We all point at Anna, and she confesses. "Yeah, I got it, but the type of cake was Vincent's idea."

Emika picks up Hulk and cuts the cake while we sing, cutting it into equal sizes. Then she puts Hulk back on the floor before picking up one piece. "We will share this," she says and kisses me.

Anna touches Emika's shoulder. "What did Vince give you?"

Emika extends her wrist. "This."

As we eat our cake, I share tales of my meeting with Alyson, Matt, and Bob.

"Why were you meeting them?" Emika asks.

Anna leans forward. "Vince was pissed when he was not allowed to hire to tenure lines, so he went ballistic. He and Philip Nardin's lawyers will free us from all the red tape."

Emika stares at me. "But why did you not tell me anything?"

I glare at Anna, and she winces as she realizes that I'd kept these matters away from Emika. I turn to Emi. "I didn't want you to worry needlessly. Also, I don't want to relive pathetic experiences when I am with you."

"OK," Emika begrudgingly responds.

I wonder how she would have reacted in the absence of the three musketeers.

Anna stands and yawns. "Thanks for dinner, Vince." She then kisses Emika's forehead, "Happy birthday, and good luck." Chris and Ravi hug Emika on their way out.

Emika turns to me, wraps her arms around me. "Thank you for the whole day."

I touch her waist. "I have one more thing for you."

I pull out the drawer under the TV cabinet and take the violin out. "This is yours. It's up to you if you want to play it."

She opens the case, and her eyes well up as she looks at the violin. "This is a rare Lorenzo Carcassi violin."

I run my fingers across her hair. "I know."

"This is Akane's, right?" She touches my hand. "Are you sure you want me to have this?"

I smile. "Yes."

"And how long have you been carrying this?"

"Thirty-two years," I say, holding back my tears.

She squeezes my hand. "One would kill to have a friend like you. What if she comes back and wants it?"

I gaze into her eyes. "I don't think she would mind at all."

Bringing my hand to her lips, she kisses it. "Well, that's because you think I am her, silly. Vince, can I play it when I'm alone? Will that be OK?"

"Sure, whatever makes you happy."

"It was a beautiful day, Vince." She hugs me. "Thank you so much."

"You don't have to thank me. Just move in with me. It's not the same here without you."

CHAPTER 13

INVENTOR

If you add all the lies, you get the truth.

(Eight to six months before today)

I RUSH INTO MY SUITE, AND Linda points to my conference room. "They are already in, Dr. A." I straighten up and enter the conference room. There are just two people—Kenji and Dinesh, both in business casual. We shake hands, and then we all sit.

I look at my watch and turn to the lawyers. "Where is the other party?"

Kenji clears his throat. "It's less drama this way. They have already signed."

Dinesh hands me the stack of papers, with the pages where I need to sign are clearly tagged. I sign in every place and hand them back the documents. They verify and give me my copy.

Kenji turns to me. "We will take your leave. We have to help the DOJ."

I put my pen back in my pocket. "DOJ?"

"The article in *The Tribune* led the DOJ to open an investigation." Kenji clasps my shoulder. "Dick Graham is in custody. Philip wants us to assist the Attorney General's office."

I raise my eyebrows. "You said Philip wants? So, where is he?"

"We don't know. We only hear from Mr. Tealeaf."

I switch on my office TV. It's the same news everywhere. The DOJ has charged Dick Graham with multiple counts of treason, crimes against humanity, corruption, bribery, and campaign funds misappropriation. The list includes fabrication of evidence, corruption from Lombard and Alleren, smuggling of intreton that crashed Flight 0606, and killing over two hundred passengers—including Elise Graham. There is no mention of Elise as an accomplice. But how long before they figure that out and come knocking at my doors?

The former CEO of Alleren and the most recent three CEOs of Lombard are in custody too. All this evidence was buried in Elise's cloud drives? Who has them now? Let me text Tabi.

Me: Watching the news.
Tabi: They caught the bastard. It would have been impossible without you.
Me: Where are the drives?
Tabi: With Philips's lawyers. They will hand them over to the FBI and cut a deal. Once the FBI figures out Elise's part, they will come to you. You should then send a text to any one of the four lawyers.
Me: Thanks.
Tabi: Take care. I am with you.

Emika enters my office without knocking. Hulk, clad in a buffalo plaid sweater, has found a home in Emika's arms. She kisses his ears and looks at me. "Doesn't he look cute?"

"He does." I pick up Hulk and kiss Emika. "If you planned on coming, we could have come together."

She grabs my lapel. "I wanted to surprise you. Also, I bought matching buffalo-plaid clothes for you, Hulk, and me. We will take pictures for home and our office." The arrangement of words—Emika, Hulk, and home—give me a sense of bliss that I have never felt before but could get used to.

I pull her close. "Of course."

After a moment, she pulls away and sits on the sofa by the fireplace. "So, what's going on?"

"As of an hour ago, I now have more control over the $950 million endowments."

She opens two boxes of *onigiri*. "So, do you feel good that your center is rich and the rest of the uni is not?"

I take her hand and look into her eyes. "It would not have come to this if the admin had chosen academics over their cushy life. They grossly mishandled funds. Do you know it took me three months of convincing to hire you, and without this freedom, I wouldn't be able to hire new faculty?"

"I understand." She places her hand on top of mine. "I just don't want people to think you are arrogant and spoiled."

"What do you think?"

She ruffles my hair with her left hand. "That you are, silly."

The news segment suddenly moves into a conspiracy mode. Some idiot starts ranting that this is a massive conspiracy by Philip Nardin, who gains from Graham's predicament. Just then, I get a text from Tabi.

Tabi: Conspiracy theories may not bode well for Philip.

Emika points to my cell. "Who's texting?"

"Tabi is updating me on the progress of Dick Graham's case. And the possible involvement of Philip Nardin."

Her nostrils flare. "I can leave if I am intruding."

I touch Emika's hand and deeply breathe. "I missed the news of Dick's arrest. That's all. You have all my attention."

She takes my phone and hers and puts them on my desk. "It's Emika time now."

We eat delicious *onigiri*. She locks the office door and licks a solitary piece of rice off my lips. Then she digs out a rose gold frame that she bought to keep the photos of our little family.

She touches my hand, smiles. "*Watashi no chiisana Kazuko.*"

At home, Emika takes several selfies of the three of us in buffalo plaid, and we print all of them. Every picture is on her cellphone. She will decide which ones go to her office, my office, and home.

In the background, the news is on. The conspiracy surrounding Philip has gained traction over the last twelve hours. Having exclusive rights to intreton did not help Philip make any friends on Capitol Hill. Everyone wants to profit from weaponizing it. The FBI has a search warrant for Philip's property. Why wouldn't Philip's lawyers stop the AG from doing that? Aren't they helping the AG? Emika gets us two cups of tea and sits next to me. She knows that Philip and I became close. "Are you OK?" she asks, pulling my sleeve.

"Yes." I put the teacup on the coffee table and pull Emika closer. I massage her neck and shoulder. Then I stop, turning back to the TV.

"Do it again."

I continue massaging until the deputy director of the FBI comes on TV. "We found no trace of intreton. We could not even locate the house." So, Philip just wanted to play with the politicians and the AG. Well done. But how is he doing all this from space?

Emika turns to me. "How could you locate his house?"

Let's play along. "I was invited."

"What?"

I lend my wrist to support her head. She shuts her eyes, and I explain. "Philip's mansion can disappear underneath the ground. He designed this with the anticipation that someone might try to seize his property."

She waves her hand at the TV. "He anticipated this?"

"According to Philip, the future has already happened, and he experiences it before most," I say as I massage her temples.

"What? That makes no sense."

I don't want to talk about the complexities of time. I bring her closer. "Have I ever talked about your beauty?"

"Yes. But I'd like a repeat."

I tuck her hair behind her ears. "Then, let's."

Text from Tabi: FBI has the drives.

I am in the office with Hulk while Emika is working in the AI lab. I have kept her at bay for her own protection. I text Jerry, Kenji, Alberto, and Dinesh. Kenji responds, "We cut a deal with the FBI director." Will the FBI director get to the agents before the agents get to me?

My phone rings. Linda is puffing on the other side. "Dr. A. The FBI is here. Three agents."

My hands are shaking. I hold my trembling left wrist with my right hand and take a deep breath. "Relax, Linda. Send them in."

Three gentlemen clad in black polyester suits enter. Hulk howls, and they smile at him. Then they introduce themselves: Agent Manning, Johnson, and Davidson.

"Take a seat, gentlemen. Can I offer you some coffee?"

Manning waves his hand. "No, we're fine." Johnson frowns at Manning's choice after glancing at my espresso machine. The agents occupy the chairs across from my desk.

Davidson takes out a notebook and a BIC ballpoint pen. "We have a few questions for you."

"Please, intrigue me."

He flips to an empty page. "How do you know Elise Graham?"

"She was my live-in partner," I answer, folding my sleeves.

Manning takes over. "Did you know Dick Graham?"

"Anecdotally, before Elise's funeral. We met once or twice after."

"What do you know of him?" Davidson asks as he leans forward.

"Just another run-of-the-mill corrupt politician."

Johnson gets his turn. "What do you know about the father-daughter relationship?"

I shrug, but deep down, my heart is beating like a drum. "Elise said she was estranged from her family. I believed her."

Agent Manning's phone rings. "I need to take this," he says, going to a corner. I can hear him utter, "Right away, sir. Absolutely, sir." Then he comes back to my desk. "We are leaving. By the way, Dr. Abajian, do you happen to know anything about the call I just took?"

I lean back as far as I can. "It's the future, Agent Manning."

"What do you mean?" He squints at me.

"It's a state that happened before you entered my office. You just had to experience it later. Good day, gentlemen. It's been a pleasure."

Two hours have passed since the agents left. I have been making changes to the works of Anna, Chris, Emika, and Ravi. Emika's writing results have improved—I taught her well. I can feel a smile develop at the corner of my lips. A smile for like nights I spent teaching her and…

A shrilling scream of "What!" from outside my office echoes through the walls and door. I had no clue Emika could scream like this. She enters my room without knocking, lunch in one hand, the other on her waist. Her face is red. "You did not tell me that the FBI was here. What the hell?" The shrillness of her voice resonates with all the metallic objects in my office. She bangs the lunch on my desk. "People share more with their pets."

These temper tantrums must be hurting her. I get up and hug her. "I would have told you when we met for lunch. I am working on our manuscript."

She calms her breathing, and we sit by the fireplace. Her hair covers her right eye, and I tuck it behind her ear. "What was it about?" she asks, and she places the lunch box on the coffee table.

I take her left hand and wind her watch. She resists smiling but then gives in. "I could tell you everything—but then you would not have deniability. And even I don't know what's going on. It's for your good that I am keeping you in the dark. When all of this is over, I will tell you everything. I promise." I kiss her hand.

She looks at me. "What if we are over before that, Vince?"

"I am begging for your patience."

Since December, Emika has been increasingly irritated and sickened by the continuous flow of news concerning the case of Dick Graham. She is spending more and more hours in her townhome. If that helps her cope better, so be it. My assurance that everything will be fine is not reaching her. Yes, I have kept her in the dark. What if the FBI questions her? If she knows nothing, she doesn't have to lie. After handing over the drives to the FBI, the case has become more intense. I understand that the FBI is not too pleased with my immunity, bargained for by the four lawyers. The exemption does not extend to my Emika.

I want this case to be over so that I don't have to conceal anything from her. We are now sitting at the opposite ends of the same sofa. Just a month back, we were on the same cushion. The news is like white noise as I rest my head on my palm. A month back, she would have come and massaged my head, offered me green tea, and lectured me about cutting down coffee. Now that's all gone. She is currently sitting at the corner, glued to her cellphone. It doesn't even seem like we are in the same reality. Why can't I get back to my simple struggles—like the one where I try to overcome the impediment to a two-way transfer of consciousness between humans and machines?

In addition to the Flight 0606 conspiracy, Dick Graham and Lombard face crimes against humanity for the company's 2006 bombing of innocent civilians. The stocks of Lombard have plummeted. Their CEO pleads the Fifth in all proceedings. The evidence against Graham is too incriminating to find refuge in the Fifth. In a turn of events, Graham stated that Ronald Burns, the POTUS, knew everything about Flight 0606. The FBI is investigating into which politicians bought Lombard stocks right before the 2006 bombing. Protesters are burning effigies of democrat POTUS, GOP Graham, and Philip Nardin.

A set of bright lights pierces through the glass and into our living room. I walk close to the glass wall, and Emika follows. The lights turn off, revealing their source—the headlights of a Rolls Royce Phantom. The driver sees me. I can only see his hat. Then he drives away, leaving nothing but a speck of dust. Emika touches my shoulder. "Are you safe?"

She still cares? I bring her close. "I am, and I won't let anything happen to you." My phone beeps. It's a text from Tabi.

Tabi: If proven guilty, he will only get twenty years.

Me: That's not nearly enough.

Tabi: He might get a presidential pardon. And then all this effort will go to waste.

Emika turns to me. "Everything OK, Vince?"

I take her hand. "Yes, it's just Tabi talking about the case."

She removes her hand, and her eyes bulge out. "What the fuck?" she shrieks. "Why are you always texting her?"

Where has my sweet Emika gone? She was right here. I tilt my head. "You wanna see the texts?"

"I don't wanna be the third wheel between you and her. Strange that you can talk to Tabi about the case but not me. I'm going upstairs. Find yourself a different guestroom."

It's getting impossible to keep it cool, and I am beginning to sense our end is near. I quickly intercept her. "She is the journalist who investigated the case. She knows about the case more than I do. Why can't you get it?"

She walks around me. "Yes, Vince, I am the one who doesn't get you. Bring her in this house. I will leave you two."

What can I do to give her some peace? Would my absence help her? I wish I could go back in time. And I wish I could talk to Philip. Would it help if she'd never asked me out? Would it help if she'd never met me? Or if Akane had never entered her? *What have you done, Akane? Can't you leave her? Couldn't you just come back whole?*

The book is now at number two on the NY Times bestseller list. There are details in the book that I don't have in my notes. How is this even possible? I have detailed accounts of everything from Victor and Amara's places to Victor's clothes on his exhibition day. I also have a thorough description of the color of the checkbook and the brand of fountain pen Olivier used to buy the painting, the exact license plates of the cars involved in the accident between Victor and Olivier, the color of the walls and bedsheets in Amara's hospital room when Philip found her.

But the book's ranking is not the highlight of the day. Today, January 2, 2024, I am taking my Emika to a concert. She left our home on December 23 for her townhome, and we spent Christmas and New Year's apart. Anna, Chris, and Ravi think that Emika still lives here. So, they never asked me to join them in their own celebrations. I did not want to dull their celebrations with my depressing story. Anna will get mad when she finds out. But they all need a break from me.

I just hope this concert and the following dinner might turn things around with Emika. Now, I am waiting for her outside her townhome. Before I can knock, she opens the door, wearing the same one-shoulder dress she wore for her birthday and Thanksgiving.

I take her hand. "You look lovely."

She runs her hands across my shoulders and chest. "Nice tux." Then she kisses me, and I can smell her perfume. I touch her waist, then her neck, hoping to put our fight behind us, hoping to take her home tonight. We get into my car.

"What's the program?" she asks, turning to me.

I start the car. "Shostakovich no. 1 and Dvořák's Concerto in B-minor op. 104."

She lifts her eyebrows. "That's heavy. Thanks for taking me."

"Who else would I take?" I say, reaching over to touch her hand.

"Well, you are a famous author, a millionaire, and a genius. You can get any date. Wasn't Tabi available?"

I look at her and squint. "Seriously?"

"I'm sorry." She shakes her head. "How is Hulk?"

"Like his daddy—misses you."

We have box seats with no co-occupants. Emika notices and turns to me. "Why isn't anyone coming to our box?"

"I booked the whole box for us." I lean over to kiss her behind her ears.

She smiles. "I didn't know they allowed that."

"It is a capitalist society, after all."

We silence our phones, and the show starts. Twenty minutes into Shostakovich, my phone vibrates. I kiss Emika on the cheek as I leave the box seat. "Excuse me."

As I step outside the box, I see people born to wealth drinking wine and talking about stock prices. These are the same ones who rebuffed me when orphanhood was my sole identity but then welcomed me with open arms after my success. Yet, they are deeply suspicious of my tan skin and my last name. They all pretend to like music and feign an interest in art. Yet, they can't tell Chopin from Joplin or Picasso from Matisse. I have one expression for them: *fuck you. I never gave a fuck about fitting into your pretentious world of utter garbage.*

"You know Shostakovich performed in our house back in 1978," says one pretentious bald chap.

A woman next to him gets all excited. "Oh, tell me all about it, Richard."

That's a remarkable feat for everyone, given that Shostakovich died in 1975 and came to the US just three times—in 1949, 1959, and 1973. Fucking liars and morons.

I look at the cellphone alerts. Lombard has agreed to plead guilty to all charges of smuggling, war crimes, and bribery and pay over $80 billion in compensation and closing the company. However, the company does not have $80 billion in cash, so it will be dissolved as part of the settlement. Its assets will be used to create a new public benefit company controlled by a trust or similar entity designed to benefit passengers of Flight 0606 and victims of drone strikes. Much to the dismay of the politicians, Nardin industries and its four lawyers will manage the trust. How is Philip orchestrating this from outer space? Did he plan all this, knowing this would happen? Can he truly see the future through the core?

I collect two glasses of pinot noir and hand one to Emika upon reentering our box. Shostakovich is done. Now there's a change and a break. Emika takes a sip. "Took you long enough to get this wine. Were you making it?"

I touch her hand. "I was just—"

"Don't bother," she says, swatting my hand away.

Now Dvořák. Fifteen minutes into the concert, my phone vibrates again. Emika shakes her head and her nostrils flare up. I collect our glasses and leave the box. It's a text from Tabi.

Tabi: Ronald Burns resigned, and Michael Williams will be the next POTUS

Me: Resigning eleven months before the election?

Tabi: It's a tactic. Michael Williams might pardon both Burns and Graham. Graham deserves to die.

Me: I know. But what can we do?

I go back to the box again, with two new glasses of Moscato. I touch Emika's hand. She removes it. We stand up, and we applaud the whole team for their marvelous interpretation of Dvořák and Shostakovich. Emika looked at me. "What are you clapping for? You missed the whole show."

I won't argue. I try to hold her hand as we sift through the packed crowd, all seemingly in haste to exit. She slaps my hand and looks at me, with eyes all read, her nostrils all flared. "Don't you dare?"

I will give her some time to cool. A nice dinner and wine may do the trick. We reach the parking deck, and we enter my car.

"I have booked us a table at Chez Giraud, but we can go to Sichuan Palace or House of Bamboo if you prefer?"

"I'm not hungry."

Maybe I can cook for her? She loved the sea bass at Chez Giraud. Perhaps I will make that for her. Yes, that could turn things around. I smile as I turn the ignition of my car. "Hey, BMW, take us home."

"Vince, drop me at the townhome." Emika turns away from me. "I don't want to be near you."

"What's wrong?" I ask, reaching for her hand.

"Don't." She slaps my hand away, lifts her index finger. "You are too invested in the investigation. And you don't share anything with me—but you do with Tabi, those lawyers, and even Philip's butler. On my birthday, it was your three subordinates who brought up the topic of restructuring your center. I fit nowhere in your life. No, sorry, I do. I am simply a mannequin that looks like a girl you fancied as a child."

She should have watched her tongue before uttering the last part. Akane is off-limits. Yet, I am driving slowly to delay her departure. "That's not true. I have shared a lot about my life. But just I can't share about this case, Emi. Not now, at least. It's for your good."

She clenches her jaw. "I don't need you to tell me what's good for me. You don't share because you see me as unfit to be your partner. That's why you did not share details of Elise's betrayal."

I shake my head. "You told me to get Elise out of my head, or you would leave me."

"That's your excuse? Well done, professor." She claps. "Your inconsideration extends beyond me. You left the concert twice. To check texts from your new beloved, Tabi, right?"

"Tabi is just a busy journalist, and we only text about this case—that's all. Follow the news. The president resigned, which means Dick Graham may receive clemency from the VP."

She turns to me as she bangs on the dashboard. "I. Don't. Fucking. Care. You ignored the tempo. The maestro worked so hard with how he communicated with the cellist. I wanted to enjoy that moment with you. I didn't expect this from you, Vince. This is something Jason would do."

"So I am an illiterate fool now?"

Her veins are visible on her forehead. "He was uncouth but not illiterate."

"Wow! A degree in student issues. Great rigor. Let's create a master's degree in how to hand tissues to students. You can master quantum mechanics through three courses, but let's make a four-year program and a two-year master's degree with this shit. Hulk's puppy kindergarten had more academic rigor."

"Your elitism has made you apathetic," she says, her face turning red.

I am running out of patience. "Apathy toward who?"

"Everyone perceives you as apathetic. Most people in the uni—the admin, the diversity office, everyone—thinks you are one apathetic, rich, spoiled brat."

"Rich? Brat?" I grit my teeth. "I came from nothing. I don't care what those fuckers think. Only what you think and what my closest colleagues think."

"I will side with them. And by closest, you mean the sycophants like Anna, Chris, and Ravi?"

I did not know she harbored such disrespect for them. I need to calm down. I take a deep breath. "Those sycophants hired you."

"I wish they hadn't. I wish I'd never known you—an elitist egomaniac."

"So now you are siding with those who were opposed to you making $155,000 as a postdoc."

She shakes her head. "It's a lot less than the $650,000 you make or the $300,000 your minions make."

"If you join us as a research scientist or a professor, you will do the same, Emi."

"I would rather be unemployed than work with you," she says, banging on the dashboard again.

I touch her hand. "Can we please go home, Emi, and discuss this?"

"That is not my home." She crosses her arms. "Bring your Tabi and start a life with her. And while you're at it, bring all your cronies to cheer both of you. We are done, Vincent."

I pull over. Then I turn to her, lowering my brows and clenching my jaw. "Done? Is that it? Leaving me at first sight of trouble? Yes, it was wrong of me to leave the concert." I point my finger at her. "But don't ever blame me for seeing someone else. I did not." I grip the steering wheel hard. "Are you in a rush to get to your townhome? Let's rush."

I start the car and reach 60 mph in under three seconds. She clutches the door handle and shouts. "Vince, slow down."

"Don't you wanna get there quickly?"

In a few minutes, I screech to a stop in front of her townhome. She gets out. "Just go back to your life of misery, memories of Akane, racing, the dojo, Elise, Dick Graham, Tabitha, and Philip. Keep ignoring what's important. You're not capable of being happy."

I grip the wheel more tightly, my knuckles turning white, and I shut my eyes. "Goodnight, Emi."

She slams my car door shut.

I wait in the driveway until she turns on her lights. Then I form a fist, cracking my fingers. I can feel all the blood rushing into my head as I punch my steering wheel. "Fuck!"

Hulk comes running with his lambchop and whimpers upon seeing me alone. I pick him up. "Am I not enough for you, bug?" He licks away my tears. Then I look outside and see a Rolls Royce Phantom. In it is sitting the man wearing a fedora. He nods and drives away. Who is it? What does he want?

How is missing a few minutes of a concert tantamount to not realizing what's important to me? Doesn't she know that I love her? Have I lost her? The woman I encountered today, is she the real Emika, without the trace of Akane? How can my Akane hurt me like this? I wish I could find a way to free Emika from Akane. But then Emika might not remember me anymore. At least I would recall my sweet Akane the way I wanted to, and Emika could be free to choose a life with or without me. Do I really want that?

I pour some 21-year-old Balvenie in a glass. I need ice. As I walk to the fridge, I notice that the post-it to the left door missing. Where is it? My hands are shaking—I can't lose it. I hunker down and find it under the refrigerator. The glue of the post has dried up. I take clear tape and paste it to the door, then apply it to the other post-it, just in case. I can't let them fall off. It's all I have of us. And one picture of us in buffalo plaid.

I switch on the burner and place today's tickets on them. Burn, you pieces of shit, as I watch the promise of hope turn to ashes. Why stop at the stubs? Take my hand, too. I feel nothing as the fire touches my skin. All I feel is a tickle in my fingertips—the sparks are back. Why do they only appear when I feel as if I'm losing Akane and Emika? Can't I get them at will? What will happen if I don't control them? Let's see what they can do. They are growing longer—ten feet, fifteen feet. Now they reach outside the wall, penetrating through the glass. What is this? Hulk runs farther away in the house and barks from a distance. I fold my palms, and the sparks in each palm are reduced to the size of a tennis ball. I push the lights together. First, they repel, then they join into the shape of two funnels combined by one neck. It looks a lot like turbulence. I insert my index finger into a funnel, and it goes through fine. Can I create turbulence? Can I bring back Akane? But what would happen to Emika, then? Can I separate Emika from Akane? The light is dimming, and then it's gone. Hulk comes running back. I need to know what these sparks can do, but I can't get them back.

I walk to my closet and open my cufflink drawer. There it is, inside the Tiffany blue box—the ring Anna helped me pick. She'd asked if I were sure. Maybe Emika was not the only one who'd rushed. I'd wanted to ask Emika if she wanted a future with me. What was it that she'd said? *A work in progress with beautiful potential.* Lies, all fucking lies. Just like my entire life. I shut the drawer.

I am staring at the metronome, hoping it will slow my racing mind.

"Would it be cruel to admit that I feel sadder at Emika leaving the house than when Elise died? Although life with Elise had less drama!"

Dr. Kauffman takes off her glasses. "It's not. But why do you think you feel sadder about Emika?"

"Well, Elise and I knew each other for a long time. I loved her. But we were not deeply in love with each other. When I see Emika, I see a life that I want to live. When I see her, I forget all my tribulations and accomplishments and immerse myself in her."

"Did you tell her this?" She puts her glasses back on and is ready with the notebook.

"I will if she comes back. Her reaction was rather absurd on January 2. The Emika I've seen since December and the Emika I saw on August 3 are so different."

"Humans are absurd, and that's what makes them beautiful. Now, if you want your Emika to respond from a select set of parameters, you can build one in your lab." She tilts her head and squints. "Will that make you happy?"

"So, you think I should go to her townhome and tell her what I told you," I ask, rubbing my hands together slowly.

"You should do what your heart tells you. But let me caution you—despite all your efforts, things may go bad. Remember, it's not your fault if they do."

I get up for my coat and then turn back. "What do you mean?"

Dr. Kauffman presses hep lips together and to hide her exasperation. "Her walking out on you may mean that she is not ready for the challenge of a serious commitment. She was too quick to move from a different relationship to one with you and then decided to buy a house together." Dr. Kauffman pauses and leans toward me. "I am risking repeating myself, Vince, but people mature differently. She may be far younger in her heart than her age suggests. Or something may have stunted her maturity."

"What do you suggest I do?" I ask as I wrap my scarf around my neck.

She smiles. "Give her time—months, years. Don't blame yourself if things go wrong."

I have accepted the deafening silence of orphanhood as a symphony. But not the silence Emika left behind—this is deafening. It's January 7, 2024.

A crisp morning with a gentle cold breeze. The sun bestows all its light on the snowcapped mountains. I am on my way to Emika's townhome with Hulk to ask her to come with me. After searching through five florists, I found her favorite blue and purple bellflowers.

As I enter her driveway, a Dodge Charger pulls in the right in front of her door. A cold breeze follows, the trees bend, and the trash box flies away. A beefy blond with crew-cut hair gets out. He is about thirty years old and wearing a bomber jacket, blue jeans, and work boots. Then he knocks on her door while holding a bouquet of red roses in one hand and a McDonald's takeout box in the other. Emika opens the door. She collects the flowers, wraps her arm around him, and kisses him. Together, they go in and close the door.

My heart begins to beat like a drum. And there she is—already on to the next guy. I was just a passing thought for her. So, this is the real Emika, free from Akane? Or is this the result of her constant battle? I don't give a fuck. I can't waste my time anymore. Instead, I should have listened to Mr. Kruger and elected logic over emotion. Which means I have no time to waste on therapy either. Sayonara, Dr. Kauffman. I wish I could think like a machine. I wish I were built in a lab.

Wait just a second—that is it. This is the key to my invention. At least something good is going to come from this pathetic sham of a relationship. Thank you, Emika, for whipping Vincent Abajian back to life. Thank you for breaking me. Now I get to rebuild.

"Good evening, Professor Abajian. It's been a while. I'm Athena."

"I know. I built you. Play my Pink Floyd playlist on a continuous loop, starting with 'Hey You.' Blast the speakers, then initiate a sequence for human mapping brains to the most advanced robots we have from Nardin robotics."

Hulk finds the warmest corner and starts to nap.

"What's on your mind, professor? You can tell me. I'm you, after all—a more efficient you."

"Yeah, don't flatter yourself. I want to see if we can create a mapping technology for a two-way consciousness transfer between humans and machines. Also, I want a detailed 3D mapping, which will show the minimum number of machine receptors we need to map all the neurons in the human brain. Can you make a 3D model of the map for every version of robots we've got from Nardin robotics? Then show me the best model in a hologram." Let's put our quantum computing infrastructure to use.

Athena announces. "Of course, professor, I can do that. While at it, I can also whoop your ass in a game of chess."

"Hey. Did Anna make any changes to your personality?"

"You bet she did. She made me sassier like her. She said that Anna is an improved Vincent."

I choose to ignore that. "Athena, can you tell me how many times Emika Amari came to this lab between January 3 and today?"

"Dr. Amari has not been here since December 20."

What was she doing all that time while staying away from work? I smirk. Probably that guy in the Dodge, perhaps even while being with me. Charming, isn't it? "What about Dr. Calimaris, Dr. Washington, and Dr. Bose?"

"They were here yesterday for the restore point creation patent."

"Perfect."

"Your 3D model is ready, Dr. Abajian."

An interactive hologram 3D model surfaces on the screen. I put on my wireless sensory gloves and pull the hologram out, then start rotating it. "How many simulations did you run?"

"One hundred thousand, as per parameters you set."

This model is useless. The mapping helps only the human brain capable of simple thoughts—politicians or worthless celebrities or Emika's dates, except for one. What if a concert pianist, a composer, or a scientist wanted to transfer their consciousness? Transistors made from silicon and germanium can't carry enough charge to be compatible with neurons. The answer must be somewhere else. Think, Vince, think. What was it that Philip said about Edward's prosthetic legs? They have a laser tech that can cut intreton-c the diameter of three nanometers. Then each strand will be capable of carrying a charge to make a perfect connection with neurons. They have not commercialized it. It's time to change that. The playlist song changes to "Brain Damage."

I can feel my pulse accelerate. "Fetch the file that has a scan of my brain. Then run another set of simulations. First, replace the composition of transistors from silicon and germanium with a theoretical 3-nanometer diameter of intreton-c. Then create a 3D mapping with my brain and run 100,000 simulations. Show me the result in a hologram." The song changes to "Comfortably Numb."

This might be it. I pull out my cellphone, scroll down to my school group, and type, "I don't say this enough, guys. But I love you, all three."

Sasha: Are you OK, bud? Just bought your book.
Me: Yep. Never felt better.
Krista: Oh boy! What is it now?
Me: Seriously, I'm fine. I'm about to invent something that will be a significant leap toward the singularity. I couldn't have done anything without you three taking care of me.
Fred: Stop thanking us and plan on meeting us. It's been too long. Is it something I said, or we did that you don't want to meet us?
Me: No, bud. You guys are perfect. I never felt I was an orphan when you guys were around. Hey, do you believe Akane would be proud of me?
Sasha: She would be regardless of our feat today.
Krista: We all hoped that she be one of the rare ones who come back from the turbulence, just to be with you.
Me: That's OK. I have learned to be comfortable with the way things are.

The last guitar verse of "Comfortably Numb" begins as I shut my eyes. A smiling image of Emika appears, but then she climbs into a grotesque Dodge Charger, winks at me, and waves her arms. "This is my new beautiful potential, Vince." I open my eyes. That cannot be Akane.

"Your 3D model is ready, Dr. Abajian."

I pick up the new hologram—a mapping between a synthetic receptor to my brain. Taking out my 50,000 pressure-sensitive digital pen, I touch portions of my brain's 3D model. It lights up, and so does the receptor.

The model can replicate feelings of pain, sight, sound, touch, and euphoria connected to ambient music.

"Athena, print out a 3D model and store this hologram in a folder. Name the folder "Vincent is back." The song changes to "Coming Back to Life." The patent from this model alone could create an industry cluster to rival Silicon Valley. Let's find the three musketeers. I want them as co-inventors. I pull out my phone again.

> Me: Can you guys come to the lab right now?
> Ravi: I can.
> Chris: Me too. I'm bored.
> Anna: Did you burn the lab?
> Me: No. But we can set the world on fire. I just invented something.
> Anna: Be right there.
> Chris: Emika is not in this group. Shouldn't we include her?
> Me: Nope. She's preoccupied at the moment.

(Third Semester at MIT)

Dr. Bovet squinted at me and smirked. "What are you willing to lose to invent that?"

I shut my eyes, and I smiled. "I have already lost everything, professor."

(Back to the present)

I sit on the floor. This is a defining moment for most scientists. Yet, I don't even feel a smidgen of joy. I finally crossed over the inventor's block, but I can't get the image of Emika with that guy out of my mind. C'mon, Vince, you have created an industry. Not too long ago, you were just an orphan being bullied. Look at you. I stare at my hands as tears start dripping on them. Everyone cannot have everything, Vince. And you have everything else. Hulk comes running and stands on his hind legs to lick away my tears.

New car: Porsche Taycan, turbo. I have my BMW decommissioned until Emika is out of my mind. This one corresponds to about 750 brake horsepower. I got it in blue with a beige interior. I can move on quickly, too—zero to sixty in under two and a half seconds.

I am working on two manuscripts simultaneously. Three knocks on the door, and she emerges even before I could say come in. Beautiful as ever, my Emika. Sorry, just Emika. She is clad in a navy turtleneck, Burberry scarf, and a long skirt with suede boots. After she hangs up her parka, she picks up Hulk and sits in front of me. She extends her hands toward mine, but my hands remain on the keyboard.

Pulling back, she covers her lips and nose. "I am so sorry for all the terrible things I said. I should not have brought Akane into it."

I tilt my head but keep my eyes on the screen. "You think?"

"Can you forgive me?"

"There is nothing to forgive. I am fine. And so are you."

She notices the duffel bag next to my desk. "Are my clothes in that?"

Yes, it is another reaffirmation that we are over. "As you wanted. It also has the Cartier box and the picture of you, me, and Hulk in buffalo plaid."

She tucks a few strands of hair behind her ear and looks at me. "You don't want the picture anymore?"

"I have no use for it. And you don't either, other than the frame."

She leans toward me. "Why?"

What the fuck is going on here? Just because she doesn't know what I know, everything has to be acceptable? "You moved on, that's why."

Bending down, she unzips the bag and takes out the picture. Her lips begin to tremble. I don't know why she is crying. I hand her my pocket square. She takes it and dabs her eyes. "You think I moved on?"

"I know you did."

"What are you not telling me, Vince?" she asks, extending her hand across the desk again.

"There is nothing *new* to tell."

She takes my pocket square away from her face. "Vince, I have been interviewed by the Alan Turing Institute. They might call you for a reference."

I look up, smile at my fate. "That's strange. You have me as a reference, but didn't you say you would rather be unemployed than work with me?"

"Vince. I don't know what came over me. You took me to such a lovely concert. I have been very confused the last few days."

"I know you are confused." I shake my head. "But you are not sorry. Turing will call me, just because you worked with me. Of course, I will give you a stellar recommendation. With that, my utility in your life will diminish."

Her eyes well up, her lips tremble. "You will just let me go?"

"Who the fuck am I to stop you? You moved on. You said we were done."

She remains silent and covers her face with my pocket square again.

"Make sure you give a status update to Anna, Chris, and Ravi about your papers and patents before you leave. Don't treat them like trash, like you did with me. They are not sycophants."

"How can I make it up to you, Vince?" she asks, lifting her tear-stained face.

I click my tongue. "How long have you been contemplating this move?"

Not meeting my gaze, she says, "The day after the concert."

"Lovely!" I roll my eyes.

She changes the topic. "You bought a new car."

"Correct."

"Do you want to tell me about it?"

"No."

"Can I stay here for a minute?" She wipes her tears. "I don't want Linda to see me like this."

"Sure."

Then she steps away and sits by the fireplace, still holding Hulk. I see her shoulders shaking. I don't want her to go. If I could, I would hug her and take her home forever. What's stopping me? She's moved on. Plus, Emika, in her most genuine sense, never cared for me.

I leave my chair and sit next to her. Bringing her hand to my lips, I kiss her fingers. Then I look into her brown eyes, behind her wet eyelashes. I kiss her forehead. "You will move on and do great things. And, eventually, I—our life—will become a memory, will fade and wither away like autumn leaves."

It breaks my heart to see Emika's sorrow. But if she wants to move on, that's the way it must be. She takes some deep breaths, then turns to me and feigns a smile. "Will you be OK?"

I can't be, but I should not stop her. Taking a long look at her, I say, "That's the thing, Emi. I am OK—even when I am not."

She collects her bag and leaves.

(November 13, 1991)

I was reading *The Tale of Two Cities* in my dorm room. A robin was chirping from a branch outside my window. Fred tapped on my shoulder. "She is here, Vince. Talk to her."

I shook my head. "I don't wanna talk to her ever."

Sasha touched my cheek. "She is crying, Vince, please. Do you really want that before she leaves?" The robin flew away.

I turned my head and saw Akane standing next to Krista. As I walked toward her, Fred, Krista, and Sasha left the room. Akane's eyes were wet. She grabbed my sleeve and pulled. "Why aren't you talking to me?"

"Every year, you're gone for Christmas. And now you'll be gone in November, too."

"Just two days, Vince." She touched my hair. "And I'll be back."

"This year, we won't even enjoy the first snow. All because of a stupid clock."

"Maybe it won't snow until I come back?" She lifted my hand and wiped her tears with my cuff.

"What if it does? I dreamt you wouldn't come back."

Touching her scarf on my neck, she said, "You have my scarf. I'll leave my violin and my photo frame. You know I never go anywhere without them. I'll come back for them." She lifted her index finger. "So, wait for me."

I lowered my head, looked at the floor. "All I do is wait. I don't like it without you."

She wiped my tears. "I know, silly."

(Back to the present)

If I'd thrown a tantrum that day or gotten myself hurt, Akane would have probably stayed. And, Emika would have never entered my life.

I get a new alert on my phone. Roland Burns will receive a pardon from current President Michael Williams. There are riots are all over DC and New York.

Today is January 15—a year since Elise left us. Hulk and I are standing before her headstone. I place twelve long-stemmed roses by the stone. A rose for each month she's been gone. It's foggy, and it's cold. Hulk sniffs the headstone, whimpers, and lies beside it.

"Hi Elise, I forgive you for lying. I asked Tabi to keep you out of her article. I want to remember you as the brilliant scientist you were and someone I shared my life with. I loved the life we had. It was peaceful." I sigh. "Also, I met a woman. She became the love of my life. But she has moved on and is in a rush to leave me, just like Akane and you. You told me that I am not an unwanted orphan. But then why do people keep leaving me?"

A gush of wind comes from nowhere. I hold on to Hulk's leash and watch helplessly the roses fly away from Elise's headstone. As the wind dies down, I notice a Rolls Royce Phantom about 100 feet from my car—the same one that's been keeping tabs on me.

Dick Graham was assassinated last night—precisely a year after Elise's death. He was transported from Loretto, Pennsylvania, to the Metropolitan correctional facility in New York on a private jet, a Gulfstream-400. The plane exploded in midair. FBI found explosives in the plane and also concluded that an M2 Browning brought the plane down. The bullets hit the fuel tank, which activated the explosives in the plane. The feds found the M2 Browning half a mile from the wreckage. Strangely, the feds did not find any other bodies besides Graham's.

The FBI did not even find any paperwork authorizing Graham's transfer from one prison to the other. The blame quickly went to disenfranchised groups in the Middle East. POTUS called it an act of terrorism that took one of our heroes. So, Dick Graham was found guilty of treason but is now a hero because a rogue terrorist brings down a plane that he was on? Mossad and General Intelligence Directorate are now cooperating with the CIA.

I call Tabi.

"Hi, Vincent."

"Where are you?"

"I'm traveling—Philly and New York. I'll be back in a couple of weeks."

"How do you feel about the news?"

"I'm ecstatic. The SOB is dead. Would it be OK if we catch up sometime? Like dinner?"

"Why not? Call me when you get back."

CHAPTER 14

POST-IT

Time is the longest distance between two places.
—Tennessee Williams

(Six months before today)

IT'S FEBRUARY. HALF A MILLION copies of my book have been sold. Anna, Chris, and Ravi have asked me for a soiree to celebrate this feat and our new invention. The new invention also prompted the three musketeers to buy new cars. I am doing this soiree only to see Emika one last time before she leaves me for good.

I've ordered a fully catered service from Sichuan Palace. The wine and champagne are from my personal collection. Anna, Chris, and Ravi are all coming, though there is no word from Emika. But Ravi is finally bringing Madelyn. And Tabi is still traveling. I've curated a playlist from the works of Chopin, Debussy, Liszt, Saint-Saëns, Satie, and Kreisler.

I am wearing my Zegna charcoal plaid suit. Let's test the theory that this will melt her heart. Anna is the first to arrive in her new Lucid-air. She's brought a chocolate pie and puts it in the fridge. "Hey Vince, Emika didn't remove the post-its yet? Do you still need them?"

I shake my head. "She left me."

Anna storms toward me and pulls my lapel. "What? And you never bothered to tell me?"

I signal Lauren, the head caterer, to offer Anna champagne. She takes a sip while I force a broken smile. "What's to tell? This is normal. The good thing was an aberration. Plus, I did not want to dull the joy of our invention."

Ravi pulls up in his new Mercedes-EQC, and a brunette emerges from the car with him. As he comes into the house, Ravi introduces the lady to me. "This is Madelyn."

She extends her hand. "Please call me Maddy. Finally, I get to meet you. Your house is more beautiful than I had imagined."

"Thanks, Maddy. Make yourself at home. I have a decent selection of drinks."

Chris is next to the dock. His chariot, a new Jaguar i-pace. Anna takes Chris and Ravi to a corner and murmurs to them while glancing at me. Before Madelyn goes over to join them, I tap her shoulder. "Hey, can you tell them not to feel sorry for me?"

She tilts her head. "I am not used to your riddles like Ravi."

"It's not a riddle."

Right then, a Dodge Charger pulls up. Emika emerges, wearing a knee-length parka, with the sapphire blue dress she wore when we went to Chez Giraud underneath. A wonderful reminder of our first kiss while bringing a different guy. She hangs up her parka. Hulk emerges from somewhere to greet her, but he stops, sensing her new company.

She pulls her date toward me. "This is Vincent."

"So, you're Vincent. You are always on her lips and mind. I'm Brad, glad to meet you."

"Pleased to meet you, Brad." How could she bring her conquest to tarnish my feat like this?

Anna squints at me after looking at Brad. I sigh, motioning, "Later."

"Hey, Vince," Chris says, "Can you show us to your den?"

"Sure, let's go down."

Everyone except Emika and Brad follows me to the den that I built after Emika left. It has a theater room, a library, a study, a wine cellar, my lab, and a studio. I switch off my classical playlist and turn on some Pink Floyd vinyl. Anna points at my Martin Logan Renaissance speakers. "They look different, and they sound divine."

"They are electrostatic speakers."

Ravi looks at my book collection. His eyes widen. "These are the first editions of Tolkien works, right?"

"Yes. They were a gift from Philip Nardin."

Madelyn comes forward. "What was it like to meet him?" Anna, Chris, and Ravi gather around her.

The song changes to "A Great Day for Freedom" as I take a deep breath. "It gives me the courage to plow through. Every heart-wrenching incident I have encountered is trivial compared to his."

Anna turns to everyone. "Guys, can you go upstairs? I need a minute with Vince."

No one questions her. I sit on the sofa. Anna takes my hand, shakes her head. "Tell me what's going on. Who is that fuckhead with Emika?"

I blink back my tears. "She ended things on January 2 and found this new guy on January 7, or maybe before. She took four days to move on—I was that insignificant. I need to reassemble myself, but I can't find the pieces. I can't even find joy in my invention."

She rubs my hand. "Shouldn't have bought that ring."

"I couldn't have predicted this." I look down. "For once, I was happy and foolish."

"How did you know it was less than four days?"

I shake my head and smile. "Remember our latest invention on January 7, when I told you that Emika was preoccupied?"

Emika intercepts me as we ascend from the basement. "Vince, do you need help with setting the table?"

"That's the caterer's job, Emi."

Brad lifts his eyes from his cellphone. "Hey, can I call you Emi?"

"No," Emika says.

I turn to Emika as she supervises the caterer. "Don't worry. They will make sure you are seated next to Brad."

I sit at the head of the table, and Emika and Anna are on my two sides. So, that was Emika's plan, sitting close to me. Why? Madelyn and Brad sit next to Anna and Emika. Chris sits next to Brad and Ravi next to Madelyn.

As the server dish, Brad comments, "Asian food, do we have orange chicken?"

The server, Lauren, bends her head. "No, sir, sorry."

"Orange chicken is an American food, Brad," Anna says, rolling her eyes.

Emika shakes her head as Brad struggles with the chopsticks.

I turn to Lauren. "Can you hand a knife and fork to Mr. Brad here?"

Brad turns to Emika. "Is this Asian food the same as your food?" Emika's face turns red.

"She is from Japan," I tell him. "The food is Chinese."

Ravi, sensing the tension, raises his glass. "How about a speech from Vincent?"

"Speech, speech!" Anna and Chris pick up, banging the table.

I stand up, straighten my pocket square. "Thank you for joining me tonight. The fact that I am an orphan does not even enter my mind when I look at Anna, Chris, and Ravi. Anna, you are four years younger than me, but you have always been a little big sister since I saw you. You are fearless and never shy away from telling me the truth. I remember what you told me, 'Vince, I can't sugarcoat shit for you.' I love your authenticity. Chris and Ravi, if I had brothers, they would never match up to you. No matter how many inventions I share with you, I can never repay the three of you." I pause and finish my drink. Then I place the glass on the table and touch my chest, smiling. "I don't say this enough. I love all of you." I turn to Maddy. "Maddy, I've only known you for a few minutes, but I'm sure we'll stay in touch. Ravi is a beautiful human being."

Lauren fills my glass with more wine, and I drink it all in one go. I turn to Emika. "I wish things were different. I wish you all the very best in life." Then I sit.

Madelyn turns to Brad. "So, what do you do?"

Brad pulls on his jacket. "I'm a claims adjuster. But my real passion is to open a sports bar in town."

I smirk at Emika's choice. "Charming."

"Hey, man, how much did this house cost?" Brad asks, turning to me.

Emika's eyes widen. "Brad, no!"

I click my tongue. "$1.7 million, but I got it for $1.5." Emika's eyes well up. Not sure why—her new station must bring her unbridled joy.

Brad squints. "Wow, man, what do you do?"

"I make jobs like claims adjustment obsolete."

Brad wraps his hand around Emika. "If Vincent does that, I can open my bar soon. Right hottie?" Emika removes his hand and frees herself.

The background song changes to Chopin's Ballade no. 4, op. 52. Emika smiles and turns to me. I clench my jaws. "Ludwig, remove this opus from all my playlists right now. Also, remove Liszt's, La Campanella."

Emika bites her trembling lips.

Maddy turns to Brad and Emika. "So, how did you two meet?"

Anna blinks at Emika and puts her elbows on the table. "Yes, Emika, please enchant us about your newfound love."

Emika begrudgingly speaks. "We met in the first week of January, in Starbucks. He sat next to me to charge his cellphone."

"I was trying to get her attention from the end of December." Brad grins. "But on January 6, she agreed to have dinner with me, and she invited me to her townhome."

"Brad, stop!" Emika bangs on the table.

Anna smirks and tightly grips my wrist under the table. "C'mon, be a sport, and let Brad captivate us with his conquest of Emika-land."

Brad continues with his tale of conquest. "This hottie is worth the wait. I was so happy that the next morning I got her a bunch of roses."

I slant my head, making sure only Emika hears me. "And breakfast from McDonald's."

She stares back at me, her jaw wide open.

Anna applauds, but her nostrils are flared. "Ladies and gentlemen, a new love ballad—Brad and Hottie."

"Wait," Chris says, lifting his eyes from his plate, "January 7th, the day Vincent made the invention?"

Anna nudges my shoulder. "He did indeed. And he put us three on the patent. So, Vince, can I tell the story of our latest patent?"

"Sure." I like where it is going.

Anna places her chopsticks on her plate and folds her arms. "So, I was on the treadmill when I saw Vince's text in our group chat."

Emika must realize now that we left her out. But she must also be OK because I am overpaid, and the other three are sycophants, after all.

"So Vince writes, 'Can you guys come to the lab, right now?'" Anna points at Chris and Ravi. "These two are always eager to please Vince, so they said yes." Then she points at me. "This one says that he has a patentable idea, so I rushed in." Anna grabs my hand. "And there he is, sitting on a gold mine. He invented a way to make a two-way transfer of consciousness between machines and humans. We are now in talks with Nardin Robotics to make hardware specific to our recommendation. We will file the patent soon."

"Vincent," Ravi adds, turning to me, "Can you elaborate on what Anna means by a gold mine?"

I place my chopsticks on my plate. "Ladies and gentlemen, we are on the cusp of disrupting computer science, robotics, neural network, and healthcare. As per our new legal documents, the uni will get nothing. And if we become independent, I will talk to the top dogs in Silicon Valley to attract investments. The sky is the limit, friends." I raise my glass. "To the future. To us."

Chris lifts his glass. "To Vincent."

"To Vincent." Ravi and Maddy chant.

Anna chimes. "My brilliant idiot."

Brad just raises his glass.

Emika's lips tremble, and she runs her finger across the corner of her eyes. She softly utters, "*Watashi no*, Vince."

I turn to her. "Why?"

Emika touches my arm. "Nothing, Vince. Congratulations!" Then she turns to the three musketeers. "Where was I?"

Chris looks down at his cellphone. "Vince said that you were preoccupied at the moment."

"So, what's for dessert?" Ravi asks, stretching his arms above his head.

Maddy touches Ravi's belly. "You have space?"

The servers get us mango and green tea mochi. Emika touches my hand, ignoring Brad, "You remember?"

I exhale. "Every last detail."

I give four hundred dollars to each of the servers tonight. Lauren thanks me, placing her hands on my shoulders. "You did a good job, and sorry for the one rude guest."

I turn to everyone, "Ladies and gentlemen, Ravi and Chris will take your drink orders. I need a moment alone." Then I say to Ravi and Chris, "Guys, help yourself. Guard my Yamazaki-55 against Brad. But you are welcome to it."

Maddy shouts, "Could we have some rhythmic music, Vince?"

I change my playlist to techno by Nigel Stanford and Kraftwerk. The first song is "Entropy." Madelyn, Anna, Chris, and Brad take the floor. Ravi decides to observe. I can't see Emika.

Feeling lonely in my own house, I go to my favorite corner just below the "Risen from Fire and Ashes" painting facing the glass wall. The music fades away, and my friends' voices become one singular noise. I sit on the chair, facing the glass wall—the view that Emika and I shared. I'd thought of growing old with her while enjoying the majestic view of evergreens, sakura, foothills, and the snowcapped mountains. Then everything just vanished. I can feel tears welling in my eyes. Hulk comes running and licks them away. He's all that I have. I run my hand over his head and kiss his nose.

"Are you OK, Vince? You forgot your drink, so I brought it." The voice of the woman whose existence is quickly expiring from my life.

I quickly blink back my tears. "I'm fine, thanks."

"The guys downstairs wanted to play Pictionary, so I set up the easel and papers. I still know where things are in this house. Do you wanna join us?"

"No." I keep looking outside.

Emika turns around and yells, "You guys go ahead. I'll be with Vince." Then she touches my shoulder. "Do you mind if I sit?"

I finally turn to her. "You don't want to be with Brad?"

She sits opposite me. "I don't care about him."

"Didn't you care about me when we were together? Or was it all a farce?"

"The thing is, Vince, I have never stopped caring about you. You and Brad aren't on the same pedestal. I'm not even sure if you two are the same species."

"Then are you with him?"

Her eyes well up as she explains. "His stupidity, his crudeness, is a distraction. Maybe that way, my transition from Abajian to Turing Labs will be less painful."

I hand her my pocket square.

She takes my hand along with it. "I'll miss you, and Hulk, and…." She looks around the house."And everything. I am so sorry for leaving."

"You must have thought deeply before making this decision," I say, placing my hand over hers.

She shakes her head. "I did not. It was impulsive. And now I have signed a contract." Her lips tremble. "Vince, I am so sorry for the concert night. The things I said to you, to my Vince. I did not realize the damage I'd done until I collected my clothes from your office."

Looking at her, I can see that she's suffering, too, with the constant conflict in her mind. What's causing this conflict?

She breathes in deeply. "Vince, I have two questions for you. Why didn't you come to my townhome after January 2? What was I working on during January 7? It was a Sunday."

My chest starts to pound as I think of that day. "I thought you would make the connection. Well, the answer to both is the same. Remember how you asked me what I was hiding the day you came to collect your clothes?"

"Yes."

"Hulk and I went to your townhome on January 7, that Sunday, thinking I'd convince you to come home. I bought your favorite flowers—the blue and purple bellflowers. As I was about to pull in, I saw a Dodge Charger already there. A guy—who's now been revealed as Brad—came out of the car holding roses. When he knocked on your door, you opened it, jumped on him, and started to kiss him. You moved on quickly. So, I concluded I didn't mean much to you. Life with me was a passing thought." I lean back and smile. "At that moment, I felt inspired to create something. I did it after running a couple of hundred thousand simulations. Then I texted the guys. They asked where you were, and all I said was that you were preoccupied."

I keep looking at her while her lips shiver. Finally, she says, "I can't imagine how you must have felt."

"You can't?" I ask, staring into her eyes while lifting my eyebrows.

She shakes her head. "And I'd thought of being with you when you invented something."

"As I said, you were preoccupied. But you were there in my mind. I just can't fathom our buying this house and what's happening now as part of the same reality."

"I'm so sorry, Vince. I was intensely conflicted, and I didn't know what I was doing. I'm still not sure what I'm doing now." She continues to dab her eyes with my pocket square, soaking it.

I gather my voice. "You don't have to apologize. I would have waited a little longer before moving on to the next work in progress with a beautiful potential. Maybe that's why you never moved in here. You weighed up other future potentials while blaming me—unfairly—for having a thing for Tabi."

She grabs my arm. "Not for one second did I think you were just a passing phase in my life. There is no potential with Brad. I did not move in because you were keeping things from me."

"You don't owe me any explanation." I smile and shake my head. "You need clarity. Do you know what you want?"

Hulk jumps on her. She pets him and glances at me with an expression of absolute helplessness. "I am split—a part wants me to be with you, and another tells me I rushed into this, and I rushed you, too. I need the space and distance to evaluate what I want. I'm sorry I dragged you into my mess. Maybe an ocean between you and me will help me evaluate what I want."

I tilt my head. "So you did give it a thought—not just all impulse."

She leans forward to touch my cheek. "Why did you remove Chopin's and Liszt's pieces from your playlists?"

"They signified the imminence of joy." I gulp down my whisky. "But you took it away. Chopin's no. 4 is still my ringtone."

"You wish I hadn't come into your life, right?" she asks softly, looking down.

I hold her hands. "You gave me the best two months of my life. And just when I was getting used to it, you showed me the reality—a lie, a beautiful lie. I don't regret anything, but at times I wish I had walked away at the start and left things at 'hello.'"

She soaks my pocket square with her tears. "I can't imagine how much I hurt you."

"Sometimes, I have this temptation to transfer a smidgen of my pain to you just so you know how much you hurt me. But I can't do that to my Em… Sorry, you." I swallow back the looming quaver in my voice. She has no right to see my tears. "What pains me today was that you brought that guy in this house—a place where we thought of building our lives. How little must our dreams meant to you? And you are telling that you don't even care about this guy." I shake my head in disbelief. "Let's change the topic from this hopeless discussion."

She wipes her tears, musters a brittle smile. "You haven't removed the post-its on the fridge doors. You still struggle to find the fridge?"

I kiss her hand and wind her Cartier Tank Louis. "I know where the fridge is. I am the one who is lost, who can't seem to find you. I am kindling a false hope that one day you will come back for good and remove them."

CHAPTER 15

OMURICE

The flames are all long gone, but the pain lingers on.
—Roger Waters

(Six to four months before today)

I RUSH TO MY OFFICE TO collect my cellphone before I meet Vikram. There is a voicemail from Emika.

"Hi, Vince. I will be vacating the townhome today and spending the night at the Holiday Inn. I have a small request. Would you be able to drop me at the airport tomorrow? I want to see you and Hulk one last time. But, I will hold no grudges if you don't want to see me again."

Her voice trembled throughout the voicemail.

I collect my jacket, overcoat, and Hulk. Then I shut my office door and turn to Linda. "I am leaving for the day."

"But, you have a meeting at two with the dean," she reminds me.

"Cancel it."

"Are you OK, Dr. A?"

I rush out of my suite. "I don't know."

I pull into the empty driveway. Then I knock on her door.

She opens it, smiling. "I wasn't expecting you."

"You want me to leave?"

She shakes her head, grabs my lapel, and pulls me in. The navy and the red suitcases are packed. On top of the navy, one is her Gurkha bag. Her black Samsonite carry-on is still open. The violin is next to it.

I sit down on the couch and pull her next to me. Holding her soft hands, I look into her eyes. "Why are you doing this? I know what you told me—but fuck that. Can't you stay? Please?"

"Why didn't you ask me this before?" She runs her hand through my hair.

"I came here twice. Each time Brad was here. And I did not want to infringe."

"If you had shown yourself, I would have asked Brad to leave." She grabs my arm. "Why couldn't you assert yourself?"

"It's difficult when it appears you've moved on." I touch her hand. "I am asserting myself now."

She looks away and swallows back tears. "I have signed a contract."

I gently turn her face toward mine. "Aren't you breaking your contract with our center? I can call Turing right now and free you in exchange for co-ownership of my new invention."

"No!" She touches both my cheeks as tears gather in her eyes. "That invention belongs to you and your team. I was just an outsider."

I swallow the tremble in my voice. "I can invent hundred more things. But there is only one Emika."

She wraps her arms around my neck and whispers. "Let's do this—let me go, and if I miss us, miss you, I will come back." She pulls away, wipes her tears, and forces a smile. "Vince, I have to vacate this place now. My Uber is almost here. It will take me to the Holiday Inn."

I tuck her hair behind her ears. "Cancel the Uber. I'll drop you there."

I load her luggage and the violin into my car, wishing that I'd been more assertive earlier, that I'd gone to her townhome before January 6. I know I am not thinking straight—it's the whole Akane-in-Emika paradox. But at this moment, I can't. I just know that I love Emika, and she is leaving me.

She gets in with Hulk in her lap. "Nice car. Do you like driving it?"

"Not really."

"Why?" she asks, tilting her head.

"I look at the passenger seat, and you are never in it."

I drive four blocks in total silence, punctuated by Hulk whimpering and then being comforted by his lovely vanishing mum.

Emika looks out the window and points. "We just passed the Holiday Inn."

"We are not going there. You will spend the last evening at home. I will drop you at the airport tomorrow. I didn't ask because you would have said no."

"Thank you." She places her hand on my arm. "I wouldn't have said no."

"Porsche, take us home and engage in autonomous mode."

She is silent the rest of the way. At some point, she reaches for my pocket square and takes it out. I kiss her hair. She is my Emika again, even if it's only for one evening.

We arrive home one last time.

Emika puts on my MIT sweatshirt and pants. As she goes to the fridge to get some water, her eyes fall on the post-its. She grabs a kitchen towel and dabs her eyes. Dinner is veggie pizza with artichoke, garlic, mushrooms, onions, and spinach. The same one that we had when we moved in. We eat in silence. I can hear the fridge making ice and the tick-tock of Philip's clocks. We both have so much to say, yet neither is willing to take the first step. After we've eaten our last slices, she grabs my cuff. "I have changed your default pizza order to this. It's healthier."

My voice quavers as I collect the pizza box and plates. "Why do you care? You are leaving me." I turn around, but she's gone. "Emi." My voice echoes across the halls. How empty this house has been without her and how blank it will remain.

I check each guestroom, but she is nowhere. Then I see that the light in my closet is switched on. And there she is, sitting on the floor, with her back to me. She's put on my light blue chambray sports jacket, and her shoulders are shaking. I sit next to her and bring her close to me. "Are you OK?" Hulk comes running and jumps on her.

"No. This is the one you wore when we went to Sichuan Palace." She touches the fabric. "Can I take it with me?"

"Sure." I kiss her hair. "What will you do with it?"

She rests her head on my shoulder. "I will wear it when I miss you."

I am not sure of our boundaries, so I set her bed in a separate guest room. Hulk keeps tilting his head as he watches Emika and I get ready in two different rooms. He follows me to my room—he can sense the transience of Emika's presence.

I can't sleep. Every time I shut my eyes, I see all the events from August 3 until this moment. Sparks dance between my fingertips. I get up and wash my hands.

A few moments after I get back in bed, I hear Emika walk into the room. She touches my shoulder. "Can I sleep next to you?"

I kiss her hand. "Of course."

We both lay awake, breathing on each other. Emika nestles her head into the crook of my neck, and I can feel her eyelashes on my skin. I touch her head and kiss her. She clenches my sweatshirt in her fist. I wrap my left arm around her. With the moonlight filtering through the blinds, I can see her eyes in the dark. "Can you make a promise?" I ask.

"Sure."

"If you feel like coming back, for whatever reason, can you just pack and come without a second's hesitation? Don't think of jobs, contracts—just come. I will take care of the rest."

I can feel a slight tickle from her lashes as she blinks. "OK."

It's Feb 14th—the day I'd thought to give her that ring. A distant dream of an improbable future, curated from a detached past.

It's 6:00 a.m. and still dark. Emika is in the shower, and I am making her breakfast. I had been practicing her favorite dish, with the hope of making it for her on Feb 15th morning under different circumstances. That hope is hope, but I may not get the chance to cook for her again.

Hulk is wagging his tail. This could be the recipe for a perfect life if she were not leaving. I dab my face with the kitchen towel hanging from my shoulder. Then I turn to the kitchen counter and see her sitting on the barstool: jeans, mustard top, Frye suede boots, Burberry scarf, and black parka by her side.

She leaves the stool to come to kiss me. "What are you making?"

"*Omurice*." I bring the plate in front of her and conceal my choking voice with a smile. "Surprise!"

Her brittle smile fails to hide her tears. "Why?"

"Food in the airport and planes are terrible. So, I want you to have something substantial before your trip." I place her plate on the counter.

"Where is your food?" she asks, picking up her fork.

"I haven't had breakfast since you left. Just a doppio for me."

She looks at me and sets her fork back down. "I can't eat if you won't."

I sit on the barstool next to hers, then cut through the egg and make a mouthful on her fork. "Open your mouth. This could be the last time I cook for you." She does so and then chews. Her tears reach her chin. I wipe them, kiss her forehead. As she takes another bite, I remind her. "Chew."

"I don't want this to be the last time."

Can I lighten the mood before she leaves? "Hey, you are the one choosing a dead mathematician over me. And I get it. I am intelligent, but not Turing material."

She turns to me. "I still can't believe my words and actions since December."

I know what she went through and is going through. I wish I could help. Maybe Philip would be able to. I touch her hair. "It's OK, you were angry. But now you have your dream job."

She shakes her head. "And despite all that, you brought me here...."

I hug her before she can finish her sentence. "It's alright. It's your home, too."

"Vince," she says, pulling back to look into my eyes. "I have a favor to ask you."

"Anything."

"Among the many reasons I chose this house was that it has a row of fifteen cherry trees in the backyard. I wanted to be with you when they blossomed. It would've reminded me of my childhood, and it was a moment I wanted to share with you. But now I'm not sure if that'll ever happen. When the petals fall, they look like flurries of snow but pink. It's a phenomenon called Hanafubuki. So, can you send me a picture when they blossom, please?"

I pick her hand from my shoulder kiss it. "Sure."

Before leaving, she walks around the home she chose. She sits in our favorite spot and rests her head on her palms. I let her be. She glances through my sketchbook, sniffs every pillow, and throws that she picked. Then she sits on the stairs, stares blankly out the windows. After a few minutes, I sit next to her. She turns to me, wiping her eyes with her scarf. "This is the readiest I will ever be." She kisses the door on her way out. "Goodbye, home. Take care of my boys. The big one, especially."

As she collects her boarding passes, I load her luggage onto the conveyer belt. She grabs my lapel and looks at me. "What have I done? I found you, and I am leaving you, Vince." Her eyes begin to flood with tears, and her lips wobble. "Now, all I will have is your sports jacket and a photo frame."

I take out my pocket square. "Add this."

"This was my home. I had everything."

I wrap my arms around her tightly. "It will always be your home."

She dabs her eyes with my pocket square and then looks at me. "*Arigato*, Vince. For life, the memories, the house, and this watch. I didn't mean a single word I said after the concert."

I tuck her hair behind her ears. "I know."

She kneels and scratches Hulk's neck. "Take care of Daddy. He only pretends to be strong."

The boarding announcement.

After picking up her handbag, she looks at me. "Can you not drive so fast?"

"I didn't, right?" I run my finger across her face.

"I mean when you are alone."

I kiss her hand. "I'll try."

She wipes her tears one more time and then inserts my pocket square inside the violin case. "I need to clear security."

I pull her in for the last time. I close my eyes and kiss her. As our lips lock, her tears touch my cheeks. Then I open my eyes. "If there is a next time, don't leave me."

"I won't."

Taking her wrist, I wind her Cartier. "Don't forget, once every two days."

She collects her Gurkha bag, the violin case, and her hand luggage. One final kiss to Hulk. "I really need to clear security."

She takes off her shoes, crosses the scanners, moves to the escalators. At the top, she turns back one last time and takes out her cellphone. My phone rings with Chopin's Ballade no. 4.

"Yes?" My voice quavers.

"Just wanted to hear your voice. Take care, silly."

"I will. You too." Will she ever remember me if there was no Akane in her?

As I walk to the parking garage, I flip my JLC Reverso and change the black dial to GMT and the white dial to Pacific. I can see the man in the fedora not too far away, sitting inside his Rolls Royce. Who is this guy? I get into my car and rest my head on the steering wheel. Hulk starts sniffing the vanishing scent of Emika in the air. He whimpers and lies down. I touch his head and kiss his wet nose. "It is not her fault, bug. It's mine." He licks my hand, and I pick him up. He licks my tears. The fifteenth is a terrible day. Akane disappeared, Elise died, and now Emika has left. I can't see or touch her anymore.

I've just lost everything once again—Emika and the Akane in her.

I switch on my car, and we leave the airport. The mountains, the hills, the roads all merge into one blur. Then I begin the climb to reach the house I thought would be our home. A place that she only stayed in for two months. When she moved out, I thought she would be back. When she found Brad, I thought she would be back. When she was offered the job in London, I thought she would turn it down. But here we are. I did nothing but stand like a silent observer, witnessing how time sweeps my life away from me.

"Porsche, open garage." Hulk and I get out, and I open the door to the house from the garage. We enter.

(November 23, 1991)

I entered my dorm room, carrying Akane's violin, the picture frame, and the scarf. I put her violin by my pillow and placed the photo frame on the nightstand. Then I sat on my bed.

I could hear quick footsteps behind me. Fred gently placed his hands on my shoulder. "You OK, bud?"

I looked up. Fred's face was blurry behind the tears flooding my eyes. I pulled his lapel and shook him. "Why did Akane leave me? What did I do so wrong? I have no one now."

Sasha and Kista sat next to me. Sasha put her arms around me, and Krista handed me her handkerchief. She said, "You have us. It's not your fault, Vince. It's OK to hurt." I wiped my tears and handed the handkerchief back. Krista folded it into a triangle, placed it in my pocket. "Here, a pocket square."

I tried to swallow my tears. "Don't you have classes?"

"We will be with you as long as you need." Sasha pinched my cheek. "Mr. Kruger asked us to be with you. And Vince, it's not your fault."

(Back to the present)

It is my fault. I should not have even started this relationship. She was conflicted from the very beginning. I throw my overcoat and jacket onto the floor. Then I untuck my shirt and sit on the floor with my back against the fridge, under two post-its Emika placed.

I scroll through my phone to find my school group. They helped me heal before. But I don't want to tell them about Emika. I don't want to reveal my failures again.

Me: Guys? All of a sudden, the memories of November 23, 1991, came back to me. I should have stopped her.

Krista: For the one-millionth time—it was not your fault. Hey, why don't you come and spend time with us? It's been so long.

Sasha: Yes. We will close the restaurant for a day, and we three will cook together.

Fred: And I will eat.

Krista: Fred, you are of no help.

Me: How about I come later this year? November?

Sasha: Sure, Vince. It's been so long. I can't wait.

Fred: Me neither.

Krista: But Vince, are you OK?

Me: I'm as OK as I was on November 23, 1991.

Krista: I'm so sorry, bud. We would come and visit, but we just opened after a long break.

Me: Thank you for looking out for me. I love you all.

Krista: We all love you. Vincent, promise that you won't do anything stupid?

Me: I won't.

What have I done? How could I just drop her off and out of my life? And why can't I control my tears? Am I still the eight-year-old boy lost in his dorm room? I get up, open the fridge, and take out a bottle of stout.

The sparks light between my fingertips again. Let's see what they do. The sparks touch the floor, and Hulk runs away. There is no damage to the floor. As I lift my arms, the sparks reach the ceiling. What else can I do? I start making circles with my left arm, and the sparks create an entrance. Then it transforms into a cylindrical passage made of light and electric charge. Is this what the inside of time turbulence looks like? I have to enter—I have to see what's in it.

As I step in, I turn back and see my room disappear. Then I move forward and walk about 40 feet. I see a boy sitting on a chair. Wait a minute—that's me. I am waiting outside the headmaster's office. "Vincent," I call. He can't hear me. I see another path. That's me in my dorm room. Can I see Akane? Everything is shaking. What's happening? Why is it crumbling?

The entire passage crumbles to pieces, then disappears. I am back at 100 Summit View.

Can I do it again? What about the other hand? I am right-handed, so it's easier. This time, I see myself frail and with a full beard. I walk forward some more, sitting next to Philip's lawyers, swearing with my right hand raised. Where is this? A courtroom, the Senate. They are asking me questions.

I turn the other way. Is that Emika holding a baby? Is it hers? So, she will move on? Can I see the past and the future? So, the end has already happened, and I am yet to experience it. Does Emika's future not include me? Will she be happy, at least? The images are disappearing, and the walls crumble again.

I am lying on my floor the next thing I know, and Hulk is licking me awake. The beer has spilled on the floor. Was that a dream, or did the sparks knock me out?

I pull out my cell phone and see a text notification from Emika.

> Emika: Reached Seattle. Off to the next flight to London. I'll text you from this number when I land there. Then I'll get a new phone. I'll use this phone again if I am in the US. Thanks for everything. Stay well. Goodbye until we meet again.
>
> Me: Try to come to the US soon. Let me know your UK number. There's a lot I need to tell you that I couldn't. I am missing you.

My mind is oscillating between Emika and my new ability. I stand up. My trousers feel loose. How did that happen? I tighten my belt as I walk across the living room. There are blue crystals everywhere. I pick one up. It looks like an intreton, and my skin dissolves it. I pick up the other crystals, and my skin dissolves them all. What the fuck? My mind starts racing even faster, coming up with what would have been impossibilities before. Am I made of intreton? Am I human? Am I the perfect vessel to transport intreton? And worse yet—what will the US government do with me if they find out my composition? Why couldn't my doctors detect this? And how come when I take a flight, there is no interference? Suddenly, Hulks comes running and looks at a solitary intreton crystal. I turn to him and point my finger. "Hulk, no!" He looks at me, takes the crystal in his teeth, eats it, and runs away. I chase after him and find him on Emikas's side of the bed, whimpering. "Why did you do that, bug?"

Fifteen hours later.

> Emika: Reached London. I'll let you know my new number as soon as I get it. This is my last text from this phone. This is so surreal, Vince. Did I do this?
>
> Me: I know you won't check this message. But Emi, whatever happens to me, just know that I love you.

Emika texted me her new number, and I could not wait a single minute to call her.

"Hi, Vince."

"How is London? And the new job?"

"Both lack warmth. They lack Vince. I'm struggling to get used to it, struggling to move past you."

"Why's that?" I'd guess Emika is fighting the Akane in her.

"The memories hurt too much, Vince. I need to move on. But the way you took care of me that last evening makes it impossible."

"Why do you need to move on? Don't you ever want to come back? Didn't you say that none of it was a lie?"

"The two months I was with you was nothing short of a fairy tale. You once told me that joy is temporary in your life. And I had never experienced happiness like that before." She is breathing heavily into the phone. "Something happened in December, and I became more and more conflicted as you got pulled into Philip, Elise, and all that. I can't do that all over again."

"So this is the end, Emi? I won't see you again?"

"We will meet at conferences and such. We have co-authored papers that I can't escape, even if I want to. I need to get some clarity, especially when I don't know the roots of my confusion."

I can sense the tremble in her voice. I need to know how I can help her—I need to find Philip. This subject is hurting her.

"Hey, I never asked you. Did you try the violin?"

"Yes."

"And?"

"You're stuck in deciphering some theories surrounding a violin. The secret was not the violin. It was far more sentient. A genius like you should have figured it out. In a way, it's good that you didn't. Anyway, take care, Vince. Have a great life. *Wakare*!"

"Hello? Hello?"

She's hung up on me. So, that's the end of Vince and Emika. Is that how she feels about me feels when the Akane in her is dormant? If those are her authentic feelings, so be it. I wish she could free herself from Akane's clutches and be free to decide what she wants. But then she would forget me altogether. The short, beautiful life we built will only reside in my memories. And how do I move on? Why do I always have to move on?

Anna, Chris, and Ravi bring in a pile of paperwork. Anna stares at me and lifts her eyebrows, then starts shooting. "Have you lost weight? What's with the full beard? What's going on?"

I shrug. "New diet, new look. Anyway, what do you want?" I can't reveal anything about the sparks.

Anna drops the pile on my desk. "We need signatures from you. There are three separate documents, each for a patent. The first one is a process of copying consciousness from one machine to another across versions. The second one is how to log the files of several iterations of the transfer. And finally, the last one is about the two-way transferring consciousness you worked on. We are co-inventors for all the patents, except Emika is not on the last one. Once you are done signing, I will email Emika for her signature."

"How many working papers do we currently have?" I ask, turning to Chris and Ravi.

Ravi takes a moment to count. "Ten?"

I close my eyes. "How many of those ten are co-authored with Emika?"

Chris makes a mental note. "Four."

I shut my eyes. After taking a deep breath, I say, "Remove me from those four papers."

Anna bangs on my desk. "Don't be stupid, Vince."

I lean back to stare at the ceiling. "It's best for her if she distances herself from me, but it would be unethical to remove Emika. I will write the editors personally regarding my withdrawal."

"Vince, you idiot," Anna says, shaking her head. "Emika is incapable of distancing herself from you. No matter what she may have told you."

"Yes, that's the problem." I press my temples with my fingers. "And she constantly suffers for it. I wish I could change that."

"You can't barge in like this, sir. Do you have an appointment with Dr. Abajian?" I hear Linda say in the stern voice she uses to keep undesirable elements out of my office. The other person responds, "We went to school together, and I need to give him something. I'll be out in five minutes."

I vaguely recognize the voice, so I open my office door. I'll be damned. It's Jean Laurent, the dormant bully. He stretches out his hand, and I notice his Yale Law class ring and his watch—Rolex GMT Root Beer.

"This is Jean Laurent," I say, turning to Linda. "We went to the same boarding school."

"I'm sorry, Mr. Laurent."

Jean just nods. "You were doing your job."

I escort Jean into my office. Hulk sniffs and approaches Jean, who bends down to touch his head and then turns to me. "Name? Age?"

"Hulk, five and a half years."

He gently runs his finger across Hulk's small head, "Hi Hulk, I'm Jean. I've known your dad since he was your age."

We sit by the fireplace, and he looks around. "You have done well, Vince."

"So, what brings you here?" I ask, crossing my legs.

He opens his briefcase, takes out a parcel, and hands it to me. "I'm here to deliver this to you."

I take the box, and my hands descend due to its weight. Upon removing the wrapping, I see a dark brown box inscribed with "AP" on the first line and "Audemars Piguet" on the second line.

I open the box to find an Audemars Piguet's Jules Audemars black dial and rose gold watch. I know whose watch this is—was, I suppose. I hold back my tears as I move my eyes from the box to Jean. "When and how?"

"He passed about two months back—advanced pancreatic cancer. But he died in peace, in his house in Basel. Our firm manages the school's trust, and we'd taken Mr. Kruger as a client. He gave all his belonging to the school, except for this watch and an accompanying letter for you."

He then hands me a white sealed envelope, with "Vincent" handwritten at the center. I open the envelope, then place it on the coffee table. Philip had mentioned he would meet an old friend from Basel who was dying from advanced pancreatic cancer. Did they know each other? Did Philip know about me?

Jean tilts his head. "You won't read it?"

"Later. So how have you been?"

He leans back. "I've been good. I got married. Made partner in my father's firm. I'm just following in my old man's path, living a life that seems already lived." He sighs. "What about you? You are in every bookstore now."

I pull my cuffs. "Different from you. I had no footsteps to follow. So, I stumbled and picked myself up, ran again."

Jean points to my picture with Akane. "Can I see that?" He holds it in both his hands, then places it on the coffee table. "Do you still have her violin and her scarf?"

"Yes." I don't want to bring up Emika.

Looking back at me, he says, "Vince, I'm sorry for siding with Luther and Rudy. Akane's adoration for you ticked off those two. How could wealthy heiress care so much for an orphan boy? And I'm so sorry that Akane went missing. Hey, your book is about Philip Nardin, and just like him, maybe Akane will return."

Shutting my eyes, I let my mind take a swift journey from August 3rd to the last phone call. Then I smile sadly at my fate. "I have given up on that." I open my eyes and look at Jean. "Also, you've apologized earlier, in 2001. It's all water under the bridge."

(August 2001)

I left a bouquet of bellflowers for Akane in the music room. I was still confused about the image of the girl in polka dot with a violin. Who was she?

I was rushing to my dorm room to collect my bags and meet Mr. Kruger one last time. Before I made it even fifty feet from the music room, Jean intercepted me. "Where're you heading, Vincent?"

I kept walking. "Dorm, then the headmaster's office."

He stopped me and shook his head. "I meant college?"

"Cambridge. You?"

"Yale, then hopefully Yale Law School."

I extended my hand. "Good for you."

"I'm sorry, Vincent, for all the times I sided with those two idiots." He clasped my shoulder. "Can you ever forgive me?"

"Water under the bridge, Jean. And good luck with law school."

He stopped me as I started to walk again. "Can I ask something, Vince?"

I took a deep breath to hide my annoyance. "Sure."

"You beat both Luther and Rudy to pulps, but you never hurt me. Why?"

"Simple—you never spoke ill of Akane." I shook my head and smiled. "Curse me all you want—orphan, bastard. But leave my Akane alone."

"You were always on her mind," he said.

"And she is on mine. If only I could tell her."

"All the best, Vince." He came forward hugged me. "I hope you find everything you want."

I kept my hands by my sides, unable to hug him back.

(Back to the present)

Jean rests his head on his palm. "Yes, I apologized earlier. But no matter how much I do, I still feel miserable and petty. I could have stopped them." He sighs. "I tried to atone. I cook and serve food in a soup kitchen. I volunteer at an orphanage. But deep in my mind, I know I should never have made fun of someone who was an orphan. I wish I could apologize to Akane for how I treated you. And I wish I could turn back time and relive my life." He looks at me, helpless. "Do you have any pointers, bud?"

I think for a second. "Why don't you adopt a child? Protect them from bullies. Love them. Make them feel that they are the happiest, luckiest child on the planet. What is being rich if not surrounded by love?"

Jean takes out a handkerchief and rubs his eyes. "I will talk to my wife." Then he stands up. "Let's keep in touch. Mr. Kruger would have been so proud of you. Maybe you'll show up at the alumni meet."

I stand as well. "Maybe I will." We shake hands, and this time I hug him. It took me almost twenty-three years. On his way out, he thanks Linda.

I come back to my sofa. My school is a mausoleum of memory fragments that I want to escape. But Akane came back in fragments, broke my heart, and took the violin. Maybe now I can return to my school and see things the way they are—buildings and artifacts. My eyes fall on the envelope, and I take out the letter inside. It's handwritten, perfect penmanship despite his condition.

Dear Vincent,

My time is near. When I look back on my years on Earth, I think of how bright, sensitive, and misunderstood you were. I was hard on you, maybe too hard. And it took me decades to comprehend the depth of your emotion toward Akane. I want to apologize for asking you to move on that day. My dying wish is that she finds you. When she does, don't let her go.

I often hear about the great things you've accomplished. And no matter how many times I say I'm proud of you, it won't suffice.

I was a headmaster to students whose futures were predetermined. You were my greatest student. My years as your teacher were the best of my life. It's not wrong to say that you are the son I never had. You became my son on November 23, 1991, but I never realized it until it was too late.

You don't need to suppress your sparks. They are key to who you are and what you can unlock. All you need is solid resolve, and the gate to the unknown will open. Once you finish your mission, you will know what you were meant to be.

Lots of love,
David Kruger

After reading the letter, I get up to lock my office door.

Both Mr. Kruger and Philip wrote about a mission. Mr. Kruger must have been Philip's sick friend in Basel. But what is this mission? When will I know it—*how* will I know it? What are the gates he's talking about? How does he know that the sparks can create some doorway? And resolve about what?

I open the lacquered wood watch box with its polished chrome hardware and look at his watch. Then I shut my eyes.

(The year 2000)

I was studying day and night for my A-levels.

"Sir, I am finished with all the calculus problems." I said as I entered Mr. Kruger's' office. "How about a game of chess?"

He took my notebook and glanced through the pages. "You should have no problem getting into Cambridge." Then he pointed at my feet. "Your shoelace is undone."

Looking down, I said, "Sorry, sir. I just tied them five minutes back." I bent down to tie them again.

"Stop. Let me teach you a stronger knot—the Berluti knot." He bent down with me and showed me the knot using my undone shoelaces. It seemed complicated, but after two trials, I mastered it. Then he stood. "Before we get to chess, I would like to show you something."

I sat across from his desk. "What?"

He opened his wristwatch and unscrewed the case back, showing me how the rotor wound the watch and stored power for forty hours, how the minute parts worked in perfect synchrony to depict the time. Then he told about the leading brands of watches.

I pointed to his wristwatch. "What brand is that?"

"It's an Audemars Piguet. The model is called the Jules Audemars. It's my favorite. If I had a son, it would be his."

(Back to the present)

I open my eyes, and I find myself holding the same watch after twenty-four years. A wristwatch he kept in pristine condition for his son. I take out my pocket square and dab my eyes. *I am sorry, sir, for not keeping in touch. You were the closest person to a father I ever had, and I ignored you because we did not agree on one thing. You should not be proud of me. You were right to tell me to choose logic over emotions. Whenever I did not, my life fell apart. And now you are gone.* Could I hear his voice one last time? I scroll down my contact list and press the dial button. An automated response in German-accented English states, "This number is disconnected." I look down and see that my shoelaces have come undone—the first time since I learned the Berluti knot. My hands shake as tears drip on my shoe. Hulk jumps on me and licks my cheeks. I look at his loving face. "Thank you for being with me, bug."

I'm sitting on a bench outside my center. Snowflakes gradually collect on my hair and fall on my scarf—Akane's scarf. The sun has set, the evening is blue, and the campus's golden lights make each snowflake visible. I left my gloves and my tweed ivy cap in my office. After a few moments, I hear footsteps—the sound of feet struggling against the snow. I look over my shoulder and see Anna coming toward me.

She sits next to me and touches my scarf. "New?"

"It's Akane's."

"Looks good on you," she says, brushing the snow from my hair.

"I am tired, Anna." I exhale and watch the vapor from my mouth. "Mr. Kruger died. Emika left."

Anna rubs my palm against her gloves. "Mr. Kruger was old, and Emika whimsical. Both beyond your control."

"It still hurts, though."

"Why don't you talk to her?"

I shake my head. "I did, but she hung up on me. She doesn't want to come back. And I think it will do her good."

"Anyone in your place would be tired. But you are not just anyone." She squeezes my arm. "You need to keep your promise to make this the best facility for AI. Stop languishing and get back to action. I can tell how much you miss her. You did your best, you gave out your heart, and she left you. But remember one thing—we all came here to work with you. Yes, you have freed us from the bureaucratic mess. And yes, the inventor is back!" She pumps a fist in the air, then looks at me again. "But the work has only begun. You are a genius, and sitting around like this is beneath you. Chris and Ravi constantly worry about you. I don't want to lose you a second time, Vince."

"Everything here reminds me of her," I whisper, gripping Anna's hand.

She stands up, tightens my scarf. "Then fucking change it. Only you can."

Tabi sits on the sectional facing the glass walls. I bring her a bottle of spring water. She places her inhaler on the coffee table, then takes a few sips of water. "You helped me a lot with the story. So, I thought I'd share a secret with you."

She fetches a small box from her handbag, then takes out a severely battered metallic piece from the box and puts it on the coffee table. "This is the bullet that killed Dick Graham. He was shot before he was taken to the G-400."

I am about to touch it, but I stop. "Isn't it evidence?" I look at Tabi, squinting.

"There is no investigation, Vince." She grins. "They blamed it on rogue elements in the Middle East. And when Mossad and General Intelligence Directorate offer to help, everything becomes legit. No one cares how Graham died. This is the election year, and it will be a hot topic for two parties. GOP has its replacement. People will forget how corrupt the parties are, and faith in our flawed democracy is restored."

Suddenly everything makes sense. Though it took me a little long to deduce. I pick up the battered bullet. "I am not an expert in weapons. Is this a .338 or a .308 caliber?"

"Why do you ask?" Her eyes narrow a bit.

"Was this fired from an Accuracy International AS-500?" I lean forward. "Did the FBI ever find such a rifle?"

"Why are you asking me all these?" she asks, unable to conceal the tremble in her voice.

I lower my eyebrows and stare at Tabi's dark brown eyes. "You are Edward's adoptive daughter."

Her jaw drops. "How could you make that connection?"

"It all came back to me as soon as I saw the bullet. The day the spaceship took off, I spoke with Edward, and then suddenly, you knew I was in my office. The assembly of a G-400 in Nardin's residence. I believe that was the plane used to transport Graham." Then I point at the battered locket she wears around her neck. "That must be an artifact from your destroyed house. You need that inhaler because your lungs may have been affected after breathing the smoke and fumes. And lastly, you have this bullet—the evidence that you've gotten your vengeance. There are no coincidences in life. I once asked Philip if he thought Dick Graham would win the GOP nomination, and he answered that Dick's end would come before that."

She drinks a few more sips and doesn't respond.

"Your secret is safe with me," I say, placing my hand on her shoulder.

Putting her hand over mine, she whispers, "Dick Graham and Lombard took everything from me."

"I know."

Tears form at the corner of her eyes, and her lips wobble. "We were poor poultry farmers who could barely make ends meet. We harbored no terrorists. We never hurt a soul, Vince."

I hand her a tissue box. After dabbing her eyes, she continues. "I was the oldest—twelve. I had an eight-year-old sister, Amina, and a little brother." She lifts her hand about three feet from the floor. "He was just three, Vince. My little Farid. We were just playing outside, and I went to the well to get water for my Farid. The next thing I knew, I was covered with rubble and stones, unable to stay awake. When I regained consciousness, a set of kind blue eyes was staring right at me, speaking a language I didn't understand. That was Edward. He looked tired, but he stayed with me every day until I recovered. He took care of me, brought me toys, food, water, medicine, an inhaler. We remained in a containment zone outside Baghdad. After I recovered, he took me to what was left of my home. We found no bodies to bury, just dust. The US military must have cleared every last evidence of a crime. They took everything from me. Edward found an empty one-inch shell, poured in some of the dust, and sealed it. 'Never forget," he told me."

She pumps the inhaler. "Then one day, he stopped coming. About a week later, he came back in a wheelchair. Looking at him made me think I had lost my family twice in two months. Mr. Nardin rescued us both. Ed owes everything to Philip. And I owe everything to the both of them."

I hold both Tabi's hands. "How did Philip find you and Edward?"

"He was on a mission to dig out intreton, and he had his private military with him."

"Where is Edward, now?"

She wipes her eyes and her face. "The Nardin residence, underground." Then she looks at the tissue, now soaked with tears, eyeliner, and foundation. "Vince, can I use your powder room?"

"Sure." I show her where it is and then come back to my seat.

Ordinarily, I would be concerned with the lack of justice in this revenge plot. But, not today, and I don't know why. I can't differentiate between justice and vengeance. Did I change because Emika left me?

Tabitha comes back. "Lots of feminine touches in the house, I must say."

"A woman with discernable taste graced this house for two months. You've met her once."

"Who?" she asks, tilting her head.

"Her name is Emika Amari. The first time we met in my office, she entered as you exited. You guys stared at each other."

She snaps her fingers. "Ah, I remember now. She's stunning. I could tell that she liked you. She had a look that said, 'Leave my Vince alone.'" Tabi takes off her jacket.

I can see the length of her burn scar that starts from her wrist and goes up to her shoulder. It must be a constant reminder of how Dick Graham stole her childhood.

I get up. "You want something to eat or drink?"

"Do you have cognac?"

I fetch a Hennessy Cognac bottle, a Hakushu 12-year-old single malt bottle, and two glasses.

"So, where is this, Emika?" Tabi asks, then gulps one whole glass and pours another.

I take a sip. "She left me. She's in London."

Tabi gulps her second glass of cognac immediately and pours a third one. She smiles at me but is struggling to keep her eyes open. "So get this. Your ex-partner's dad, Dick, bombs my family—BOOM. All gone. Then Edward takes care of me. Then Dick bombs again and takes Edward's legs." She stretches her arms and yawns. "And then he also kills his own daughter, your ex-partner. And now Edward kills Dick. Imagine that? And you and I are sitting together getting drunk. At the center of it all are Philip and you. Did you ever think that genius?" She is struggling to coordinate between the bottle and her glass. I collect her drink from her and place it on the table.

"Yes, I thought about that the moment I saw the bullet." Am I just a silent observer in this onslaught of shit? What is my mission that Philip wrote in his letter? And why can't I remember where I've heard this before?

I look at Tabi and her lack of coordination. "You are in no shape to drive. Why don't you spend the night here?"

She can barely open her eyes. "Are you sure?"

"Of course, I'll make a bed for you in one of the guest rooms. You should have everything you need—temperature-zoning control, toothpaste, brush. I'll give you a change of clothes. Though you may need to make do with my Cambridge sweats."

She covers her eyes. Her shaking shoulders reveal her tears and her vulnerability. I sit next to her, bring her head close to my shoulder. "It's not your fault."

She moves her head from my shoulder and stares at me through her tear-stained eyes. "Vengeance and rage drove me. So where do I go from here?" She pulls the lapel of my robe. "Tell me, Vince, what do I do now? You are the genius."

If I were a genius, I would not have rushed a relationship with Emika. I look into Tabi's eyes. "Throw away that locket and that bullet. You start living now. A life free from pain, guilt, and distress."

"This is all I have of my family." She pulls at her locket. "How can I throw it away?"

I take her hand from her locket. "Your family lives in you. Not in that locket."

"Tell me, Vince, how do you put your past behind you?"

"You can't. It's a constant battle where you have to choose your life over your past. And it's a fight I lose every single fucking day. I want you to do better."

Ravi serves a perfect ace. Chris stretches his arm out and tumbles. Ravi and I high five as we sail through the set 6–0. Anna, instead of helping Chris, stands beside him with her hands on her waist. "What's the point of your height when you can't even hit a fucking ball back." She continues as Chris shakes his head and stands up. "I have seen sloths move faster than you."

"What the fuck? It's just a game." Chris turns to me. "Hey, Vince, I can't take her temper anymore. I want to change teams."

Anna touches Chris's shoulder and begins to smile. "Sorry, I was insensitive." Chris starts to accept the apology, but Anna interrupts and bats her eyes. "Sloths have feelings, too."

We all move to the towel station. I throw a bottle of water at each of them. "How about we take ten minutes to break while I ask you guys something?"

I take off my t-shirt and put on a new one. Anna points her racket at me. "Exactly how much weight are you gonna lose?"

I smile. "Leanness suits me." Then I straighten my cap. "I need to know your goals. Primarily, how would you utilize your time if there were no students to teach?"

Ravi sits on the bench, puffs, and wipes sweat from his forehead. "I would spend time on research and inventions. And maybe spend time with firms on the practical applicability. Also, in the last two years, we have seen a decline in the quality of doctoral student applicants."

Chris inspects his new tennis racket and swishes it in the air. "We have an abundance of patents, and we hardly see any commercial applications. We are sitting on a gold mine, but we are spreading ourselves too thin to look beyond teaching undergraduate and graduate classes."

Anna takes off her hairband and looks at Chris. "Stick to air tennis." Then she turns to me. "If I'm freed from teaching, I'd be able to take more time explaining our research to larger firms and even move on to corporate training. But Vince, what exactly are you thinking?"

I smile. "Thanks, guys. I don't want to do anything drastic till our doctoral students graduate. But I want to set the ball in motion for something radical. And I'll be doing it in the next several months."

"And what's that?" Ravi asks.

I inspect my tennis racket and stretch my neck. "I plan to sever us from this university. We have enough funds for a seed fund. But can we strengthen our finances and technological reach? Starting May, I'll travel to Silicon Valley, Seattle, and Boston to meet with some of my angel investor buddies. They want to partner with some institute that sits on top of patents as we do. So that's how I'll pitch us. I'll also make some stops at MIT, Carnegie, UT-Austin, Stanford, Caltech, UC-Berkeley, and UW. I'll be talking to their intellectual property divisions to see if we can collaborate." I pause. "But in the meantime, I'll speak with the legal division of Nardin industries to see if any matching funding is possible. How does this sound?"

Chris comes forward and shakes my hand. "What prompted you?"

I look at Anna and smile. "I couldn't bear to see you guys losing hope in me."

"We never lost hope in you, idiot." Anna touches my shoulder. "Also, we could have discussed this in the office."

"I don't like that office anymore." I pick up a tennis ball and serve it across the net. It hurls through the air, making a wooshing sound, cracks the brick wall, and then drops—all in the blink of an eye. I look at my hand and see blue markings slowly receding. Intreton? I've never served that fast before. What's happening to me? I hope Anna, Chris, and Ravi did not see the markings.

They are staring at me with their jaws dropped. I pick up another tennis ball. "One more round, guys?"

Anna looks at the cracked wall and then looks back at me. Slowly, she raises her hand and crumples her lips. "Can we draw straws? I don't wanna play against you."

While tossing my tennis gear in my trunk, I feel a nudge on my shoulder. I turn around and see a blond guy in his twenties. He looks like those guys who spent their college years playing beer pong and bullying the nerds.

He takes out an envelope from his messenger bag and begins to butcher my name. "Are you Vincent Aba… Abaja…"

I shake my head. "I am. And you can quit struggling." Either he can't read, or he makes a mockery of those who sound different. Remarkably, he made it this far in life and could locate the country club.

Handing me the envelope, he says. "You have been served." Then he abruptly walks away.

It is a subpoena by the US Senate regarding the whereabouts of Philip Nardin, calling me to be a witness on April 13, 2024. I take a picture of the subpoena and send it to the four lawyers.

As I get into my car and put it in reverse, Kenji calls. I begin to drive as I answer. "Hi, Kenji."

"Vince. I'll prep you in the next four or five days. It's nothing new to us. All of us will accompany you. You don't have to worry about getting tickets or taxis to DC. Our corporate jet will pick you up, and we will arrange your stay."

"I'm not sure how to say this, but… is Philip still paying for all this?"

"Yes, son. Philip wants us to represent you, and we can't disappoint him. I urge you to do a bit of research on the Senate committee—it's a corrupt, bipartisan gang that is united in destroying Philip."

"Do you know where Philip is?"

"I can't say anything. We cannot have the risk of you lying in the Senate hearing. Have a good day, Vincent. Get plenty of sleep."

"Thank you, Kenji."
"My pleasure."
After hanging up, I say, "Porsche, call Tabi."
She picks up after one ring. "Hi, Vince."
"I am due on the Senate floor on April 13. Can you help?"

CHAPTER 16

SAKURA

It's easy to stand in the crowd,
but it takes courage to stand alone.
—Mahatma Gandhi

(Four months before today)

APRIL 13, 2024. CAPITOL HILL, Washington, DC.

I riding with Dinesh and Kenji in a blue Bentley Mulsanne. The other two lawyers are riding in front of us inside a Maybach. Dinesh is arguing directions with the driver. Kenji pulls out a bottle of Balvenie-21 and pours a glass. "Relax, Vince." Kenji squints as I take my first sip. "Are you OK, Vince? You have lost weight."

Dinesh turns back. "I was wondering the same."

"I'm fine, gentlemen."

I look the window and see some questionable but understandable signs: "Burn the Senate," "End the Corruption," "People over Profits," "The World is Watching." But as we near the building, the slogans get a little more incomprehensible with "Justice for Dick Graham," "People vs. Nardin." Eight armed men line up with umbrellas to protect us from tomatoes, eggs, and milkshakes before we step out.

The four lawyers help me dodge the journalists and photographers, and we enter the designated room. It is crowded with more journalists and photographers. I can barely keep my eyes open with the constant flashes. I can hear someone instructing someone else to swear in the witness.

Kenji turns to me. "Stand, Vincent."

Someone announces. "Please raise your right hand."

I stand up and raise my right hand.

The voice continues. "Do you swear that the testimony you give will be the truth and nothing but the truth?"

"I do."

"You may sit now."

I am sitting between Jerry and Kenji. Dinesh is seated on the other side of Jerry, and Alberto is next to Kenji. Being flanked by the most feared lawyers in the business gives me a confidence boost that I haven't felt in a long time. GOP Senator Rosenthal chairs the committee, and the vice-chairman is from the Democratic party—Senator Cohen. Tabi helped me research the committee members and their genuine allegiance, which is money. What if they knew I could absorb intreton? Would they tear me apart?

"Can you state your name for the record?" asks the chairman.

"Dr. Vincent Abajian."

"What's your profession, Dr. Abajian?" asks Senator Cohen.

"Professor, scientist, tech-adviser, inventor, author."

After every reply, I shut my eyes due to flashes from the camera. My head is pounding from the cameras' clicking sounds, the blinding flashes, and the typewriter's noise. Jerry whispers. "Now they will ask about Philip. Do your best. We will do the rest."

Rosenthal takes a sip of water and flips through his notes. "Dr. Abajian, do you know Mr. Philip Nardin?"

Did he need his notes for that? I lift my eyebrows. "I do."

There is a pause for a moment. I hear coughing, the typewriter, random camera clicks. Senator Cohen takes off his glasses. "What was the nature of your relationship with Mr. Nardin?"

I straighten my lapel. "Professional."

"Did you write the book, *The Time Fixer: Three Lives of Philip Nardin*?" asks Senator McCarthy from Georgia. If Graham were to be the presidential nominee for GOP, Tabi told me this clown would be his top choice for the VP ticket.

I rest my chin on my palm. "Yes."

McCarthy continues. "When was the last time you saw Philip Nardin?"

I scratch my beard. "October 2023."

"Did Mr. Nardin ever mention Dick Graham to you?"

I pause to assess the risk. My answer could change the direction of questioning. I turn to Kenji and follow his recommendation. "I don't recall."

"Do you think Mr. Nardin had anything to do with the assassination of Dick Graham?" Tabi was right. McCarthy is the protagonist in this circus.

A lot is at stake here. A little lie will save Tabi. Both she and Edward had to deal with terrible tragedies. I believe they want to link Philip Nardin with fictitious rogue elements that killed Dick Graham. "I don't think so," I say, shrugging.

McCarthy taps his desk. "What's the basis of your opinion?"

I am breathing heavily. I sip from a bottle of water and calm down. What a colossal waste of time this is. I lean forward, my nostrils flaring. "Mr. Nardin did not come across as someone capable of such an act. Moreover, Dick Graham was too insignificant to him."

A GOP senator from Mississippi, Mr. Blunt, asks "Have you been to the Nardin residence, Mr. Abajian?"

"First, it's Dr. Abajian. Second, yes, I went to one of his residences."

Then the senator continues. "Why do you think agents of the FBI couldn't locate his residence?" I leer at his question, and Mr. Blunt points his finger at me. "Dr. Abajian, please wipe that smirk off your face and answer the question."

My smirk transforms into a chuckle. "Commenting on the incompetency of your agents and the outdated locating techniques they use is outside my realm of expertise." I slant my head. "Respectfully, sir."

Kenji and the other lawyers struggle to keep the smiles off their faces, and so do the journalists. With every answer, the photographers are turning their cameras from the senators to me. I'll have to go off-script if the questioning line doesn't remain professional.

Floridian Mr. Franks decides to wake up. "What do you think we are doing here, Dr. Abajian?"

"You're wasting taxpayer dollars and a precious resource—my time."

He waves his glasses at me. "You think your time is more precious than ours?"

I lean forward. "Yes. And your time is bought by the lobbyist who represents weapon manufacturers. Your intention isn't to find Philip. Now that Lombard is dissolved, you are showcasing your resolve to find a new employer—a new DOD contractor who might be interested in weaponizing intreton. And in return, you will get your mansions, yachts, and more money in your Swiss accounts."

McCarthy bangs the desk. "That's preposterous!"

I can feel my pulse inching toward a hundred per minute. As I am about to reach for my jacket pocket, Jerry grabs my hand. Kenji leans toward the microphone. "Can we have a five-minute recess?"

Jerry whispers. "Let's stick to the script, Vince."

I stare at McCarthy and Franks and think of Dick Graham's atrocities. These motherfuckers killed over 200 innocent lives. They killed Elise. They took everything from Tabi. She was just twelve. My pulse continues to rise. If it weren't for these guys, Emika would still be with me. Stick to a script for these criminals? Never. They will get the complete Vincent Abajian treatment. I turn to Kenji. "We don't need a recess. Philip would have wanted this."

Kenji turns to Jerry. "Let him do it. If there is any damage, we can manage it."

I take out a folded paper from my pocket. "Dick Graham was just the tip of the iceberg. If one carefully looks at who funds your campaigns and could hack into your private routers, they'd know how loyal you truly are to the people you're supposed to serve." I point my finger. "I'm talking to you two, McCarthy and Franks. Haven't you received five million from Lombard to vote in their favor that their casing is as good as Nardin's? The evidence will be in print tomorrow. I have the account numbers with me." I tilt my head and lift my eyebrows. "You want me to read it?"

Republican McCarthy takes the gavel from Democrat Rosenthal. "This hearing is over." He points at my lawyers. "Your client is in contempt."

"Contempt of what?" Jerry says into the microphone. "You will hear my client."

I stare at McCarthy. "Your vote of confidence for Lombard cost the lives of over 200 people. *The Tribune* will publish the names of each victim and the details of the bribes you received. Yes, you murdered those people. There were American, British, Japanese, Indian, South Korean, Australian, and Chinese citizens. A couple who were about to celebrate their fiftieth wedding anniversary. Two pregnant women. There were students on exchange programs." I pause and gulp and continue, "And fifteen children under nine. You took everything from them, their lives, their dreams, even their death. You want me to read their names and their ages?"

I need a lie that is more powerful than all the truths. However, it's not a lie but false speculation that will deflect attention from Philip to McCarthy and Franks. It will help Tabi and Edward. I lean toward the microphone and point at the two senators. "Maybe you two feared that Graham would squeal your names as co-conspirators. Maybe you orchestrated his assassination and blamed it on the Middle East. After all, you two stood to lose the most if he confessed."

Senator Frank's jaw drops. I don't think he can even fathom this turn of events. Democratic senator Cohen looks at McCarthy while pointing at me. "What is he saying? Is that the truth?" McCarthy ignores Cohen and bangs the gavel. "We are done here." He starts whispering to Senator Franks, breathing hard through his microphone. Senator Blunt is staring blankly at his "esteemed colleagues" while wiping his forehead. I smile at Senator Blunt and shake my head. "I guess your colleagues Graham, McCarthy, and Franks didn't even tell you that you could make money from your vote in favor of Lombard."

The world is witnessing this circus, as every camera now turns to me. I cover my eyes to block the flashes and can't tell which senator makes the following statement. "You, sir, have a lot of contempt for us and the important work we do."

I sigh. "You just proved the point that one doesn't need a functioning brain to be a politician. You just need two types of talent. The first is begging for votes from people and money from lobbyists. The second is deception. If I program deception into a minimally functioning machine agent that's capable of, say, basic actions like sit, roll over, shake hands, I can automate your job instantly. However, you've wasted one day of my life. I usually accomplish more in a day than you do in your entire pathetic lives smeared with mediocrity and corruption. I am done." I stand up.

Alberto, Dinesh, Jerry, and Kenji fold their papers in their briefcases and follow. Senator McCarthy goes to his microphone. "We are not done with you, Dr. Abajian!"

I turn back. "I thought you said the hearing was over."

Then I feel a tingling in my palms, and as I lift my cuffs, I see blue intreton markings. I form a fist before the sparks come out. The markings retract. So my sparks are detached from heartbreaks. I'd thought it would be impossible, given they first appeared the exact moment Emika was born and the moment I learned of Akane's disappearance. Maybe I can move on now.

I have received five calls from Dr. Rebecca Kauffman. I am not returning them. The liberal media celebrated that I am an immigrant, which I never found to be an achievement. The conservative media found a way to use my heritage to propagate immigration obstruction for international students to come to the US. And Anna, Chis, and Ravi keep sending me memes from my Senate hearing. I am now an emoji called Vi-Moji, which spits fire from its mouth, burning people. My Senate performance made my book climb to the top spot in the NY Times best seller's list.

My phone beeps. It's my school group.

> Krista: Saw you on TV. Is that the Vince we knew from school?
>
> Me: Why?
>
> Sasha: That was a sweet Vince who would cry at the very mention of Akane. This one is a badass who ran out of fucks to give.

Me: I still cry when I think of her. Hulk is the only witness.
Krista: You still plan to come here next year?
Me: Yes.
Fred: Awesome. We need to catch up.

I can hear the beginning of Claire de Lune. After opening my eyes, I turn off the alarm. It's 6:30 a.m., April 15, 2024. I've woken up in my guest room. Hulk is nowhere to be found. "Hulky?" I yell. No response. I leave the guestroom and find him sitting on Emika's chair, staring outside, looking at the mountains. Emika would sit there with Hulk on her lap, singing to him, and together they'd watch the hills. It's been two months since I dropped her at the airport.

"Wanna go out, Hulky?" He comes running to me. I pick him up, and he licks me. I change into my robes and dress Hulk in his warm buffalo plaid woolens. Then we venture out to the backyard. As I reach the glass walls to the backyard, my eyes are riveted to the scene outside. My heart skips a beat. The cherry trees have turned pink, and petals are falling in flurries. I release Hulk, and he runs around the trees, hoping to catch a few flying petals, barking at them. Pink flurries dance in front of the snowy foothills and snowcapped mountains that look golden against the morning sun. I stand beneath the cherry blossoms and open my palm. A couple of petals land on it. They may be from the same bloom—they may spend all the time together for a season, and now they will never meet again, forget each other, and wither away in solitude. Yet, they seemed inseparable until yesterday. My hands are cold. They miss the warmth of Emika's touch. I wish she were here to witness this with me.

I take a four-minute-long video, choose Aoi Teshima's "Spring Breeze" as the background score, and send it to her with the subject line "*Hanafubuki*: Keeping my promise." The video has the sakura, Hulk running around, and what used to be our home. But it does not have me in it. My phone beeps after a few minutes.

Emika: *Arigato*, Vince. The song perfectly complements the video. It reminds me of the conversations we had on the day I discovered you were an artist. You know, when you talked about language barriers and music. Saw you at the Senate hearing. I'm beginning to understand what you were going through all this time and why you concealed everything from me. I'm sorry, Vince. I hope one day you will forgive me.

Me: You're welcome. Good to know.

I don't think our hearts will move even an inch closer if I write how I feel. And, I don't want to add to the conflict between her feelings and Akane's. I wish I could extract Akane from her. But, how? Is the answer linked to my sparks? Mr. Kruger did write that they open a gateway to the unknown. That must be the turbulence. If he knew what it was, why did he insist that I should distract myself from it? At times, I've tried to use the sparks to create small turbulences and pierce through them. But, each time, it collapses, and I keep losing weight. My phone vibrates.

Tabi: Your performance put McCarthy, Franks, and Blunt in custody.

Me: Your research and their acts did it. I just used speculation to show the truth.

Tabi: Hey, I would like to buy you dinner sometime.

Me: Sure. But I do the buying.

Tabi: OK. We'll fix a date.

Me: Let's do it soon because I'll be traveling for three months.

Tabi: Well, I will be traveling, too. It would be awesome if we met in a different city.

Me: I will share my itinerary.

The doorbell rings. Anna is the first to enter. She starts firing as soon as she sees me. "So now if I need to see you, I have to switch on the TV? You have a center, you know." She hugs me and touches my face. "Are you OK, bud? You looked so furious. If only we'd known what you were going through. You made the senators shit their pants."

"I'm fine. Planning my travel itinerary and making appointments. This Senate thing came out of nowhere."

Chris, Maddy, and Ravi patiently wait outside the open door for Anna to be done with me. Chris and Ravi enter with three boxes of pizzas from Godfathers. I collect everyone's jackets, then take a seat on the sectional. Chris and Ravi place the boxes on the kitchen counter, and Anna opens the cabinet for plates. Ravi turns to me. "Can we?" pointing at the bar.

"Of course." I smile. "Pick whatever you like."

Chris winks. "Including the Yamazaki-55?"

"Of course, man."

I can faintly hear their whispers. Ravi is asking Anna, "Why don't you talk?" Anna responds with, "Why is it always me?" Then Chris takes charge. "Because you are close to him, and you still talk to Emika."

I turn to them. "Guys, I can hear you. I'm fine."

Anna brings me three slices of my pizza and sits next to me. Chris follows and sits next to her. Madelyn and Ravi occupy the two chairs perpendicular to my position. Anna looks at my slice. "Why have you changed your regular order?"

"It was Emika's doing. I need to change it back."

"For once, she was right." Anna rubs my arm. "Hey, we had a watch party in the college gallery for your Senate hearing. About fifty faculty members attended, including us three, Madelyn, Linda, and Vikram. Vik commented, 'That's why you don't mess with Vince'." Then she starts scrolling through her texts and suddenly pokes my arm. "Even Emika saw it live, and she texted me. 'If I had only known what he was going through all these months. I feel so terrible.' Do you wanna know what I wrote back? She also called me too."

I click my tongue. "Not really. I don't care."

"Suit yourself," Anna says, rolling her eyes.

Awkwardness looms across the house. I can hear the ticking of Philip's clocks and the chewing of pizza.

After a few moments, Anna removes my empty plate. Suddenly she asks, "Did you love Emika because you thought she was Akane?"

"Why is this important?"

Anna lifts her legs into a lotus position and turns to me. "Because all your actions indicated that you looked for Akane in her."

"I was drawn to her because of Akane," I say, looking at Anna. "But when I looked into her eyes, I always searched for an Emika, free from Akane. That's the woman I loved. And that's the one who did not want me."

"Did you ever tell this to her?"

I sigh and shake my head. "She left too soon."

"Then why did you gift her the violin, idiot?" Anna asks, pulling at my robe.

"Emika had challenges playing some violin pieces that Akane used to play. I thought uniting her with Akane's violin would help her overcome that obstacle. It has nothing to do with me finding Akane in her."

Madelyn had been quietly absorbing all this, turns to me. "Vince, I am not privy to most of this. But can I say something?"

"Sure."

"Since you did not get the chance to explain, Emika must have thought that all you cared about was whether she was Akane. Do you think she chose this house and life, with you thinking she was a fragment of Akane? The violin gifting may have been heartbreaking for her."

I click my tongue. "Then she should not have accepted the violin. I would have kept it."

"She did not want to break your heart," Ravi argues, agreeing with Madelyn.

"Shocking." I lift my eyebrows. "Emika must have been repelled by that."

Anna grabs my robe again. "Listen, idiot, remember our dinner at Sichuan Palace?"

"Yes?"

"Well, around October last year, I asked Emika why she'd turned so gloomy upon learning that you were an orphan," Anna says, letting go of my robe.

I am staring at the floor. "Go on."

"She always had a vision of life in the Alps, where she used to hang around with a kid that looked like the young Vince in your picture with Akane. In her vision, that kid had no parents. So, the first time she found out you were an orphan, she got emotional, thinking that it could've been you who came into her visions. After all, she had no vision of an adult man. Everything was confirmed when she saw that picture of you as a kid."

My jaw drops. "She never told any of it to me."

"Telling you all this would only ensure you'd only seek Akane in her," Chris adds in. "She just wanted to be Emika in your eyes. Plus, you kept her at bay from all the turmoil you were facing. She thought she had no place in your life besides someone who looked like Akane."

I turn to Chris. "She was Emika in my eyes. Always has been. I had to keep her away from all this political shit." I look down and form a fist. "I couldn't let those fuckers interrogate my Emi." Then I look up Anna, Chris, and Ravi. "Same with you guys. I had to protect all of you. I couldn't drag you into my shit."

Madelyn stacks the pizza boxes, and I collect them for recycling.

Ravi twists the cap of a stout and looks at me. "Why don't you tell her that you always searched for Emika, who is free from Akane?"

"I cannot ingratiate myself anymore," I say as I sit back down on the sofa. "Besides, she is deeply conflicted. I am confident that Akane in her initiated the relationship with me. She has to disregard that and know what she wants from life. I really don't want to mess things up for her by asserting my presence. I wish I could extract Akane and her haunting memories out of Emika and free her. But I can't. And I haven't a fucking clue where Philip is."

I gather my thoughts and stand up. "Since all of you are here, I want to tell you that, from May through August, I'll be traveling for my expansion plan. Anna will be the acting director while I'm gone." I turn to Anna. "Yes, you can park in my spot while I am gone, but I need another favor from you."

She blinks. "Anything."

I pick up my Hulk. "Can I put you as an emergency contact with Little Paws while I am away?" I swallow the shake in my voice. "Also, if something were to happen to me, can you adopt my boy? He is all that I have."

She puts her hands on my cheeks. "What the fuck? Nothing will ever happen to you. You will not do anything stupid. Second, yes, I can adopt him, but I won't have to. And he will not be in Little Paws for three months. He stays with me."

CHAPTER 17

AUGUST 13

The wound is the place where the light enters you.
—Rumi

(Two days before today)

MY ARMS ARE SPREAD OUTWARD as sparks from my fingers create a circular path. I enter the turbulence. Suddenly, a Vincent from the future appears and pokes my chest. “You are wasting time. It will be dawn in London soon. You have to free her before she wakes up. Complete your mission and become the Time Corrector.” I close my eyes, and an image of my Emika appears. She is smiling through her teary eyes. “See you later, Vince,” she says, waving.

And I smile. “Goodbye, Emi.”

That's been my recurring dream since I came back from my three-month-long hectic trip. I have secured an excess of two billion in funding. The center will be how I want it—free from this stupid university and free from the memories of Emika. Tomorrow, I will meet with Anna, Chris, and Ravi to start looking at office spaces. I will be the guest on *What's Tonight, with Maurice Johnson*, two days from now. He is traveling all over the country and hosting shows outside LA. I guess my book and stunt in the Senate made me a celebrity. I'll have to drive to Seattle for that show.

I roll my sleeves up as blue intreton markings appear on my skin. Then I snap my fingers with both hands. Sparks! So, I can transfer all my energy through a snap of a finger and create a spark. I roll the sparks in both hands into balls. That's the core. I circle my fingers around the balls to make them bigger.

I turn to the sphere on my left hand. I see a lady putting her child to sleep while humming Kreisler's Liebesleid. As she gently touched the child's chubby cheeks, it grabs her fingers, whimpers making the mother smile. Yet, her tears roll down her cheeks. She knows that her time with the baby is ending. She is the lady from Philip's painting that I have—she is Amara. Gently, she swings the broken bassinet in which the child is sleeping. Then she tucks her child inside a torn quilt and picks up the baby. The child whines and stares into the loving eyes of its mother. Amara doesn't know that she will be meeting Philip soon—someone who she knows as Victor. She doesn't know that someone from the future will tell Philip what to do with the child. As she smiles at the child with twinkling eyes, I can see the actual color of her eyes and the texture of her hair. They are identical to her child's. They are identical to mine.

I turn to the sphere on my right hand, and I see my Emika. She sits next to a crib, putting a child to sleep while humming Aoi Teshima's "Spring Breeze." Her eyes are shut, with tears rolling out, reaching her chin. But why is she crying? What does she want but can't reach? How far in the future is this? Is she still conflicted between her desires and Akane's? I close my palm. The intreton markings retract.

I am sitting facing the glass wall—Emika's favorite corner. The horizon before me is getting dark. A series of lightning hits behind the mountains, reflecting on the evergreen trees, making them white and purple. It starts to rain, and streams of water run down the glass wall. I hold Hulk tightly in my lap. "It's just you and me, two orphans." He digs his face between my arms and waist.

I have everything that I want, yet I feel a vacuum inside of me. I felt empty in every hotel room, the airport lounge, the airplanes, and even when I presented my work. Scrolling through my entire calls list, I excavate our last conversation, buried deep between pointless exchanges with university presidents, IP lawyers, angel investors, Vikram, Edward, Kenji, my publisher. What time is it in London? I turn my JLC Reverso.

I hit the call button and stumble into her voicemail. "Hi, you have reached Emika. Please leave me a message. Thank you!"

"Hi, Emi. I am weary of trying to move past you, and I can't lie to myself anymore. I am surrounded by objects that tease me of our brief time together and what could have been. Now, I'm sitting with a cup of Genmaicha tea and watching the rain splash on the window. I can see the mountains and the lake in the rain, and how everything changes as soon as the lightning strikes. Yesterday, it was sunny, and the golden light touched the snowcapped mountains, the hill, the trees, the grass." Breathing deeply, I shut my eyes. "Hey, you know the bellflowers never bloomed in spring, but they did yesterday. The setting sun shone on them, and it was gorgeous to see how the light danced around them. I could almost picture you picking them and placing them all over our home. Yes, our home. I know the conflicts in your mind. But I think you may get some clarity tomorrow morning. And after that, if you feel we are still the work in progress with beautiful potential, I will be waiting for you right here. And, Emi, I love you."

Will she ever check this voicemail? Since I left school, I found myself continually searching for something. It was someone. The very moment Emika walked through my office door, I knew it was her. But that's just my feelings. She deserves to be free. I can't get Akane back, but I can free Emika from her memories. And, if Emika forgets me, I will have my peace with it. We will become a memory, just like all other good things in my life. Emika deserves a life of her own, free from the memory of a child that made her find me—a worthless orphan.

I just need to make another call.

"What's up?"

"I need a favor, Anna."

"What?"

"Can you call me tomorrow morning? And, if I don't pick up, can you take Hulk home with you?"

"What the fuck, Vince?"

"Hey, nothing serious. All I need is for you to promise to check on me tomorrow morning."

"I will, and I also want to watch you live on *What's Tonight*. So, don't do anything stupid."

"I won't."

All my involvement with politics and the university funds helped me see the discord in Emika. My not sharing anything with her was a mirror, showing me what she was going through. Now I know what Philip meant in his letter. I know my mission—I have to free Emika.

I prepare Hulk's favorite food with chunks of tuna and steak. I don't know if this is the last time I will see him. Picking him up, I kiss his head, trying to hide the tremble in my voice so he doesn't sense it. "Be a good boy." I lift my cuff—it's 7:00 p.m. The rain has stopped, the grass is wet, reflecting tiny droplets of water on their tips.

I wrap Akane's scarf around my neck as I walk into my backyard, leaving Hulk in the house. Then I walk to the farthest edge of the property. I extend my arms in the direction of the house, taking a deep breath. The blue markings of intreton appear, and with them, the sparks, unabated. The sparks grow brighter, their white light illuminating the whole backyard. I move my hands to create a circular path with the sparks while the background disappears. My house is now a haze, and Summit View is barely visible. It's just me and a bright circular doorway—a gate to the core, the unknown. The past and the future merge and bend to converge into this moment. The gate does not want me to enter—it knows my mission. It's hurling a storm toward me, making my hair, jacket, and scarf fly, trying to throw me off the cliff. *Not today, pal. You have controlled my life for so long. You have taken all that I hold dear. You took the only one who loved me, and then you made another one suffer for years. It all changes today.*

I cover my eyes, tighten Akane's scarf around my neck, and enter the turbulence. Dust, wind, and pieces of rubble all come flying toward me. In the very next moment, my jacket, hair, and scarf all fall into place. The storm is gone. And so is the ground underneath my feet. I am levitating. I float for a few hundred feet and encounter a world I have never seen before. As I land on the ground, I look at my shaking palms. The intreton markings are all gone. Looking in front of me, I see green meadows and gigantic trees as far as the eye can see. I see the seasons changing instantly, from spring cherry blossoms to lush summers, fall colors, and winter white. What's causing them to change so frequently? Suddenly, a gigantic tourbillon appears right in front of me. It's bigger than my house. The tourbillon encases a movement whose center, other than a balance spring and an escapement, is a massive sphere of shimmering white light, just like the sparks in my hands. That must be the core, pure energy. Did I summon something? Or did I create a path to the North Sea?

The sparks at the outer edge of the core are connected to the tourbillon. The core is throbbing—expanding and contracting like a living object. Its reverberation radiates a pulse that shakes my jacket, hair, and scarf, and there is a change of season with each throb. But there is some peculiarity. The trees expand with each vibration, but they start back again from a sapling after a while. I begin counting. The trees reach maximum height after 164 beats, and then they go back to being a sapling. I understand it now. It's a depiction of forty-one years of my pathetic life in a loop.

The whole apparatus—the tourbillon, the movement, and the core slowly move at a 66-degree angle, making a deep swooshing sound. I have seen several tourbillons in watch shops and museums, but none this majestic. The entire apparatus is made from platinum and gold, and the escape wheel has intreton crystals size of bricks. But would Philip build a tourbillon? Is the core susceptible to the effects of gravity, and the tourbillon neutralizes it? Or does the tourbillon fix the problem with time turbulence?

As I walk closer to the apparatus, a baritone voice welcomes me.

"Welcome, Vincent." The deep bass shakes the trees and their leaves.

I look around, but I can't see anyone. So, I look up. "Who are you?"

"I am Chronos, protector of time, and keeper of the core."

"How do you know me? What is this place?"

"I have been waiting for you. Your struggles, trials, and triumphs have led you to open the door to the crossroads of all realities—a place outside the space-time continuum. Only two people on this planet can access it, but only you can summon it."

My pulse rises rapidly. "Me? Isn't Philip the Time Fixer?"

"He uses borrowed abilities, but you were born with it."

"Borrowed from whom?" I ask.

"You."

How could Philip get this from me? "How?"

"You will soon find out."

I crane my neck up more. "Tell me how Emika was born in the same reality that Akane was taken from?"

"You wished her back, that's why. The core granted it."

I can feel the pulse from each of my heartbeats. So I am responsible for Emika's suffering? "Why was it granted?" I ask, struggling to hold back my tears.

"It was a pure selfless wish from the prospective Time Corrector. That's all. You never wished for anything else in your life. Instead, you worked and toiled for everything else. And now you here to undo your wish—another selfless act."

"How can I access Emika's past that is linked with Akane?"

"Float toward the core and enter it."

"I don't see an entrance."

"You don't need one. You are the Time Corrector."

I look at the core. "And what will I see when I enter?"

"Everything, even minute details from your past and your future. But Vincent, the core will fight back if you make any changes. It will tempt you to not do this."

I jump toward the core. A hole opens up as I pierce through it, floating with my right hand forward. I look back and see the pathway close behind me. How do I get out? Not important right now. The spherical core changes into a luminous golden tunnel with endless red doors on my right and left. All the doors are marked with the names of people who came into my life—Amara, Philip, David Kruger, Akane. I put a brake on my flight, and I stand before her door. I want to enter this door, to see her one last time. Should I?

As I touch the door, I feel a knot in my stomach, just like I felt on the day I learned of her disappearance. *I am sorry, Akane. I would give anything for just a minute with you. But, I have something more pressing today. I need to free someone from you. Please forgive me.*

I move on, passing every person who came into my life. And then there it is—a door, marked in hiragana, with the name "Emika." I turn the knob and enter. The room has a red and black tint to it. It looks painful. There she is, sitting on a chair, holding her violin and massaging her temples. Perhaps she is not much older than nine and is wearing a knee-length navy dress with white polka-dots and puffed sleeves. Her shoes are pink with a white bow. This is the girl whose image I saw in my school's music room at my graduation in August 2001. So that was Emika?

As I come near her, she looks up. Her eyes are filled with tears. "*Anata wa dare?*"

I kneel down to reach her height. Then I wipe her tears with my scarf and kiss her forehead. "I am nobody. Is there something troubling you?"

"I have this headache when I try to play four pieces," she says, waving her violin. "I hear voices." Her voice trembles and she presses her temples hard. "*Sore wa itai.*"

"Do you want those voices gone?" I place my hand on top of her head.

She nods. "*Hai.*"

I stand up and tighten my scarf. "Then let's get rid of them."

Looking past her, I see a black tree with red leaves on it. It's riddled with a complex tapestry of stems and branches. As I walk toward it, I start decoding the branches and see a particular stem, which looks like another tree attached to the main one. It slanted the tree in one direction and stunted the main tree from growing. The whole tree, led by the stem, is inclined toward me. As I move left, the branch along the entire tree slants toward the left. When I move right, the same thing.

This branch must have attached itself to the main tree in August 2001. Akane must have heard my plea. *All I want is to see you—maybe just for a minute. Is that too much to ask?* And then she'd rushed into Emika. Which made Emika pick the violin and attach herself to me. It is all my fault. I am the one who caused her suffering.

I take off my jacket and roll my sleeves up. Gripping the stem, I pull with all the strength I can muster. I brace my right leg against the main tree, and I keep tugging. Every vein in my arm is bulging out. They will burst open if I pull harder. I pause to catch my breath. Was the extra strength that I discovered during the tennis session for this? I can't let it go to waste. I can't give up. So I start again, and with every pull, the stem separates from the tree, bit by bit. And, with each tear, the room's color changes from red to purple to blue, and grass begins to grow on the floor. With each pull, the gloom in Emika's face fades away by a smidgen, and she begins to glow.

Emika comes running. "Can I help?" she asks, pulling at my shirt.

"You have suffered enough. It's my turn."

I take the deepest breath of my entire life, grab the branch with both hands, and create a fulcrum with my right leg against the main tree. And I pull. I feel the blood rushing to my head. I can feel my eyes bulge out. "Come on, you son of a bitch. Leave her alone." With one mighty yank, I find myself on the ground five feet away from the tree, holding the severed stem.

I stand up. As I look around, the room transforms into green meadows, rolling hills, and snowcapped mountains in the distance. The tree, free from the stem, transforms itself into fifteen cherry trees, each blooming pink. This is the scene from my backyard that she wanted to share with me—the magnificence of *hanafubuki*. Emika's violin disappears. I look at my hand. The branch has transformed into a luminous orb the size of a tennis ball. All her memories connected to Akane, and perhaps her feelings for me, reside in this core. She may not remember me anymore, but she is free. I look at Emika. Her gloom is gone, the beauty mark has disappeared, and she is glowing with joy. She spreads her arms and runs around the cherry blossoms as tiny bits of cherry petals land on her hair like pink snowflakes.

Then she rushes toward me and hugs me with her tiny arms. "*Arigato gozimasu.*"

I kneel down and kiss her forehead as I swallow my tears. "You are free. Now live your life."

As I leave the room, Emika grabs my sleeve. "When will I see you again?"

"Whenever you want."

I take the glowing orb and leave the room. Looking back, I see Emika's room get engulfed within the walls. I smile and shake my head. So, she will forget me. Across from me, a door marked "Crossroads" opens up. I walk in. It's a circular hall with equal-sized sections along its perimeter. Each unit is separated by sparks, just like those from my fingers. I walk into the first one, and I see a young Philip holding a little baby in his arms. I know now that baby is me—Amara's son. Philip turns to me, squints. "Vincent?"

Before I can respond, another person walks in. He is wearing the wristwatch Philip made—he is me from the future. He looks at Philip and points at me. "Yeah! That's me, from three or four years back."

I touch the other guy's shoulder, and he smiles at me. "Hey, Vince. You look like shit." He then turns back to Philip. "Can you build him a suit so that he doesn't lose any more weight?"

"Of course."

I am gasping for breath, trying to absorb all this. "How is this possible? How can the three Vincents occupy the same space?"

"You are the Time Corrector," Philip says to the future Vincent. "Go on."

Vincent looks at me. "Vince, this is the crossroads of reality. The past and the future are co-occurring. You have earned the key to it."

"He has the key too?" I ask, pointing at Philip.

Philip nods. "Yes, I am the caretaker of the Time Corrector." He smiles and shrugs. "You know the Time Fixer."

"How did you get the key?"

"Watch closely." Vincent creates a spark without even snapping his fingers. He takes little Vincent from Philip's arms and transfers the spark to Philip, touching only his right hand. Then he looks at me. "Like that." He hands little Vincent back to Philip.

"You see, Vince, I can never summon the core," Philip says. "That's why I had to build a station. Can you guess who asked me to build the station?"

"I did?"

Vincent claps. "Bingo."

I look between the both of them. "So, what brings all of you here?"

Vincent shakes his head and smiles, turning to Philip. "Name him after my favorite artist and give him my mother's last name. There is a man in Basel, David Kruger, the headmaster at a boarding school in Montognola. He will raise Vince." Future Vincent pauses, and his voice quavers. "He is tough, but he will love him like his own son, in his own flawed way." He turns to me. "Right, Vince?"

I shut my eyes to hold back my tears. My lips tremble. "Yes."

Then Vincent points to a room across the hall. "If you are more curious, go in there."

As I enter that other room, I see Vincent and Philip playing chess. Vincent moves the bishop and says, "Checkmate." Then he looks at Philip. "You need to create a synthetic intreton and name it intreton-C. I will let you know of its widespread applications. But you must cut it to 3 nanometers to help Edward's legs and to help me create a path-breaking invention." Vincent turns to me and winks.

Philip takes off his glass. "Edward?"

"You will meet him in 2006," Vincent says, smiling.

I approach them. "When is this taking place?"

Vincent turns to me. "Philip here is from 2005, and I am from 2028. We are playing chess in a time removed from past and future." He starts setting the pieces on the board and looks at Philip. "Ford and Shelby must put Bruce Mclaren and Ken Miles as their drivers. If Ferrari keeps winning, the arena will lose its charm. I have already created a simple navigation path across realities in 2025."

"You got it," Philip responds as he inspects the board.

"When did you guys had your first conversation?" I ask.

Philip leans back and smiles. "1992."

"I have no memory of this."

Vincent points at the orb I am holding. "It will come to you after you finish the mission."

I look at both of them. "Can't I see that memory here?"

"I have removed it from here." Vincents stands up. "It should not be tinkered with."

"Why can't I recall it?" I clench my teeth.

Vincent walks toward me with his eyebrows furrowed and pokes my chest. "Because you created it from the future. You wanted to safeguard it even from yourself." Then his voice becomes more baritone, like Chronos's. He lifts his cuffs and points at his watch—the one Philip made. "You are wasting time. It will be dawn in London soon. You have to free her before she wakes up. Complete your mission and become the Time Corrector. Then, you will remember everything."

The room begins to fade, and with it, the tunnel. The hole opens up again, and I fly through it until I reach the core's periphery, right before the tourbillon. I land on the ground gently.

I place my palms on the orb and expand it to see all of Emika's memories linked to Akane's. I see her picking up the violin the first time, her struggles with the four pieces. I see her attending my lecture in Tokyo, coming to the US, applying for the postdoc job, and entering my office. But are these memories the only reason why Emika was drawn to me? I shouldn't watch any more. If I do, I will lose my resolve. I have to end it. So I look away.

Chronos asks, "Why did you stop looking?"

I wipe my tears with Akane's scarf. "Because I must destroy this."

"Memories can't be destroyed. But they can be transferred."

"Then how do I make sure this does not go back to her?" I ask, breathing hard.

"There is only one way. But, remember, the one you love may not remember you."

My heart is racing. I take some deep breaths and smile at my fate. "Chronos, it's still worth it."

"Place the orb against your heart. Your body will absorb the memories. Those are now your burden. To balance this extraction, minute portions of Emika's past will change, and memories of those will come gradually in her mind." Warns Chronos.

The orb rests in my right hand, and I am about to place it against my chest when I feel a tug on my left sleeve. I know that pull—I haven't felt that in years. What now? I look down and see the sweetest face I have ever known. I kneel to reach her. Her eyes are wet. She is holding a violin case in her right hand, and she touches my face with her left hand. "You don't want me anymore?"

I gently place my hand on her head. "I will always want you."

"Then why are you doing this?" she asks, moving her hand from my face to run her fingers over the scarf.

I kiss her tiny hand. "You've got to stop hurting Emika, alright? She did nothing wrong. Just like you, she was a little girl."

She moves back and stomps her feet. Her face turns red, and she crumples her eyebrows. "It's not fair, Abajian. I waited so long to find you."

"Life is unfair." I stand up and stare down at her. "And besides, you are not Akane."

Her voice changes from sweet to hoarse. "Why do you say that?"

"My Akane would never knowingly hurt me by hurting Emika. My Akane would never call me by the name Abajian. It was always Vincent, Vince, or silly. My Akane carried her violin case on her back or in her left hand. You are just a cheap imitation."

Her face turns into molten wax, and she begins to disappear, but not before uttering, "You will suffer."

What's new about that? I clench my jaw and stare at the core. "If Akane wants to meet me, she has to come back whole—not by infecting an innocent soul."

I place the orb again on my chest. It illuminates my chest as my skin begins to absorb it. I can't keep my eyes open. As I let them close, an image of my Emika appears. She is smiling, but her eyes are wet with tears. Waving her slender hands, she says, "See you later, Vince." The light stops glowing as my Emika disappears.

I open my eyes. The orb has been entirely absorbed into me, though the load I had been carrying is gone. I look at my hands—they will perhaps never hold her. But she is free at last. I wipe my tears with Akane's scarf. "Goodbye, Emi."

I created this turbulence, and I made this adjustment. Can a Time Corrector create turbulence across realities? I look up. "Chronos, who was the Time Corrector during the times of Victor Constantin and Olivier Journe?" I grind my teeth. "Who took my Akane?"

"It's immaterial who a Time Corrector is and at what time. They can make any adjustments, even those that are beyond their time. Those turbulences resulted from an act that hasn't taken place yet."

I shake my head. "The future predicts the past—a future that hasn't happened, at that? What action?"

"Yes. Future actions of Time Correctors can lead to experiencing an effect in the past before the future even takes place. You will experience the act."

"Can these actions be undone?"

"You can try when the time comes," Chronos says. "But you have to wait. You have already rewound time and reality, which will result in a long-winding course correction. Doing more tonight will break time. It is like resetting a mechanical watch between 9:00 p.m. and 3:00 a.m., which is catastrophic for a movement."

"What course correction?"

"Every human infected by a time-turbulent survivor suffers—they just don't get freed. Your freeing Emika deviates from normality, and to balance that, the cause of her suffering will change. The course correction will result in an outcome that will alter the reason for Emika's suffering and justify your freeing her. The outcome will have minimal consequences to the world—except for you."

Someone taps my shoulder, and I turn to see another older me. He has a *tanto* in his right hand and a journal in his left. He shakes his head and smiles. "I wish I could tell you that it gets easier." I notice streak marks of intreton on his neck and throat. Why? He catches me staring and guesses my thoughts. "I am from 2033, and by the time you are there, you will know everything." Then he hands me the journal. "It's a brief history of Time Correctors. Don't rush into reading it." He touches my shoulder as I take the journal. "Take your time with it."

I point at his hand. "What brings you here? And what's with the *tanto*?"

"It's just a device." He smiles. "I can't reveal anything else."

"Anything you can you reveal?"

His smile widens, almost reaching his ears, yet his eyes remain moist. "You are neither unloved nor are you worthless." His voice trembles. "If you were, I wouldn't be here, preserving all that you did."

I tilt my head. "Like what?"

"Take care, Vincent." He snaps his fingers.

Everything disappears.

I open my eyes to find that I lie in the backyard, covered in dirt and grass. The journal is in my right hand. So, it wasn't a dream. I brush myself off and shake my head. As I stand up, I notice that my trousers have come loose once again. I tighten the belt to the last hole, then look up and see Hulk peering through the window, wagging his tail, and scratching on the glass. It's still 7:15 p.m. on the JLC Reverso, but 10:00 p.m. on my cellphone.

I drag all the mud with me into the house, and Hulk follows me to my bedroom. I place the journal on my bedside table. Then I take out all my watches from my winder. All the three watches have stopped at 7:15 p.m., with both the Omega Seamasters changing their dates erratically. Philip's clocks are perfectly ticking. Going into the bathroom area, I stand on my scale—five pounds lighter. I feel the sweat beginning to form on my brow.

I put all my watches in my jacket pockets, harness Hulk's leash, lower the thermostat by 4 degrees and leave the property. When I reach my neighbor's driveway, I check all my mechanical watches. They have all autocorrected themselves to the right time, with the Omegas displaying the correct date. So my house is outside the reality now? Why didn't this happen when I created turbulence on February 15? Maybe because it collapsed. When will this one collapse? How can Hulk be between two realities? Is it because he swallowed an intreton crystal on February 15? Hulk wags his tail as I kneel down and kiss his button nose. "I love you, bug."

I stand up and wrap Akane's scarf around me. How many time loops have I created to learn the future and tell Philip to forge it? Suddenly, a jolting pain hits my head, and I shut my eyes tight. I remember it all, just like the future me said I would. The first time I heard the name Emika, saw the TIME-FIXR license plate, got the Breguet watch, my mission, and wrapping Emika with my scarf. It's only been coming in fragments over the past thirteen months, starting the day I entered Philip's house. Now I know why he winked at me when he asked if the directions had worked, back when I visited his house for the first time.

CHAPTER 18

1992

Everything makes sense if the future and the past bend and converge into the present.

(My memories)

I AM SITTING ON THE BENCH outside Headmaster Kruger's office, clad in my school uniform and swinging my legs, which are too short to touch the floor. Beside me is a little suitcase that I packed, with Akane's violin case on top. I am wearing Akane's scarf around my neck. From behind the closed door and through the vents, I can hear two voices—Mr. Kruger's and someone else's. I can pick out every word.

"Here are your million Swiss francs. How are you distracting him?" asks the stranger.

Mr. Kruger assures, "Drawing, culinary arts, math, and chess."

"Slowly, introduce more complex things like watchmaking. He needs to appreciate the art of the time," the stranger says. "He is the true Time Corrector, unlike me. He will have a hard life, and he will have to make difficult choices, Dave."

Mr. Kruger's voice croaks, "Tough choices? Don't you think he has had enough? He is just a child."

The stranger's voice deepens. "And listen, don't treat him like a snowflake child of some insignificant duke or worthless celebrity."

"Snowflake?" Mr. Kruger's voice booms through the door. "You were not there when I broke the news to him. That girl was all he had. You were not there when the sparks came out that day. That day he became an orphan all over again."

There's a loud bang on Mr. Kruger's desk, and then the stranger continues. "He is no ordinary boy. And I have always watched him. I watched his past, his future, and the past through the future. You need to teach him to suppress his gifts. And when the day comes, he will be ready to summon the core at his will. That is something I can never do."

"How will he know when he is ready?"

"The moment he frees himself from all the doubts surrounding what he should do, he will be able to summon the core. And then, he will be able to bend time, converging the past and future. He will be able to exist in multiple realities and seamlessly travel between them."

"How can he travel across realities?"

"Intreton runs through his veins."

"What?" Mr. Kruger shouts. "There is no such peculiarity in his medical reports?"

"It won't appear in any scans. It only gets revealed in the presence of time turbulence. So, he can seamlessly walk and glide in it."

"What else can you share?" inquires Mr. Kruger.

The stranger pauses, and silence engulfs the room. I can even hear Mr. Kruger's pendulum. "I know the exact date he gets his power, and I know that he completes his mission and becomes the Time Corrector on August 13, 2024."

"That's thirty-two years from now. How do you know it's Vincent? What mission?"

"I can't tell you the mission. Vince must find out himself. And, I can spot him among a hundred thousand at a Pink Floyd concert. He is the spitting image of Amara. He is all that I have of her. And he is the closest to a child I could ever have."

After a few moments, Mr. Kruger breaks the stillness. "Which year are you traveling from?"

"July of 2023, just a day before the interview. I am using a navigation path that Vincent created in 2025. Vincent from 2027 asked me to come here and tell him about this mission. And when he wakes up on the day of the interview, the memory will come in fragments and puzzles, which he will solve after completing his mission. After meeting him today, I will go back in 2023 and finish a painting of Amara. Vincent won't remember any of it till he becomes the Time Corrector."

I hear the screeching sound of chairs being pushed back and a forceful tap on the desk. "Take care, Dave. Enjoy the money and buy him some nice clothes."

The conversation stops, and I hear footsteps nearing the door. The doorknob turns and then clicks. The stranger steps out of Mr. Kruger's office and looks at me. He stoops down and touches my right shoulder. "Ah! You must be Vincent." I look up at him. He is wearing a linen suit and a fedora. His beard is white and pointy, and he is carrying a tan briefcase in his left hand.

"Yes, sir. How do you know?"

He touches my hair, looks at my eyes, and smiles. "I can tell from those Turkish blue eyes and that wavy hair." Then he reaches into his jacket pocket. "Let me give you something." He takes out a pocket watch. "This is yours now."

I take the watch, and my eyes widen with joy. It's too large for my small wrist. "Thank you, sir." The gentleman shows me how to keep the watch in my jacket pocket. Then he shows me how to wind it.

I look up. "What if it stops one day, sir?"

He lifts his eyebrows. "Well, then you come and find me."

"Where?"

"You will have the directions," he says, smiling.

"When?"

He runs his hand across my hair and stares at me with glinting eyes. "I have already given it." He winks. "You should have it today, only thirty-one years later."

I tilt my head as I look up at him. "Huh?"

He smiles. "You will know." Then he kneels down to reach my height. "So, Vincent, who are your friends in school?"

I grab Akane's scarf and look down. "Akane was the closest. My other friends are Fred, Krista, and Sasha."

He touches my head. "Was? What happened to her?"

My hands begin to shake, and I feel a throbbing in my head and tears in my eyes. "She went to Berlin to see some stupid clock. Time turbulence took her from me. I miss her all the time." Sparks form at the tip of my fingers. The stranger takes my palms and kisses them, absorbing the sparks. Then he wipes my tears and kisses my forehead. "Sweet boy. One day you will know how to use them. Everything I have is because of you." He points at the violin. "Yours?"

"It's Akane's. When I find her, I will give it back." I touch her scarf. "This is also hers. She gave it to me when I was hurt and cold."

The stranger's voice quavers. "What do you want to be when you grow up?"

I shake my head. "I don't wanna grow up. When I do, I must leave this place. And I have nowhere to go."

He stands up, puts his fingers under my chin, and lifts my face. "Look up." His voice becomes firm. "If you don't leave this place, you can never do great things with your life. You have to be at the top of your field. And that will make Akane find you—though she may have a different name. Will you recognize her?"

I grab Akane's violin case and squeeze it hard. "Yes."

"So, work hard, get out of this place. Let Emika find you. And when she feels cold, wrap that scarf around her. But before that, you must free her. That's your mission."

I am still lost in the beauty of my new possession. It has a clean white porcelain dial, an independent second hand, a golden case, and a striking logo. The word "Breguet" is written in cursive, and underneath is inscribed "Depuis 1775." Who's Emika? I lift my head. "Who's Emika, sir? What mission?" But the gentleman is gone. I run toward the stairs, but he is nowhere. Then I turn around and run across the hall to the large window. The sound from my little shoes echoes across the walls. As I look down from the closed window, I see a red car parked on the driveway. It has a license plate that reads TIME-FIXR. Before entering his red Ferrari, the stranger looks up at me, smiles, and nods, tipping his fedora. Then he drives away.

CHAPTER 19

TODAY (FINALE)

He who has a why to live for can bear almost any how.
—Friedrich Nietzsche

(August 15, 2024)

I RUSH BACK TO THE DRESSING room to collect my briefcase and the scarf. It's 5:35 p.m.—no notifications from Emika. Of course. At least she is free. Why am I rushing to get back home? Is it because of Hulk or my dream this morning where Emika came back? Will she? Even for a minute? I run into Jim on my way out.

I catch my breath and touch his shoulder. "I need my car."

He points across the hall. "End of the hallway, turn right, and you'll see the valet."

"Thanks, Jim."

"You're welcome, sir."

I run across the hallway and finally see the valet. "Blue Porsche Taycan, license plate HULKSDAD," I shout from ten feet away.

He nods. "Couple of minutes."

Every second feels like a minute, every minute like an hour. I wait helplessly outside the revolving door until I see my car appear. I can breathe now.

My mind is racing as I struggle through the traffic rush. So, I asked Philip to alter my memories of 1992 to help Emika in 2024 and become the Time Corrector. Yet, Akane wouldn't even enter Emika until 2001. Why 1992? To induce a will to be the top of my field? At that age? So, the Breguet watch is a totem for this alteration? That's why I could not remember it—because it was a part of altered memory. I did it all from the future, and I kept it safe from myself. Nothing could come between me and freeing Emika—not even me. The future me is a genius, far greater than the one who invented the two-way transfer of consciousness. What price must I pay to earn that genius? Why were the eyes of Vincent from 2033 filled with tears? Why did he have a *tanto*? What did I ever make that is worth preserving? I should have at least glanced at the journal. I have to make time to read it. The future Vincent can make the whole core disappear with a snap of his fingers—that's some power.

I am weaving through the traffic, prompting everyone to honk at me. Why do people drive below the speed limit? What's the need for a traffic signal every quarter of a mile? Why the fuck would anyone buy a minivan? Why can't the government tax this slow-moving sloth of a monstrosity? One more mile before the exit. Why is it taking forever? There's a semi-truck blocking me. I will pass it and come back to the lane. There is a tight spot right in front of a BMW X5M. I accelerate, reach 80 mph under 4 seconds, cut off the X5M, change lanes, and come back right in front of the semi for my exit. The X5M honks. *Fuck you, too. If you have an X5M, don't drive it like a minivan.* Now I am on the highway, moving at 110 mph, weaving between cars.

I see a cop car pointing his speed gun at me. I snap my fingers and create a spark. *C'mon motherfucker, stop me and spend your life outside the space-time continuum.* He targets a white sedan—a wise decision.

Finally, I pull up at Little Paws. I collect Hulk and harness him to the front passenger seat. He falls asleep like a baby. Then it's the final ascent to 100 Summit View. "Porsche, play Chopin's Ballade no. 4. It's time." So, that explains the dream this morning. Is my entire life foreshadowed from the past and future? So, whatever I will experience has already happened? Maybe the journal has something on it. It's 8:00 p.m. according to my JLC Reverso. Will it stop when I enter my property? I don't want to find out. Up ahead, I see my brightly lit Pacific-Northwest house peeping through the evergreens.

"Porsche, open the garage door." Hulk lifts his head and begins barking and wagging his tail. He wants to go out and investigate. I wrap my scarf before we disembark, and I keep the garage door open.

"OK, bug, let's inspect."

Hulk leaves the garage and runs toward the bench near the front door. I follow him. The setting sun shines its last drops of light on the bellflowers by the bench. I see a figure slowly moving away from the bright bellflowers and come toward me. She leaves the shadow of the house and emerges into the light. I know that face. It's the one I was perpetually searching for and hoping would appear since last February. Even though I knew she would not be at the airport gate, at the waiting lounge, at the bookstores, my meetings, the hotel lounge, or among the audience tonight, I kept hoping. She's wearing a tan suit and an untucked white-chiffon shirt underneath. But, what is she doing here? She is free. Akane—the part of her that found me—is gone.

I notice the bulge of her belly as she comes closer. I shake my head and smile at my fate—it is the fifteenth, after all, and she has moved on, swiftly as always. But that's a long flight just to tell me it's over. This is worse than my nightmare this morning. A strong breeze picks up, its intensity like January 7, but warmer, much warmer. She holds her hair against the wind.

Hulk jumps around Emika's legs and whimpers. She sits in the grass and lets him lick her face as she nuzzles her nose in his fur. Hulk keeps wagging his tail and won't stop licking Emika's face. "I know, baby." She pouts. "Mum was stupid."

Why is she toying with Hulk? She glances at me with glinting eyes and pats the grass. After I sit, she turns to me and wraps her arms around my neck. I want to kiss her—but she has someone else. And she is someone else. She moves her head back and looks at me. Her beauty mark is gone.

"That was quite the show, professor! So, you thought your love was unrequited?"

I lock her fingers with mine and stare into her eyes. "Evidence supported the conclusion."

"Evidence?" she asks, narrowing her eyes. "Who picked this house? Who initiated us? You are wrong, genius." She touches her belly and stares right into my eyes. "Vince, this little girl is living, breathing evidence of what you are to me."

That baby is mine? I squint. "When? How?"

She points at our house. "February 14, this house, the night before I left. Ring a bell, professor? How? You studied biology in your elitist boarding school, right?" She extends her right arm. "Help me." Grabbing my arm, she heaves herself up.

I stand up and point at her belly. "Can I touch?"

"Why not?" She rolls her eyes. "It's your doing." I gently place my hands on her belly as she touches my face with hers. Her voice trembles. "How much weight have you lost? What have you done to my Vince?"

"Fifteen pounds. And I am still the Vince you left." I take her wrist and wind her watch. Her watch does not have a second hand—the only way I can only know if it's ticking is by placing it against my ear. Should I? She presses her trembling lips together and shuts her eyes. "I missed that." She opens her eyes again as tears pour out and pulls the pocket square from my jacket. "Do you know why I am here?"

"Why?" I ask, kissing her wrist.

She dabs her eyes and breathes deeply. "I could play those four pieces on any violin after I met you. Akane's violin was not the cure to my discord. It was your voice that I heard, the voice asking me to find you, and finding you cured my headaches. I sensed it the moment I walked into your office. It was confirmed when I saw your picture with Akane. The life whose image haunted me had you in it. I wanted to tell you this." She pauses while dabbing her eyes again with my pocket square. "But, from the middle of December, I felt conflicted. Did I move in too quickly? Why doesn't he tell me what's going on with the case? Does he not care? Why is he glued to the TV, his cellphone? Why is he so distant? My headaches were back. It was like, there were two people inside my head. And, I made terrible decisions." She's breathing quickly now.

"Can I get you some water, Emi? You wanna come in? Please?"

She shakes her head. "You need to hear me out." Then she points into her Gurkha bag. "Also, I have water." Taking a deep breath, she continues. "After our last phone call, I thought that my missing you would fade away with time. I was wrong. I couldn't stop looking at your jacket, your pocket square, our photograph. All I could do was picture a life that could have been mine. Then you removed yourself as an author from our papers. I sensed your pain, but I kept quiet. I read your book and saw you in the Senate. I could see the rage and the pain in your eyes. When I apologized on April 15, all you texted was, 'You're welcome. Good to know.' At that moment, I knew I'd lost my Vince. A week later, I felt sick and found out about the baby. I kept the news to myself because I knew you were trying to move on."

She covers her eyes with my pocket square. "But deep down, I kept hoping you would want me. It's selfish, I know. The next four months went quickly. When I woke up yesterday, August 14, I felt new. I dreamt that I was standing in our backyard, witnessing the perfect cherry blossoms with the backdrop of rolling hills and snowcapped mountains. And in the middle of all of it was you, smiling and telling me, 'You are free. Now live your life.'

"My beauty mark was gone, and with it, all the doubts in my mind. And then I noticed a voicemail from you. I listened to it about 100 times. I was about to return your call, but then suddenly Nardin Robotics called me about a job. Within ten minutes of the call, they sent me a ticket to fly here for an interview. So, I thought I would surprise you instead of calling you."

I fetch the water bottle from her bag. She drinks while holding onto my sleeve, and I rub her back. After a few sips, she puts the bottle back. "When I landed here, I switched my US phone back on. I saw only one message, dated February 16. It read, 'I know you won't check this message. But Emi, whatever happens to me, just know that I love you.' I had my interview today, and the job is mine if I want. So, I listened to the voicemail again." Her lips tremble. "Vince, I love you. Can I come back? I have packed all my stuff, like I promised I would, on February 14. I don't care if I moved too quickly. But I don't want to waste another day without you."

Now I notice her luggage and the violin case by the bench. I touch her face. "You should have called me about the baby. Growing up, my parents had nothing to do with me. Do you think I would do the same to my child?"

She grips my sleeve tighter. "I thought you'd moved on, and I did not want to impose."

I tuck her hair behind her ears. "Did I ever make you feel like you were imposing, even during our worst times?"

Her voice quavers. "No."

"Let's go in." I kiss her forehead. "I kept everything the way you like, including the post-its on the fridge."

Suddenly, the sprinklers turn on, soaking our shoes and trousers. Emika puts her arms around me and locks her lips to mine. She sees my tears for the first time. Taking my pocket square, she wipes them away and says, "Tears in Professor Abajian's eyes. Who would have thought?"

As we turn to the house, I notice a brown cardboard package by the front door. "What's that?"

She shrugs. "It was here when I arrived."

I collect the package and open the door.

Emika picks up Hulk and whispers, "Mum is back."

I bring her luggage and Akane's violin. Finally, she is moving in. I breathe in deeply to absorb this. Then I open the cardboard package. Inside is a piano-black wood box bearing an exquisitely marked logo, "Philip Nardin." Inside the box is the only wristwatch Philip ever made. Next to that watch rests my Breguet pocket watch from my childhood. They've been perfectly synchronized. There is also a handwritten note.

Dear Vince,

I have your fixed pocket watch. Do you now remember how you got it? Also, the only wristwatch I made is now yours. I never found the occasion to wear it. But, as of this moment, you've got what you sought the most—a beautiful life. This is the fitting moment I spoke about. The reset time for this watch is August 3, 2023, as with all the watches you've received from me.

I have noticed that you massage your temples. They're not migraines. A part of the core is in you. The dreams and the headaches are symptoms when the core is trying to connect with you. You and I have the strongest connection to the core among all humans. That's how you could write so many details in your book that I never dictated. The core could allow you to tap into my mind. The beautiful lady standing next to you also had a connection with the core. It helped her find you the first time.

To walk inside turbulence, you need a suit powered by intreton-c, which will inverse the polarity between the intreton in your body and the turbulence. Without it, you will keep losing weight. Come and find me. I will have a suit ready for you.

Love,
Philip
P.S. You still owe me a race.

How does Philip know Emika is standing next to me? I peep outside, and there it is, the Ferrari Enzo, with the TIME-FIXR license plate. The driver is wearing a fedora. He nods and tips his hat. As he turns on the headlights, I hear the rumbling of the V-12 resonating through the floor of our house. Then he drives away. So, it was him in the Rolls Royce Phantom all along. He never left—his autopilot system worked.

Emika looks out as well. "Who was that?"

"Philip Nardin."

She sits down and looks at the watch. "Did you know he was here? The senators asked you."

I sit next to her and touch her hair. "Philip never revealed to me where he was so that I didn't have to lie." I kiss her hand. "I did the same for you."

She runs her fingers through my hair, blinks. "I am so sorry, Vince." Then she points at Philip's wristwatch. "What's that?"

I smile. "It's the only wristwatch Philip ever made."

She picks up the pocket watch. "What about this?"

"My first inheritance."

Emika looks at the note. "I have so many questions," Emika says, looking at the letter. "What's a core?"

I stand up and snap my fingers—sparks form instantly. Emika's eyes widen. I roll the sparks into a ball and make it levitate an inch above my palm. "This is the core. I can create time turbulence. And I can view the past and the future and all possible timelines. I can alter realities."

Emika stands but remains speechless. She is not even blinking. Then she grabs both my lapels and shakes me. "Vince, tell me this is our timeline." She looks around. "Vince, tell me everything is real."

I dissolve the core and touch her neck. "Are you real?"

She lets go of my lapels. "Yes."

I touch her belly. "Is she real?"

"*Hai.*"

"Then everything surrounding you is real." I kiss her.

"Does it hurt?" she asks, touching my hand.

"No."

"You will tell me everything. How did you come across this ability?"

"How about we talk during dinner? Where do you wanna go?"

"Nowhere." She puts her arms around my neck. "Can you make me the *omurice* that you did on February 15? Only this time, I won't leave you."

I pull her closer. "Sure."

She looks up and points toward the second floor. "Can we furnish the master bedroom?"

"Sure." I look into her eyes. "It's your home."

"By the way, why is it so cold?" she asks, rubbing her arms.

I take off Akane's scarf and wrap it around her neck. "Is this warm?"

She touches the scarf to feel the texture. Then she smiles and dabs her eyes with my pocket square. "*Attakai desu.*"

Her phone rings, and she turns to me. "It's Nardin Robotics."

I leave to get my briefcase from my car. She hasn't called me silly even once. She is free—and my Emi is home. I turn back to see her waving her slender hand. "See you later, Vince."

Upon returning from my car, I see Akane's violin case by the front door, resting where Philip's watch was. Didn't I already take it in? How could I miss it? I open the case and see Akane's violin and my pocket square from February 15. I touch my chest and find the pocket square still there. Didn't Emika take it out and dab her eyes with it? Why do I still have Akane's scarf wrapped around my neck? Why is Hulk outside with me? Didn't' I leave him inside with Emika? I take out my cell phone—the current time is 8:30 p.m. The wristwatch had stopped ticking at 8:00 p.m. I shake my head, collect my belongings, Hulk and enter the house. There are no tears in my eyes as I look outside my property. I smile. "You are free from Akane. Now live your life, free from me. Goodbye, Emi."

CHAPTER 20

FOUND YOU!

Silent forest weeps, misty river bends,
timeless dawn awakens, anew.
—Unknown

(November 15, 2024, thirty-three years after the Alexanderplatz incident)

A PRIVATE GULFSTREAM G-700 LANDS IN Seattle, carrying just one passenger. She is wearing a bespoke cobalt-blue jumpsuit and bespoke 6-inch-high heels. On her left wrist is a 37-mm platinum Philippe Dufour watch. Her long hair is tied into a bun, held by two jade chopsticks. One flight attendant helps her fetch the 22-inch Dior and Rimowa blue cabin luggage. She places her Birkin handbag on the luggage. A second flight attendant helps her put on her bespoke trench. Both the flight attends bow. "See you in a few minutes, ma'am."

She steps out of the plane, takes a deep breath, and walks onto the bridge. Two almost 7-foot-tall bodyguards flank her.

Following the events of the time turbulence on November 15, 1991, she was in a coma until August 2001. It took years of physiotherapy to revive her muscles and motor functions. But she had no memory of her past. Finally, the doctors reached a breakthrough when, around December 2023, she started to get her memories back. Since then, it was a constant struggle plagued with headaches and mental collapses until the momentous afternoon of August 14, 2024 (Japan Standard Time), when she got all her memories back. At this moment, all she wants is to see someone special. Everything else can wait.

She must clear immigration before her final destination. She follows the signs and waits for the TSA agent to call her up. A caucasian male TSA agent gestures to her that she's next. His name tag reads "Brandt."

Brandt points his finger at the lady. "Ma'am, can I see your passport?"

One of her bodyguards hands over the paperwork to Brandt. He looks at the passport and then looks back up to verify her face as she impatiently taps her shoe on the floor. *Come on, Sherlock. Hurry up. Don't you have a burger and fries waiting for you?*

Brandt stares at her. "What's the purpose of your visit, ma'am?"

"Travel and to meet an old friend." She smiles.

"Travel and what?" Brandt puts his palm behind his ears. "I couldn't catch your accent."

She clicks her tongue. "Just travel."

Brandt squints. "How do you pronounce your name, ma'am?"

Oh boy, he can't read. She smiles. "Just the way it's written, sir."

Brandt turns a page in her passport. "Ma'am, can you confirm the date and place of your birth?"

"September 18, 1982. Tokyo."

"Ma'am, what do you do for a living?"

"I co-own a media conglomerate."

Brandt places his palm behind his ears again. "Media what?"

She smiles and tilts her head. "It's like AT&T, but bigger," she says, spreading her arms.

Brandt stamps her passport and slides her documents under the glass window.

As she walks toward the exit, she meets her pilot. He bows. "Egami-*san*, we are ready. Please follow me."

She looks at her watch and counts the hours before she sees her favorite person after thirty-three years. *Will he remember me? Does he have our picture, my violin, my scarf? Does he recall the pieces I played for him? Is he still silly*?

She takes out a pencil sketch encased in a platinum frame from her handbag as she sits in her plane. It is a portrait of her from when she was nine years old. The date of the drawing is September 18, 1991. She gently runs her fingers over the signature below the sketch. Then she holds the frame to her chest, shuts her eyes, and smiles, envisaging the shock on her friend's face when she surprises him. She reaches into her handbag and pulls out the book *The Time Fixer: Three Lives of Philip Nardin*. Then she turns to the back cover and runs her fingers over the picture of the author. Tears form at the corner of her eyes. She wipes them away, and she whispers, "Found you, silly. *Watashi no ai. Watashi no amai*, Vincent."

To be continued...

CPSIA information can be obtained
at www.ICGtesting.com
Printed in the USA
BVHW030117260122
627087BV00004B/5